TO KILL A UNICORN

CHRONICLES OF CAIN BOOK ONE

JOHN CORWIN

RAVEN HOUSE

KILL A UNICORN OR DIE TRYING

The gods are dead. The fae rule Gaia.

Cain used to kill for the fae. The only human to become a member of the Oblivion Guard, he killed one time too many and had enough. Leaving it all behind wasn't as easy as turning in a resignation. But the fae had trained him well and soon it was they who bargained for him to leave Feary and live in exile in Gaia.

Now a tracker for an assassination and bounty hunting agency, Cain doesn't kill anymore. When his mission to track a teenage girl goes horribly wrong, he and the girl end up on the run from powerful forces the likes of which he's never seen before.

That's because the fae have been hiding a terrible secret. The gods aren't dead. In fact, they're very much alive and killing humans they deem too powerful to survive. The girl is in their crosshairs and now he is too.

To make matters worse, Cain discovers he's dying from the curse of

Cthulhu. The cure? Eating a living, beating unicorn heart. Cain thought unicorns were extinct, but a mystery party offers him salvation: a unicorn for the assassination of the leader of the Mages Guild.

With the gods, the fae, and the rest of the supernatural world hunting the hunter, the odds don't look good. But Cain has survived too much to give up now. And the high and mighty are about to find out what real fear feels like.

BOOKS BY JOHN CORWIN

CHRONICLES OF CAIN

To Kill a Unicorn

Enter Oblivion

Throne of Lies

THE OVERWORLD CHRONICLES

Sweet Blood of Mine

Dark Light of Mine

Fallen Angel of Mine

Dread Nemesis of Mine

Twisted Sister of Mine

Dearest Mother of Mine

Infernal Father of Mine

Sinister Seraphim of Mine

Wicked War of Mine

Dire Destiny of Ours

Aetherial Annihilation

Baleful Betrayal

Ominous Odyssey

Insidious Insurrection

Utopia Undone

Overworld Apocalypse

Apocryphan Rising

Soul Storm

Assignment Zero (An Elyssa Short Story)

OVERWORLD UNDERGROUND

Soul Seer

Demonicus

Infernal Blade

OVERWORLD ARCANUM

Conrad Edison and the Living Curse

Conrad Edison and the Anchored World

Conrad Edison and the Broken Relic

Conrad Edison and the Infernal Design

Conrad Edison and the First Power

STAND ALONE NOVELS

Mars Rising

No Darker Fate

The Next Thing I Knew

Outsourced

For the latest on new releases, free ebooks, and more, join John Corwin's Newsletter at www.johncorwin.net!

CHAPTER 1

I sighted the target through the true-sight scope of my oblivion staff. One shot. One kill.

A simple focus of will could release a blast of magic that would penetrate flesh and burn the heart to a cinder. But this was no ordinary target, and I was no longer an assassin.

My hands trembled, and the scope lost its target. I laid the staff in the grass and took a long, deep breath. *Why in the hell is my target a teenage girl?* I'd asked myself that question a lot over the past few days. Tracking her down had been my toughest assignment yet. The foster system had done a good job of losing her in piles of red tape and misplaced folders.

Eclipse, the agency I freelanced for, hadn't given me much to go on—just a picture of a little girl, her mother's surname, and their original address. No birthdate to approximate an age and no explanation as to why someone would want her dead or captured.

I picked up my oblivion staff and found the target again with the scope. I felt like a complete creeper stalking a kid at high school. Even though the tall grass camouflaged me, I used an obfuscation illusion—a wall of camouflage—as a blind so anyone looking this way would see nothing but grass.

Disguised as a janitor, I'd sneaked into the school and triggered the fire alarm to get the kids into the parking lot. Now they milled around aimlessly as teachers tried in vain to account for everyone in their care. The target stood near the back of the crowd, trying to stay as far from the others as possible.

She was tall for a girl, five feet, six inches, with light brown skin and jet-black hair. She'd gotten that from her Arabic mother. There was no information on the father. Her bright green eyes hinted at European ancestry from the father's side, but that was just supposition on my part.

I traced a finger on the edge of the scope, shifting to thermal. Just as the last time, her body temp looked normal. It would have been a few degrees higher if she were a lycan, and room temperature if she were a vampire. Of course, if she were a vampire, she would've burned up in the sunlight.

I tapped the scope again, switching to astral view. Her physical body became transparent, revealing the gentle off-white nimbus of her soul. As before, the girl had no magical aura to indicate she was a mage of any kind. The only oddity was the faint silver lining around the edges of her soul.

I didn't know what that meant.

The other students possessed the typical dark-gray edges of nubs—non-supernatural humans. The girl was unusual only in that aspect. But she hadn't exhibited the behavior of a malevolent supernatural entity who needed to be tracked and bagged.

I lowered the scope again. "What the hell am I doing here?" I scoffed at myself. "Maybe I should just ask Janice why the client wants her marked." My handler wouldn't tell me, of course, but she'd know I'd found the target and was holding out. That sort of behavior was frowned upon. *They must have a good reason.*

I'd tracked kids before, of course. But most of the time, they weren't really kids. Some were vampires over a hundred years old. Others were shifters disguised as children. Some were even rogue mages using illusion.

The true-sight scope on my oblivion staff could see through any kind of illusion as far as I knew. The only thing it couldn't penetrate was fae glamour, but that was by design.

"Just do it, dammit." I snapped the scope back to my eye, found the target, and focused my will. The spell, a small transparent orb of energy, hit the target in the base of the neck. The girl flinched and slapped her neck as if bitten by a mosquito. There was no damage, no visible mark on her skin. But the tracker spell broadcast her location to anyone with the proper sigils. Only the agency and the client had access.

I felt instant regret.

What if she's innocent? I gritted my teeth and fought off old memories. *Don't think about it.* Trying not to think about it made me think about it. My hands trembled, and the scope swayed around the target.

Voices whispered in the back of mind. Some were sad, others angry. Most were confused, and it was my fault.

Three other kids drifted near the target, two girls and a painfully fat boy. Another group of kids paced behind them, faces sneering. Two were tall, muscular boys, and the third a pretty blonde girl with tanned skin.

The fat boy bumped into the target. The target backed away as if trying to escape. She didn't make friends and avoided talking to people whenever possible. Her current foster home wasn't a bad place, but some of the records I'd uncovered indicated physical and mental abuse in previous homes.

I twisted my fingers in a pattern, cupped a hand, and flicked it across my ear. I angled my head to pick up the conversation.

"Ever heard of a dermatologist, Jan?" The blonde smirked at one of the girls in orbit of the fat boy. "Or deodorant?"

"That's not her stink," muscle boy one said. "That's all the sweat trapped in Thomas's fat rolls."

His companions burst into laughter.

Fat boy Thomas looked as if he wanted to shrink to nothing, but that would be one hell of a feat, given his girth.

"Leave us alone, Karen!" Jan shouted. "Just because you're pretty doesn't give you the right to call us names!"

"You're so fucking ugly you hurt my eyes," muscle boy two said. He was graced with a thick brown mane, a chiseled jaw and probably didn't have a worry in the world. And yet he wasn't satisfied with that. He had to demonstrate his superiority to the ugly kids.

I'd never been in a normal school, so bullying fascinated me. I'd seen it on television and in movies, but rarely in reality. The fae didn't have a lot of children, and the few I'd met treated me like human trash. In other words, they barely acknowledged my existence.

"Brent, please leave us alone," Thomas pleaded.

"Then stop torturing my eyes, you fat fuck." Brent elbowed his male companion. "Am I right?"

The other guy grinned and nodded.

Brent's gaze flicked to the target. "What the fuck you looking at, bitch?"

My target froze, fists clenched, but she quickly looked down.

"I asked you a question," Brent said. "What the fuck were you looking at?"

The target shivered violently. "Nothing," she whimpered.

"Look at me when I'm talking to you!" Brent shouted. "Even your ugly-assed friends give me that respect."

The target froze in place. The silver edges to her soul seemed to glow a little brighter.

"Look at me!" Brent shouted again.

"Yeah, look at him," Karen said.

"Shut up," the target said. "Shut up, shut up, shut up!" Her sentence rose into a scream that nearly ruptured my ear drums through the amplification spell.

Brent, Karen, and their male companion went into convulsions, their screams tangling with that of the target's. Ghostly figures stretched and distorted from their bodies, tearing free and flying toward Thomas and the other girls. Their bodies abruptly arched and went into spasms as something ripped from them and streaked toward the bullies.

The target stopped screaming and went still, fists clenched, shoulders tight, body rigid. Tears streaked down her cheeks. The silver lining to her soul thinned to almost nothing.

Thomas shook his head. He looked at Brent and his eyes flared. He looked at his hands and back at Brent. Jan and the other kids did the same thing, as if seeing something impossible. The bullied kids began screaming and crying. The pretty kids burst into shouts of their own, inspecting their bodies as if in disbelief.

"What in the hell is going on?" I muttered.

The target backed away, forehead pinched in confusion. She covered her ears and began trembling violently. Then she convulsed and went down in a heap.

A teacher rushed toward the commotion. "What's wrong?"

The kids kept screaming.

The teacher saw the target lying on the asphalt and rushed to her side. "Someone get help!" the woman seemed reluctant to touch the girl, but gingerly put her fingers on the target's neck.

Thomas launched himself at Brent. "What the fuck did you do to me, you fat fuck?"

Brent stumbled backward, eyes wide with fear.

"Stop fighting this instant!" The teacher stood and held out her hands, but Thomas ignored her and swung a fist at Brent. Brent jumped back.

Brent's buddy looked down at his hands and clenched his fists. Then he reared back and cocked Thomas in the face. The fat kid yelped. Arms windmilling, he staggered back and fell hard on his ass.

Jan fell to her knees, sobbing uncontrollably while her female friend shrieked like a gods-damned banshee.

I'd never seen anything like this before, but in retrospect, it seemed obvious what had happened. And the target was the cause. Judging from the shocked look on the girl's face before she collapsed, she didn't have a clue what kind of havoc she'd just unleashed. But now I knew why the agency wanted her.

"Holy fuck." I stared at the girl's still form and my mind filled with unwanted images from the past. Cold sweat broke out on my forehead. I took calming breaths to quiet my nerves, but it didn't help. The whispers in my head grew to an unrelenting susurrus. They hadn't been this loud in years.

I banished my oblivion staff and it vanished back into the pocket dimension where it resided until I needed to summon it again. Then I started shambling down the hill before I knew what I was doing. I barely had the presence of mind to put on an illusion mask so I didn't scare anyone. I dug the counterfeit school ID badge from under my shirt, identifying me as Bill Jones, part of the janitorial staff.

By the time I realized what I was doing, I'd already slid through a cut in the chain link fence and was halfway to the target. The obfuscation spell was the only thing keeping anyone from seeing me approach. If anyone had been remotely observant, they would've wondered at the strange shimmer in the air gradually approaching.

But the bedlam surrounding the bullies and their victims was more than enough to keep attention firmly away from me.

I hid behind a bush for an instant and dispelled the illusion. The next instant, I focused an image in my head and patterned another illusion sigil to make my clothes resemble a gray janitor's uniform. I usually preferred using actual clothes. Even perfect illusions sometimes flickered or didn't quite match up. I hoped with all the confusion no one was observant enough to notice.

When I stepped into plain view, no one even glanced my way.

A school resource officer had come onto the scene and was restraining a red-faced Thomas. "He stole my body!" the kid screamed. "Thomas stole my body!"

Brent's companion giggled and stuck out his tongue. "Don't be jealous, you fat fuck."

Brent looked wide-eyed from Thomas to his friends, mouth hanging open.

Jan stared at the pretty blonde. "What happened to my body? How did I get in here?"

Everyone was so focused on the struggle they didn't notice me slip in next to the target. I could have used a medical disguise, but there were only two nurses at the school, increasing the odds of someone quickly noticing an impostor.

I wove an avoidance sigil on the target and all nearby gazes averted elsewhere. Then I scooped her up and backed out of the crowd. I reached the edge of the asphalt, still backing up to keep the avoidance spell between me and the crowd.

I almost made it.

A kid with platinum-blond hair stared at me from the far edge of the parking lot a hundred yards to my right. The sigil should've diverted his attention, but he was looking through it and directly at me.

He was no ordinary kid, but I didn't have time to summon my staff and have a look at him through the scope. I'd never seen him before. He wasn't with the agency and he wasn't one of the freelancers on the official list. He also wasn't an approved and accredited bounty hunter. I always kept up with both lists so I didn't accidentally cock block someone from doing their job.

The kid's forehead wrinkled. He cocked his head like a curious dog. If he knew who I was, then he knew I wasn't just breaking protocol, but smashing through it with a sledgehammer. I tracked targets. I stalked targets. I marked targets for the agency. Then they took it from there. At no point in that process was I to apprehend targets myself.

Those weren't even their rules. They were my rules. I told them I wouldn't take part in retrievals or assassinations. But no one else could find someone as fast as I could. No other freelancers had my skillset or training. Because very few in my former profession survived the exit interview.

The kid walked my way, bright eyes locked on me like a beacon.

"What the hell am I doing?" I muttered to myself. I rarely gave in to impulse. Today I'd given in twice and fucked myself both times. The smart thing would be to set down the mark and leave her for the kid. But my legs refused to stop walking, and my arms wouldn't release the girl.

Once of the voices in my head rose above the others. *Will you kill her like you killed us?*

Sometimes the ghosts that haunt us are our own conscience. Sometimes they're memories so vivid and awful that they dig scars deep into our souls. But sometimes those ghosts are real. They're ghosts of our own making. And they haunt people, not places.

In my case, I was haunted by all the above. And those ghosts were leading me down a dangerous path that would probably make me one of them if I didn't drop the girl and leave.

But I didn't drop the girl. Keeping the sigil between me and the crowd, I kept backing up one step at a time. Four, three, two, one. My back hit the hole in the fence. An obfuscation spell would've worked to get me over the small hill, but the blond kid was closing fast.

A few kids glanced curiously at him as he jogged past. The teachers and security were still trying to subdue Brent and his friends. No one seemed to notice or care that one of their supposed wards was making an escape attempt.

And I knew right then I wasn't going to get out in time.

CHAPTER 2

I almost turned and ran. Almost gave everyone at the school a nice view of a janitor kidnapping a student. But I'd been through too much to yield to pressure. I kept an eye on the kid pursuing me and backed up the hill one step at a time. He was maybe a hundred feet away when I made it over the ridge and out of sight of the school.

Then I turned and ran. I activated the sigils tattooed on my body and magical energy propelled me faster. It didn't make me as fleet of foot as a lycan, but I could've beaten even the fastest normal human. I ran through the woods, not glancing back to see if I'd left the kid behind.

The power sigils strengthened my arms and steadied my grip. I was only a few yards from the edge of the woods and Dolores when it felt as if someone reached into my chest and squeezed my heart with a steel vice.

My knees turned to jelly. I stumbled and plowed face-first through leaves and pine straw. The girl tumbled from my arms and rolled to a stop. Gasping, I pounded a fist on my chest to release the tension. It didn't help. I ripped open the top of my shirt as if that would help, revealing black veins webbing my flesh.

The grip on my heart abruptly went slack. Breathing became easier and oxygen returned to my blood. I took a long, deep breath, and held it in for several seconds, then stood and turned to meet my pursuer.

He walked toward me, expression curious but not angry. "Who are you?"

Unencumbered by the girl, I reached across my shoulder as if pulling a sword from a sheath across my back and summoned my staff. It slid from the pocket dimension with a crackling thrum. I flipped up the scope and sighted the boy. He wasn't hiding anything behind illusion, and he wasn't a shifter. That meant he really was a kid. The only thing out of the ordinary was his soul—it shined like polished silver. I'd never seen anything like it before. Then again, two firsts in a day wasn't exactly a first for me either.

I loaded a spell in my staff and then checked myself. What was I going to do, fire on someone who was just doing their job? The voices in my head began muttering again. I released the power and let him approach.

"You're here for the girl," I said.

The kid's head twitched from side to side as if the question surprised the hell out of him. "You're Ghostwalker?"

"I've never seen you before." I banished the staff. "Who are you?"

"I've heard stories about you." The kid seemed relaxed, as if he didn't have a worry in the world about facing someone with my reputation. "You always did your duty until the day you didn't." He laughed. "Is this like that time?"

I blew out a breath. "Look, kid, I don't play twenty questions with anyone. I found the target and made the mark. I'm taking it in myself."

"Taking *it* in?" He laughed. "That's a girl, not a thing."

"Yeah, and what do you plan to do with it?" I asked.

He shrugged. "I have to kill her. It sucks, but I don't have a choice."

"For what?" I risked a look back and saw the girl still unconscious not far from me. "As you said, she's a girl—an ordinary girl. She's not a freak." At least like none I'd seen before.

"I've heard stories about you." The boy seemed to ignore everything I said. "I wish I'd been alive to see the war."

"War isn't a spectator sport, kid." I made a shooing motion with my hands. "Now skedaddle and keep your mouth shut about this. I'll handle the mark myself."

He stuck out his tongue and made a raspberry. "Sorry, mister, I can't let you do that. I've got to take pictures of the body or they'll punish me."

"How old are you anyway?" I looked him up and down while gradually easing backward. "Sixteen?"

He shrugged. "I don't know. They don't care about mortal stuff."

I wondered if he was talking about the fae. They proclaimed not to care about the passage of years, but even immortals still liked to track their ages, if only for bragging rights. I took another step back.

"Okay, that's enough." The boy held up a hand. "Please stop so I don't have to hurt you."

I scoffed. "Hurt me?"

He nodded. "Yeah. Just go away and leave the girl."

I straightened my shoulders and braced myself. "I said I'd take care of it, kid. Now, go."

"Fine, have it your way." The boy balled up a fist. Crackling blue energy coalesced around it. A thick bolt of lightning arced out and sawed a sapling in half. Acrid smoke drifted from the scorched bark.

I was fast, but I wasn't lightning-bolt fast.

I flicked my fingers and cast a shield a few feet in front of the boy. The next lightning strike exploded in his face.

He flew backward with a startled shout. I scooped up the girl and ran to the edge of the forest where Dolores, my black vintage station wagon waited. I powered the sigil on the rear passenger door, and it sprang open. I tossed in the girl, shut the door, and then raced around to the driver's side.

The engine thrummed to life at a thought from me, just as the boy ran out of the woods. I jumped in the seat and hit the accelerator. Dirt and grass churned into his face before he could unleash another lightning bolt. Rubber met asphalt and Dolores surged ahead.

Dolores had the body of a nineteen-seventy Dodge Coronet Super Bee, but her big-block engine was powered by liquid mana. She was the longest relationship I'd had, and for damned good reason. But right now, Dolores was giving me some bad news. The kid was in my rear-view mirror. He wasn't a tiny dot a few hundred yards back like he was supposed to be, but an almost life-sized figure maybe thirty feet behind.

I was doing fifty, which meant that kid had to be booking it. But Dolores wasn't without her feminine wiles. A row of buttons ran beneath the eight-track player. I located a suitable one and pressed it.

The kid's arms flailed, mouth agape in shock as his feet found the slick potion I'd just released on the asphalt. He flew off the road and smacked into a pine tree so hard, splinters rained down.

"Oh, shit." I almost stopped to see if he was okay.

The ghosts whispered in my head, anxious, but not upset about what I'd done to the boy. Maybe that was because he was trying to kill the girl.

The boy staggered to his feet, his face a mask of blood. Then he started running again.

"Holy fuck." I jammed the accelerator to the floor. The kid was fast, but he wasn't a hundred miles per hour fast. At least I hoped he wasn't holding back. It played into my favor that the school was outside of town near a state highway. There wasn't much traffic, and plenty of open road.

There was just one major problem with my strategy.

The mark I'd placed on the girl wouldn't come off easily, even though I'd designed it and knew how to dispel it. I'd have to untangle the weave and that would take a good fifteen to twenty minutes. Until I did that, the agency would know my location within a hundred-yard radius.

I didn't understand how the kid had arrived on scene so fast. There weren't any fast-travel nodes nearby, and I hadn't given anyone at the agency my location until I cast the mark on the girl. The only other method of fast travel was plane shifting, but it was extremely dangerous. If the kid was capable of that, then he could jump ahead of the car at any time.

Since he hadn't done that yet, I figured someone had sent him to the target. It meant he would keep chasing after me on foot and give me some time to dispel the mark. I had to untangle the mark while driving, and that was going to be damned hard with the girl in the back seat. Hell, it'd be hard with her in the front seat. But I had to touch the sigils to untie the pattern.

The kid wasn't even a speck in my rearview mirror, but that didn't mean anything. He was damned near as fast as a lycan in wolf form, so he'd be on me in a hot minute if I stopped too long. But it was a risk I had to take. There were no cars behind me, so I hit the brakes and skidded to a stop on the shoulder.

I jumped out of the car, ran around to the passenger side, and opened the front and rear doors. The girl wasn't too heavy, so it only took a moment to drag her from the back and toss her in the front. I fastened the seatbelt—a modified shoulder harness I'd installed for high-speed safety.

She slumped, head lolling forward. That was just fine since I needed to reach her neck to untangle the mark.

A bolt of lightning arced into the asphalt two feet away, reducing it to bubbling tar. The boy had just hit the top of the hill about fifty yards back. If he hadn't stopped to take a shot, he probably could have reached me before I even knew it. I jumped in the driver's seat and punched another button beneath the eight-track.

The magical afterburners where the dual exhaust used to be roared to life. Dolores surged ahead. No screech of tires, because the locomotion wasn't coming from the wheels this time. More lighting struck where I'd been a split second ago.

I stared at the boy in the rearview mirror. "Just stop it, kid. Take a breather and go home."

He didn't. Drawing from a seemingly bottomless reservoir of endurance, the boy raced after us. Unfortunately for me, an obstacle loomed on the horizon—namely, the town of Spearhead, North Carolina. It wasn't a big place. Hell, it only had two traffic lights. But the speed limit was twenty-five and I couldn't just roar through there at top speed. That meant lightning boy would be on me in a flash—pun intended.

I had maybe three minutes before the city limit, so I got to work on the girl. My tracking marks were a combination of sigils. Untangle the sigils in the wrong order and you'd get a series of warnings. The first warning was a nasty shock, like sticking a fork in an electrical outlet. The next warning would punch a grown man hard enough to send him across a room. The third attempt and any after that would knock you out.

Most targets were taken out or picked up by bounty hunters well before the targets even realized they were marked. It was one of the reasons people came to me for particularly hard-to-find people. My marks were discreet, and the sigil encryption was nearly unbreakable.

On the downside, it meant I hadn't inserted an easy backdoor to allow instant dissolution of the sigils. It meant I had to manually decrypt the sigils while driving at high speed. Even though I knew exactly what to do, it wouldn't be easy.

I stopped thinking about it and got to work.

Sigils are patterns of varying complexity imbued with power and purpose. The more complex the purpose, the more intricate the sigil. The more powerful the purpose, the denser the pattern. My marks didn't require much power. If left alone, the power would fade after three weeks and the mark would dissolve on its own. The complexity of my marks was only to make decrypting them harder.

Keeping one eye on the road and one hand on the steering wheel, I traced a pattern around the mark and imbued it with power. The mark faded into view, a tangled mesh of black lines. Those lines were four sigils woven together. I reached toward the top of the weave but the bumps in the road made it hard to keep my finger on target.

Focus, damn it!

I held a breath and steadied my fingers. It found the correct line. I plucked it like a guitar string and the mark rose from the skin, hovering in the air above the girl's neck like a hologram. I rolled the specific section of the same line between thumb and forefinger and the sigil it belonged to shaded red. I found the proper section of the next pattern and tapped it with my pinky. The sigil turned green.

The three sigils were now red, green, and black, allowing for easier decryption. But I was less than a minute from the town. Even under perfect circumstances, I'd need ten minutes for decryption. This was going to be a neat trick if I pulled it off.

I finessed the top part of the red sigil up to the left, moving the line a fraction of an inch. Then I moved to the green sigil and manipulated its lower right section. Using my middle finger and thumb, I spread the inner circle of the black sigil outward by a millimeter. To make things as complicated as possible, I used metric and imperial measurements in most of my designs.

By the time I got to that point, it was too late to do anything else until I made it through the town. I disengaged the thrusters and slowed to a relative crawl. With my eyes back on the road, I realized I'd slowed down too late. A police cruiser sat at the corner of town, a radar gun pointed at me.

I'd been doing forty over the speed limit only a moment ago, so there was little doubt the cop clocked me. Any remaining doubt was erased when the cop pulled out behind me the moment I hit the first traffic light.

Driving at high speeds with an unconscious girl in the passenger seat was going to look mighty suspicious to the lawman. I cast a quick obfuscation spell over the holographic pattern so the cop would have one less thing to freak out about. The girl would be much harder to hide without something more complicated, so I decided to act natural and hope for the best.

My biggest worry was that lightning kid would swoop in and fry all of us before we even knew what happened.

I pulled into a small gas station right after the traffic light and parked facing the other exit to allow a quick getaway if the kid showed up. I set the car windows to max legal tint to obscure the inside as much as possible and got out.

The writing on the side of the patrol car told me the occupant was a deputy. He looked about twenty-five and wore a wide-brimmed hat over a shaved head. He took his time getting out of the car and then sauntered over to me.

"Why'd you get out of the car?" He looked past me and into the window.

"My daughter's asleep. Didn't want to wake her." I gave him an easygoing shrug and glanced at his name tag. "I picked her up from school because she's feeling sick, Deputy Haines."

He grunted. "You know why I pulled you over?"

"No, sir." I wove a sigil behind my back and cast it at his car. The siren whooped, the horn honked, and the lights on top sparked and went out. With a fading wail, the patrol car went silent.

The deputy jumped like he'd just seen a live hand grenade. "What in tarnation?" He stared at his car like it was possessed.

"Technical difficulties?" I kept one eye on him and another on the hill outside town.

"Naw." He shook his head and turned back to me. "I clocked you going ninety in a fifty-five. That don't leave me much choice but to take your driver's license and hold you for bail money."

"Wow." I clucked my tongue. "Sounds like I'm in a lot of trouble, Deputy Haines. Mind if I see the proof?"

"Be my guest, sir." He seemed very self-assured. After all, I hadn't just broken the speed limit—I'd shattered it. It was almost gratifying to see him deflate when he opened the door to his car and saw the computer inside.

The computer screen and radar display were blackened and burned. Smoke drifted from the console, and the inside reeked of fried electronics.

A silhouette appeared atop the hill outside town. Lightning boy had caught up. The shit was about to hit the fan.

CHAPTER 3

Was lightning boy's next move to swoop in, fry me and the girl, or was he bound by fae rules of conduct like everyone else? His long pause at the top of the hill seemed to indicate the latter.

Still keeping an eye on him, I shook my head sadly at the deputy. "What a shame. Looks like there's no proof after all. Guess I'll be going."

"I saw it plain as day," the deputy said.

I shrugged. "You still need the radar reading, right?"

He grumbled, hemmed and hawed, and just when he seemed ready to give up, his shoulders straightened. "Sir, I want to see your license and proof of insurance. And I want to speak to your daughter."

It seemed he was going to make things as difficult as possible.

I spread my hands imploringly. "Deputy Haines, you have no proof I was speeding. Therefore, you have no reason to hold me."

"I can damned sure get you on reckless driving," he said. "Follow my orders or I'll arrest you."

Two old men sat outside the gas station on a bench, watching us as if they hadn't seen such quality entertainment in years. That made getting out of this situation a little harder. On the other hand, their presence gave me a safe place to remove the mark from the girl, because lightning boy had slowed his roll and was jogging at a normal pace toward town.

It'd take him a few minutes to reach us—plenty of time to remove the mark, provided Deputy Haines followed protocol.

I dug into my pocket and pulled out my license and insurance.

He looked at them and grunted. "This is a local address, but I ain't never seen you before."

"You know every single person in the county?" I said. The documents were forgeries, of course, but he didn't need to know that.

He narrowed his eyes. "Most of 'em." Then he did what I'd hoped he'd do and sat in his car. He probably did it on instinct, forgetting that his computer was a smoking pile of garbage. Or maybe he was going to call it in on his radio and hadn't realized it, too, was trashed.

For whatever reason, Deputy Haines dropped into the seat of his car and gave me the opportunity I needed. I shifted my body to block the view of the old men on the bench and in one quick motion, jabbed two fingers into a nerve on the deputy's neck, delivering a mild jolt from a spell. He shuddered once and slumped.

I remained in position for a moment, nodding as if the deputy were still talking to me. Then I said, "Sir, I'll go see if I have that information." I took back my documents and closed the patrol car door.

A quick glance back told me the old men were still watching but didn't seem suspicious that anything out of the ordinary had happened. Lightning boy was about halfway to town. I'd be cutting this close.

I slid back into my car and closed the door, then adjusted the tint a little darker to hide activity from prying eyes. I wiped away the obfuscation spell over the tracking mark and began deftly plucking, twisting, and manipulating the sigils. It took as long as expected. About ten minutes later, I unknotted the center holding the sigils together and the pattern faded.

The girl was free of the mark, but her assassin stood about twenty feet away in front of the car. Dried blood caked on his face, and his t-shirt was shredded and covered in splinters. He looked like a damned zombie.

The old men stared wide-eyed at the kid. One of them looked nervously toward the deputy's car. The other pulled out a phone and started dialing. This situation was about to go bad six ways from Sunday.

It was possible the boy might just let me drive away. If he hadn't used magic in front of the nubs yet, it was likely he wouldn't attack if I drove away. The deputy's car blocked me in from behind, so the only way out was forward, right over the kid.

The boy walked toward the car, head shaking. "Why are you making this so hard?"

I couldn't just run him over, mainly because he'd only get back up. One of the old men was recording us with his phone now. The only way out was to defuse the situation long enough to open another avenue.

Or I could just do my damned job and hand over the girl.

I glanced at her slumbering form and regret attacked me from multiple angles. I'd just fucked up hard. Word would spread, the agency would blacklist me, and my time providing tracking services would come to an end. If it weren't for the damned ghosts in my head, I could have just let nature take its course.

If I hadn't tagged the girl with the tracker in the first place, none of this would've happened. I could've taken her, explained the situation to my handler, and found out what in the hell made her worthy of execution.

I got out of the car and leaned casually on the door. "What's your name, kid?"

Lightning boy stiffened. "They call me Sigma."

"Like the Greek letter."

He nodded. "Now, if you'll—"

"What are you, Sigma?" I frowned. "Never seen anything like you."

"It's a secret." He wiped some of the caked blood from his face, revealing undamaged skin beneath. "Why didn't you just mark her and leave? I would have finished my mission already and gone on to the next. Now I'm going to get in big trouble."

Just when I thought he couldn't surprise me anymore, he had to go and say that. "Jesus, kid. You've got more assassinations on your plate for today?"

"Not today, but—" he shook his head as if realizing he shouldn't give me any more information. His fists clenched. "You're making this really, really hard!"

"Give me a damned good reason for all this and I'll make it easy." I glanced at the old men. They were both recording on their phones now. I didn't want to risk another hex because if they were streaming live, the video would survive on the internet whether their phones died or not.

"I can't say." Electricity sparked on his fingertips. He lowered his voice to a whisper. "Don't make me kill all these people too."

I stiffened. "Why would you do that?"

"To keep the law."

"That's a violation of Article Four, Sigma." I stepped around the car door. "Besides, those nubs are recording everything. You use magic, and it'll be all over the internet."

"The what?" He looked genuinely confused.

I scoffed. "They didn't tell you about the internet, social media, and smart phones?"

"Oh, yeah, I know about the phones." Sigma glanced at the old men then back to me. "You can't leave while I'm standing here, so give me the girl."

If it had just been me, I could've escaped a dozen different ways. But I wasn't leaving Dolores, and getting her past the kid wasn't so easy, especially when he had supercharged regenerative abilities. Magic was out of the question and I couldn't attack him physically. Sirens wailing in the distance told me my options were narrowing by the minute. I had to turn one of these obstacles into an opportunity.

Or I could just cheat.

My hand drifted to my chest and touched the orb hanging from a chain beneath my shirt. Sigma might be strong, but I could probably move him out of the way with enough power. If I got back in the car, I could cast the spell without the men even seeing me. It wasn't the best plan, but it was the only thing that seemed feasible.

I should've been paying better attention.

Dolores roared to life. Tires screeched, and the driver door caught me in the back. I used the impetus to spin and caught a glance of the girl behind the steering wheel just as the door slammed shut.

Sigma braced himself and held out his hands just before the car hit him. Metal groaned and rubber screeched. For an instant, Dolores stopped. But while Sigma had the strength to hold the car in place, his shoes weren't up to the task. The rubber soles couldn't hold their grip and Sigma began to slide backward.

Anger boiled my blood. "You dented her hood, you little monster!"

The old men were on their feet now, shouting in surprise. I took a risk and hexed their phones while they were pointed away from me. They cried out again and dropped their smoking devices. And then the rest of the sheriff's department screeched around the corner toward the gas station.

By now, Sigma had been pushed well past the gas pumps. There was plenty of room to escape, but first I had to reclaim my car. I activated the sigil on the driver door, and it sprang open, revealing the girl. Face red, mouth wide open and screaming, she looked like someone who'd just woken up in a bed full of roaches.

I pinched a nerve in her shoulder, and she released the steering wheel with a cry of pain. Still in motion, I used my body to shove her across the bench seat. Then I cast another sigil, this time drawing power from the orb beneath my shirt and broadsided Sigma with it.

He yelped and flew sideways twenty feet before skidding across the asphalt. Fire and ice pumped through my veins and seemed to constrict around my heart. My vision blurred and I slumped against the steering wheel. The pain vanished as quickly as it had come. I sucked in a breath and jerked upright.

The girl clawed at the door handle on the passenger door, but it was magically locked. No getting out without my permission. Sigma climbed unsteadily to his feet just as every cop in the county converged on the parking lot.

Thankfully, they all came from one direction. I hit the accelerator and peeled out of the parking lot.

"Let me out!" the girl tried rolling down the window, but the handle was locked. "Let me out!"

Pain constricted around my chest. I gritted and bore it, focusing on the road through the haze of oxygen deprivation. My heart pounded faster and faster. Waves of heat and cold pulsated across my chest.

Somehow, I managed to talk. "Calm down. Someone's trying to kill you."

"Yeah, you!" The girl shrank against the door. "You're that creepy-assed janitor I noticed watching me the other day."

I must have really been slacking to be that obvious, or she was more perceptive than most teens. With a flick, I unbound the disguise sigil and the uniform faded, replaced by shirt and slacks.

She gasped and cowered against the door. "H-how did you do that?"

"Magic." I glanced at her and back to the road. "There are some heavy hitters in the magic community after you."

"Magic?" She scoffed and flicked her gaze to the side, like someone considering a desperate plan and deciding to do it. Then she climbed over the seat and into the back where she tried her luck on the doors and windows back there.

I didn't like having a potential threat at my back, especially with the pain in my chest, but there wasn't much I could do. Flashing lights appeared on the road behind me. The police had probably radioed ahead for a roadblock.

Instead of trying to fight me from behind, the girl had crawled into the back of the station wagon and was trying the back door and window.

"You need to get in the seat and buckle up," I said. "You've got ten seconds."

"Let me go, you fucking pervert!" She lay on her back and kicked the window.

Like everything about Dolores, it was a lot tougher than it looked. Her ten seconds expired, and I did what I had to do, veering right into a residential neighborhood. The girl rolled and slammed into the side with an explosive grunt. Shrieking, she rolled and hit the other side when I took another sharp turn.

A car parked on the road looked about the same shape and size as Dolores. It wasn't a station wagon, but it'd do. I screeched to a halt and jumped out. I didn't see anyone outside and at this point didn't really care if they saw me. In quick successive strokes, I scrawled a sigil on the dirty hood of the parked car and infused it with power.

The faded gray paint turned glossy black. The trunk became a station wagon hatch, and the front end went from rounded to square. In the span of seconds, the other car looked identical to mine. Then I turned to

Dolores and empowered the illusion sigil on her hood. Her paint faded, the rear end bubbled up and out, and the front end rounded like a modern car. She'd morphed from station wagon to SUV thanks to the power of illusion.

The girl was already trying to climb over the seats and out of the open door, but I hopped in, closed the door and hit the gas before she made it.

"Let me out!" This time she slapped my face and grabbed my short hair from behind. I let her have at it and calmly drove down the street until I could make another turn. I stopped, shifted my body toward the middle of the seat, and grabbed her wrists in one quick motion.

I wasn't about to talk sense to this girl, not in her frame of mind. Couldn't blame her either. She'd passed out in the parking lot at school and woken up in a stranger's car. I had too much to worry about without her screaming bloody murder in my ears and hitting me. I jabbed her in the neck same as I'd done for Deputy Haines.

But she was struggling too much and I didn't hit the exact spot. Instead of knocking her out, I hit her throat. Her eyes flared and she started gasping for breath. It wasn't an ideal situation, but it'd do for the moment. I let her wrists go and she slumped in the back seat, grabbing her chest and sucking air.

I drove the speed limit toward another road. I knew from my extensive exploration of this podunk town that it connected back to the highway. I tootled on down to the stop sign and stopped to watch police cars blur past, sirens wailing. Several turned down the road I was on and zipped right past me. Others turned down the street I'd been on earlier. It seemed they wanted to box me in. The road was clear, so I turned right and headed on out of town. I'd had enough adventures for one day.

Unfortunately, my passenger had other ideas.

She lunged over the seat and tried to jerk the steering wheel to the right, so we'd veer off the road. I knocked her hands away before she even got close. I entertained a few options—knock her out and find a place to stay the night, knock her out and drive all the way back to Atlanta, or stop the car and let her go.

The last option would be a death sentence. Sigma would probably find her walking back home and turn her into a charred corpse. The ghosts in my head stirred again. They were angry and adamant. This was my fault, not the girl's.

I'd made a terrible choice and would have to suffer the consequences.

CHAPTER 4

The rural countryside offered me another option. I turned down a narrow road with no houses in sight and located a dirt road a few hundred yards later. The dirt road led into the woods, so I followed it a good distance and stopped. The girl made me fight for every inch, screaming, punching, and even trying to choke me.

I batted her hands away for the umpteenth time and yanked her over the seat. She unceremoniously tumbled over and rolled onto the floorboard. I opened my door, gripped her arm, and dragged her out after me. I dumped her at the edge of the road. A quick spell bound her knees so she couldn't get up or run.

"Help!" she screamed. "Help!"

I slapped another spell over her mouth to keep her quiet.

She touched her frozen lips, eyes flaring with surprise. And that was when I realized another strange thing about this girl. She hadn't cried, not once. She was furious, but not afraid. Most kids her age would've shat their pants by now. But not her, not this girl.

I leaned against the car and folded my arms. "You're bound with magic.

That's why you don't see any ropes on your legs or duct tape on your mouth."

She stopped struggling and stared at me.

I took that as a good sign and continued. "I was supposed to mark you for termination. At first, I didn't understand why. Then I saw what you did to those kids."

She made muffled sounds, unable to open her lips. Since she wasn't screaming, I figured I could risk letting her talk. I unbound the spell and held a finger to my lips. "No screaming, or I'll silence you again."

Her eyes narrowed to slits. "Are you going to rape me?" The question sounded so matter of fact, it threw me for a loop. But it wasn't surprising, given what I'd found in her records.

The look in her eyes was all too familiar. I'd seen it on the faces of targets just before I ended them—the look of acceptance when you know there's nothing you can do to change your fate. Seeing it on the face of someone so young was really fucking sad.

"Jesus, no." I spat on the road as if that would clean the bad taste from my mouth. I had second thoughts for the third time about what in the hell I thought I was doing. I'd broken code, was acting unprofessionally, and had nearly exposed nubs to magic. Explaining myself to someone who should be dead right now felt completely alien.

She continued to stare at me. "Do you get your jollies killing people then?"

"There's nothing enjoyable about killing." I'd just done it, keeping emotions out of the equation, at least until my big fuckup during the war.

She flinched, apparently receiving a response that surprised her. "What in the hell does that mean?"

I wasn't sure where to begin, so I boiled it down to essentials. "I'm a tracker. I locate missing people. In some cases, I find them for relatives.

In other cases, I find them for bounty hunters and assassins." I folded my arms across my chest. "I find the target, mark them, and leave the rest to the client. In your case, it seems they want you dead."

She stared at me. "Bullshit."

"Yeah, I suppose it sounds like it." I shrugged. "Look, I don't know what the hell I'm doing. I should've just marked you and left. Instead, I've done everything wrong and pissed off some powerful people." I blew out a breath and stepped away from the car. "This is the most idiotic thing I've done in a while."

Her forehead furrowed. "Kidnapping?"

I snorted. "No, that's kid's play." I swiped away the binding spell on her legs and pointed down the road. "Just call the police and have them pick you up. I removed the tracking spell, so maybe Sigma won't find you for a while."

Suddenly free, she sprang up and ran into the woods.

"Wrong way," I shouted. I threw up my hands and sat in Dolores. I knocked my shoes together to get rid of the dirt and swiveled into the car. I felt eyes on me and looked left. The girl stood at the edge of the woods, watching me forlornly.

"I don't have a phone," she said.

I sighed. "Just follow the dirt road back to the highway. I'm sure someone will find you." *Hopefully not Sigma.* The chorus of voices bubbled up in my head. *Killer. Murderer.*

"You went through all the trouble of kidnapping me and now you're just abandoning me here?" She threw up her hands. "What kind of a monster are you?"

That was a question I didn't want to answer. "You think this is about some pervert kidnapping you, and yet you're standing there talking to said pervert instead of running for the hills." I closed the car door and rolled down the window. "Just start walking." I almost told her to be careful, to watch out for creepy blond boys on the way home. It didn't matter. She'd be dead before nightfall.

The girl bit her bottom lip. "Why would someone want me dead? I'm a nobody."

"Yeah, you are." I shrugged. "At least I thought you were until I saw what you did to those kids at school."

Her forehead pinched. "What did I do?"

"You swapped their souls." I leaned back in my seat and looked down the winding dirt road. "Never seen or heard of anything like it."

She scoffed. "What kind of bullshit is that? Do you really think magic exists, or are you crazy?"

I got out of the car, summoned my oblivion staff and focused power down the smooth black metallic wood. A fireball streaked from the end and splintered a sapling. Then I wove a sigil and cast it at her, lifting her a couple feet off the ground by her neck.

She choked and gasped, legs flailing wildly. I released the spell and she dropped to the ground, eyes wild.

I banished the staff. "Guess I'm crazy either way."

The girl climbed to her feet and stared at me. "You're for real."

I pointed down the road. "Follow the road to the highway." Then I got back in the car and started the engine.

The girl ran around to the passenger side and tried to open the locked door. She pounded on the window. "Let me in."

I stared at her for a moment. *What are you doing?* I thought to myself. I powered the door sigil and it opened. *Apparently, letting her in.* "Knock the dirt off your shoes."

She frowned but did as requested before putting her feet on the floorboard. It was vinyl, and easy to clean, but there was no reason to just dump debris in my clean car. The girl closed the door and looked at me expectantly. "Who's trying to kill me?"

I pursed my lips and stared at her for a moment. I'd already violated my agreement with the agency and fought the assigned assassin. Even if I gave up the girl right now, I was too far over the line to find forgiveness. That just wasn't a thing in my line of work. I might be the best, but it all went down the crapper the minute someone pulled a stunt like this.

At this point, I couldn't really make matters much worse. But I was probably wrong—dead wrong.

"I don't know who the client is. The agency keeps that confidential." I leaned my elbow on the windowsill. "The assassin is a kid named Sigma. But he's something I've never seen before."

She frowned. "Something?"

"Yeah, some kind of freak I've never seen." I shrugged. "Don't know of anyone who can shoot lightning out of their hands."

"A freak?" Her eyes widened. "You're saying he can do more than blow up trees with fireballs?"

"Way more." I patted my hand on the windowsill. "Never even seen fae use that kind of power. They're strong in other ways."

"What's a fae?" she said.

The kid was completely in the dark and I didn't have all day to explain. Then again, that depended on our next steps. "Look, what do you want to do? At this point, I've screwed myself so bad, I might as well help you keep breathing."

She gulped. "I-I don't know. Anywhere is better than here."

"Because you're being hunted?" I said. "Or something else?"

"Because of everything else." She seemed to shrink in on herself. "I don't give a shit about my foster parents, and this is the third school I've been to this year."

"Third?" I didn't know a lot about regular human schools. "Is that a lot?"

She snorted. "Yeah, it's a lot."

"So what are you saying, kid?" I waited for an answer.

Her eyes flashed. "Don't call me kid."

"Fine. Tell me what you want to do."

"I want to live, but not in this shithole." She leaned over and put her arms around her knees, as if about to pull them up on the seat but stopped when she saw the indignant look on my face. "I'll go with you."

"A complete stranger," I said.

"Maybe that tells you something about my current situation." She leaned back in the seat and started messing with the buckles. "God, why are there two shoulder straps?"

"It's a harness." I took one of the two straps. "Click them both in the middle buckle."

"But why?" she said.

"Pray you don't have to find out." I shifted into drive. I'd removed the stock manual and replaced it with an automatic after converting the fuel to liquid mana. "Tell me about your situation, kid." I backed down the dirt road since it was too narrow to turn around. I knew some nasty details about her past but hadn't dug much deeper. Once I found the first bread crumb leading from an orphanage to her first foster parents, I'd just followed the trail. Some people liked knowing everything about who they tracked. I found it unnecessary unless there was a good reason to know all the details.

It was best not knowing a target too well. It made it easier, knowing their future just got a whole lot worse, or a whole lot shorter.

"Stop calling me kid." She bared her teeth. "My name is Hannah."

I winced before I could stop myself.

"Something wrong with my name?" she said.

"No." I reached the paved road and oriented the car toward the highway. "Go on."

"Why'd you look like that when I said my name?" She stared at me, unblinking.

It didn't bother me, but I also didn't really care if she knew. "I already knew your name. I just don't want to use it."

"Ah." She tapped a finger on her temple. "You don't want to humanize your targets. It's easier that way."

"Yeah." I arched my eyebrows. "So, what's your situation?" I wasn't sure why I wanted to know. I didn't need conversation to keep me entertained. Knowing her background would only humanize her more. Then again, I'd just saved her from assassination, which was a lot more humanizing than anything I'd done in recent memory.

"My mom was born in the US, but her parents immigrated from Iraq. They were super religious and wouldn't let her date anyone because they'd already arranged for her to marry some old dude when she was fourteen years old." The girl shrugged. "My mom didn't like that, so she ran away, met some random guy and got pregnant." She scoffed. "She tried to have me aborted, but it didn't work. She used to tell me that a lot when I was little."

I raised an eyebrow. "Really?"

The girl nodded. "But then she met this great guy who really liked us. Mom finally accepted my existence, and everything was great for a while." Her shoulders slumped. "But then bad things started happening around me."

I grunted. "Like what?"

"This boy tried to steal my lunch at school. He hit me, and I got so mad, I screamed at the top of my lungs." She looked down. "All the windows in the cafeteria shattered at once."

"Early manifestations of your abilities," I said. "It's normal, at least for mages."

"Mages?" she said.

"Wizards, sorcerers, witches," I said.

The girl nodded. "Oh, okay. Other weird things happened, but I didn't think it was really me causing it." She sighed. "One day Mom came home really scared and said we had to leave."

I frowned. "What about the boyfriend?"

"She was crying. I think maybe something happened to him because she never talked about him again." The girl's lips trembled. "We started travelling. We went so many places I can't even remember them all."

I wondered if it had something to do with the people who wanted her dead now but didn't mention it. "Rough life. What happened to your mother?"

"She died," the girl whispered.

"Then you went to an orphanage," I said.

"I was ten." She watched me as if looking for a reaction. "It was actually better than moving around all the time like I had with Mom, but then they put me with a foster family."

"Not so good?" I said.

"They had multiple kids. The older boy would sneak into the girls' bedroom at night and molest us." She shivered. "He choked me when I tried to resist. Said he'd kill me if I told anyone."

"Did you tell anyone?" I said.

"No." The girl looked out the window. "One of the other girls did. She went away, but he stayed."

I'd heard rough life stories before. The girl's wasn't any worse than most, but that didn't make it good. I felt sorry for her even though I tried not to. My training taught me that connecting with targets was the worst thing I could do if I wanted to sleep at night. There were others who enjoyed befriending targets and then killing them. I thought that was fucking sick, but it didn't make me any less of a killer.

"Things got worse?" I said.

"At first they got better." She stared at the road. "Then the boy started doing it again."

"No justice in the world," I said.

"Except what we make," she whispered.

I gave her a questioning look. "Explain."

"He liked to jerk off when he played with us," she said. "Sometimes he'd pull it out right in our face. I stabbed him in the balls with a fork."

I shuddered. "Jesus."

"He hit me so hard I blacked out for a minute." A smile crossed her face. "But the screams woke up everyone. The fosters saw him holding his bloody balls."

"How old was the boy?" I asked.

She shrugged. "Fifteen or sixteen. The state took him after that."

I knew she'd been through multiple fosters. But I didn't push for more information. I didn't want to know—didn't want to care. Once we got back to Atlanta, I'd find the girl a safe place to stay and cut her loose. Then I'd have to deal with the ramifications of my poor decision making.

I activated a secure connection app to connect me with the agency messaging system. I was curious about what they'd have to say about my sudden disregard for protocol. But there were no new messages in the app. Did they not know yet, or simply didn't care?

"You even listening to me?" the girl said.

I put my phone down. "Yeah."

"Bullshit." She crossed her arms over her chest. "Your eyes went all distant like you were thinking about something and then you got on your phone."

"Truth is, I don't want to hear anything else." I checked the rearview mirror for the tenth time since reaching the highway and was happy to see nothing but open road behind us. "You're sixteen, right?" I didn't need to ask, but figured it was less creepy that way.

"Yeah, why?"

"I'll set you up with a new identity and some starter cash," I said. "You can go back to school, or just get a job." I shrugged. "Whatever works for you."

The girl stared at me. "How much starter cash?"

I ignored the question. "I know a place you can live for cheap. Don't worry about it." I flashed a smile. "Better than dying, right?"

The girl looked away. "Sometimes I wonder."

"Valid point." My chest tightened and my vision went blurry for an instant. The potions my healer gave me weren't helping. I hated to do it, but it was time to call in a favor and find out what in the hell was wrong with me.

"You okay?" The girl watched me closely.

I nodded. "I'm fine. Gonna be a long trip, so just entertain yourself."

Her lips trembled. "You just told me you don't give a shit about my past and that you're going to drop me off in a strange city to fend for myself. How in the fuck do I entertain myself when I've got nothing to look forward to?"

"Think happy thoughts." I shrugged. "Or whatever it takes."

She glared at me. "Do you even have friends?"

"I do, as a matter of fact." I sped up to pass a slow-moving truck. "Look, there's no need to get personal. You'll be in good hands when we get to Atlanta. I promise."

"Fuck you." She leaned against the door window. "If you hadn't marked me, I wouldn't be here right now. My life wasn't great, but it wasn't a dumpster fire until you stepped in."

She was probably right. I bore responsibility and would have to make sure she was taken care of. My decision had fucked up two lives. Once the agency got involved, things would get a lot worse.

And by worse, I meant deadly.

CHAPTER 5

After an hour of me not responding to her attempts at conversation, the girl climbed into the back seat and eventually fell asleep. We hit the Atlanta perimeter around eight. I still hadn't heard a peep from Eclipse which made me wonder if Sigma hadn't reported the incident yet. Then again, he could've been detained by the police, unable to break the law and use magic to escape.

Whatever the case, it bought me some time.

It was too late to go downtown and drop off the girl, so I headed home. The girl was still asleep, but I cast an obfuscation spell around her head so she couldn't see or hear anything that might give away the location of my secret lair. I headed just inside the city perimeter and turned into a residential neighborhood. Another left took me toward a wooded area where farmland used to be.

A tall iron gate blocked the road ahead. Chain link topped by razor wire blocked access to the woods on either side, forming a perimeter around eight acres where farmland used to be. The former owner had been an old coot who refused to sell to developers even though he couldn't keep up the farm any longer. The place had been in his family for generations, dating back to the eighteenth century.

In my hunt for a safe place to live after my tumultuous exit from the fae realm, I'd tracked rumor and substance to locate a place where no one could find me. But sometimes I wondered if I'd found this place or if it had found me. When I'd first arrived here, the old farmer acted as if he'd been expecting me. Considering the bizarre and morbid history of the land, that wouldn't have surprised me.

I powered the sigils on the locked gate. Metal clinked and rattled as the gate slid open. I drove through and paused to watch it close and lock again. Old-growth oaks and maples leaned over the narrow road, forming a tunnel of thick branches. I continued onward until I reached a dead end. Nothing but forest extended past the abrupt cutoff in asphalt. I didn't slow down, driving straight into the trees. There was a brief flicker of darkness as I passed through the illusion and then the road reappeared ahead.

I drove past the burnt-out shell where the farmhouse used to be. The other outbuildings were covered in vines and vegetation, and the fields were overgrown with saplings and bushes. I continued into the heart of the eight acres and reached a clearing of old stumps and clumps of grass in hard-packed earth.

Faded tombstones jutted at various angles from the ground on the left and right of the road. There were three hundred and thirty-three of them in all, several generations of the farmer's ancestors and other community members—at least that was what he'd told me.

Past the gravestones rose a church, an octagonal building with a sturdy granite foundation and a frame of thick timber. An eight-sided tower rose from the center of the peaked roof, reaching thirty feet high.

The farmer's ancestors had built the community church, but something had happened, and it had gone from a Christian church to something not quite so mainstream. The farmer hadn't been alive when it happened. He never told me what the place had become, or much about it.

When his parents died, he destroyed all their religious texts and demolished the statues. He'd closed off and hidden passageways, making it impossible for even me to find them all. He'd taken the secrets of the place to his grave. "My forefathers were fools," he'd told me on his deathbed. "All the gods are dead."

I knew it to be true. The fae had gone to war for their freedom and killed the gods. For better or worse, they were the only gods left. They were the ones running the show.

Whatever the church had been, the consecrated grounds protected me from the undead. It didn't matter which god or goddess they worshipped—anything consecrated in a divine name worked just fine against vampires and zombies.

The worshippers had also carved a giant sigil in the ground and filled it with silver. When Atlanta burned during the American Civil War, this place remained hidden from nubs and supers alike. Lycans would instinctually stay away from the silver even if they couldn't see it, and the sigil hid the church from prying eyes.

The gods might be dead, but my prayers had been answered when I found a place for me and Fred to live. This chapel had become my sanctuary.

The girl stirred from her slumber and immediately panicked. "I can't see! I can't hear! What the fuck did you do to me?"

"Calm down." I pulled into a wooden outbuilding that served as a garage and turned off the car. I dissolved the sensory deprivation spell. "Welcome to Sanctuary."

She gasped wiped her eyes. Then she looked around. "We're in a shed." She backed away, eyes wide. "Shit. This is the part where you kill me, isn't it?"

"Hardly." I opened the door and stepped out. "Sanctuary is this way."

The girl narrowed her eyes and hesitated a moment, then scooted over and climbed out of the car. She followed me out of the garage and toward the chapel.

"Wow, it's actually beautiful." She pressed her hand against the granite foundation. "I've never seen a church like this."

I kept walking, eyes forward. "You've been to a Christian church before?"

"Yeah." She caught up with my long strides. "It sounds weird when you put it that way. Most people in the South assume churches are Christian."

"Not where I'm from." I disarmed the sigil on the thick wooden door. It flashed and disabled the trap wards. "Never try to open this door yourself or you'll die."

She gulped. "What kind of fucked up world do you live in?"

I grinned and waved a hand around at the outside. "This one."

The girl stared at the graveyard. "Yeah, I guess it's all shitty."

I closed the door behind us and enabled the traps again, then disabled the wards on the inner door. "Oh, and this door will kill you too."

"Damn, you're paranoid." She followed close on my heels into the former sanctuary.

When I'd first seen the place, it had been completely empty. The farmer had chopped up all the benches and burned them, and then taken a sledgehammer to the giant idol that once sat in the middle of the room.

It had taken months, but I'd hired day laborers and brought them out to remodel, sectioning off an area into a master bedroom and bath, a kitchen, and a living space. There were even guest rooms, though I never used them. And that was just the upstairs.

The workers had lived in tents outside and I brought them the materials they needed. While they might have tales to tell of a strange man, they'd never be able to find this place again.

"Wow." The girl stopped and took in the open floor plan leading from the living space into the chef's kitchen. "Are you rich?" She scoffed. "You're an assassin. Of course you're rich."

"Money isn't a problem," I said. "And I'm not an assassin anymore."

She scoffed again. "You're delusional. You mark people, they die. Same thing no matter how you try to rationalize it."

"You're perceptive for someone so young." Or was she? I hadn't dealt with many nub kids, but they were usually pretty stupid at this age. Just as I'd been. The fae had never let me forget that.

"There's something weird about your face." The girl peered at me. "The skin looks weird when you talk."

"It's an illusion," I said. "A mask."

"You don't want me to know what you look like." She shrugged. "I get it."

I shook my head. "I just don't want to frighten you."

"Oh, yeah?" The girl stepped a little closer. "Now I really want to see what you look like."

"Maybe tomorrow." I went over to the fridge and took out a frozen dinner since the leftover lasagna I'd made last week was long past its expiration date. I paused and grabbed another dinner. It had been some time since I'd had an unexpected guest.

The girl walked around the couch in the living space and jumped back with a shout. "Jesus!"

I tossed the dinners in the microwave and started heating them. "Birds or mice?"

"Both!" Forehead pinched she stared at me. "How did you know?"

I walked around and looked at the corpses. Two sparrows and two mice formed a square on the area rug. "Sorry, Fred's weird like that."

"You've got a cat?" The girl shook her head. "What kind of fucked up assassin are you?"

Then a section of the rug reached out and wrapped around her leg. She screamed and ran into the kitchen.

"Nice one, Fred." I picked up the mice and birds. "Still don't know why you think I like these things."

A larger section of carpet changed color from mottled gray to black. Fred looked up at me with his golden eyes for a moment, then perched up on his tentacles and walked to a dark pool in the far corner. He slid in with a small splash and then floated to the surface, regarding me.

"That's Fred?" The girl came up behind me. "You've got a pet octopus? How in the hell does an octopus kill birds?"

"He's not a pet." The microwave beeped so I headed back to the kitchen to see if the meals were done. "He's a rescue."

"A rescue?" The girl followed me. "Normal people rescue dogs and cats, not octopuses."

"He doesn't talk much," I said. "That's why I like him."

"You're so weird." The girl sat on a bar stool and rotated on it. "You've got this really nice house, but it's a church on the outside. You're an assassin who doesn't kill, and you rescued an octopus from—from where? Illegal octopus breeders?"

The food seemed warm enough, so I plopped hers down in front of her along with a fork. "These are mail order meals. Let me know what you think." I checked the label on mine. "Backyard BBQ. I hope it's good."

"You've got death wards on the doors, but you let them deliver mail here?" She scoffed for at least the fifth time. "This one says turkey meatballs."

"Nothing is delivered here," I said. "I have another property for that." I opened the lid and tested the barbeque pork. "Hmm. It's tasty."

She stabbed a fork into hers and nibbled. "Too salty."

"I'll take that one off the list then." I filled two glasses with water and gave her one. "All the water is filtered, even from the tap."

The girl nodded toward Fred's pool. "What about that?"

"Salty," I said. "Just like Fred likes it."

She stared at me. "You going to tell me where you got him, or just change the subject like you do for everything else?"

I shrugged. "What's the point? You'll be somewhere else tomorrow and we'll never see each other again."

"At least show me your face." She put down her fork. "Let me see the face of the person who saved me from himself."

I dismissed her request without a word and took another bite of pork. Then I reconsidered. It wasn't a big deal. I used illusion to disguise myself on jobs, so it didn't really matter if she saw my face. Life had hardened the girl so it would probably disgust more than scare her. I dissolved the illusion.

The girl recoiled. "Oh, shit." She gagged. "What happened to your face?"

I unbuttoned the top of my shirt and pulled it back to show where the black veins started around my heart. From there, they moved up my neck and branched out over my left cheek and ear. The veins on my chest pulsed and squirmed like worms beneath the skin sometimes, but they were still now.

Fred emerged from his pool and lay on the edge, his golden eyes shading to pools of black. I'd had him for years, but it still creeped me out when he did that.

"I happened." I buttoned up my shirt and put back on my mask.

"How old are you?" the girl asked. "Fifty? Older?"

"Thirty-eight," I said.

"You haven't aged well at all." She stirred the meatballs with her fork but didn't seem to have an appetite anymore. "I guess killing people is hard on the body."

"Fae magic is hard on the body," I said. "It's even worse when you amplify it."

"You use fairy dust to kill people?" She tried another meatball and grimaced.

I snorted. "Pixie dust," I said. "Fairy is considered a derogatory term."

The girl swallowed the meatball with some difficulty. "What do fae look like? Likes elves from *Lord of the Rings*?"

I'd binged human movies and television shows even during my time in the fae realm, so I knew what she meant. "Elves are a different species. The fae were created to oversee nature and take care of the planet." I shrugged. "At least that's what they say."

"What do they look like?" she said.

"Like humans, but better," I said. "Imagine a race of supermodels."

"Even the men?" she asked.

I nodded. "Not that you ever know exactly what they look like. They use glamour—the strongest kind of illusion magic—to change their appearance." I traced a finger along my cheek. "My mask is convincing, but it's not perfect."

The girl risked another meatball. "So the fae are perfect."

"They wish. They love bargaining and tricking others into accepting lopsided deals." I stared at my food and wondered why I'd become so chatty suddenly. I finished off my food and tossed the empty container. "Trash is here." I pointed to the bedrooms on the other side of the space. "You'll find blankets and toiletries in the closet over there."

"Wait, that's it?" She reached for my arm but checked herself before she grabbed it. "What's so awful about telling me about the fae?" This time she did grab my arm. "You just thrust me into a world I didn't even know existed and expect me to survive without any information?"

I looked down at her hand and she released my arm. "I hope you like to read." I walked to a door with a rounded top set at the back of the kitchen. I opened it and flicked on a light, then walked down the spiraling stone staircase. We descended a hundred and three steps, the air growing cooler around us until we reached an opening at the bottom.

"My god." The girl stared in awe at what lay beyond.

The library was cavernous and mostly empty. The farmer had destroyed all the literature down here, much to my regret. I couldn't imagine how large the collection had been. The only remnant I'd found was a torn piece of papyrus with *Codex Oblivionis* neatly inked across the top.

The Latin translated to Oblivion Codex. It likely related to the Oblivion Guard, though I'd never heard of such a document in all the time I'd served. I couldn't exactly ask the fae what it was, so I'd stuck it in a chest and forgotten about it. Over the past years, I'd amassed a decent amount of human literature, mostly about the history of the human world and its nations.

I'd tried reading some of their fiction, but aside from romance novels, found very little that interested me. I assumed romance appealed to me only because it focused so much on interpersonal relations between the genders.

The low fae acted like the characters from romance novels, often stabbing others in the back to get what they wanted. But the high fae were cold and impersonal. If any such activities went on among them, it was out of sight of lesser beings.

I took the girl to a section across the cavern, well away from the human sections. I dug out an old leather tome originally written by an elf named Alinar Carzowryn and later translated into English by some unknown scholar. The book was huge and heavy, so I lugged it to one of the reading tables and set it down.

The girl stared open-mouthed at the towering shelves even though barely a quarter of one of them was filled. "Jesus, dude. What is this place?"

"A library." I pointed to the book. "*The History of Feary,* for your reading pleasure." I started back toward the stairs. "I'm going to bed."

"Feary?" She tried to pronounce it as I had. "Why isn't it spelled f-a-e-r-y?"

"That's just the way they spell it," I said.

She scoffed. "What, am I supposed to fear the fae?"

"Yeah, you should." I started walking again. "Be very fucking afraid of the fae. You and me?" I motioned toward me and then her. "We're barely insects to them."

But as dangerous as they were, the fae were probably the least of her worries.

CHAPTER 6

"Wait!" The girl held out a hand. "You're just leaving me alone down here?"

For the first time, she looked vulnerable and kind of cute like a kid should. I felt...sorry for her. Maybe that wasn't the right word. It was that same feeling I'd felt right before saving her. As if helping her made me feel good. It was bizarre and dangerous as hell.

The ghosts murmured in assent.

A simple emotion made me throw away years of training and professionalism. The ghosts in my head whispered furiously, but I couldn't make out anything they said. They seemed pleased with my poor decision.

I purged the emotions and turned away. "You'll be fine. Sanctuary is the safest place you could be."

Looking small and defeated, she sat down at the table and watched me forlornly. "But I'm chilly."

"There are blankets in the closet upstairs." I pointed up. "But don't take the books out of here. The underground environment preserves them." I stopped again. "When you go to bed, lock your door. Fred sometimes like to mess with guests."

"Can't imagine you have many," she grumbled.

I nodded. "I don't."

"Last thing I want are tentacles picking my nose in the middle of the night." The girl sagged.

I tried not to envision that and headed upstairs. Tired as I was, I still had a few things to do before going to bed, and I wasn't looking forward to them. I confirmed Fred was still perched on the edge of his pool before closing the door to the library. He'd never gone down there that I knew of. I couldn't imagine why he would, considering how dry it was and how difficult the stairs would be for an octopus.

Then again, he stayed out of water a lot for a creature that supposedly needed it to breathe. The apothecary I'd rescued him from had abused him and treated him with all kinds of experimental potions. For all I knew, Fred could breathe air. He was certainly no dummy. I'd found that out soon after taking him home.

That had been long before finding Sanctuary.

I went into the door leading to my bedroom. The master suite was roomy, decorated with posters I'd collected over the years. *Star Wars* and *Star Trek* movie posters took up one wall. Fantasy movies dominated another. The nubs were great at science fiction. Sometimes I wished I could leave this planet behind and find something else far away from the fae.

Romance posters dominated the other wall. *An Officer and a Gentleman, Dirty Dancing, When Harry Met Sally,* and *Ghost,* to name a few. I'd found that romance movies were also a kind of fantasy, because no nub I'd met had ever found the kind of love and devotion portrayed in books and movies. It was something I'd never find, mainly because I couldn't afford to risk it.

But sometimes it was nice to make believe.

I sat down at my desk and opened my laptop. Since the agency still hadn't messaged me, it seemed prudent to check the job status online and see if it was in default. I sigil-encrypted all my internet traffic, making it nearly impossible for anyone to trace. I doubted many mages had the depth of knowledge to crack the code, but I still changed them frequently in case.

I pulled up the agency website on the dark web and logged in. A couple of clicks took me to my account where a long list of jobs was marked completed. The other two were listed as in progress.

A chat window popped up.

Janice wants to chat. Accept?

I stared at it for a moment then clicked to accept.

Janice: Did you complete Alpha 809?

That was the girl's mission.

Anon: No. In progress.

Janice: You haven't logged in for weeks. You don't usually take so long.

Anon: Sorry. I have very little information to go on.

Janice: That's not why I contacted you.

I waited without responding.

Janice: Per your request, I found a healer who might be able to help you. Fitzroy Simmons.

An address followed. I stared at it, apprehension building. Seattle was the last place I wanted to go. But I didn't have much of a choice.

Anon: Why this guy?

Janice: He's a shaman.

I grunted and stared at the screen.

Anon: He's legit?

Janice: Very.

Her word was good enough for me.

Anon: What about the druid you mentioned in Arizona?

Janice: He's not responding. He's been on the run from the fae for centuries. It's possible they found him.

Anon: And the wizards you mentioned? The ones in Chicago and St. Louis?

Janice: Neither can help.

I groaned. Seeing a shaman wasn't exactly on my bucket list. I'd put a lot of hope in the druid. Their kind could cure many afflictions, but there weren't many of them left these days.

Anon: The shaman it is, then. My health has been affecting Alpha 809 progress. Will delay while I consult.

Janice: Client has paid for escalation. Agency will assign other partners to assist.

Anon: I'm exclusive.

Janice: Exclusivity expires at the end of week. Finish the job.

Agent disconnected.

I leaned back. This was mostly good news. For whatever reason, the client hadn't advised the agency about my fuckup. My condition gave me a perfect reason to bow out, and once the girl was with my connection downtown, she'd be safe. Most of the trackers I'd met could barely find their own assholes, much less a girl with almost no paper trail.

I disconnected the laptop and powered it off. Pinpricks of pain worked up my chest and into my cheek. I dissolved the illusion and stared at myself in the mirror. The girl was right. I looked super old now. The change had been so gradual over the years I hadn't even noticed until the black veins appeared.

None of the healers I'd seen knew what was wrong. I'd been examined from head to toe and even been to see some nub doctors. Their technology couldn't identify the problem. I knew that it was magic related, but not exactly how. The more power I used, the likelier it was that I'd have severe chest pains. That was why I used the pearl so sparingly now.

"It's not so bad," I told myself. I looked like a monster on one side of my face. The rest of my face looked fine, but the veins were slowly spreading across my nose and would soon reach the other side. I needed this fixed soon.

I WAS WELL into cooking breakfast the next morning when I remembered I had a guest. I decided she could have oatmeal since I hadn't cooked enough bacon and pancakes for her. I finished eating and went to her bedroom. The door was open, the bed empty. I went downstairs and found her in the library, wrapped in blankets, head down on the table.

She'd made it about a third of the way through the book I'd given her, which was kind of impressive given the dense text. Much of it was anecdotal history, spread by word of mouth through the generations, so it took up a lot more space than a few paragraphs of dry facts.

I left her alone and went back upstairs to make a call. I used sigil encryption just like with the internet to mask my location. Anyone who tried to trace would bounce all over the cellular network before settling on a random location.

A man answered. "Sandy's Pub, Andrew speaking."

"Sandy in? This is Cain."

A pause. "She's out of country. Want to talk to Phyllis?"

"Sure." I waited.

The phone clicked a moment later and a woman spoke. "What do you want?"

Phyllis didn't like me. Then again, most humans in the supernatural community didn't. But Sandy and Phyllis owed me, so it didn't really matter how they felt. Besides, they didn't charge favors for this kind of service. "I have someone, a girl, who needs disappearing. Can I drop her off today?"

"You can help all the girls in the world, and it won't make you a better person, Cain." Phyllis made a spitting noise. "Why do you even bother? Not like you give a shit."

"It interests me." The girl wasn't the first girl I'd taken from a bad situation, but she was the first I'd broken a contract for. "You'd rather they be left alone than rescued by someone you hate?"

"You're just a twisted fucker." Phyllis blew out a breath. "Is this one unconscious like the rest? Last time you forgot to unbind the sigil and she didn't wake up for a day."

"I'll bring this one in conscious," I said.

"It'll have to wait until Sandy comes back." Phyllis cleared her throat of phlegm. "I'm headed out this morning and won't be back until next week."

"When is Sandy getting back?" I asked.

"Four days." She coughed, chest rumbling with heavy congestion. "Call back then." And she hung up.

I heard a faint noise and turned to see the girl coming up the final bend in the stairs, still wrapped in blankets. She yawned and then noticed me looking at her.

"Do I smell bacon?" she said.

"Yeah, but I ate it all." I pointed to a container of oatmeal. "Milk is in the fridge."

She grimaced. "God, you're a terrible host. Do you make Fred cook his own food too?"

I hated that I'd be stuck with her for four more days. I'd just have to keep her locked up here alone. "The people who are going to help you are out of town for a few days, so you'll have to stay here until then."

"Can I at least cook my own bacon?" she said.

"Cook whatever you want." I pointed to the pantry. "There's more food in there."

The girl blew out a breath. "And I thought *I* had bad interpersonal skills."

"I have to go out of town," I said. "I'll probably be back tomorrow, but it might be the day after."

She threw up her hands. "You're leaving me here alone?"

"You won't be alone." I nodded to the tentacles poking from the pool. "Fred will be here."

The girl shuddered. "Going to kill someone else?"

I shook my head. "It's personal."

Her eyes narrowed. "It's about your ugly face, isn't it?"

I locked my gaze on hers, but she refused to turn away. I nodded. "I need it diagnosed."

"I kind of hope it's killing you." The girl crossed her arms. "You probably deserve it."

"Yeah." I pocketed my phone. "I probably do."

"I read that the fae call mages, vampires, werewolves, and all the human supernaturals mutants." She shook her head. "You definitely look like a mutant."

I considered that a moment. "I'm the mutant the mutants hate." And then I went into my room and packed.

Seattle was a viper's nest, thick with vampires. The frequent cloud cover and rain made it the perfect place for them to live. In fact, it was their stronghold on the North American continent. It was a dangerous place for mages to visit, and even more so for me. I packed light, but smart. Blades weren't allowed on commercial airlines, so I took my dueling wands. My staff was always with me, waiting to be summoned from its pocket dimension.

I wished I could do that with all my stuff, but it was a built-in feature of the staff, not a spell I could cast on my own.

I got on my computer and purchased an airline ticket under the name Marcus Lynch. I selected the proper ID from my stash and put on the appropriate illusion mask. Then I picked up my duffel bag and slung it over my shoulder.

The girl looked up from cooking her bacon when I walked out. "Fred isn't going to kill me in my sleep, is he?"

"Not unless you're a rodent," I said.

"You never told me how it's possible for him to kill birds." She shivered. "It's creepy."

"You'll have to ask him." I kept walking to the door. "I've never seen him do it."

"Wait!" She ran over to me and tried to take my hand, but I kept it out of her reach. "Are you sure I'll be okay here?"

"There's enough frozen food to last a month. You'll be fine."

"What if you die?" she said.

I studied the worry lines on her face. "I won't."

"You might." The girl tried to take my hand again, but I tucked it behind my duffel bag. "Maybe you could give me some money and put me up at a hotel instead. I don't want to be trapped here."

"The door wards will run out of power in thirteen days if I don't refresh them." I couldn't decide if that was fear in her eyes or anger. For a child, her emotions were hard to read. "On the fourteenth day if I'm not back, just walk out."

Her eyes narrowed. "Is that the truth? Or will I kill myself?"

"The truth." I stepped away as she made another play for my hand. "Just lock your room at night if you sleep up here."

"But—"

I disarmed the inner door ward and left. It automatically snapped back on when the door closed, as did the outer one. I tossed my bag in Dolores and took off for the airport.

Despite heading to vampire central, I was looking forward to the plane ride. Normal humans made me feel uncomfortable, but also right at home. They were ignorant and stupid, yet full of themselves, as if they were the final authority on life. As if by knowing a little, they knew everything. I was highly skilled in many forms of fighting, both physical and magical, but I sometimes regretted not having a normal human upbringing.

I knew the fate of the human world was guided by the fae. That the seat of all power was in Feary and not in the governments of the human nations. The nubs only perceived themselves as having power when, in fact, many were merely puppets. It was illusion without fae glamour—manipulation on a grand scale.

I accepted my ignorance of how the fae managed such a feat. *Accepting and acknowledging ignorance brings about self-awareness. Self-awareness leads to knowledge. Knowledge leads to wisdom.* Cormyn Dran's words still echoed in my head. He'd often dispensed such useful knowledge during my training in the Oblivion Guard. That was before Torvin Rayne, the head commander of the guard, told him simple creatures like humans could never comprehend such things.

In that one instance, I didn't entirely disagree with him.

The ghosts grew angry at the thought of his name. They despised me, but they hated Torvin even more. I understood completely, but it seemed they were stuck with me just as I was still tormented by memories of Torvin.

I reached the airport and stood in a long line to check in. I could have easily used a kiosk, but it was more interesting to speak to the tireless airline workers behind the counters. Despite dealing with so many rude and foolish customers, they managed to keep a professional air about them. With such mental stamina, they'd do well to train as assassins.

"Any luggage to check?" The middle-aged woman behind the counter glanced at my duffel bag.

"No." I smiled and handed her my ID. "I just need my boarding pass."

She smiled. "For future reference, the digital kiosks can print your boarding pass without the need to wait in line."

"You're doing a great job," I said reassuringly. "It's hard work."

Her smile faltered with a touch of confusion. "Oh, well, thank you, Mr. Lynch." She typed on her terminal and produced a printed pass a moment later. "Enjoy your flight."

I smiled harder. "Thank you, Miss Dawson." I thought using the name on her tag was a nice touch to the interaction.

Her smile trembled. "You're welcome?"

I walked away feeling proud about my success. Had I not been a trained assassin, I might have had a skip in my step as well. I tested a little skip just to see how it felt. A girl looked at me and giggled.

It wasn't that I never dealt with nubs, but there was something refreshing, something authentic about mingling with the ignorant herd. Despite their shortcomings, nubs were interesting. And there were so many, I didn't have to make friends simply to be among them. The fae called normal humans *kine,* an ancient term for cows. There was definitely something comforting about being in a herd.

And so I sat back and enjoyed the flight, watching a plane full of nubs exist in their own worlds—worlds made even smaller when they retreated behind the screen of a laptop or tablet, or put on earphones and shut out everything around them.

I was jealous they had such luxuries. If I dared walk around with headphones buzzing music in my ears, it would likely be the death of me. I relaxed, fully vigilant. Napped fully awake, and feigned being oblivious while noting every detail and quirk of all two-hundred and twenty-three souls aboard.

I noted the first signs of danger the moment I exited the plane and spotted a vampire. He was dressed like a baggage handler, but his pale skin and slightly bluish lips gave him away immediately. Most vampires used compulsion to make those around them perceive them as normal, but this vampire was obviously new or not very good at it. I was also trained to resist compulsion, so it was possible he simply wasn't very skilled or strong.

The way his eyes scanned all the passengers walking down the terminal, it was also obvious that he was on the lookout for someone. I sat down in a chair and pretended to be among those waiting for the next flight. It gave me a moment to identify any other dangers.

I counted six more vampires, three of them disguised as police. It seemed an unlikely coincidence that they just happened to be here today of all days, and far more likely they'd been sent here for a reason.

And that reason was me. I'd been burned.

CHAPTER 7

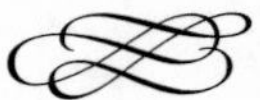

The agency burned me.

That was my first thought. Janice had played along so she could set me up. The healer didn't exist. It was a ruse to bait me into a vampire stronghold so they could capture or kill me. The agency knew that I'd abandoned the job but had kept the information quiet so they could deal with me this way.

But I wasn't done just yet.

Vampires have no powers that allow them to see through illusion. But it was possible they had devices which might allow them to penetrate my disguise. Given the current state of my face, I would stand out like a beacon if they saw through my mask.

I remained seated next to a man watching porn on his cell phone.

My phone buzzed, startling me so much I nearly flinched. All my outbound calls were sigil encrypted and anonymous. No one had my direct number except for the most insidious group of all the humans—telemarketers. It wasn't a call that rang my phone, but a text message.

The man watching porn was visibly aroused and drawing a few looks from nearby mothers with children. Acting as casually as possible, I scooted over a seat and gave him a look of disgust. He didn't see me, but the women did. So did the vampire dressed as a baggage handler. His eyes lingered on me a moment, then moved to the man.

I leaned back in my chair, crossed a leg, and looked at the text.

Communication compromised. Don't go to Seattle.

"How convenient," I muttered. I typed back a message. *You set me up, Janice. Bad decision.*

Not me. Coms tapped on my end.

Janice was trying to play me again. Then again, what if she wasn't? What if she didn't know what I'd done with the girl? It seemed best to play both sides against each other if possible, so I sent another message. *Vampires here. I avoided them. Leaving the front entrance now.*

Then I sat back and waited.

Janice replied almost instantly. *Leave Seattle. Do not visit healer. They know.*

The vampires remained in place, furtively watching disembarking passengers. If they knew I was coming, all they had to do was watch any planes arriving from Atlanta. Which was why I'd flown to Chicago first, purchased another ticket, and flown from there. The instinct to always cover my tracks seemed to have paid off again.

In the past minute, I'd gleaned two vital facts: The vampires couldn't see through my disguise, and since the vampires hadn't raced toward the airport exit, Janice was not the mole. It meant I might escape without confrontation.

Vampires were difficult to fight, especially without magic. They'd intentionally chosen police disguises so they could take me without a struggle. Because if I followed the rules, they thought I couldn't use magic against them. With their physical superiority, they assumed I'd be easy to subdue.

They were wrong.

Even so, confrontation was off the table, especially in a public venue versus police imposters. I didn't want the nub police force on high alert during my visit. The smartest policy in this case was avoidance.

I checked the airport schedule on my phone. A plane from Atlanta was due to arrive in thirty minutes. Sitting around and waiting for the plane from Atlanta wouldn't be prudent even though it would be interesting to see what the vampires did. I stood, stretched, and moseyed on down the terminal, walking toward the baggage handler vampire. It was probably overkill, but I did it anyway. The crowd bumping past him made it so easy, it was barely an inconvenience.

I timed my steps and passed the vampire just as a large group split to go around him. I lifted his cell phone and kept on walking. The screen wasn't even locked, so a quick swipe opened the phone. The picture of a man long gone stared back at me. I hadn't seen that face in years—at least not without all the blackened veins and bluish skin mottling the left cheek.

It was me.

The picture was zoomed into my face, making the image blurry and pixelated. But even so, I looked worlds better back then than I did these days. I pinch-zoomed out as I continued to walk down the airport terminal and discovered I was not the only person in the picture.

Next to me stood a tall, fair-skinned man with Disney princess eyes and long golden hair. His full lips and high cheekbones gave the impression he was royalty, which was precisely the truth. The female next to him was just as tall and even more beautiful. Her hair was silver, her eyes frost white, and her gaze as cold as an arctic wind. Prince Onwin, a child of summer, and his bride, Princess Frezia, the daughter of winter.

I was merely one among six others dressed in the black and gold armor of the Oblivion Guard. We surrounded the couple, a semi-circle of trained assassins, ready to annihilate anyone and anything that might harm the glorious rulers of Feary and Gaia. One might think no one would dare attack such well-protected people, but one would be wrong —so very wrong.

A tall figure to the right stood next to a group of fae from the winter court. His black hair, bluish skin, and pointed ears told anyone he was a dark elf. But this guy was darker than dark. Just seeing Torvin's face sent a chill down my spine and bad memories racing through my mind.

I remembered the occasion the picture was taken—the winter solstice, celebrating the longest night of the year when the winter fae were at the height of power. It was also a celebration of peace between the courts, something that had lasted for over a thousand years—at least that's what the fae told us.

"You've looked better, Cain."

Only training kept me from shouting in surprise. Besides, I'd been expecting this visit. I looked at the man pacing me. He looked ordinary enough in his navy blue business suit, a leather briefcase at his side. But there was nothing ordinary about him.

I slowed to a stop near a sandwich vending kiosk. "Glad you noticed. Something I can help you with?"

He peered at me with perceptive blue eyes. "Your ghosts are rather restless. It seems you've done something unexpected."

"Me, unexpected?" I scoffed. "Nah."

"They're more bound to you than ever, Cain." He pursed his lips. "We should get a drink soon."

"What brings you to Seattle?" I said.

An old man walking nearby gasped and clutched his chest.

A woman screamed. "Someone help!"

"He's having a heart attack!" Someone else shouted.

My old acquaintance shrugged. "Oh, you know." He winked. "Business." He tipped a hat I hadn't noticed before. "See you soon." He walked over and knelt next to the man on the floor. His hand seemed to grasp something. He smiled, nodded, and spoke. No one else noticed him as he helped someone invisible rise to their feet. For a moment, his hand turned to bones, and his briefcase became a scythe. And then he was gone.

I could have seen exactly what was happening with my true sight scope, but now was no time to draw attention to myself. Thanatos often greeted me when he was in the neighborhood. He held a sort of fascination for my ghosts. Having the attention of such an entity didn't seem like a positive thing. Judging from the progress of my disease, he'd probably be visiting me soon enough for entirely different reasons.

I started walking again.

The picture was still on the phone screen. I took one last look at Torvin and tapped the back arrow to go through the gallery of images on the vampire's phone. He had pictures galore, but no more of me. A quick look at random images told me he was into sex and blood. No surprise there. The airport wasn't large, and I was nearly to the exit, constantly scanning for more vampires. It seemed they'd placed all their bets on capturing me in the terminal, because there were only three watching the exits out of baggage claim.

The text messages on the phone provide no useful information, except to further reaffirm the vampire's love for sex and blood. The image of me had been sent in a text from his blood master. It simply said, *Capture him alive*.

They no doubt wanted to drain my blood for as long as possible before killing me. Once they got a look at my skin, they probably wouldn't want to sink their fangs into my flesh. I'd probably make them as sick as me.

I skirted past the vampire guarding the nearest exit and went outside to the taxi line. There was one more thing to do before I could trust Janice wasn't lying to me, even if it was risky as hell. She'd sent two more texts since I'd swiped the vampire's phone.

Leave Seattle.

I did not betray you.

An elderly woman and two men in business suits waited in the taxi line ahead of me. I could have used a rideshare company, but their apps kept sensitive information and could be hacked. I stuck to the old-school methods of transportation. I checked the settings on the vampire's phone and found they were set to my satisfaction.

When the elderly woman began lugging her suitcase toward the taxi, I hurried over and helped her load it in the trunk before the taxi driver got out.

"God bless you, young man." She patted my hand.

I smiled back. "So say we all."

Her forehead wrinkled with mild confusion, then I helped her into the back seat.

"I hope you don't think that means you can skip to the front of the line," the next man in line said.

I let my gaze settle on him and wished I could show him my true face. Apparently, the look in my eyes was enough. He flinched like a sheep seeing through the wolf's disguise. But I wasn't here to cause a scene, so I went to the back of line.

The other businessman turned and cupped a hand over his mouth. "That was nice of you," he whispered. "Don't listen to that jackass."

I smiled. "Thanks." I'd done what I needed to do anyway. Hopefully the old woman would be out of the car long before the vampire realized his phone was missing and tried to track it. The odds that the vampires would follow the phone were slim, but within the realm of possibility.

When my turn came, I gave the taxi driver an address a few blocks from the healer. It was time to see if Janice had lied about this or not.

It took about forty minutes to reach Green Lake. I exited the taxi at the address I'd given the driver and headed onto a trail circling the lake. Dark gray clouds covered the sky, but it wasn't raining. Even so, it was good weather for vampires. Such thick cover blocked about ninety percent of ultraviolet rays, which meant vampires could wear heavy sunscreen and walk around as if it were the middle of the night.

I pretended to sightsee while keeping an eye on my surroundings. I counted eight vampire pedestrians on my walk, but none of them seemed interested in anything except enjoying the day. It wasn't until I grew closer to the healer's address that I found three vampires diligently watching the house.

Janice wasn't lying.

Or perhaps she was, and the house was the final trap in case I escaped the airport. There was one way to find out. I walked around the block and found no one watching the rear of the house. I normally would have taken a few hours to thoroughly case the surroundings, but since the flight from Atlanta had probably arrived by now, I didn't have much time to spare before the airport vampires realized I wasn't on it.

Hopping a couple of fences was all it took to reach the back yard. A dark-skinned man tending a garden looked up at me in surprise. I smiled reassuringly and waved. "Janice sent me."

He blinked. "Oh, your secretary." Another blink. "You're Mr. Cain."

"That's me." I held out a hand. "Sorry about jumping the fence, but I need to keep this visit discreet, Mr. Simmons."

He took my hand and shook it. "Call me Fitz, please."

"You're Jamaican," I said.

"Yes. I practice Obeah as it was from the old country." He led me to a door set in the ground and opened it. "Janice tells me you've got an ailment that resists all treatment."

"Yeah." I followed him through a cool underground passage until we reached a root cellar. Only wooden beams held up the dirt walls and ceiling, but there were also shelves built along the walls, each one bearing heavy loads of jars and containers of all shapes and sizes. I felt mostly good vibes from this place unlike some of the witch doctors I'd visited over the years.

Janice had told me the truth. The healer existed and he'd been expecting me. I saw nothing in his eyes that indicated he was lying or preparing to betray me. Now all I had to worry about were vampires descending on this house once they realized I wasn't on the flight from Atlanta. Of course, I might get lucky and they might assume I was on a later flight or even coming on a different day.

But I'd learned it was best to never rely on chance for a positive outcome, especially when the odds were artificially stacked. The faster Fitz helped me, the better. "How long will this take? I have an early flight to catch."

He stopped in front of a workbench. "An hour. No more."

I nodded. "Then let's proceed." I dispelled my mask and unbuttoned my shirt.

Fitz hissed and backed up a step. "Aye, man, you've been working dark magic, haven't you?"

I frowned. "There's no such thing. Magic is neutral. It can be used for good and bad."

He shook his head. "Do you use planar magic?"

"Yes."

Fitz raised an eyebrow. "Which plane?"

"Feary." It was a partial lie, but close enough to the truth.

His lips peeled back. "Direct from Feary? How is that possible?"

I waved off his question. "I answered your question. What does this have to do with my face?"

"I've seen many cases similar to yours, mostly from those accepting power from demons." Fitz removed a thick album from a shelf and thumbed through pictures. Every page labeled and displayed ailments ranging from bruises all the way to putrid growths as large as heads.

I knew when he'd reached the page pertinent to me because the men and women in the pictures bore blackened veins much like mine. Fitz pointed to one particular picture. "This nub accepted charms from demons so he could work magic. By the time he came to me, the demon was able to possess him at will."

As if in answer, the veins in my chest tightened around my heart. "But I've never used demon magic."

"You've never used unknown charms or anything of the sort?" he said.

I touched the white pearl around my neck. "I have, but I didn't receive it from a demon."

Fitz stared at the pearl but didn't touch it. "Where did you get that?"

"My octopus." I shrugged. "I thought it was just a normal pearl at first, but then I discovered it amplified my power exponentially."

He hissed between his teeth. "Is your octopus a demon?"

"Hell no." I scoffed. "I even had him tested at a veterinarian. He's just an octopus."

"This pearl must be tainted." He turned to a nearby shelf and found a mason jar filled with filthy water. Fitz unscrewed the lid and poured a trickle of the liquid into a petri dish. "Place it in here, please."

I undid the clasp on the chain and put it in the water.

He retrieved several more ingredients from his shelves and began mixing them. "I fear for you, friend. There is something different about the markings on you. Somehow, you have become the patron of a powerful demon."

"No way." My response wasn't a denial, so much as an admission of my stupidity. The changes I'd suffered had been so gradual over the years I'd never once connected them to the pearl. If anything, I would have connected them to my oblivion staff or a bad interaction between fae magic and my human body.

Fitz ground herbs into powder, mixed them with liquid, and then boiled the concoction. When he was done, he stirred the thick liquid with white powder. "It's sea salt," he explained. "Pearls come from the ocean, so this will help me track its origin."

"How would that help you find out if a demon cursed it?" I said.

"I already know it is not demon cursed." He pointed to the liquid. The holy water did not boil or interact with it. Some demons are powerful enough to overcome holy water, but most are not."

I put a finger in the water, half expecting it to burn me. It felt tepid, but that was all. "I'm not demon cursed?"

"Let's find out." He scooped some of the muddy mixture onto his fingers and traced it along the veins on my chest.

I stiffened. My mouth opened as if to shout out in surprise, but no sound emerged. The world went dark, but I hadn't passed out. Waves lapped on a shore. Frogs croaked in a grand chorus and something slimy slithered past my feet. My eyes grew accustomed to the dim light from glowing fungus and the environment came into focus. I stood barefoot on the shore of a vast underground sea.

Massive shadows stirred offshore and began trundling my way. The waves grew larger as the silhouettes came closer. Fear built in my chest, growing tighter as it climbed up my throat. I'd not felt such fear in years. Not since my early years of training. My body shook and my mind told my mouth to scream. Something vast, something terrible was coming to claim me.

I shouted. The darkness vanished. Fitz's bulging eyes were right in front of me. My hand gripped him around the throat. His hands pried futilely at mine. His legs thrashed a foot above the ground. I gasped and dropped him.

"Shit, I'm sorry." I held up my hands. "I don't know what happened."

Fitz rubbed his throat and backed away. I expected him to point to the door and demand I leave. But he simply took a moment to catch his breath before speaking.

"Mr. Cain, I'm sorry to tell you this, but you gonna die."

CHAPTER 8

I dropped back onto the chair. "Die? There's no cure?"

"It's no demon that's got you, man." He massaged his throat and swallowed hard. "What you've got is a god relic."

"The pearl is divine?" I felt even more confused.

"No, man." Fitz looked at the pearl. "The relic is too powerful for you. It was made for some other being, not a human. By using it, it's used you up and put a claim on your soul." He retrieved a small vial from a shelf and uncorked it.

"What's that?" I asked.

"It's gonna tell me how long you got, man." Fitz winced. "It ain't long, I know that for sure."

My knees should have gone weak, and my breathing should have become difficult. But I'd faced death all my life. Most in the Oblivion Guard never made it five years, much less ten in service to the fae. It seemed best that some self-inflicted malady would be the end of me instead of someone else's sword.

I nodded calmly. "I'm ready."

Fitz sprinkled me with the liquid and began chanting in another language. His hands made circles in the air around my chest and then grabbed something invisible. It was as if someone tugged on a string tied to the very center of my being. I resisted the reflex to kick him away and endured the discomfort for a moment as he examined whatever unseen force in his hands.

He let go, and my body relaxed from head to toe. "What the hell was that?" I asked.

"Your aura." Fitz hissed between his teeth. "Mr. Cain, if you stop using this pearl, you have at most, another month and a half. The infection has spread into your heart like a cancer."

"Can't you cure it?" I already knew the answer but couldn't stop myself from asking.

He shook his head. "I have worked with ingredients from many planes. Even the most potent elements from Feary would not cure this." His lips pressed together. "This is god-level cancer, Mr. Cain. The only thing that might cure it is, unfortunately, not available."

I narrowed my eyes. "And that is?"

Fitz grimaced. "A unicorn heart, eaten while still beating."

I stared at him blankly for several heartbeats. "Unicorns have been extinct for years. The last ones were killed in the war as retribution against the fae."

He sighed. "Very sad times, Mr. Cain. The unicorns were among a few of the original creatures in this universe. Their bodies contained the original magic of creation. It was those godlike properties that made humans hunt them to near extinction."

"Yeah, I've heard stories." I'd never given unicorns much thought except when the last ones were slaughtered. It had been one of the few times I'd seen high fae weep for the death of something that was not a personal pet. "In other words, I'm a dead man walking."

"Yes." He deflated. "I can ask my sources, but I don't think there is much hope."

"Are there any other creatures with the same kind of magic?" I asked.

"If there are, I've never heard of them," Fitz said. "Give me your number and I'll contact you when I have news."

I gave him an internet phone number he could text. I still didn't know how Janice had gotten my actual number and it made me question everything about my security practices. It made me wonder if the agency could track my phone. I'd been so preoccupied with meeting Fitz I hadn't even stopped to think about other ramifications to Janice having my number. It was possible she could track me.

Fitz nodded at the pearl, still in the holy water. "I would stop wearing that around your neck. The less temptation there is to use it, the longer you'll live."

I stuck the pearl into my duffel bag. "Thank you, Fitz."

He gave me a small leather pouch. "These pills will help with the pain and perhaps keep your heart beating a little longer."

"How much do I owe you?" I asked.

He waved a hand. "It was an honor helping the legendary Ghostwalker."

I frowned. "That's literally the first time I've ever heard a human say that."

"The fae are despised by humans, because humans are greedy, a cancer on Gaia." Fitz spat on the dirt floor. "Humans destroy and the fae preserve. I would rather they remain in charge instead of giving more power to humans."

I didn't know if I agreed with him, but I also wasn't going to sour the first compliment I'd received in years about my past. "Thank you. Let me know if I can return the favor sometime."

Fitz led me upstairs. "I have no desire for anyone to die."

"That's not what I do anymore," I said. "I'm just a tracker."

He didn't comment.

I went to his fence and surveyed the neighboring areas for signs of vampires. Seeing none, I hopped the fence and took a circuitous route to the lake. I didn't call a cab right away. Instead, I sat on a bench and stared at the lake, reflecting on everything that brought me to this moment. The fact that the agency might be able to track my phone and that vampires were waiting at the airport to pounce me seemed like insignificant little things.

One way or the other, I'd soon be dead. And the worst part was that I had no idea what I wanted to do with the rest of my life. Did I want to take a long vacation? Did I want to drink and party until I passed out? Or did I just want to walk into the lake and float on the surface until I sank out of sight and drowned?

The possibilities seemed endless with my newfound mortality.

I had plenty of money to spend on entertainment. But no matter how much fun I experienced, it was all so fleeting. Moments came and were gone with barely a memory to hold onto.

I typed a message to Janice. *I'm going to die.*

She responded faster than expected. *That's the prognosis?*

Yes. I scoffed, unable to believe I'd ever be sending someone what I sent next. *Unless I eat a beating unicorn heart.*

Her response was delayed this time, probably because she'd either laughed her ass off or wondered if I was bullshitting her. *Unicorns are extinct,* she replied a moment later.

So I've heard. Nice knowing you.

Janice was apparently made of sterner stuff than me. *I'll see what I can find with our dark market contacts.*

I scoffed and put my phone away.

A little girl walking down the path gasped and stared at me. Her mother flinched, eyes wide, then she scolded her daughter and dragged her away. It took a moment for me to realize why the girl gasped. I'd been so preoccupied with my predicament I'd never put my mask back on after leaving Fitz's.

A quick scan of the area told me the vampires watching Fitz's place had already noticed. There were too many witnesses for me to openly use magic, so I covered my face with a hand and slid back on the illusion mask. Then I stood, leaving my duffel on the bench. I touched the place where the pearl usually rested on the hollow of my throat and felt a brief flash of panic when remembering it wasn't there anymore.

Three vampires closed in from different directions, all of them talking on their phones. Backup was no doubt on the way. I left my dueling wands in their leg sheaths and waited.

"Come with us peacefully." A tall vampire with a mop of blond hair held out a hand and stopped the others from coming closer. "The Shadow King would like word from you."

I raised an eyebrow. "Is that what Lothar goes by these days?"

"Surrender and we won't hurt you." The blond vampire's pupils swelled larger. "Drop your weapons and come." His suggestions sounded so reasonable, I almost wanted to believe him.

Almost.

Vampire compulsion works because it's so subtle, in many cases, you don't even realize you're being finessed. This guy wasn't trying to brute force his will on me, which was good for him. My response was to do a little magic of my own. I powered a sigil tattooed on my shoulder—a white skull with a black snake threading the eyeholes.

The reflection spell flickered on invisibly around my head. I let the vampire keep on talking.

"Drop your weapons," he said. "Come peacefully." His eyes glazed over. He reached behind his back, drew a gun, and dropped it on the asphalt, much to the chagrin of the other vampires.

I wasn't even surprised to see vampires packing heat. They got into so many turf wars with lycans, some had taken to carrying guns loaded with silver bullets. The bullets wouldn't outright kill lycans, but they'd put them out of a fight in a hurry.

"He's magicking us!" One of the other vampires shouted an instant before he launched himself toward me.

Vampires are so fast they look like a blur to the human eye. While I could magically enhance my physical abilities, I hadn't figured out a way to make my eyes see faster. Thankfully, I didn't rely entirely on any one sense to help me fight. Otherwise, I would have failed to protect the fae under my care from the variety of creatures that wanted them dead.

The disturbance of air caused by such speed told me exactly where the vampire was coming from. His body language just before the attack showed me his intent to grab me from behind. I could have powered a shield sigil, but his other companion was already leaning toward me, hands outstretched.

I powered my body sigils, giving me enhanced speed and strength. I wasn't vampire fast or strong, but it was enough to make a difference. After a quick sidestep, my left hand grasped the vampire by the wrist and yanked it down. The vampire's upper body changed direction too fast for him to handle. He flipped forward, skidded across the ground, and splashed into the lake. Vampire number two was already in motion. I didn't dare try to trip or hit him. Vampires were hard as stone to my human hands. I wouldn't hurt them, but I'd probably break my arms or leg.

There is such a thing as power without skill. Brute force without finesse. Many of the physically strong supernatural types rely too heavily on their power to achieve results. Granted, it works most of the time against less powerful beings like nubs.

However, it was their extreme physical power and their willingness to use it without skill that gave me an advantage in such a situation.

I redirected the second vampire's hands toward his blond companion and let his impetus do the rest. He smashed into the other vampire with terrific force. They tumbled across the ground about twenty yards before striking a tree hard enough to shake loose a squirrel and a shower of leaves.

I picked up my duffel and walked over to the woozy vamps. "Leave me be and no one has to get hurt."

By now, a crowd of nubs had gathered a safe distance away. As usual, cell phones were out and a new internet meme was ready to be born. I didn't need the attention, even if I was in disguise. I flicked a hex their way and watched several thousand dollars' worth of smartphones go up in smoke.

People shouted in alarm, throwing their smoking smartphones as far away as possible. Their attention now drawn away from me, I walked past them and lost myself in the crowd of pedestrians strolling the path. Unfortunately, the vampires had already gained their feet and were following a discreet distance behind.

It wouldn't take long for their backup to arrive. Without the use of my wands or staff, I wouldn't be able to hold off a swarm of them. Once again, it seemed avoiding further confrontation was for the best. I crossed the road, walked down the residential street, and took another right, heading back to the address where I'd had the taxi drop me off earlier. I'd chosen that spot with care and now it would provide a safe place for retreat.

Unable to use their supernatural speed or even chase me at a normal pace without making a big scene, the vampires paced behind at a brisk walk. But when I crossed the road and stepped onto the property there, they could come no closer.

The Seventh Day Adventist church and its grounds took up nearly two blocks. I walked straight down the middle of the property while the vampires had to circle around one way or the other. They did the smart thing and split up to cover both sides so I couldn't go left or right to lose them. But because of the buildings, they also couldn't keep eyes on me the entire time.

The front door of the church was unlocked, so I walked inside. Organ music and a woman's voice filled the sanctuary. I walked down the aisle on the far side, acting as if I was supposed to be there, and entered a back foyer through the door. I picked up a bible from a pile inside the room and tucked it under one arm, then cast an illusion to change my appearance completely.

My cargo pants and t-shirt morphed into a dark business suit and my duffel bag became a briefcase. I wiped away my current mask and replaced it with a new illusion: a chubby face, round glasses, and shaved head. I thought the stolen bible was a nice touch. I could have made an illusory bible, but the less I had to concentrate on, the better.

Once outside, I waited for a group of people to walk past on the sidewalk and merged into them. I spotted the blond vampire hurrying down the sidewalk across the road. I didn't see his compadres, which meant one of them had probably stayed behind in case I doubled back, and the other was pacing the sidewalk on the other side.

I didn't think the blond vampire could see through my disguise, but there was no sense taking chances. I slowed my pace, so the vampire was well ahead of me, and then crossed over to his side of the road. I cut between some buildings and emerged back on the main road near the lake. A taxi passed by before I could wave it down. Keeping a wary eye on my surroundings, I waited for another taxi to come past. The minutes ticked by.

I saw the blond vampire and company appear across the street. They'd figured out I hadn't emerged from the church grounds and were probably backtracking to see if I'd done exactly what I had done. One of them ran his gaze right over me without stopping. A taxi drove past, but I didn't dare wave it down, not with them lurking.

A man just down the street whistled and waved it down, and the vampires reacted as I'd thought they would. They knew I could disguise myself, so they didn't know what I looked like right now. They assumed that I'd try to make a fast escape and what better way than by hiring a taxi?

They ran across the road heedless of the traffic and managed to jump in front of the taxi to stop it from leaving. The driver shouted at them, but the blond vampire ignored him and jerked open the back door. I used the incident as a diversion and started walking the opposite way, back toward Fitz's house.

A black car that hadn't been there earlier had parked on the brick pad near Fitz's driveway. The front door hung open. By getting caught with my pants down in front of his place, I'd let the vampires know that I'd been there. That meant Fitz might have useful information for the vampires to extract. Despite the rules outlawing violence among the factions, the Seattle vampires were far more powerful than any other supernatural groups in the area. They could have their way with Fitz, and no one would stop them.

My lack of diligence might cost the witch doctor his life.

CHAPTER 9

I didn't know much about the mage community in this area, but I doubted they'd go out of their way to help a witch doctor. Mages considered sorcerers and wizards top shelf. Witch doctors, shamans, and warlocks were looked down upon. They might all belong to the local mage guild, but that didn't mean they were treated as equals.

I'm a moron. I'd proven it to be fact by using a mysterious pearl for nearly two decades without divining its true nature, and then doubled down over the past twenty-four hours by rescuing an assassination target and letting my guard down. Now I was a dying moron, but there was no sense in letting Fitz die as well for my stupidity.

I went up to the open front door, knocked, and said, "Jehovah's Witness. Do you have time for me to talk to you about our lord and savior, baby Yoda?"

The vampires looming over Fitz in the den just inside didn't look like they wanted to invite Yoda into their hearts. The one behind Fitz bared his fangs, ready to drain Fitz's lifeblood. Like any good proselytizer, I barged in and tried to force religion onto them. Opening the bible to a random page, I started reading aloud in my best televangelist voice.

"But I say unto you, love your enemies, bless them that curse you, do good to them that hate you, and pray for them which despitefully use you, and persecute you that ye may be the children of your Father which is in heaven. For he maketh his sun to rise on the evil and on the good, and sendeth rain on the just and on the unjust."

A big thick goon of a vampire glowered at me. "Get the fuck out of here, preacher!"

"Lord Jesus, forgive this man for his sins!" I thrust the bible toward the three vampires, and they leapt back like kids fleeing a spider. "Accept him into your loving embrace!"

"He said get the fuck out of here!" A slightly smaller vampire lunged at me.

I threw the bible in his face, drew my dueling wands, and unleashed hell on his sinful ass. I flashed the wands through precise patterns and fired golden orbs into the biggest one. He screamed as concentrated sunlight burned through his flesh like hot pokers. Then I scattered another volley of orbs at the other two bloodsuckers.

It wasn't enough to kill them, but it was enough to put them down and out.

"What the hell, man?" Fitz jumped to his feet. "They was gonna leave, and now you come in here and piss them off!"

"They were going to kill you if you didn't give them what they wanted," I said.

"I told them you was gonna die! I told them everything I knew." Fitz bared his teeth. "Now they gonna kill me for sure."

"They were already going to kill you before." I booted the squirming vampire who'd been behind him. "He was about to drain your blood."

"Mother of fuckers." Fitz banged a fist on the wall. "You've ruined me!"

I felt like an even bigger moron than earlier. Everything and everyone I touched suffered. Judging from Fitz's collection downstairs, he'd been at this for decades. His collection was probably priceless, irreplaceable.

"I'm sorry." I watched the injured vampires in case they managed to overcome their pain and attack. "You helped me, and I destroyed your life." I hesitated, then forced myself to offer him help. "I have money. If you come with me, I'll help you set up shop elsewhere."

Fitz sighed and seemed to deflate to half his size. "My life's work is ruined."

I frowned. "I'm sorry, I really am."

He sighed. "I can replace my business, but not my life." Fitz growled. "I accept your offer. Now get us the hell out of here."

I nodded toward the door. "Let's go."

No more vampires waited outside, so I took the car Fitz's attackers had come in and started driving. Going back to the international airport was a bad idea, so I set my GPS for Renton Municipal Airport. There weren't a lot of flights out of there, but it was the best available option.

There were few people and zero vampires at the small airport. There were also no flights to Atlanta leaving from there. I purchased tickets for the next flight out to Portland at the counter.

Fitz sat glumly on a bench in the small terminal, arms crossed over his chest, eyes unfocused.

I sat down next to him. "I'm sorry. Finding out I'm going to die distracted me and I forgot to put on my disguise."

"You didn't tell me vampires were watching my house." He glared at me. "You didn't even mention once that my life might be in danger."

"Look, when we get to Atlanta, I'll make this right."

Fitz shook his head. "I don't want to go to Atlanta, man. Do you know how long it took me to build a life here? To afford the house I have?"

"Will the mage council here help you?" I said.

He shook his head. "I don't have enough money to make them care."

"How much would it take?" I asked.

Fitz grunted. "Too much."

"Tell me," I said.

"It cost me ten grand just to get a license to practice here," he replied. "And my annual dues for the local council are twenty. That's four times the price they charge wizards, and sorcerers don't pay anything."

"They can get away with that?" I said.

He scoffed. "Who gonna stop them? The national guild don't care. They think we trash because we practice natural magic."

"Twenty grand doesn't buy you any protection?" I said.

"Not, here, not in Europe." Fitz scoffed. "Especially not in the vampire capital of North America."

"How about a hundred grand?" I said.

He scoffed again. "Yeah, of course. But where I gonna get that much money?"

I took out my phone. "Give me your bank information."

His mouth dropped open. "You serious?"

"As magic cancer," I said.

"Holy shit, man." He gave me the information, and I wired the money from one of my overseas accounts.

"You've got two choices." I wrote names and numbers on a piece of paper. "Talk to these freelancers. They're some of the best magical security money can rent. Or, you can go to the guild and offer them a huge bribe." I shrugged. "Personally, I wouldn't give them shit. Mage guild knights are excellent fighters, but they're pompous assholes and might not be willing to help you."

"Freelancers it is then." The tension in Fitz's shoulders visibly melted. "You're a better man than most think, Ghostwalker." He shook his head. "You could have left me to die, but you went above and beyond to save me."

I looked at the floor. "Saving lives isn't my forte. The world will be a better place when I'm gone."

He put a hand on my shoulder. "Well, maybe you can do some good before you die."

I scoffed. "There's no balancing my scales no matter how much good I do."

"Maybe not." He stood. "Hey, maybe you can get your money back for my ticket."

A laugh escaped me. "Eh, losing five hundred bucks isn't going to kill me."

Fitz offered a small smile and left. I hoped he was able to persevere.

I sighed. "Figures I'd fuck over the one person in the supernatural community who actually likes me."

After arriving in Portland, I took a direct flight from there to Atlanta. Unless my enemies knew exactly when and where I was coming from, Hartsfield Airport was simply too huge for them to find me.

It was a pleasure to climb back inside Dolores and drive home. I wasn't ready for what I saw when I walked inside. Blankets and pillows were strewn all over the place. Food and dirty liquid stained the kitchen floor. An unopened bottle of bleach lay next to Fred's pool. A glance inside the guest room showed me it was trashed.

I sucked in a lungful of air and shouted, "What the fuck happened?"

No answer.

"Girl, where are you?"

Still no answer.

I jogged downstairs into the library. There were two empty frozen dinner boxes on one of the tables and several empty bottles of water, but still no girl. I jogged past the tables, looking down each row and found her on the far side in the magical section. She lay on pillows and blankets piled on the stone floor, a book in hand.

The girl looked up. "Why are you shouting?"

My face burned and my fists clenched. "What in the hell happened to my house?"

Her eyes averted from mine. "Your fucking octopus happened."

"Fred?" I gripped a shelf to keep myself from strangling her. "Aside from dead animals, he never leaves a mess."

She blew out a breath and set down her book. Looked up at me as if this conversation was a major inconvenience. "I decided to lay down in bed since I didn't sleep well last night. I closed and locked the door and went to sleep. Then I started having nightmares. I woke up to a cold tentacle over my mouth and nose!" The girl shivered. "I think your pet was trying to kill me."

"That doesn't explain the food on the floor." My hand gripped the shelf tighter. "Or the blankets and pillows everywhere."

"I threw pillows and blankets at him because I was scared!" The girl huffed. "Then he tried to attack me again when I made food. So, I came down here to escape him."

"Fred doesn't attack people," I growled.

"Yeah?" She tilted her head. "How often do you have guests?"

"Often enough." I jabbed a finger toward the stairs. "Go clean up your mess." I remembered one more thing. "Were you going to poison Fred's pool with bleach?"

"Bleach?" The girl frowned. "I didn't even know you had bleach."

"Well it didn't move to the side of his pool by itself."

She scoffed. "I think Fred is trying to frame me, because I didn't do it."

My knuckles cracked. "Go upstairs and clean up your mess. Now."

"Or what?" She raised an eyebrow. "You'll toss me to the wolves?"

Oh, I was tempted to. But it was my fault she was even here in the first place. I wanted to threaten her, but the mess upstairs was a direct result of me not doing my job. "No." I shook my head. "But I'll be really disappointed."

The girl's mouth dropped open. "Wow. In what reality does an assassin use a guilt trip to get his way?"

"I'm not an assassin anymore." I sagged a little. "I won't be much of anything much longer anyway." I turned and left.

I'd done very little work during the flight back to Atlanta. I should have contacted Janice and asked her how she got my number. I should have destroyed my phone and gotten another one. I should have figured out if the agency could somehow track me.

But none of it mattered anymore. I'd soon be dead, and the world would keep on going without me. The cancerous growth tightened around my chest as if to reinforce my hopelessness. I didn't want to be home anymore. I needed a distraction.

"I'm leaving." The girl probably couldn't hear me from her nest in the library, but I said it anyway like a good host.

I drove to Little Five Points and circled the block for ten minutes before finding a parking space on the street. I activated a shield sigil to keep Dolores safe from thieves and random scratches. Her hood might still be dented where Sigma tried to stop me with his bare hands, but that didn't mean I couldn't keep the rest of her body safe.

I walked past the bars on Euclid, went right on Colquitt, and walked around the back of the building. An illusion hid a stairwell that took me twenty feet down to a steel door. I gave it three quick raps, paused, and then two slow knocks. The speakeasy panel opened, revealing a set of eyes with horizontal slits.

I gave him the password. "Feary."

He opened the door and I walked in. The eyes belonged to a bridge troll named Durrug. He stood seven feet tall, every inch of his green skin bulging with muscles. There weren't a lot of his kind on this side of the Feary portal these days. Most had left Gaia in the late nineteenth century when mankind's spread across the globe made it difficult for beings who couldn't easily disguise their appearance.

Durrug barely glanced at me and dropped back onto his stool with a loud creak. I'd tried to say hello to him once, but he just ignored me like he did everyone else.

The dimly lit tavern bustled with activity. A group of rowdy men and women, most likely lycans, played pool in the back. Young mages in tight-fitting robes played darts. Vampires crowded around a table sharing a bottle of vintage blood.

Voltaire's wasn't the only local tavern that catered exclusively to the supernatural community, but it was by far the most popular, partially because of location, but also because it was an officially designated neutral zone by the Fae Accords. Anyone within a furlong radius was considered under the protection of the high Fae.

Only one person in recent memory had broken the rules by punching another patron over a game of darts. No one had reported the incident and the other party laughed it off since he was winning. But moments later, a diplomatic pixie had flown in and delivered a summons to the offender. The next time anyone saw the man, his offending hand was gone, neatly severed.

My mask had vanished the moment I crossed the safe zone, part of the fae magic that protected the place. It didn't allow compulsion, illusion, or even fae glamour. When it came to neutral zones, the fae didn't play around.

A group of middle-aged mages scowled when they saw me. A female vampire hissed at my passing.

"Betrayer," someone said loud enough for me to hear.

"Why do they even allow him in here?" someone added.

I didn't care who hurled insults at me. Sticks and stones were far worse than anything they could say. I found an open seat at the bar and the seats to the left and right of me cleared out within seconds.

"Take a shower sometime, Cain." The red-headed elf behind the bar grinned at me.

I smiled back. "You think I stink, Aura?"

She sniffed the air with her pert nose. "It's not as bad today. So, the usual?"

I nodded. "A mangorita."

"You and your girly drinks." Aura laughed.

"I suppose I could have a nasty old dark and stormy." The name fit my mood perfectly. Drinking something so bitter would only worsen it. "Or I could drink something with fruit and tequila that actually tastes good."

Aura's laughter tinkled across the room, causing a brief lull in the roar of conversation. She tucked a lock of hair behind her pointed ear and winked. "You're so weird, Cain. All the men want their manly drinks, while you're over here sipping on something with plastic swords and toothpick umbrellas." She sighed. "How about I make you an elf specialty you'll love?"

"Sure, let's try that." I rubbed my hands together. "Making my mouth water already."

An old man with a potbelly stepped out of the kitchen and surveyed the crowd. His gaze turned sour when he saw me. "Fucking hell. Can't you just go away and die?"

Agreeing grunts and cheers echoed around me. Nearly everyone in this bar would kill me with their bare hands if they could. Because, to their reckoning, I'd betrayed humanity.

CHAPTER 10

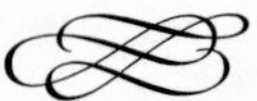

"Hey, Bill." I managed a friendly smile. "I'll be happy to oblige after a few drinks."

"Your face looks half-dead already." He made a spitting noise. "Traitorous shitbag."

"Hey, don't mince words." I winked. "Tell me what you really think."

Aura hummed to herself as she made my drink, seemingly oblivious to the entire exchange.

Bill strode directly across from me and leaned on the bar. "I even told the fae you came here. Told 'em they could probably pick you up without too much of a fight." He scoffed. "They didn't care."

I shrugged. "Guess I'm not that important to them."

He made another spitting noise. "Guess they decided they didn't want trash guarding their royalty."

"And here we are!" Aura announced brightly, revealing a tall glass filled with blue slush and chunks of oranges and pineapples. A little plastic pirate sword jutted from an apple wedge on the rim. There was so much fruit crowded around it, I wasn't sure how I was supposed to drink it.

Aura solved the problem before I could ask by producing a long curly straw and plunking it down in the middle.

"Um, wow." I stirred the contents and sniffed them. "Definitely fruity."

"You're going to love it." She leaned on the counter next to Bill, waiting to see what I thought.

Bill gave her a disgusted look and left.

I took a sip. The sweet taste of fresh blueberries greeted my tongue, enhanced by the mild sting of rum and something else I couldn't quite identify. I took another sip and nodded. "It's amazing."

"Glad you like it." Aura's smile faded. "You're looking kind of haggard, Cain."

I touched the tainted side of my face. "I'm not long for this world, Aura. On the upside, I won't be driving away business much longer."

Her brow furrowed. "Are you serious?"

I took another sip and wondered if my tongue was turning blue. "Yep. Magic cancer."

Aura's eyebrow rose. "Never heard of such a thing."

"Me either." I shrugged. "Apparently, I got it from a tainted artifact."

"I'm so sorry, Cain." She put a hand over mine. "I always liked you."

"Probably because you're not human," I said. "Elves tend to side with the fae."

Aura's eye twitched as if I'd hit a nerve. "My kind killed a lot of humans during the war, but the humans still hate you more."

"I was a human fighting for the fae." I stared into my drink and stirred it with the straw. "I'll always be a traitor to them."

"But you were sworn to fight for the fae." She patted my hand. "You're the most interesting human I ever met."

I met the gaze of her dark blue eyes. "Why?"

"No human ever served in the Oblivion Guard." Aura shook her head in wonder. "I'd like to know how you qualified."

I could have told her the truth—I'd cheated. But I didn't want to spoil the way she looked at me. The pearl had given me a magical advantage, but I'd passed the physical tests all on my own. So maybe I'd partially earned my place in the guard.

Instead of saying all that, I just shrugged and took another sip. "I'd like to know how you make such perfect alcoholic beverages."

Aura laughed. "Elf magic, of course."

Another patron banged his empty glass on the bar. "Hey, can I get some service down here?"

"Duty calls." She rubbed my hand one last time and went to help others.

I'd felt eyes on my back ever since arriving, but my instincts told me the owner of one set of eyes was coming closer. I turned and found a group of three men in fitted burgundy robes striding toward me. Each wore a silver sword at their side and a staff across their back. I knew who they were even before spotting the silver flame insignia on their chests.

Mage Guild knights—the Keepers of the Light.

I leaned my back on the bar and took another sip of Aura's concoction through the curly straw. Guild knights enforced the laws of the local mage guild, kind of like wizard cops. Unless, as my visit with Fitz proved, those members were witch doctors or other undesirable members.

I'd never joined the local council or the umbrella organization, the Mages Guild. There seemed no point in paying to be a part of an organization that would just as soon see me dead. But since I was classified as a mage, I was technically under their purview.

I took another sip of my drink. "Sir Colin, what a pleasant surprise. Would you like to join me for a drink?"

Their glorious leader scowled and folded his arms over his chest. "You failed to appear in court to answer for your crimes. I'm here to serve an arrest warrant."

"Again?" I frowned and looked around the room. "I don't see any wanted posters with my name on them."

Sir Francis, one of Colin's henchmen, growled and punched a meaty fist into his palm. "Let me shut his smart mouth, Sir Colin."

Colin put up a hand to stop him. "Nay. I will give him one more chance to come peacefully."

I loudly slurped the final drops of my drink and then plucked the plastic pirate sword from the apple wedge. Holding it between thumb and forefinger, I pointed it at Colin. "Approach me at your own peril, sir knights, lest I strike ye down with the fabled sword of Captain Jack Sparrow!"

Colin bared his teeth. They looked like yellow bits of corn caught in his bushy black beard. I'd never seen a guild knight who didn't have a beard down to his nipples and hair down to his shoulders. I'd also never met one who didn't think he was the cock of the walk.

Colin's fists clenched, but even with all his perceived power, he couldn't do a damned thing. It didn't matter who you were or what you'd done, no one could molest you in a fae neutral zone. They could call me all the nasty names they wanted, but they couldn't assault or arrest me. Dragging me out of here against my will would be considered the same as physical assault. Even drugging or using magic on me was against the rules.

I thought about rubbing it in with a smirk. Instead, I stabbed the apple wedge with the pirate sword and ate it. Then I turned to the bar and waved at Aura so I could order another. I felt hot breath on my neck and shuddered with revulsion. "Colin, please. I'm not in the mood for sex right now."

Colin took the seat to my left and his companions claimed the stools to my right. Colin sneered, showing his corncob teeth again. "There is no escaping justice, traitor. Sooner or later you'll have to leave, and we'll be right here waiting."

"You realize this is a tavern with rooms for rent, right?" I stabbed another apple wedge with my pirate sword. "I could stay here indefinitely."

"I have a hundred men at my disposal," Colin said. "There will never be a time of day or night when we aren't watching and waiting."

I rubbed my hands together. "Ooh, exciting. I love being stalked by a bunch of grumpy old men."

His aggressive companion slammed the bar top hard enough to make my glass jump. "Come outside and see if your sharp tongue is any match for my sword, scum."

"Calm, Sir Henry." Colin held up a hand. "We must follow the rules in here, but outside, the traitor will follow ours." He scooted his stool over until we bumped elbows. "While we're here, we might as well enjoy our evening."

Colin wasn't the brightest person in the world, but he sure knew how to get under someone's skin. Drinking with these buffoons crowding me took the wind right out of my sails. Admitting that, however, would give them a victory I could not allow.

Aura returned, an amused smile on her face. "Well, it looks as if you'll have company for your bed tonight, Cain. I didn't know burly, bearded men were your type."

I snorted. "Their huge beards compensate a great deal for their small manhoods, but I will make the best of the situation." I patted Henry's hand. "Right, darling?"

Henry jumped up from his stool so fast, it clattered across the floor. He reached for his sword, but Francis grabbed his arm and held it. "Not here, Henry!"

I moaned. "Oh, Henry. I can't wait."

"I will kill you!" Henry roared.

Colin jumped up to help the other knight subdue their enraged fellow. "Sir Henry, you will calm yourself this moment!"

"What kind of homophobic garbage do you allow into your organization, Colin?" I rolled my eyes and shook my head. "Sad."

Aura laughed so hard she doubled over and started gasping

Colin held up a fist. "We'll be here waiting for you, traitor." Then he and the other knight dragged Henry away from the bar.

For a moment the bar was quiet except for the laughter of the amused elf. Then the roar resumed, but this time with a great deal more excitement. It seemed my little encounter had granted everyone quite a thrill.

"Oh, goodness." Aura leaned on the bar, chest heaving as she fought to catch her breath. "I had no idea you were so funny, Cain. Usually you just sit around and sulk."

"I don't sulk." I stabbed a piece of pineapple repeatedly. "I brood."

She snorted. "You don't come out of your shell very often, but it's nice when you do."

"I guess it takes a group of burly men to really bring me out." I put the slice of pineapple out of its misery by eating it. "May I have another drink?"

Aura's forehead pinched. "You usually don't have more than one drink when you come in. How often do you get drunk?"

I shrugged. "Don't remember."

"Well, I put a triple shot of rum in that drink." She leaned closer and looked into my eyes. "Sure you want another right now?"

"I'm barely buzzed." But I felt pretty good. And I really liked looking into Aura's big blue eyes. "You're pretty."

She quirked her lips. "Yeah, you're more than buzzed." Aura nodded toward the table the knights had taken. "You don't care about them stalking you?"

I sighed as a sudden melancholy wave washed over me. "I'll be dead in a month, Aura. I don't really care about much anymore."

Her smile vanished. "There are a million better ways to spend your final days than in the holding cell of those assholes."

I shrugged. "They couldn't take me anyway."

"What if a dozen or more are waiting outside for you?"

"Within a furlong radius?" I scoffed. "They can't cover all that ground."

Aura shook her head. "So, want another drink then?"

"My usual," I said. "A mangorita. I'd like to get girly drink drunk tonight."

Her smiled returned. "I definitely like this side to you better. How come I've never seen it before?"

I shrugged. "I don't have friends, and I don't get out much."

"Wow, that's a sad admission." Aura turned her back to me and started mixing my favorite mango-infused concoction. "Well, sounds like you won't be leaving behind much of a life when you die."

I snorted. "Damn, that's harsh."

She nodded. "Yeah, but it's true."

I leaned my elbows on the bar. "Do elves believe in an afterlife?"

"Sure." She nodded without looking back at me. "There are all kinds of places to go when you die. It just depends on what you believe. Dark elves believe their spirits join a great army that will burn the world in the end of days. Many light elves believe in a paradise."

"I don't believe in much," I said. "Does that mean I'll go nowhere?" I wondered where Thanatos would take my soul on that fateful day.

"Oh, you'll probably go somewhere." Aura garnished the new drink with strawberries to match the red liquid inside. "I'd imagine most assassins don't go to the good place, though."

I nodded glumly. "Yeah, I'm definitely going to the bad place."

Aura reused the straw from my last drink and slid the glass to me. "Well, bottoms up, then."

I held up my drink. "Here's to the bad place."

Aura's lips twisted with amusement. "If you'd like a taste of the good place, my shift ends in an hour."

My mouth went dry at the implications. "Are you serious?"

She nodded. "You make me laugh, and that's kind of a big deal to me."

My hand wandered to my left cheek. "Even though I look like this?"

Aura grinned. "You're ugly, but I can make it work."

I took a long sip of my mangorita. "Yes. I would definitely like a taste of the good place."

Another laugh. "Well, then, enjoy your drink, Cain. Just don't drink too much. I don't want it to hurt your performance."

I grinned. "Okay."

After she went to a customer at the other end of the bar, I allowed myself a fist pump. My life didn't allow for romance or relationships. Members of the Oblivion Guard were forbidden to marry or have children whether they were male or female. Casual sex, however, was condoned and encouraged.

I had a few women to visit should I want a fling, but I liked Aura and that made it a big deal. Normally, I would have turned her down. Emotional entanglements were bad. But since I was going to die, sleeping with a woman I liked sounded like the best idea in the world.

I could hardly wait for her shift to end.

The mangorita went down sweet and left me feeling warm and fuzzy all over. I was going to die, but knowing I was about to have carnal relations with a cute elf made everything feel just fine.

"God, you're pathetic." Layla Blade slid onto the stool next to me. Her form-fitting yoga pants and tank-top weren't capable of hiding weapons, but I knew better. She hadn't given herself the last name "Blade" just because it sounded cool. She banged on the bar top. "Aura, get me a mojito, babe."

The elf flashed her a grin. "Coming right up."

I raised an eyebrow. "I think mojitos are way more pathetic than mangoritas."

"Cain, are you drunk?" Layla scoffed. "I don't care about your girly drinks. I'm talking about the lovey-dovey eyes you're making at Aura." She turned her dark gaze on me. "No way in hell she'd go for someone with a face like yours."

"Gee, thanks." I polished off my drink. "I haven't seen you in a couple of weeks. Off on assignment?"

"Yeah." She turned her back to the bar and propped her elbows on it, casting her gaze around the room. "Are those fuckwit knights making another go at you?"

"They seem even more serious about it tonight." I turned sideways and leaned on the bar. "I'm going to die."

Layla glanced at me. "Yeah, when I catch you outside this place."

"No, I mean, I'm dying." I slapped my bad cheek. "Magic cancer. Doc gave me a month or so to live."

She spun back around to the bar, eyes staring at the liquor bottles on the shelf. "So, you're saying I don't have much time to kill you."

I nodded. "Yeah."

"Well, fuck." Layla gave me the side glare. "I haven't been trying very hard. There are too many easier targets for the money."

"I don't doubt your ability," I said. "Maybe you'll get lucky and catch me when I'm too weak to fight back."

She made a raspberry. "I prefer a challenge."

Aura slid the mojito in front of Layla. "Let me know if it's not sweet enough for you."

Layla stirred the drink with her small straw. "How come Cain gets a curly straw and I get this dinky little thing?"

"Because I like him more." Aura winked. "Enjoy." She left the bar and went through the kitchen door.

"What a brat." Layla took a sip. "But damn, she makes good drinks."

"Yes, she does." I stared at my empty glass and wondered if I should get something else. My phone vibrated. I held it out of Layla's view and looked at the text that had just come in from Janice.

New client. Payout-unicorn heart.

I stared at the message unable at first to process what that meant. I sent back a message: *Are you serious?*

Yes.

I almost dropped my phone. If this wasn't bullshit, someone out there had the cure that would save my life.

CHAPTER 11

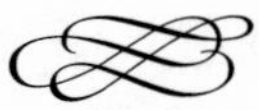

"I'll be right back." I got up and went into a stall in the restroom. A lot of things suddenly seemed way more important than drinking right then.

Janice, how did you get my number?

A minute ticked by before she answered. *You once sent a message directly from your phone instead of through the proxy number. I kept it in case.*

I'd caught myself almost making that mistake a few times. It seemed I'd slipped up without realizing it. *Only you have it?*

Yes.

I hoped that was the truth. *How did the vampires know I'd be in Seattle?*

Someone tapped communications on this end. You were not compromised.

That made me feel a little better. It meant whoever listened in hadn't hacked my computer or phone. But knowing someone in the agency wanted me dead wasn't exactly reassuring. *How in the hell did you find someone with a unicorn heart?*

Dark market connections came through. An anonymous agent contacted me for the owner. We negotiated an agreement.

Janice didn't seem to be the type to fuck with me, so I decided to take her seriously. *What's the catch?*

List of three people. Find them. End them. Proof of death required.

I blew out a long breath. *I have to kill them personally?*

Yes, she responded.

I hadn't killed in years. The ghosts in my head might not like it if I started doing it again. *I need proof of unicorn.* It was hard to believe I'd typed that out.

I can fae certify. Shall I proceed?

I felt short of breath, and it wasn't from the magic cancer. It was the thought of killing again. I left the stall and went to the sink to splash cold water on my face. Either I faced my demons from the past and killed again, or I just quietly let myself die.

Will they take money for the unicorn? I asked.

No.

If real, a unicorn was priceless. Whoever the client wanted dead had to be hard targets indeed. I just hoped they were some evil mother fuckers. I fought back the anxiety. *I'll do it.*

Janice replied a moment later. *Will certify and contact you tomorrow.*

I typed out a response and almost deleted it, but then sent it anyway. *Why are you helping me?*

She didn't reply.

But it was still a damned good question. Why stick her neck out for me? Hell, I didn't know her real name, what she looked like, or where in the world she lived. Eclipse was as big of a mystery as she was. I'd been approached by an agency proxy and offered a job not long after I'd left Feary and come to Gaia. When I refused to kill for them, I figured that opportunity was gone for good. But a little over a month later, another proxy offered me a job as a tracker. I didn't need the money, but I was bored out of my skull, so I took it.

I'd never really considered tracking down the whereabouts of the agency. They'd given me something to do and I'd made easy money. But now I had reason to find out who there had a bone to pick with me. But first things first. I needed to cure what ailed me. Janice and her reasons for helping could wait until then. That meant getting out of here and getting straight to business the moment Janice certified the job.

I went back out to the bar and waved down Aura. "I gotta pay my tab."

Her jaw went slack. "You're leaving?"

"I'm sorry. Something came up."

She scoffed. "That was supposed to be my job."

"Gods be damned, elf." Layla groaned. "Are you really that bad off that you'd sleep with him?"

Aura rolled her eyes. "You know, there's a lot more to Cain than just an ugly face."

"Bad breath?" Layla sniffed. "Yeah, definitely bad breath."

"Jesus, you two are the worst." I slapped some bills on the bar. "It's like a game of fuck, marry, kill, except I'm the one getting fucked and killed."

"No marriage for you." Layla slashed a finger across her throat.

I jabbed a thumb toward her. "I'll get her tab too."

"Still going to kill you," Layla said in a sing-song voice. "But thanks."

Aura sighed. "Cain, my offer is only good tonight. Sure you want to bail?"

I grimaced and hissed a breath between my teeth. "I'd love to stay so much, but a matter of life and death came up."

"Oh, really?" Layla pursed her lips and looked me up and down. "You found a cure?"

"Maybe." I tapped my fingers on the counter. "Check, please."

Aura scoffed. "Wow. I've never had anyone turn me down before."

"I'm not turning you down!" I tried to figure out how to reason my way through this disaster and realized I couldn't. On the other hand, what was my big rush to leave? I could have an enjoyable night and get to work in the morning. If anything, I should celebrate the potential cure to my disease. I took a breath, nodded. "Okay, I'll stay."

"Men and their dicks." Layla snorted. "Pathetic."

Aura beamed. "You made the right decision, Cain. But now I'm kind of pissed at you, so I'll have to think about it."

Layla burst into laughter. "Classic reversal!"

I sank into my chair, defeated. "Fuck this. Fuck this so much."

"Well, you spurned me, Cain." Aura patted my hand. "Make it up to me before my shift ends and maybe I'll decide in your favor."

"Yeah." I planted another bill on the bar. "Not going to happen." I got up and turned to leave.

Aura grabbed my hand. "Wait! I was just kidding."

Layla groaned. "Really, girl? You were in a position of power and now you're just throwing your elf pussy at him?"

I kissed Aura's hand. "I would dearly love to fuck you tonight, but I'm at my limit of fucks to give." I let go and bowed. "I bid you adieu, ladies."

Layla flipped me off. "Thanks for the drink. Kill you later, okay?"

Aura's lips tightened into a pout. "Fuck you, Cain."

"That's the plan." I winked and headed for the door.

Sir Colin and his buddies got up and started following me. I stopped and turned to face them. "Do you really want to do this tonight? Have a drink. Enjoy yourselves. Don't get your asses handed to you."

"You will face justice, traitor." Colin bared his nasty teeth. "Just try and escape us."

I pursed my lips. "Do you have backup waiting, or is it just you?"

Henry's chin rose a good four inches, probably three inches more than his dick could. "I could take you myself."

Colin's fierce expression faltered at the boast, but he didn't try to correct the other man.

I nodded. "Okay. Let's go. I waved goodbye to Durrug, who opened the door but otherwise ignored me. I stomped upstairs and to the parking lot. My car was parked right at the edge of the safe zone, so I started walking in its general direction. There was a small park where the homeless crowd liked to sleep. I figured it'd be a good spot to take care of business.

I looked over my shoulder and saw the knights a few paces back.

"Just try and flee," Henry said. "You cannot outrun justice."

"And no one can outrun that mouth of yours," I grumbled. Within a couple of minutes, I saw the line marking the edge of the zone. Nubs couldn't see it or the peace seals that magically enforced the zone.

I stopped just inside the safe zone and turned toward the knights. "You absolutely sure you want to do this?"

Henry cracked his knuckles. "There is no doubt."

"Submit peacefully." Sir Colin produced a pair of silver manacles from his leather satchel. "There is no need to add to your crimes."

"I never got the memo about my crimes." I tapped a finger on my chin. "What are they exactly?"

"Too long to list," Colin assured me. "Now cross the line and submit."

"I'll cross the line, but I won't submit." I winked at Henry. "Ready to take me down, big boy?"

Henry drew his sword and roared, "Test me!"

"Okay, then." I stepped across the seal and backed up several feet to enter the park. A few homeless folks milled around, but most of them weren't paying attention just yet. I figured it wouldn't take long to notice the big man with the sword and his two compadres.

Henry rushed me. I reached toward my back and summoned my oblivion staff. The cool metallic wood of the hilt met my grasp and sang when I swung it forward to meet Henry's sword. Metal clanged as if it hit stone. I figured if they were going to swordfight me in public, I could spice things up a bit myself.

My mind reached for the pearl only to find it absent. For an instant, my concentration faltered, and Henry nearly took my head off with a well-timed swing of his sword. I leapt back and pressed a sigil on the hilt of my staff. The brightblade hummed to life, bright blue power crackling along the top three quarters of the staff.

"Using magic in public!" Sir Colin pointed out my brightblade as if no one would notice it otherwise. "You add to your crimes, traitor!"

"Hey, you're the ones sword fighting in public." I swung the staff around and enjoyed the electric hum. "Plus, this is really cool."

Henry came at me again, and I figured it was best to end this early. If his sword had been normal steel, I could have cleaved it in half. The knights used magic-resistant blades for obvious reasons. But there wasn't much that could withstand repeated clashes with a brightblade.

His blade met my staff. I sent a jolt of magical electricity through the brightblade and Henry convulsed like a two-year-old who'd successfully jammed his first fork in a power outlet. A dark stain spread across the crotch of his robe and his greasy hair started to smoke. I pulled back my brightblade and let him fall. Then I deactivated it and tucked it back in the pocket dimension. I grinned at Colin and cracked my knuckles. "Let's finish this."

Colin's other pal came at me first. I ducked beneath his sword, punched him hard just beneath the armpit, spun, and jabbed two fingers in his throat. The man went down like a rag doll. I kept moving, ducking and dodging Colin's flashing sword. The man knew how to handle the blade, but his fighting style wasn't cut out for this.

I powered the sigils on my arms and caught Colin's sword wrist on the downswing. A quick twist and chop to his arm sent the sword clattering to the ground. Continuing to use the other man's momentum against him, I flipped Colin onto his back, twisted his arm, and put a foot on his neck.

I stared down at him. "Yield, sir knight."

"Never!" He gasped.

"Say uncle." I twisted his arm a little more, eliciting a cry of pain from him.

"Never!"

I felt the tightness in my chest growing and my breaths came harder. I didn't have time to play games. If I had a bad moment right now, Colin would make me his bitch. So I kicked the other man in the side of the head and sent him to dreamland.

Some of the parks' denizens gathered a safe distance away to watch the scuffle. A shadowy figure beneath a tree clapped slowly and strolled toward me.

"Impressive for someone who's nearly dead." Layla came into the light, a dark smile on her face.

There was no way I'd get back over the seal to safety, so I straightened and tried to act as if I weren't on the verge of a heart attack. "Did you even finish your Mojito?"

"I did, thanks." Layla looked down at the unconscious Sir Henry as she walked around him. "And now it seems I have you all to myself, Cain."

I'd met Layla in Voltaire's nearly a decade ago when I'd just left the Oblivion Guard. I'd nearly been booed out of the place before she patted a stool next to her and asked me to sit. In the months that followed, we hadn't exactly become friends, but we also weren't enemies. She knew a hell of a lot more about me than I knew about her.

I knew that someone had hired her to kill me about seven months after my first visit to Voltaire's. I knew she had a reputation as being deadly with blades and arrows. I suspected she was a part elf, part human, due to the slight point in her ears and the shape of her nose. And the last thing I knew was that she hadn't tried to kill me—yet.

It seemed that was about to change.

"Yes, I suppose you do." The tumor in my chest tightened painfully, but I managed a smile. "Did you decide to fuck instead of kill me?"

Layla chuckled. "I'm afraid not." She knelt and felt Henry's neck. "He's still alive."

"What a shame." I shrugged and began to back up ever so slowly. Dolores wasn't parked too far away, but I wasn't about to run any wind sprints with my heart being choked out. "Decided to finally collect the contract, then?"

"That would be in my best interests." Layla pulled a short, silver rod from a sheath at her side and gave it a flick. It lengthened to about four feet. She bent it and strung it so fast, I barely saw her do it. "I'm curious to see if you're as good with blades as I've heard."

"I didn't bring my blades." I produced my dueling wands. "Just these."

She shrugged. "Good enough."

"Would you mind rescheduling the demonstration?" I said. "I've got a lot going on."

"I've waited years, Cain." Layla's hands flashed and an arrow was suddenly nocked in her bow. "I think it's time." She'd barely finished talking when her hands blurred, and the arrow streaked toward me.

CHAPTER 12

I'd been shot with arrows and still had the scars to prove it. Elven archers were formidable, but even they didn't shoot as fast as Layla Blade. I preferred blades to wands when it came to this, but my reflexes made do with what I had.

I flicked the wands through a pattern, charging them with energy, then slashed the first arrow in half—straight down the shaft from the arrow-head to the nock. Twisting and turning, I slashed another six arrows to pieces, working my way closer to the target.

Layla began to run circles around me, hands blurring, arrows flying even faster. My heart pounded, and my lungs wheezed. This fight would be over before she landed a single arrow. I flicked a wand into its holster, still slashing with the other one, and cast a sigil at Layla's feet. A puddle of water turned to ice.

She lost her footing for only an instant, but it was enough.

In the moment she stopped firing, I cast a binding on her bow. The bowstring went stiff. I cast a shield ahead of her trajectory. Layla must have seen the air ripple, because she dove to the side, casting her bow away from her. Two silver blades sang through the night air. I tried to sway backward, but my knees turned to jelly, and I fell instead. I rolled onto my stomach and pushed up to my knees.

I panted and wheezed, desperately trying to get my breath, even though my lungs weren't the problem. Cold steel on my throat told me it was too late for that anyway. A hand gripped my hair and jerked my head back far enough to look up into Layla's face. Her dark eyes were black pits in the night. I imagined it was the last thing I'd see.

"Gods damn, you're impressive." Layla tapped her knife on my neck and then poked the hollow of my throat with the pointy end. "Too bad you're on your last legs."

I tried to talk, but the angle of my neck and the lack of oxygen to the brain just made me dizzy. "Ungh."

"Yeah." She pushed the knife a little harder into my neck. "Wish I could've fought you in your prime." Then she thrust fast and hard.

I was so winded I didn't even feel the pain. Didn't feel the spurt of blood leaving my artery or feel my face hit the ground. Then I realized that was because she hadn't actually stabbed me. I wheezed a query. "Huh?"

Still holding my hair, Layla leaned down. "Do you solemnly swear that you're my little bitch?"

I couldn't nod thanks to her grip on my hair, but I made a noise. My chest knotted with pain and the world began to fade.

"You're going to show me where you live so I can find you when you're finally able to fight again." She pressed the knife to my neck again. "And also in case you die of whatever's wrong with you. I still want the bounty on your head."

She had me by the balls and I was in no condition to argue, so I made an affirmative sound.

Layla nodded. "Good bitch." Yanked me to my feet. "Let's go." She retrieved some items from the ground and then took my arm again. "Which way?"

Able to nod again, I did so in the direction of Dolores. I barely remembered walking to the car or opening it. Layla made me punch the address for the church into her phone and then she drove. I fumbled with the glovebox where I'd stashed the pills Fitz had given me.

"Hey, cut it out." Layla slapped my hands away and opened it. "Don't go for a weapon."

The knife in there wouldn't do me much good against her anyway. I found the pouch but couldn't loosen the strings. Layla opened it for me and jammed a couple of pills in my mouth. They melted like chocolate and warm liquid trickled down my throat. The knots in my chest loosened and my breathing returned to normal. I wasn't a hundred percent, but I also wasn't about to pass out.

Finally, I was able to talk. "I didn't say you could drive Dolores."

Layla's mouth opened, but she seemed at a loss for words. "That's seriously the first thing you say to me?" She burst into laughter. "Jesus, Cain. You turn down free pussy from Aura and then worry about your fucking car after I almost killed you? Do you even know what priorities are?"

I straightened in my seat and tried to recover some dignity. "I'm not begging for sex from anyone, and I don't like people taking liberties with my property."

"With your girl, Dolores?" Layla stroked the dashboard. "Where's the clit, baby?"

I smacked her filthy hand. "Stop it!"

"You've been getting it from your car, haven't you?" She glanced back. "Right up the tailpipe?"

"Fuck you." I tried to calm my breathing. "I should've just let you kill me, so you never got to touch my car."

Layla eased to a stop at the gates around the woods. "Open sesame?"

I reluctantly unbound the sigils and opened the gate. She continued and didn't even stop at the dead end.

"How'd you know that was illusion?" I said.

She shrugged. "Because the wind is blowing but the bushes aren't moving."

I made a note to fix that problem.

When we reached the church, I guided her to the garage. When she turned off the car, she gave me an expectant look. "Invite me inside?"

I groaned and climbed out of the car. "Please be my guest." Then I headed to the front door. I fancied the idea of letting her try to open it and getting rid of her once and for all. But I also kind of liked Layla, even if she'd made me her little bitch tonight. So, I gave us safe passage through the two doors and went inside.

The kitchen was still a horrible mess and the girl was nowhere to be seen.

"You're a slob," Layla announced as she inspected the strewn blankets and food. "But turning a church into a house is smart." She looked at me. "Where in the hell did you find a place like this?"

"Right here," I said.

She rolled her eyes. "I mean, how? It looks ancient."

"For real?" The girl stood at the top of the stairs, a blanket wrapped around her. "Did you bring home a prostitute?"

Layla looked from the girl to me and back again. "You've got a daughter?"

The girl laughed. "Oh, daddy. You and your silly prostitutes."

"Watch it, kid." Layla stared daggers at her. "I almost killed your dad tonight. I could end you too if you piss me off."

The girl stiffened. "Oh god. Is he into snuff porn or something?"

I held up my hands. "Shut up, for god's sake!" I leaned against the couch. "The girl is not my daughter, and Layla is an assassin, not a prostitute."

The girl blanched. "Why exactly did you bring home an assassin? Is she going to kill me since you didn't?"

"My, oh, my." Layla smirked. "Cain, were you supposed to kill a little girl?"

"I'm not a little girl." The girl stomped a foot. "And my name is Hannah!"

Layla ignored her outburst. "Your life is so much more interesting than I thought, Cain." Her eyes locked on something else. "Is that an octopus?"

"That's Fred," I said. Fred perched on all eight tentacles at the edge of the pool, his eyes big and black. "Fred, can you say hi to our new guest?"

He kept staring.

"What a rude octopus." Layla frowned. "Cain, I think you owe me some backstory. What's the deal with the girl and Fred?"

"Hannah!" the girl shouted. "Fuck you people!" Then she grabbed a box of cereal from the pantry and stormed downstairs.

A dull headache in the back of my skull climbed to a sharp crescendo. I filled a glass with water, stumbled into my bedroom, and went straight to the medicine chest in my bathroom. I mixed a pinch of anti-pain powder into the water and drank it. Nub medicine couldn't compare to the stuff shamans and witch doctors made.

Layla watched me from the doorway. "What's really wrong with you, Cain?" She held up a hand. "And don't hold back. You owe me your life."

"Only because you chose not to kill me." I brushed past her and went to the kitchen. "Would you like water or milk?"

"No." She looked at my liquor shelf. "But I'll try some of that aged scotch. Neat."

"From a mojito to scotch? Classy." I poured her a glass then took my water to the couch. Fred was gone, probably back in his pool.

Layla sat in the armchair opposite me and took a sip of the scotch. "This is good shit."

"Yeah." I gulped some water and took a deep breath. Telling other people my business wasn't easy. But I'd agreed to her terms.

I told her the brief tale about the girl, and she was as amazed as I'd been by the series of events.

"A soul-switching girl and a kid who can cast lightning." Layla leaned back in her chair. "You've wandered into unknown territory."

"Most mages would pass out from exhaustion after just a couple of lighting spells," I said. "This kid threw them out like a clown tossing candy in a parade."

She tapped a finger on her glass. "The gods had power over souls and the elements, but they're dead."

"Yeah." I shrugged. "Well, she won't be my problem much longer. I'm taking her to a safe place soon."

Layla leaned her elbows on her knees and met my eyes. "I understand not killing kids, but what in the actual fuck were you thinking to mark her and then save her from Sigma?"

"I wasn't thinking." I slapped my forehead. "I think cancer is affecting my brain."

"It's affecting a lot." Layla pursed her lips. "They say you're called Ghost-walker because you're haunted by the ghosts of innocents. Maybe that's why you did it."

"Sure." I agreed without really agreeing. I'd heard all sorts of explanations for that nickname.

Layla finished her scotch in one gulp. "Here's the deal. This is the most interesting shit I've heard of in a long time, and I would kill to see a live unicorn." She stood. "You let me know what's up with this list of people and I'll help you for free."

I blinked. "For free?" I stared at her. "You almost killed me tonight."

"I'm glad I didn't." Layla put the glass on an end table and then patted my head like a dog. "I think this is going to be a lot of fun."

I stared at her for a long moment. "You're crazy. You know that, right?"

She shrugged. "Yeah, so?"

"How much for my head?" I asked.

"Ten million."

I whistled. "Why in the hell haven't you killed me yet?"

"Money isn't everything, Cain." She mussed my hair. "Am I right?"

I shoved her hand away. "Yeah. It sure hasn't given me a life."

Layla headed toward the exit. "Open the door for the lady?"

"You're no lady." I unbound the sigils protecting the inner and outer door and walked her outside. "How in the hell are you getting home?"

"Just drive me outside the gate," she said. "Then I'll get an Uber."

I was tired as hell, but I offered anyway. "I can just drive you home." It wasn't about being nice, but about knowing where she called home.

Layla tutted. "Oh, Cain, you sly devil." She patted my cheek. "I'm going back to Voltaire's. My evening is only just starting. Did you see those cute witches at the back table?"

"Yes." Of course, I'd seen them. But they'd been among the many in the bar who looked like they wanted me dead. I regretted leaving in the first place. If my ego hadn't interfered, I'd be balls deep in Aura right about now instead of playing host to an assassin with a contract on my head.

I drove Layla back outside the gate and to the main road to wait for her driver, then went back home.

I was exhausted and looking at the mess the girl had made of the kitchen just made me want to stop adulting for the day. So I brushed and flossed my teeth and went to bed without showering.

JANICE GOT BACK to me early the next afternoon.

Unicorn verified. It's amazing! I could have looked at it all day long. It's the most beautiful creature I've ever seen.

I read and reread her message a few times because it was completely out of character for her to text more than short and to the point messages. *Good to hear. You okay?*

Better than okay. It's a life-changing experience, she wrote back.

And I was going to eat the beating heart of this magnificent beast. *Definitely not an illusion? No tricks?*

Fae authenticated.

I grunted. *You have fae on the payroll?*

Lower fae, yes.

That was still impressive. That meant the agency had some heavy hitters. It meant I'd have to be even more careful with one of them out for my blood.

Official channel is compromised, Janice sent. *How do you want info?*

I gave her a secure email address.

Sent, she replied.

I went to my laptop and opened the target dossiers. The first two were scant on information—just a few pictures of a middle-aged man in one and a woman in the other. The man's name was Albert Ingram and the woman, Greta Mead. Judging from the pictures, they were both humans. I assumed they were part of our community because why else hire me?

I knew right away they had to be hard to find and dangerous. I still didn't understand what made their deaths worth a priceless unicorn. The third dossier was nice and thick. The moment I opened it I knew why. The target inside would be easy to find, but nearly impossible to reach—at least for most assassins.

Because the target was the current Mage Supreme.

CHAPTER 13

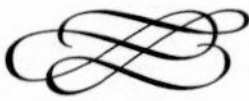

"Holy shit." Mason Digby, the Mage Supreme, was probably worth a unicorn heart by himself. Even after penetrating his security personnel and wards, his personal defenses and abilities would be formidable.

The Mage Supreme was to magic users what the pope was to Catholics. While the fae didn't draw many distinctions between human magic users, the supernatural community drew dozens of lines among them. Mage was the umbrella term for magic users, but they subdivided themselves into sorcerers, wizards, witches, warlocks, and more –mancer categories than anyone had time to learn.

I hadn't bothered to learn all the categories, but the sorcerers tended to be the upper crust and wizards the more common magic users. Witches and warlocks utilized natural magic, much like shamans and witch doctors, but that didn't mean they were benevolent. I'd avoided becoming part of such cliques, not because I wanted to, but because most human magic users despised me.

On the upside, I saved a few thousand bucks a year on membership fees.

On the downside, assholes like Sir Colin and his knights still tried to hold me accountable to the laws of their communities.

What connects Digby to Mead and Ingram? I wondered.

Nothing in the dossiers indicated such connections existed, but I had to assume they were linked even if the client didn't admit it. Very rarely did anyone order hits on multiple targets for completely unrelated reasons.

The scant info in Ingram's and Mead's dossiers gave last known locations from two years ago. No known associates or family listed. Which meant these people habitually covered their tracks like I did, or the client intentionally truncated the information. The latter seemed unlikely since clients typically desired success.

I had to assume that taking one of this trio off the board would alert the others. Digby was so high profile that I certainly couldn't take him down without raising an alarm. The ideal strike would remove all three pieces from the board at once or in quick succession. But how to pull that off?

"Help!" The girl's screams echoed distantly.

I groaned and ran out to the living area. Another shout emanated from the library stairs. I ran down the spiral staircase, white light strobing from somewhere down below, just like flashes of lightning. Had Sigma somehow found my place? Had he slipped past me and into the library?

Impossible!

I couldn't imagine him possessing the skills to find my house. Not unless Layla gave me up. I reached the bottom and found the source. It wasn't Sigma. The girl hovered ten feet off the ground, spinning erratically. Sizzling light waves poured from her eyes and open mouth. The beams from her eyes left scorch marks wherever they struck, threatening to obliterate my collection of mundane books if she hit them just right.

I reflexively cast a shield toward the shelves, blocking them the best I could and then shielded myself.

"Help!" she cried again. "I can't stop!" The light from her mouth vanished each time she spoke.

I had no idea what to tell her. She looked possessed, but no demon had this kind of magic. The shields rattled, pinged, and cracked from the onslaught every time the beams from her eyes raked them. The light coming from her mouth seemed harmless, but I didn't want to get caught in it regardless.

"Close your eyes!" I said, unsure if that would work at all.

The twin beams vanished behind brightly glowing eyelids. "Now what?" she said.

"I'm trying to figure that out." I resisted the urge to pluck her from the air by her foot. The glow around her skin looked dangerous and there was no sense in discovering that the hard way. I summoned my oblivion staff and flipped up the scope for a peek.

The silver border to her soul was thicker than last time, but quickly dwindling down to a thin edge. She began to descend slowly, a balloon losing its helium. The glow from her skin grew dimmer and she abruptly dropped the final foot, sprawling on her back. The silver edge to her soul whittled down to nothing.

The girl groaned but seemed unconscious. I knelt next to her and gently slapped her face. "You okay?"

She didn't answer.

The chairs and nearest reading tables lay in smoking pieces, as if sliced up by laser swords. My shield had protected the shelves, but scores of books looked damaged beyond repair. I walked over and identified which ones. The *Fifty Shades* trilogy was ash, as were most of the *Fever* series. They could be replaced. But some casualties of the fire were irreplaceable antiques.

I found an intact chair and pulled it up next to the girl. "This is bad. Really bad." I couldn't just hand her off to someone else. If this happened again, she'd not only light up like a beacon to Sigma, but probably kill innocent bystanders in the process. That meant, until I figured out what was going on with her, she was my responsibility.

"Fuck!" I kicked a smoking chair and it crumbled to pieces. I had way too much going on right now to worry about another burden. But that was life. I had a month, more or less, to get this shit sorted and assassinate three people if I wanted to keep on breathing.

I drew in a calming breath and accepted my fate.

I look up into Beywin's golden eyes, my vision blurry with tears. "Why did you bother saving me? I'm human trash!"

She smiles at me. "All life is precious, little one. You have it within you to rise to any heights you desire."

I still didn't know what Beywin and Erolith had seen in me when they found a filthy little human baby in the ashes of his home. They'd never told me what killed my parents or why they'd been there in the first place. I probably could have demanded answers, but sometimes the past is best left in the past.

It was an important reminder that someone once took mercy on my pitiful little soul, fed me, cared for me, and trained me so I wasn't completely helpless among the Fae. They'd so affected my life that I'd risen to become an elite among the mightiest of beings.

But this girl was a danger to herself and others. I had to figure out what sort of magic she possessed and train her how to use it before she burned my library and possibly me to the ground. It might have taken me years to identify and control my magic if not for the fae training method. All I needed was to give the girl a little bit of control—just enough to keep her contained.

The girl gasped, back arching. Her eyes flared open. Lips trembling, she climbed unsteadily to her knees and stared miserably at the ground.

"What's happening to me?" Tears dripped off the tip of her nose, puddling on the floor. "I'm trapped in an assassin's house with a maniacal octopus and my body is going crazy." Her shoulders shook. "You should have just let me die."

It seemed I'd found the girl just in time. A few days later and she would have had an episode like this and killed dozens of classmates. Sigma would have found her on his own and ended her before she caused any further destruction, which made me realize that finding her when I did had been no coincidence at all.

The girl should have died before her bizarre powers activated. But the agency knew damned well about my past. They knew that once I identified the mark as a teenaged girl that I might have a problem carrying out my job. The event that triggered my resignation from the Oblivion Guard was almost common knowledge among the supernatural community.

I tapped out a quick message to Janice. *You know about the girl, don't you?* I tucked away the phone and walked over to the girl. "Do you really want to die?"

Shoulder shaking with sobs, she looked up at me and shook her head. "Sometimes. Other times I just want to beat the shit out of the people who fucked up my life."

"I understand." I sighed. "Life hasn't given you many choices. But I'm going to give you a choice now."

The girl's brow pinched. "A choice?"

"Yeah." Everything in my head screamed not to do this. I didn't have time to play babysitter to this girl while my life dwindled to nothing. But my choices had brought her here. I was one of those people who'd fucked with her life. "I don't know how yet, but I'm going to train you to control your powers."

Her mouth dropped open. "Y-you're going to train me?"

I nodded.

The girl's eyes grew hopeful. "To be a badass assassin?"

"To not destroy everything around you." I held out a hand. "Is that a yes?"

She took my hand and pulled herself up. "Yes."

I looked around at the mess in the library and groaned. "First, we need to clean this up."

The girl grimaced but nodded. "Okay."

We spent the next two hours moving books to unburned shelves, and removing the charred remains of books, tables, and chairs.

The girl examined the ruined romance novels. "You read this junk?"

I nodded. "I enjoy drama."

She laughed. "That's not something I hear much."

The girl seemed excited and happy. I wondered how long that would hold true once we started training. The physical aspects might be interesting, but other parts were mind-numbingly boring.

Once the library was spic and span, I unlocked a door behind the spiral staircase and took her into another chamber.

The girl whistled. "Holy shit. There's an entire gym in here!"

My training room had just about everything, from kickboxing bags to tumble mats to gymnastic rings, and a complete set of free weights.

"Do you really use all this?" she said.

"No. I collected it over the years to switch up my workouts." I patted a vaulting bench. "Otherwise training became so boring that it was a struggle to make myself do it."

"So even assassins hate working out," she said.

I nodded. "It's the worst."

The girl frowned. "You're nothing like I'd expect an assassin to be."

I shrugged. "Television and movies don't portray us very accurately." I remembered that I'd texted Janice earlier and checked my phone. No response yet. She had to know or at least suspect something went wrong with the job. And I was almost certain it had been by design. I tucked my suspicions away for the time being so I could get to work with the girl.

"Do you dance?" I said.

She blinked. "Dance? What does that have to do with anything?"

I whistled. "Get out here, dummy!"

"Wow, really?" The girl scoffed. "I just asked a simple question."

A female form jolted upright from its place in the corner and jogged over to us.

The girl shrieked and jumped back. "There's someone in here!"

"No, it's a golem." I tapped a sigil on the dummy's forehead and the illusion giving it a human appearance vanished, revealing a rubber mannequin beneath. I activated the sigil again and the emotionless female face appeared again.

The girl cowered behind me. "That is super creepy."

"I suppose." I shrugged. "But it's great for practice."

"How?" she said.

I snapped my fingers three times in quick succession. Six plastic bins lined up against the wall began to shake. Their lids popped open and golems dragged themselves out, bodies unfolding from positions impossible for humans.

The girl shrieked again. "Stop scaring me!"

I grinned. "I'm not trying to." I made a motion with my finger and the golems surrounded us. "Find a place to sit."

Looking uneasily at the golems, the girl slipped between a pair and sat down on the bench vault.

"Practice mode eleven," I said. The golems attacked.

I blocked the first blow. Dodged a fist and used its momentum to strike another golem in the face. The golem cried out and blood burst from its nose. I swept the feet from beneath another golem and used the same spin to deliver a kick to the chest of the next. I heard the air whoosh behind me and ducked. Grabbed the foot meant to strike me and punched the golem in the crotch. I jumped, grabbed another attacker by the arm, twisted it and flipped over its shoulder. A quick yank broke the neck.

I shoved the body into the remaining two golems. They spread out and attacked from opposite sides. I jumped back, grabbed their wrists, and assisted their impetus, smashing their fists together. They roared in pain. My hands slid up to their necks. My thumbs found arteries and squeezed. Using the sigils on my legs and arms, I thrust the attackers to the ground and punctured their arteries.

Blood spurted and pooled over the tumble mats as the last of the attackers died.

The girl clapped her hands. "Okay, that was cool."

I turned to her and bowed.

"But god, what a mess." She shuddered. "How do you make them bleed?"

I reset the illusion sigils. The blood vanished along with the wounds on the golems. "Practice mode end."

The golems stood, faces impassive.

"Okay, that's the coolest thing I've ever seen." The girl got up and walked around one of the golems, poking and prodding it. "Do I get to fight them?"

"Later," I said. "First, you need to learn control over mind and body."

"I'm yawning already." The girl faked a yawn. "But I guess you're right."

I shrugged. "Yeah, it sucks, but control is the foundation of everything else."

She rubbed her hands together. "Okay. What's first?"

"We can do this the normal way, or I can bind a memory sigil to you." I tapped my forehead. "It will accelerate your learning."

Her eyebrows rose. "So I can learn everything in a single musical montage?"

I grunted. "I wish. This technique is discouraged because it affects your mind."

The girl's eyes narrowed. "Um, so how long does the normal way take versus this way?"

"It helps you focus and remember," I said. "It might cut your time in half unless you're really stupid."

Her lips pursed. "But there are risks."

"Your mind will tire faster. If your vision starts blurring or you start slurring your words, then it's time to stop for the day." I shrugged. "If you keep pushing, it can permanently damage your brain."

"So as long as I don't push myself too hard, I'm safe?"

I nodded. "I've got no idea what your limits are, so you'll need to tell me if anything feels off, okay?"

The girl tapped a finger on her lips. "Okay, I'll do it."

I nodded. "Okay, so this next part is kind of weird." I pulled out a small dagger. "I need a little blood."

"What the fuck?" She jumped back. "What for?"

"The sigil works better if it's bound in your blood." I mimicked poking my finger. "Just a prick, okay?"

The girl shuddered but held out her index finger. "This is all kinds of messed up."

I gave the finger a quick jab.

Her eyes flared. "Jesus, I didn't feel a thing!"

"Because it's a tiny prick," I said, instantly regretting the joke.

The girl guffawed. "Good one."

I took her finger and used it to trace fine lines on her forehead. With the sigil complete, I powered it. White light flashed in her eyes and faded.

"What's wrong?" The girl frowned. "You look like you saw a ghost."

I shook my head. "I've never seen that before."

"Seen what?"

I shook my head. "Your eyes lit up when I activated the sigil."

She grunted. "Yeah, well have you ever seen anyone flying and shooting lasers from their face holes?"

"No." I had a feeling her training would be a learning experience for both of us.

CHAPTER 14

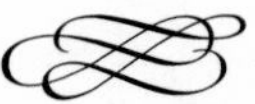

"You're going to learn a little salsa today." I activated one of the golems. "Dance mode Cuban salsa, beginner, female."

Its female appearance flickered and changed to that of a young Latin male. It faced the girl. "We will start with the basics. Please watch my feet." It went through the steps once slowly and stopped. "Please repeat."

I copied the steps. The girl tried but didn't quite get it. The golem repeated and waited. The girl tried and flubbed them again. Cursed, and did them again, this time getting them right.

"I still don't understand how salsa is going to help," the girl said.

I stood on tiptoes and pirouetted, kicked out with a foot and pulled it in to spin faster. I bounced across the floor on my toes, flipped forward, and landed in a split. I pushed up, balancing my body on my hands and flipped back to my feet. "Fighting is all about control and grace. It's literally a dance with death."

She raised an eyebrow. "You're saying every fight is a dance-off with death?"

I nodded. "I was required to master fae shadow dancing before they'd even admit me into soldier training."

"Shadow dancing?" the girl shook her head. "Sounds freaky."

I nodded toward the golem. "Less talking, more practicing."

She opened her mouth as if to protest, then turned back to the golem. "I'm ready."

"Very well," it replied. "Please watch my feet and mimic the movements."

While she practiced, I went upstairs and retrieved Mason Digby's dossier. I took it downstairs to the training room so I could watch the girl and read at the same time. I was about halfway through the folder when Janice responded to my text.

What girl?

I chewed the inside of my cheek and considered her response. She'd gone out of her way to help me more than once. With someone at the agency out to get me, Janice had to know she was putting herself at risk by helping me, especially through a backchannel like this. Which meant she had ulterior motives.

Don't play stupid. Tell me everything right now.

Janice had to know I'd found the girl the moment I marked her. While it was true my handler didn't automatically get a notification of a mark, the dispatcher at the agency did. I suspected Janice knew by now that I'd marked the girl, but that there was no confirmed kill. What that meant, I didn't know. But I suspected there was a lot more to this than she'd told me.

After a long pause, Janice replied. *You did more than what I hoped.*

I waited for her to elaborate, but she didn't. *Enough with the vague responses. Explain.*

The girl must live. Protect her.

"You've got to be kidding me." Those two sentences told me everything. *You set me up. You knew I wouldn't go through with the job.*

Her response came faster, as if she'd been typing it out while I sent her mine. *I hoped you'd just leave her be. But then you marked and took her. Please keep her safe.*

Why? This girl has powers I've never seen before. What is she?

We should meet, Janice sent. *Will explain everything.*

My insides went cold. Meeting with a handler was forbidden. The agency thrived on anonymity. Everyone used fake names and only a select few in the central office knew who worked there. I'd learned more about the agency in the past two days than in all the years I'd done work for them. But the rules had gone out the window the second I decided to save the girl.

I watched the golem lead the girl through a series of simple spins and twists as salsa music played in the background. They ended with the golem dipping her toward the floor.

"I did it!" Face flushed with pleasure, the girl clapped her hands. "Did you see that?"

I nodded. "Good work." Then I turned back to the phone and responded to Janice. *When and where?*

4 PM. Voltaire's. Bring the girl.

Another dangerous outing to Voltaire's was just what I needed. *Too dangerous. Pick somewhere else.*

I can't. Must be Voltaire's.

I groaned. *Fine. See you there.*

I watched the golem teach the girl another routine. She picked up on it quickly—almost too quickly, even with the help of the memory sigil. They continued for another thirty minutes before I called a break.

Breathing heavily, the girl took a seat next to me. "This is way more fun than I thought it would be."

"I'm glad you're enjoying it." I closed the dossier and laid it on the table. "You're picking it up a lot faster than I anticipated."

The girl tapped the bloody pattern on her forehead. "Yeah, this memory sigil is the bomb."

"I mean, you're learning fast even for someone with a sigil." I nodded toward the stairs. "Let's go get you cleaned up. We've got to go meet someone."

She frowned. "Who?"

"Someone who can help, I hope."

The girl looked down at the dossier. "What's that for?"

"New job." I scooped up the folder and stood.

"Cain." The girl took my other hand and squeezed it. "Thanks."

I nodded and took my hand back. "Yep."

She looked down, shoulders slumped, and started up the stairs.

I swallowed a lump of guilt. Just because I was helping the girl didn't mean I had to get attached. The moment she learned enough control to keep her powers from killing everyone around her, I'd find her a safe place to live and that would be that.

Killer, the voices whispered in the back of my mind. *Killer, killer, killer!*

Despite the control I had over my thoughts, I still couldn't repress the ghosts. I had a feeling they'd grow stronger once I started this next job. Once I closed in on a kill.

By the time I got upstairs, the girl had already closed the door to her room. I heard the shower going, so at least I knew she wasn't sulking inside. I went and cleaned up too. I refreshed the protection charms on some cargo pants and a long sleeve shirt and outfitted myself with dueling wands and silver blades just in case.

The girl was in the kitchen eating a sandwich when I came out. She looked clean, but she wore the same dirty clothes I'd rescued her in.

"Shit." I blew out a breath. "You look like a homeless person."

"Yeah, you think?" She put a finger through a blackened hole in her shirt. "You took me straight from school, so it's not like I had spare clothes with me."

We still had a couple of hours before the meetup, so I grabbed my keys. "Let's get you something decent."

The girl watched me for a moment, as if trying to find something that wasn't there. She sighed and put down the remains of her sandwich. "Okay."

We didn't have to drive far. I took her to a Goodwill and let her figure out what she needed.

"Make sure you get something practical," I told her. "Something you'll be comfortable in while fleeing assassins."

The girl laughed, but her smile faded when she saw the look on my face. "Oh, you're being serious."

"I've got a guy who makes enchanted clothing, but we don't have time for that right now." I motioned toward some jeans and cargo pants. "I'd suggest that and some tennis shoes."

She shrugged. "Sure, whatever you say." Then she tried on half a dozen dresses and a godawful hybrid of coveralls and shorts she called a romper. She paired a green romper with tennis shoes and wore it out of the store.

I carried three bags full of clothes while she skipped alongside me, happy as a jaybird that just shit on three clean cars. "Well, at least you can run in that thing."

"Don't hate on my romper, dude." The girl smiled at me. "Thanks, Cain."

I avoided her smile and looked for Dolores in the parking lot. "It was necessary."

She sighed. "No one's taken me clothes shopping since my mom died. I know I'm a burden, but it kind of meant something to me."

I rolled my eyes and stopped to face her. "Yes, you're a burden, but that's because I made two bad decisions in a row. I want you to go on to have a life, but that doesn't mean we get to be buddies, okay?"

A giant tear welled in her eye. She blinked and it rolled down her cheek. "Fine, Cain. Thanks for not letting Sigma murder me." The girl wiped her cheek angrily. "Let's just get on with this so we can go our separate ways faster, okay?"

It took all my training not to feel guilty. I nodded. "That would be best."

I powered the illusion sigils on Dolores, turning her into a banana-yellow station wagon, and then disguised the girl as a young boy. Once we entered the safe zone, our disguises would vanish, but at least they'd keep us hidden from prying eyes before then.

When I parked in Little Five Points, I opened a bag of things I'd purchased and handed the girl a ball cap and sunglasses. "Put these on." I slipped into a disguise of my own, including glasses and a fake mustache.

The girl laughed. "That mustache looks ridiculous."

"Doesn't matter," I said. "It's the best I could do on short notice."

"And it's crooked." She reached toward me hesitantly as if I might bite her and made some adjustments to the mustache. "Still stupid, but at least it's straight now."

I inspected her work in the rearview mirror and found it satisfactory. "Looks good."

The girl scoffed. "For a seventies porn star, maybe."

I raised an eyebrow. "What would you know about porn, much less seventies porn?"

"Foster dads." She shuddered and opened the car door.

I watched her for a moment, resisting the urge to ask for elaboration, then shook it off and climbed out. We were just outside the safe zone, so Dolores's illusion was intact. If anything happened to us at least she'd be okay. Voltaire's might be a safe space, but as Colin and his knight bros proved, it wouldn't stop people from following us out. I wondered why Janice insisted on meeting here.

We approached Voltaire's from a residential neighborhood to the northwest, keeping to the sidewalk. We reached the peace seal about thirty feet from Dolores and our illusion disguises vanished. A nearby nub did a double take but then shook it off as if perhaps he hadn't seen us clearly the first time.

The girl snorted in amusement. "Do you ever feel better than them —the nubs?"

"Not better. Just different." I scanned the area for hostiles or watchers but found nothing suspicious. "Sometimes I envy them."

"I wouldn't be jealous of them." The girl scoffed. "I kind of hate them."

"There are good and bad nubs, just like there are good and bad supers." I shrugged. "Don't hate everyone just because you personally dealt with the shitty ones."

"Easy for you to say," she muttered.

"Yeah." I shrugged. "I've got more experience than you."

"No one ever called me super." She grunted. "They just called me a freak."

The girl kept talking about people from the various schools she'd been to and how awful most of them were. I acknowledged her yammering with a few nods and grunts but continued to keep vigilant. We reached the door and were admitted without incident. Inside I found a trio of day drinkers, but the bar and other tables were empty.

Bill looked up from wiping down the bar with a smile, but it died along with the greeting on his lips when he saw it was me, even through my fake mustache. "Gods damn you, traitor. Wish I could ban you."

"Guess my disguise didn't work too well," I murmured to the girl.

"Duh." She scoffed and looked around. "This is a supernatural bar? I'm not impressed."

"Not much to be impressed with," I said. "Same kind of bar, different kind of assholes."

The girl laughed.

My phone vibrated. I checked the message. *Room 201.*

I walked past Bill's glare and went down the hall toward the bathrooms. A wooden staircase took us down to the rooms. We went down another level and emerged a few doors away from the room. Despite my best calming techniques, my nerves were in knots. I was excited and anxious to meet my handler in person for the first time.

I knocked. The door clicked open and a voice called out. "Come inside."

We entered.

A candle on a table provided the only light. Shadows hid the face of the figure sitting in a chair across the room.

"You look ridiculous," the figure said in a harsh whisper. "Planning to star in an adult film later?"

The girl barked a laugh. "That's what I said!"

I closed the door behind me. "Why meet in person if you're going to hide in the shadows?"

"Just a precaution," she whispered. "I can't use magic to hide my voice or face, so I had to improvise."

"Well, we're here." I reached for the light switch. It didn't work.

"I turned off the power to this room," she said, still masking her voice.

"Gods damn it, Janice." I flicked my fingers and cast a small ball of light. "Enough with the secrets. Step into the light and tell me what all this is about."

Janice rose and came closer, but a hood concealed her face. She was medium height. The cloak she wore hid her body shape and size, but she didn't look fat. Janice walked to a metal panel in the wall and flicked on a breaker. The lights came on. Turning toward me, she reached for the hood.

My breath caught in my throat. I expected an older woman. Someone matronly with glasses and gray hair. That would be in keeping with the bossy but wise handler I'd come to know over the years through text. I still didn't even know what her voice sounded like.

The hood slid back, and it took all my restraint not to punch her in the face.

CHAPTER 15

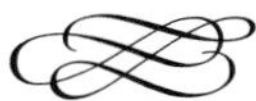

"What kind of joke is this?" The dueling wands were in my hands out of sheer reflex even though we were safe from attack here. I grabbed the girl's arm and guided her toward the door.

"What's wrong?" she said.

"We've been tricked." I sheathed my wands but kept backing toward the door.

The woman held up a hand. "Cain, it's not a trick. It's really me."

But it couldn't be Janice. There was no way in hell this person had been Janice all along. Because Janice didn't act at all like the woman in front of me.

"You can't be Janice." I shook my head. "You're Aura!"

Aura gave me an apologetic smile. "Yes, I am. But I also work for the agency under the code name Janice, and I've been your handler for years."

"Whoa, you know her already?" the girl said.

"Yep." Aura held her hand out. "I've been his bartender and handler all this time."

The girl shook Aura's hand, an awed expression on her face. "You must be something else to outsmart Cain. He doesn't even tie his shoes without making sure someone's not sneaking up to kill him."

"Fuck this. You take care of the girl." I stormed out of the room alone and slammed the door behind me. I felt stupid. I felt blind. Worst of all, I felt betrayed. I thought Aura genuinely liked me all this time. But it was obvious it had all been an act. Even her asking me to have sex last night was probably a pretext for a meeting to talk about the girl.

I stopped in front of a mirror. The mustache didn't come close to hiding the blight covering half my face. Even illusion barely hid the ugliness. I'd fucked myself by using the pearl all these years. Or maybe I'd just been fucked from the start of my miserable life. If I'd been smart, I would've just left everything behind and become a reg. Now I had all the money I could ever want but no time to appreciate it and no one to enjoy it with.

"Just leave it all behind right now." I jabbed a finger at the ugly face in the mirror. "Go enjoy the last month of life and let it end."

Greedy. Corrupted. Evil. The voices in my head didn't like what I was thinking. It seemed they wouldn't even allow me to enjoy the little time I had left.

"Cain."

Aura's voice startled me. I'd been so consumed with my thoughts I hadn't even sensed her approach.

She put a hand on my arm. "Cain, I'm sorry."

"You have nothing to be sorry about." I moved my arm. "This is all on me."

"Not entirely." Aura smiled, but her eyes were sad. "Please come with me. Let me explain."

I scowled and the face in the mirror grew even uglier. "You've got five minutes." I went back inside the room.

The girl looked at me with big eyes from her seat on the bed but said nothing. Aura dropped into a chair next to her.

I closed the door and leaned against it. "Talk fast." I snapped my fingers. "Straight to the point."

Aura stiffened but started talking. "There is a secret organization that kills special children like Hannah. They've used our tracking services before, but they always send one of their own to complete the job. I've tried to get these jobs assigned to you, but the agency knows your profile, Cain. They don't think you're a good candidate for marking kids."

My throat went dry, but I managed to speak. "They're right. Does the agency know the identity of the assassins they use?"

"Only the handlers know real names," Aura said. "They try to keep everything compartmentalized for good reason. But we do build profiles, and you're rated as non-lethal. Your past actions made it clear you wouldn't kill the girl or possibly even mark her, so they wouldn't choose you."

"Make sense," I said.

The girl watched me, concern etched in her forehead.

"I landed this one only because no one else could find Hannah." Aura glanced at the girl as if seeking forgiveness and then back to me. "I hoped you would at the very least leave her be. But you actually took her in and protected her."

"It was a mistake." My knuckles cracked. "I marked her and regretted it. Now she's my responsibility."

"I can take care of her from here if you'd like," Aura said. "I know some people who could take her in."

"Some people?" The girl glared at Aura. "Your brilliant plan is to shuffle me off just like Cain wants to?"

I interrupted before the argument began. "What's this about an organization killing kids?"

Aura tore her eyes off the girl. "Special kids."

I grunted. "I found her spinning in the air, shooting death rays out of her eyes earlier today. You can't just dump her with someone else until she learns to control that."

"Cain's helping me." The girl crossed her arms over her chest. "He hates it, but at least he's not just dumping me somewhere."

"Not yet anyway," I amended. "Don't get too cozy with me, kid."

"I know where I stand with you, Cain." The girl put an emphasis on my name. "And you're helping me. So even if you don't give a shit about me, at least I've got that going for me."

"Hannah, I wouldn't just dump you." Aura reached out as if to pat the girl's hand, then seemed to think better of it. "The people I know would be happy to train you."

"So, you, a handler for assassins is suddenly all noble and wants to save kids?" I scoffed. "Tell me what's really going on."

"That is what's going on," Aura said. "I only found out about these people a year ago. I still know next to nothing about them except that their assassin is named Sigma."

"Yeah." Another thought occurred to me. "Are you in cahoots with Layla?"

Aura's forehead scrunched. "Why would I conspire with her?"

I grunted. "Just making sure."

"We met Sigma," the girl said. "He's got powers you wouldn't believe."

"Just like you," I said. "I saw you swap souls between six people at once. That's more impressive than shooting lightning out of your bare hands."

"Lightning?" Aura's eyebrows arched. "Sigma shoots lightning from his hands?"

"He melted asphalt with it." I shook my head. "Looks like this organization uses a special kid to assassinate other special kids."

"Fucking sickos," the girl said. "Why do they want us dead?"

"Damned interesting question." Aura's five minutes were up, but this mystery felt like something I could really sink my teeth into. "Guess I've got a month, give or take, to figure it out."

"You're really dying?" Aura said.

I slapped my blighted face. "Can't you tell?" I scoffed. "Did you plan to tell me all this last night when you offered me sex?"

The girl's eyes flared. "You conniving bitch!" She lunged at Aura, but the other woman's hand blurred with elven speed and stopped her. The girl stared at Aura's ear, no longer concealed by long hair. "Oh my god. You're a Vulcan."

Aura's face pinched with disbelief. "I'm an elf, not a member of a fire cult."

"That's not what she meant," I said.

"Fire cult?" The girl wriggled free of Aura's grasp. "What does that have to do with pointy-eared aliens, you green-blooded bitch?"

"Vulcan was a Roman fire god," I said, a little impressed that she could quote *Star Trek*. "He's got a cult following in the pyromancer community." I didn't want to get sidetracked, so I got back on subject. "So, about last night."

"Yes," Aura said. "I'm sorry I tried to use feminine wiles to talk to you in private."

I was more disappointed than I should've been. "I figured." I blew out a long sigh to soothe the pain my heart. "Is that all you wanted to talk about?"

"Mostly, yes." Aura fidgeted in her chair. "Also that I think that someone from the agency complained about you to the Black Hand."

"The Black Hand is an assassin." I shrugged. "You're saying someone hired him to kill me?"

"He's not just the world's most dangerous assassin," Aura said, "he's also the director of Eclipse."

I scoffed. "You're telling me the biggest, baddest assassin in the game outed me to vampires instead of coming for me himself?"

Aura grimaced. "The only reason you've been able to maintain a relationship with the agency this long is because no one knew you who you were, Cain. Somehow, the Black Hand figured it out."

"Sigma probably told him," I said.

"Yeah, well someone anonymous sent out a directive to have you killed by any means necessary," Aura said. "But then today, the Black Hand sent out another directive saying he would personally handle it."

I pointed to my impassive expression. "This is my worried face."

Aura bit the inside of her lip. "Cain, I know something of your past even though a lot of it is under seal. I think you might want to worry more about this."

"What does my past have to do with this?" I said.

This time she bit the outside of her lip. "Because I know the Black Hand's real name."

I raised an eyebrow. "Oh, that's not his real name?"

Aura groaned. "No. His real name is Torvin Rayne."

My jaw went slack. "I should've known that evil mother fucker would be up to no good."

"You know him?" the girl said.

I nodded. "My old boss from the Oblivion Guard. He makes other dark elves look like the Keebler elves."

Aura sighed. "You need to be extremely careful."

I scoffed. "I thought I was being extremely careful. Then I find out my bartender has been gaming me for years."

"It isn't like that, Cain." Aura flicked a hand as if dismissing the line of conversation. "Torvin doesn't know who I am. I've successfully kept a wall of privacy between me and the agency."

"I haven't exactly been off the radar," I said. "The local guild knights have been trying to arrest me off and on for years. I'm sure Torvin already knows I'm around here. I'm actually surprised he hasn't made a move on me already."

"Does he have a reason to?" the girl asked.

I snorted. "Oh, he's got plenty of reasons. Maybe he's got better reasons for leaving me be." I walked further into the room and looked for another chair, but Aura had the only one, so I sat on the corner of one of the heavy wooden end tables. "At least now I know why you wanted to meet at Voltaire's and how you keep such a low profile. A safe zone makes for a nifty hideout."

Aura held up a key. "I have the run of the place."

"Let's get one thing straight," I said. "This is the last time I'm coming here until this shit is sorted. There's way too much heat on me if Torvin is on my ass."

"I understand." Aura sighed. "I'll miss seeing you at the bar."

"Enough of the bullshit." I pounded the flat of my fist on the table. "This is the last time you get to use me, *Janice*." I scoffed. "Your good deed burned me at the agency. My reputation is toast."

"But it's good toast," Aura said.

"And you're free now," the girl added.

"Yeah, free to die." That brought up another horrifying question. "How do I know this unicorn job is legit?" I rose to my feet. "Aura, if you're bullshitting me about that, I will end you."

She jumped to her feet, hands raised defensively. "It's a hundred percent real and fae authenticated. It's not a trick."

I narrowed my eyes. "I want to see this unicorn."

Aura shook her head. "You can't. The client only allowed us to see it because we brought a fae to verify it. We had to sign a non-disclosure agreement."

"Which you broke into a million pieces." I scoffed. "Whatever. The girl and I are leaving. Next time we meet on my terms, not yours."

Aura nodded. "I understand." She reached out, took my hand, and kissed it.

I jerked it back. "What the hell?"

Aura smiled. "I wish you'd stop behaving like a badass long enough to admit you're a decent person, Cain."

"I'm barely decent," I shot back.

"Ugly, but decent," the girl said.

"No one asked you." I headed for the door. "Let's go." I left without looking back to see if the girl was following me or not. When I emerged upstairs in the bar, something felt different. Aside from the girl's shoes clomping behind me, there were no other sounds—no voices, clinking of cups or silverware. Another scent mingled with the odor of food and drink—ozone.

I stopped and grabbed the girl's arm. Gave her an urgent look and put a finger to my lips.

Eyes wide, she nodded. I mimicked tiptoeing with my hands and stepped forward. Treading silently came naturally to me, but the girl scuffed the soles of her shoes against the wood almost every step. No one could hurt us here, but that didn't mean I wanted them following us outside.

I crept down the hallway next to the bathrooms and peered around the corner. The three men at the corner table were gone. I couldn't see the entire room, but the bar looked empty. I flicked a pattern with my hand and cupped my ear. The girl gripped my arm and tried to look around the corner with me. I shoved her back with my elbow and gave her a stern look.

No one spoke, but I heard someone breathing. Whoever it was had the lungs of a smoker, judging from the hoarse rattle with every intake. It seemed to be coming from the bar which was just out of sight. The loud breathing nearly concealed another presence. The other lurker's breaths were so soft as to be almost silent.

I released the amplification spell and went over my options. Were they out there waiting for us, or was it just another drinker sitting at the bar? I discarded the latter notion. The raspy breaths likely belonged to Bill, and he couldn't go more than two beats without talking to someone whether he liked them or not.

Unfortunately, there was no other exit from Voltaire's except through the front door. I couldn't use illusion to mask our presence and it would be damned hard to get the girl through the room unseen and unheard. The only option was to fake it and try to make it.

I put my mustache back on, lowered the ball cap a bit, and started walking toward the door as if everything was hunky dory. I noticed Durrug wasn't in his usual spot. I hadn't made it ten steps when Bill spoke.

"There he is."

"Don't turn around," I whispered to the girl. "Keep walking."

"Stop!" a familiar voice shouted.

We kept on walking.

The air crackled. Intense heat flared and something struck me so hard in the back, I thought I'd been rammed by a bull. If not for the shield sigils on my clothing, I would've been cut in half. I was in so much pain, I almost wished I had been. I barely had time to tuck and roll before smashing into a wooden beam.

The girl screamed.

Somehow, I staggered to a kneeling position and saw Sigma at the bar, eyes sparking, blue electricity arcing across his fingers. He looked like a teenaged thunder god ready to unleash the might of heaven on my ward. Jagged bolts speared out and slammed into the girl. She flew back, hit a table and upended it before flipping over and landing behind it.

"This is a fucking safe zone!" I shouted. "The fae are going to murder you!"

Sigma looked at me grimly, eyes still crackling with power. "No. I have an exemption."

"A what?" There was no way the fae would allow that. "You're full of shit."

Bill poked his head up from behind the bar. "What the hell is going on?"

"Good question." I didn't have time to figure it out. The girl and I would be long dead before the fae acted. I ran a trick play and cast a shield right in Sigma's face, just as I'd done the first time.

He held back another attack at the last second, reached out and felt the transparent barrier in front of him. "Not this time, assassin."

Still dizzy from the blast, I staggered over to the girl. Her hands and arms were blackened and burnt, and smoke rose from her hair. I couldn't tell if she was breathing. There was no time to check if I was picking up a corpse or not. I reached into my jacket and popped open one of the hidden pockets inside. Grabbed a handful of dice and threw them across the floor between Sigma and the door.

The dice didn't have pips on them—they had shield sigils. I powered them as they skittered across the floor and a barrier projected from each one. Then I hefted the girl, powered the sigils on my body for extra strength, and ran for the door.

Sigma blurred toward us and smashed into the first shield. He roared in anger, smashing fists against the barriers, trying to find a way through. I wished I had time to give Bill a nasty look before I left, but I felt the blight in my chest pulsating, ready to squeeze my heart and leave me helpless.

If Sigma didn't catch me in the next couple of minutes, it looked like I was going to die all on my own.

CHAPTER 16

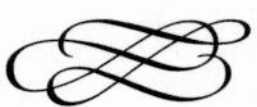

Panting, I jogged up the concrete stairs to street level and threw one last die into the stairwell. Another shield blocked the exit. I got my bearings and started toward the car. A man getting out of his car in the parking lot stumbled back when he saw me.

"Jesus Christ!" He took out his phone and started recording me.

I should have hexed it, but it was all I could do just to put one foot in front of the other even with the magical assist. Sigma's screams of rage echoed from the stairwell and the guy rotated his phone that way. The blight snaked around my heart, squeezing tighter with every step. There was no way in hell we were making it out of here. I needed another option. I ducked behind a windowless van and tried the double back doors. They were locked. I didn't have time to finesse them, so I jammed the end of a dueling wand into the lock and blasted it with a quick burst.

I yanked open the right door. The insides were crammed with carpenter tools and building materials. I shoved aside a shop vacuum and dumped the girl inside, then climbed in after her. With the latch broken, the door wouldn't stay shut, but a stray piece of wire wrapped around the door handles solved that problem. I situated the girl so she wasn't lying awkwardly on power tools and then crawled between rows of junk so I could peer through the windshield.

Sigma burst from the stairwell, lightning crackling along his body. The man with the phone shouted in alarm. Rage boiled in Sigma's electric eyes. He turned in a circle, looking for us, then glared at the man. "Where did they go?"

"Jesus Christ!" The man with the phone tried to run. He made it two feet before a bolt of lightning arced into his back and burst from his chest. Boiling blood and innards exploded across the asphalt.

No longer the calm kid from before, Sigma screamed at the sky in the shrill voice of an enraged teenager. "Cain, you mother fucker! They tortured me because of you. They fucked with my mind. Told me they'd do worse if I didn't kill the girl." He continued turning as if I might pop out of nowhere.

He'd somehow made it past my shields in thirty seconds, maybe less. The long building and locked rear doors blocked access to the street. There was nothing but parking lot for fifty yards in either direction—too far for me to have made it out of sight in a short amount of time. Sigma seemed to know that, or he would've picked a direction and given chase.

Sigma held up his hands and dark clouds formed overhead. Lightning coursed into his body but didn't exit his body. I wondered if that was how he charged himself.

He eyed the cars and I felt like a cornered rabbit. But I couldn't scamper to safety even if I wanted to. That lightning blast to my back had triggered my condition. The blight had a firm grip on my heart. If I didn't rest, I'd be gasping for breath after a few feet.

"Just bring her to me, Cain." Electricity arced between Sigma's fingers as he flexed them. He pointed at a nearby car, and a thin stream of lighting struck the hood. The tires exploded and the hood sprang open. Sigma raked the front row of cars with lightning, causing a cascade of erupting tires and car alarms.

More power flowed into him from the thunderclouds above.

"Shit." I ducked behind the power tools and tried to calm my racing heart. Rubber tires usually protected vehicle occupants from electricity, but I didn't want to bet against Sigma's raw power. It'd be so much easier if I just got out and gave up the girl. Then I could go on with my life and get my gods damned unicorn heart.

"What are you doing?" A female voice outside startled me from my reverie.

I poked my head up and saw Aura at the top of the stairs leading below-ground to Voltaire's.

"Are you insane?" Aura said. "There are security cameras all over the place. The nubs are going to see your little lightning show!"

Sigma snarled and aimed a finger at her. A bolt of lightning caught Aura in the chest. She screamed and vanished down the stairwell, leaving only a puff of smoke where she'd been.

Aura! I barely stopped myself from screaming. "Aura," I whispered. "Mother fucker." Tears burned my eyes. I sagged against a pile of construction materials and stared blankly at the girl. She was breathing, barely. Aura was dead. The girl and I were going to join her very soon.

I shook my head. Wiped my eyes. "Why the fuck am I crying? That bitch is the entire reason I'm in this mess." My heart hurt, and it was no longer because of the blight. My knuckles cracked and heat built in my face. Despite all my rage, I was impotent—powerless to do anything. Even at full health, I'd have a hard time bringing down Sigma, but at least I could have escaped.

Sigma blasted another row of cars. Police sirens wailed the distance, but what the hell could they do against power like that? The boy had discharged enough electricity to power a small town and didn't look tired at all. He seemed able to draw endless power from the clouds.

Kid lightning walked around the smoking cars, approaching our row. In a minute, he'd fill the metal frame of this van with enough power to cook us alive.

In the middle of all the junk I saw a slim ray of hope. It was rubber lining—the kind builders used for tiling bathrooms. The roll was five feet wide and thick. I didn't have time for anything else, so I did the only thing I could. I balanced myself on top of the roll and pulled the girl on top of me.

The scent of her burned flesh and hair filled my nostrils.

Tires exploded and more car alarms began to blare. The van rocked. The bare metal roof and floor sparked. The van shook and it was all I could do to stay balanced atop the fat rubber roll. I instinctively put out a hand to keep us from falling off and my hand met scalding metal. I stifled a shout of pain and jerked my hand back. My feet planted to either side and the stink of burning rubber filled the interior. The heated metal made the interior feel like an oven.

Police sirens blared above the car alarms. Tires screeched and people started shouting. I tried to move my feet, but the melted rubber stuck to the metal floorboard and with the girl flopped on top of me, I was afraid to force the issue. Lightning crackled. Something exploded and it didn't sound like tires this time.

The girl's blackened face lay on my chest. I touched her neck and felt a pulse. Despite the burns and other injuries, her heart still beat.

Guns popped. People shouted and screamed. With all the car alarms and sirens, it sounded like a warzone. Sigma's handlers had turned the mostly polite kid assassin into a raving lunatic. I didn't know what the hell they were thinking or if they even cared about what they'd just unleashed. And how did he have exemption from fae law? Even the damned fae couldn't violate a peace zone without punishment.

My mind went back to Aura and tears burned my eyes again. Pain gripped my heart, sharper than even the cancerous blight. "This is what you get for breaking the rules, idiot." I stopped trying to suppress the pain and let it wash through me. "Fuck me for caring." My tears sizzled against the hot metal.

Despite all my precautions, I'd allowed myself to like Aura. Now I was all alone with a problem she'd created for me. I brushed hair back from the girl's face and looked at her through tear-blurred eyes. Someone I genuinely liked had paid a blood price for this girl.

Sigma had killed Aura without even a second thought. Blasted her chest. Burned her heart to ash. She might have played me for a fool, but gods damn it, she'd been my favorite bartender. I hadn't let emotions cloud my judgement for a long time. It seemed I was really shitting the bed these days, because now this had become about as personal as it could get.

"I'm going to kill that little shit." Provided I didn't die in the next five minutes.

It was still hot as an oven in the back of the van, and fumes from burning construction materials filled my lungs. At least death was giving me options. Did I want to die from poisonous fumes, heat, or a heart attack? Maybe I could catch a stray bullet from a cop or a lightning bolt from Sigma.

I peeled my shoes off the floor and scooted across the rubber roll toward the door. The power tools and other crap made it hard to maneuver with the girl sprawled on my chest. I kicked the back door open. The protective sigils on the back of my jacket were toast. Only a few inches of the rubber roll remained to protect my back, so I'd have to just burn my ass the final feet.

Careful to keep the girl from falling on the hot metal, I used my feet to drag me off the rubber roll and onto my rear end. The armor enchantment on my pants helped a little, but the heat began to penetrate it before I started moving.

There weren't any flames, but it certainly felt like someone lit a fire under my ass. I moved a lot faster than I thought possible with the girl flopping around on my chest. I tumbled out of the van and lost my grip on the girl. I sprawled face first onto the asphalt, gasping for breath. The girl landed spread-eagle on her back.

Black smoke from burning tires drifted across the parking lot. The place looked like a warzone. I climbed to my knees and peeked around the side of the van for any sign of Sigma. Lightning flashed to the south-west. I slung the girl over my shoulder and hoofed it due north. When I finally reached Dolores, I nearly cried with relief.

"Oh, baby, I missed you." I thought she was the only one I'd kill for. My, how the times had changed. I was so tired it took a moment to realize I was the focus of shocked looks from bystanders. Many of them looked from the smoke in the distant parking lot and back to us.

"We got caught in an explosion," I said. "I'm taking her to a hospital."

"Call nine-one-one," a woman said. "It'll be faster!"

"The lines are all busy," I said. "It'll be better if I take her." I laid the girl down in the back seat, then dragged myself around the car and slid into the driver's seat. A deep breath helped me collect my remaining strength, and I shifted Dolores into gear. I took a few random turns and reset the illusion sigils on Dolores, so she looked like a white sedan.

Then I pulled to the side of the road and waited. It didn't take long for me to spot a car I'd seen a few turns back. I couldn't say why it had caught my attention, but I'd learned to trust my instincts. I altered the illusion to make Dolores look empty. Unless someone pressed their face to the window, they wouldn't see through it.

I summoned my oblivion staff and flicked the scope to magnification mode. Two men in black suits occupied a gray sedan. The driver looked both ways and hit the passenger on the shoulder with the back of his hand. The passenger bared his teeth and started talking to the other guy.

I switched modes on the scope to check the auras of my stalkers. They were no longer human when I looked back through. Though they wore human clothing, their faces were scaly and green like lizards. They weren't reptiles at all, but goblins. The passenger goblin held a small black circle to his eye. I realized at the last second that it looked exactly like the true sight scope on my staff.

"Oh, shit." I didn't know how lowly goblins got their hands on fae devices, but the moment they looked my way, they'd see that Dolores was shrouded in illusion. I quickly disabled the sigils and Dolores's appearance reverted to her curvy black form.

The goblin with the scope slowly turned our way. There were plenty of other cars parallel parked between us and them, but I held my breath and hoped he didn't know what my car looked like. The goblin slowly turned the other way, still peering through the scope. I thought about pulling onto the road and making a run for it but didn't dare take the chance.

"Fuck, shit, fuck!" I ducked behind the seat and held in a breath to calm my heart again. When I peeked over the seat again, the goblin car was turning in the opposite direction and driving away.

I nearly pissed my pants in relief, but also because I had to use the bathroom something fierce. Making sure there were no curious passersby on the sidewalk, I leaned over the back seat and examined the girl. A soft moan escaped her lips and her eyelids fluttered.

I gently patted her cheek. "Hannah? Can you hear me?"

She moaned again but didn't open her eyes.

We couldn't go back to my place. I had to get her to a healer. If the burns weren't treated, she might get an infection or worse. I texted the only person I could trust.

I need a healer I can trust ASAP.

Layla responded a moment later. *What's the emergency?*

Electrical burns, I replied.

What are your coordinates?

I hesitated, then gave her an intersection near me. Layla responded a moment later with a link to a map location. I looked back to ensure the car with the goblins was gone, then pulled out and headed toward the coordinates. The healer was only five miles away, but with traffic and stop lights, it'd take twenty minutes to drive there.

Plenty of time to think about just what in the hell happened back at Voltaire's.

I opened a password-protected app on my phone and checked the bounty boards. My name wasn't listed. So how did Bill know I was a wanted man? Surely Sigma hadn't coincidentally shown up moments after I had and asked about me. It seemed more likely that the people controlling Sigma had other people on the ground asking about me and probably offering rewards. When I showed up to Voltaire's, Bill had probably called them, and they'd sent Sigma.

There was no telling how many eyes they had looking for me, so I'd have to be extra careful visiting any other supernatural establishments.

The girl moaned. I reached a hand back over the seat and touched her hand. Her skin was cold, clammy, and covered in goosebumps. She shivered violently and moaned again.

Traffic going in my direction was at a near standstill and we still had three miles to go. At this rate, we'd never make it in time, and the girl would die.

CHAPTER 17

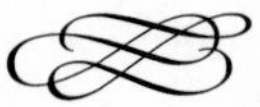

As usual, the road going the opposite direction was almost empty. I had a trick, but it was risky to use. It might get us there faster or draw more attention than I wanted. At this point, I had to take the chance. I powered the illusion sigils on Dolores and pressed one of the buttons under the eight-track player.

Dolores slipped into a police car disguise and the button activated a siren. Nearby drivers looked at me in confusion, as if wondering how in the hell a police car suddenly appeared out of nowhere. To anyone outside looking in, they'd see a policeman behind the wheel and not me. Slowly but surely, the sea of cars began to part. Traffic was so thick most of them couldn't go anywhere, so I took a chance and darted into the oncoming traffic lane.

Cars screeched to a halt, jerking out of my way when they saw the flashing lights. I slowed at the intersection and eased through the red light. Traffic was marginally lighter on the other side, so I dodged back onto my side of the road and forced other cars get out of my way.

On most occasions, I took the GPS arrival time as a personal challenge and tried to beat it. Cheating like this cut the drive time by ten minutes.

But it also attracted a hell of a lot of attention. I was sweating bullets, hoping I didn't pass a real police officer. Then I'd have a real problem on my hands.

A moment later, I turned onto a residential street and quieted the siren and deactivated the illusion sigils. Dolores shimmered back to normal and a kid on a bicycle did a violent doubletake, twisting his handlebars so fast he flipped over.

I didn't like how reckless I'd become lately. Using magic in front of nubs was bad policy, but Sigma and his handlers hadn't given me much of a choice. I pulled up to the address on the GPS and turned into the empty driveway. It led around to the back of the house and into a carport with an entrance hidden from the eyes of prying neighbors.

An older woman sporting long gray hair and mom jeans opened the door the moment I pulled in. I jumped out of the car and pulled the girl from the back seat.

The woman's forehead pinched into a V when she saw the girl's condition. "This way." She hurried inside. I followed down a dim hallway and to a room with a hospital bed and gear. The woman tapped the girl's wrist, found a vein, and inserted an IV. Then she began spreading gelatinous green goop over the girl's burns.

"What happened?" the healer asked as she worked.

I was a little hesitant to tell her since, up until a couple of days ago, I wouldn't have believed stories about a kid who could throw lightning from his bare hands. So I kept the details sparse. "Magical lightning burns."

She nodded and kept working. Once the burns were covered, she picked up a pestle and mortar and began mixing something else. "How long ago?"

I ran some quick calculations from the time the girl had been hit, to the time trapped in the van, the walk to the car, and the drive over. "Maybe thirty-five minutes."

The healer wrinkled her nose. "I'll do my best, but there will be scarring."

"The girl's got worse scars already, believe me." I found a chair in the corner and got out of the way.

The healer looked up from mixing as if someone tapped her on the shoulder.

"Someone trip your wards?" I said.

She nodded. "Please answer the back door for me so I can keep working."

I bit my bottom lip and stared at Hannah. She looked bad—really bad. "Will she live?"

The healer glanced back and frowned. "The back door, please."

I huffed. "Okay." Got up and went back down the hall to the door. Layla was just raising a fist to knock when I opened it. "Surprise, surprise."

"You look rough, Cain." She looked me up and down. "I guess the girl got the worst of it?"

"Yeah."

"What happened?"

A knot formed in my throat, making it difficult to talk. Fists clenched, I took a deep breath and swallowed. "Sigma killed Aura. Nearly killed us too. The healer is working on Hannah."

Layla's eyes widened. "Jesus, you're using her name now, Cain? What happened to you?"

"Shut it." I leaned against the wall and crossed my arms over my chest. She was right. I'd started using the girl's name and hadn't even realized it. "I'm fucking emotional right now, okay?"

She patted my arm. "Hey, it's okay. Assassins have feelings too, even the female ones."

I scoffed. "You mean male ones?"

"Nah. Guys are super emotional all the time." Layla winked. "So that goes without saying." She leaned against the opposite wall. "Tell me what happened."

I gave her the story, complete with discovering that Janice and Aura were one and the same. Telling someone everything felt better than I wanted to admit. I usually told Fred everything, but he didn't really give a shit.

"Didn't realize the elf was so sneaky." Layla shook her head. "She had us both fooled, and that's saying something."

"I'm so fucking pissed that Sigma killed her." I almost banged the wall before remembering I was a guest in someone's house. "I'm pissed that I liked her too."

Layla shrugged. "You caught feelings, Cain. It happens, so just get over it and move on."

"I'll move on when I find out who's behind this and kill them."

"Provided you don't drop dead from your cancer first." She stepped closer and put a hand on my cheek. "Let me see the dossiers and I'll help you."

I grabbed her wrist and held her hand at bay. "Layla, lay off the bullshit and tell me why you're really helping me. No assassin in her right mind would turn down ten mil and get buddy-buddy with her mark. Not unless she's an absolute savage."

"Well, I am savage." Layla didn't try to free her wrists and stared me in the eyes. "But I'm really conflicted about killing you."

"Why?" I said.

"Because you're the first human ever in the Oblivion Guard. Because you're the first being to ever leave the guard and live to tell the tale." Layla peered into my eyes as if trying to see my soul. "Almost everyone on this side of the fence hates you, and no one on the other side even acknowledges your existence."

I released her wrists. "So I'm an enigma." I scoffed. "That's not a good enough reason to turn down ten million."

"Cain, don't get me wrong." Layla's hand suddenly gripped my throat, digging into the flesh with something sharper than fingernails. "The moment I want you dead, you're dead. So just shut the fuck up and let me enjoy seeing you eat a unicorn heart, okay?"

I grinned and leaned harder against her hand, letting the dagger-like nails dig deeper. "Now that's a good enough reason."

Layla jerked back her hand and examined spots of blood on her fingers. Her fingernails were trimmed like a man's, but tiny blades retracted into rings she wore on almost every finger, explaining what had poked me.

She wiped the blood on my shirt. "Don't give me your cooties, Cain."

I scoffed and walked back down to the girl's room. The healer had spread thick, blue liquid on the patient's forehead and was drawing sigils in it with a feather quill.

"Gods be damned." Layla gripped my wrist. "It looks like she plowed face-first into a nuclear reactor."

I nodded. "Sigma's powers are no joke."

The healer sighed loudly and looked back at us. "Please go wait in the lounge down the hallway. I need to concentrate."

I looked down at Layla's hand still wrapped around my wrist. "Want to just hold hands or is that too forward?"

She snorted and let go. We moseyed on down the hall to the next room over and sat on plush leather chairs.

Layla leaned forward, elbows on knees. "Tell me more about the dossiers."

I gave her everything I had and summed it up by saying, "Two of them are ghosts. The other is a rock star."

She pursed her lips. "Connections?"

I shrugged. "Haven't had a chance to do much research yet."

Layla leaned back. "That's it?"

I nodded. "Can't figure how Digby connects to two complete unknowns."

She pursed her lips. "Who in the hell wants the Mage Supreme dead?"

I scoffed. "Besides vampires, lycans, and the population of Ratham Penitentiary? Not to mention his political enemies."

"You've got a point." Layla walked to a table with an assortment of teabags and started sorting through them. "I doubt the client cares about gaining power. They've got a grudge to settle."

"I don't know the why, just the who." I touched a tender spot on the back of my neck where Sigma's attack had gotten past my protection. "They all need to be hit at the same time."

Layla held up a purple tea bag and read it. "Yeah. The minute one of them dies, the others will be on high alert. That's the way these conspiracy groups work."

"Need to find what binds them together." I wanted to go check on Hannah. We'd only been in here a few minutes, but it felt like longer. "If we find the common thread between them, we can use it to draw them together in one place."

"I know how it works, Cain." Layla tore open the package and dropped the teabag in a cup. "I'll follow you home when we leave so I can read the dossiers myself." She poured steaming water from the teapot into the cup.

My heart skipped a beat just thinking about allowing her back in my formerly secret lair, but I simply nodded. "Sure."

"Aw, that's cute." She looked at me like a mother doting on a baby. "You just hate the idea of anyone penetrating your sanctum."

"Take me to your place," I said. "Let's see how you like it."

Layla waggled a finger. "Not until you have dinner with me and my parents."

I rolled my eyes. "So witty."

She sat down while her tea steeped. "Tell me everything in Digby's dossier. I want a head start."

I spent the next twenty minutes doing just that, using a privacy ward so the healer couldn't hear us plotting the assassination of the Mage Supreme. The ward was one-way, so I heard the healer coming down the hall and dispelled it.

"She's stable and recovering." The healer held up a jar of green gel. "You'll need to spread a fresh coat of this over her wounds every two hours. It'll minimize scarring. The healing sigils will keep her sedated for another twenty-one hours. If her wounds don't show signs of recovering by then, bring her back."

"Thanks, doc." I reached for my wallet. "How much?"

Her eyes moved from me to Layla. "Off the books, I assume?"

I nodded. "You don't want to meet the people after this girl."

"Okay. No invoices then." The healer seemed to think about it for a moment. "Three hundred, please."

That seemed pretty low, so I rounded up and gave her five hundred cash.

She frowned. "Why the extra?"

"Because I wanted to." I walked to the other room and looked the girl over. She was breathing normally, and her skin wasn't covered in goosebumps anymore. Green goop covered her wounds, and the blue stuff was on her forehead and the top of her chest.

"The wards on the clothing protected her from worse," the healer said from behind me. "I measured the voltage that hit her. It was off the charts."

"You can measure that?" I said.

She nodded. "I can treat trauma better if I know exactly what happened." The healer shook her head. "It should have cooked her insides. I guess your wards are just that good."

They were good enough, I supposed. "Thanks, doc."

"You're welcome." She looked at my cheek. "At first I thought your face was burned, but then I realized it was your veins."

"Yeah, magic cancer." I raised an eyebrow. "Shaman told me it was a god-level curse eating me up."

The healer grimaced. "I can deal with minor curses. Shamans and witch doctors are the experts on more powerful afflictions."

"Yeah." I shrugged. "Well, thanks."

I lifted Hannah off the bed, cradling her best I could, and Layla helped me get her into the car. I headed back home, Layla following me in a beat-up old pickup. When we got to my lair, I made the girl comfortable in the guest bedroom and came back out to find Fred creeping across the floor.

I got in front of him. "Hey, leave her alone. She's had a rough day."

He stared up at me with creepy black eyes and didn't back down.

"Fred, can you just lay off?" I bent down to pick him up, but he scooted past faster than I thought possible for an octopus on land.

Layla snickered. "You're a master at training pets, aren't you?"

I jogged after Fred, but when I got to the bedroom door, it was closed and locked. "What the fuck? I didn't close the door."

"What?" Layla came over and tried the doorknob. "Your octopus closed the door and locked it?"

I threw up my hands. "Jesus, I guess so. Like I said, I didn't do it."

Layla examined the lock. "Where's the key?"

"I don't need one." I flicked a pattern with my fingers and deactivated the lock sigil. The doorknob clicked.

Layla turned the knob and opened the door.

Fred was on the pillow above Hannah's head, two of his tentacles draped over her face. His big black eyes widened, like someone caught doing something bad. In this case, I didn't know what the hell he was doing. Hannah's back arched and she screamed.

I raced over and lunged at Fred. His tentacle lashed out, extending further than should have been possible, and smacked me in the face. Suddenly I couldn't move. All I could do was stare at the screaming girl on the bed.

CHAPTER 18

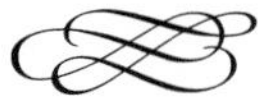

"Cain, what the hell is going on?" Layla came up beside me and another tentacle smacked her face. She froze just like me.

The world around me blurred in reverse. A crowd of students surrounded me. We ran backward into a building. I saw lockers and realized we were in a school. We rewound faster and faster. My world became a blur of colors, sounds and scents.

Suddenly it stopped.

Sad hazel eyes looked down at me. The face belonged to a Middle Eastern woman—Arabic to be exact. It was Esteri, Hannah's mother. Tears poured down her cheeks as she took a handful of pills and shoved them toward my face. I choked and gagged, trying to spit out the bitter mouthful, but she clamped my mouth tight and rubbed my throat.

"Swallow them, my sweet. All will be well." I choked them down against my will. She gave me a glass of water. "Now, wash it down."

Then she took another handful of pills and put them in her mouth.

"But mama, I'm not sick," a little girl's voice said. "And neither are you."

Esteri shook with sobs. "I have to do it. I can't run anymore."

I felt dizzy. The world spun and I collapsed to the carpeted floor. Esteri lay next to me and kissed my forehead. "Sleep, my love. Sleep so the demons will never find you and drag you to hell."

I couldn't keep my eyes open any longer. I slept.

I heard vomiting and realized dully that it wasn't part of the vision. It was me retching in real life. Whatever the hell Fred was doing made it almost impossible to separate reality from this fever dream.

Light returned. My head ached as if a blunt object slammed it repeatedly. The first thing I saw through blurry vision were Mommy's glazed eyes staring back at me. I was so dizzy I could barely think. Smoke filled the room. I looked around and saw a fallen candle beneath the curtains. Flames licked their way up the surface.

"Mommy!" My tiny hands touched her face. Her skin was cold, face frozen. "Mommy!" I screamed in pain and fear. "Mommy!" I grabbed her, but she was limp and too heavy for me to move. I knelt beside her, screaming, afraid, alone. Something was wrong with Mommy. We were going to burn up if I didn't move her.

My little hands gripped her shirt and pulled and pulled, but I couldn't move her. The curtains and carpet were ablaze. Flames licked at Mommy's toes. A terrible odor filled the air. I ran from the room, screaming at the top of my lungs.

"Help! Help!"

I ran outside the house. I didn't know where we were. I didn't know anyone here. Mommy had just moved us here to escape the demons. Everything was dirty and rundown. I ran to the next house, but the doors were boarded up. Same with the next one. I screamed until my voice went hoarse. I ran until my legs could run no more.

I fell and didn't get back up.

"Stop!" I shouted in my own voice. "For god's sake, stop!"

My vision didn't return, but the dream did.

An old black woman looked at me sadly. "She hasn't said a word in five days. We don't know who her parents are or where she came from."

A police officer stepped into view. "I'm sorry, Mary. We don't have the resources to track down her parents. I asked the newspapers to run her picture in the afternoon edition."

"The only one that matters is the Detroit Free Press,*" the woman said.*

"They promised they would." The officer sighed. "Third stray kid this week. What the hell is happening to our city?"

The world fast-forwarded in a blur. When it stopped, I was alone in a room. A middle-aged man, tall, thin, and balding locked the bedroom door. It was Bob, my foster dad. He looked at me and licked his lips. "It's playtime again, sweetie."

"I don't want to." My voice was older, nearing puberty. "Please don't make me."

Bob's lips curled into a sneer. He took off his belt and brandished it. "What did I tell you about talking back?"

"No," I whimpered.

He unbuttoned his pants and came closer. "Shut up or daddy will punish you."

"No!" My voice rose louder.

Without warning, he lashed out with the belt. It cracked against my cheek.

Pain inflamed my cheek. Anger exploded and something inside me awoke. I felt the bad stuff roiling in my chest. I couldn't control it. I didn't want to control it. I just wanted this man to pay for everything he'd done.

I stood on the bed and screamed. "No!" Brilliant light exploded. Bob's eyes went wide with shock. Ghostly white tendrils wrapped around his body, gripping, twisting, and pulling.

Horrible screams tore from his throat as his bones snapped and crunched.

I suddenly felt weak and collapsed on the bed. Bob folded into a jelly-like heap, bones spearing through flesh, blood spurting. I struggled to my feet and ran from the room Bob shared with his wife. I ran into my room, closed the door, and fell onto the bed, sobbing with relief and fear.

My bad stuff had come back. The demons would find me again. And this time, I didn't have Mommy to help.

The real world flashed back for an instant. "Fred, let me go!"

His black eyes regarded me for a moment, and another reality appeared.

Torvin stood in front of me, his large eyes emotionless black pits. "You're weak, Cain. You don't have what it takes to win this war."

"Mass murder doesn't win wars, you sick bastard." Anger boiled in my chest. What had I done? How could I have trusted Torvin after everything.

"Destroy your enemies and none will rise against you when the war ends." Torvin tilted his head slightly, as if peering into my soul. Wind whipped his long black hair around his face. "Other assassins are carrying out my orders across Gaia and Feary. If you wish to remain in the guard, you will complete your next two missions. Otherwise, I will kill you myself."

My brightblade suddenly appeared in my hand. Torvin's appeared just as quickly. The glowing blades clashed with a hum of power. I thrust out a hand, casting a kinetic sigil. His feet skidded back ten feet, but his elven reflexes kept him upright. Blades flashed. I drew on the power of the pearl, amplifying my strength and drove the dark elf back.

"Halt!" Three of Torvin's personal retinue raced across the field toward us.

I could barely take Torvin, much less three more Oblivion Guards. I cast a smokescreen and raced into the forest.

I fell to the floor, suddenly back in reality, now free of Fred's tentacles. The octopus watched me with his black eyes and then slithered past faster than possible for an octopus on dry land.

Layla thudded to the floor next to me, shivering, eyes filled with tears.

Hannah had mercifully stopped screaming.

The blight ached in my chest, but the pain went much deeper than that. I identified with the girl now. I'd lived a small part of her life and felt what she'd felt. It was bad—maybe worse than anything I'd been through as a child in the care of heartless fae.

I was crying too.

Aura was dead. I was dying. And now I knew that the people who controlled Sigma had been after Hannah for a long time. Esteri had been so frightened of them, she'd tried to kill herself and her daughter just to escape.

I sat up, trembling violently, wishing I could unsee everything. Wishing I could purge these awful feelings that weren't mine. Layla sat up and hugged me, soaking my shoulder with her tears.

"Gods be damned, Cain." She shivered. "That was fucked up."

"Yeah," I rasped. "It was."

Layla flinched and pulled away, as if suddenly realizing assassins had no business crying and hugging no matter how traumatic the experience. She cleared her throat and stood. Offered me a hand.

I accepted and she easily pulled me to my feet. I looked down at a small puddle of vomit. Then I saw another puddle that was too far away to be mine.

Layla rolled her eyes. "I got motion sickness, okay?"

"Yeah, me too," I lied. I needed to clean it up, but first there was something else I needed to do. I went over to Hannah and put a hand on her forehead. The sheets were soaked with sweat, but she didn't feel too hot. I stroked her damp hair and sighed.

"You're being manipulated, Cain." Layla put a hand on my arm. "Your fucking octopus is playing with your mind."

"You think the visions were all lies?" I said.

She hesitated. "Maybe they really were her memories. But that doesn't mean you have to care, gods damn it."

I flexed my jaw, unsure what to feel. What to say. "Maybe I'm here for a reason." I stood and faced Layla. "Maybe I have a purpose in life besides tracking, hunting, and killing."

Layla shook her head. "We have no purpose, Cain. We live. We kill. We die. That's all there is to it."

"No!" I pounded my fist against the wall.

She nodded. "Cain, just be yourself. It's okay."

I worked my jaw back and forth again, trying to come up with a rational response. But I couldn't. "I don't give a shit. Fuck Fred, fuck Sigma, and fuck you. I'm going to save her meaningless life even if it costs me my meaningless life. Why? Because I want to."

A tiny smile lit Layla's face. "Then let's do it. Just as long as you realize all life is meaningless and nothing we do matters."

"I'm painfully aware of it, thanks to you." I glanced at the girl one more time, then left the room and stormed over to Fred's pool. It was a good thirty feet deep and twenty feet wide, full of crap I'd pulled from the ocean just to make my thankless octopus happy.

I'd suspected he was no ordinary octopus the moment I rescued him from a dark arts shop when I was barely twenty. I thought it was because he'd been magically modified and experimented on like the other animals there. But now he'd just shown me something I'd never seen before. Something that couldn't be explained away with anything rational.

Layla joined me at the pool and stared into the black water. "What are you doing?"

"I am a fucking fool." I blew out a breath. "Fred isn't a regular octopus. He's someone's familiar."

She whistled. "That would explain it. Never heard of any normal animals with telepathic abilities."

"When his eyes go black, it means his master is watching me." I clenched my fists and growled. "Gods, I'm so fucking stupid!"

"Meh." Layla patted my shoulder. "I've got a soft spot for animals too. Now, if it was a cat, a rat or a raven, I'd call you an idiot since they're the most common familiars. But who the hell would suspect an octopus?"

I scoffed. "Thanks for trying to make me feel better." I knelt at the water and splashed it with a hand. "Why would his master reveal himself so blatantly? If he's spying on me, why not keep on spying covertly?"

"Maybe his master is intrigued by the girl," Layla said. "Do you think Fred's master can track you through the link to his familiar?"

"I doubt it, but anything's possible, as my pet octopus just illustrated." I stood up. "I use fae magic to hide this place, so it would take some serious power to pierce the protection."

Layla's eyebrows rose. "You know how to use fae magic?"

"You have to learn it to be in the guard," I said. "But I'm not nearly as strong as high fae when it comes to using it."

"It's sigil-based, too?" she asked.

"Some is. But the high fae use a combination of blood and planar magic." I stared at the water and wondered if Fred was just going to hide down there the rest of the day. "Some say they stole their powers from the gods."

Layla pursed her lips. "What was it like being a guardian?"

"It made my adoptive parents proud," I said. "That's what it was like."

"So you just did it out of duty?" she said.

I gave up on Fred for the time being and went to the dining area to sate my rumbling stomach. I went around the counter and removed a loaf of homemade bread from the breadbox. "I don't know anything about my real parents—how they lived, or how they died. For some reason, the fae decided to adopt me and train me to become like them."

"Maybe your parents were fae," Layla said.

I scoffed. "I wish. I was physically inferior to even the low humanoid fae, and the high fae are like gods compared to almost everyone."

"You're sure they didn't do something to you?" she said.

"I secretly had myself genetically tested when I was younger. I'm human through and through."

Layla shook her head. "Then how in the hell did you qualify for the Oblivion Guard?"

"I worked my ass off day and night. I took enhancement potions and everything I could." I sliced a couple pieces of bread. "You want a sandwich?"

"Sure." She nodded. "But keep going with the story."

"Even with all that, I was barely in the bottom rung of trainees." I hated to admit the last part, but Layla had seen me cry, so admitting another weakness didn't really matter at this point. "Then I found Fred at a dark arts store. He was about half the size then that he is now and destined to be chopped up for parts. So I bought him."

Layla smirked. "How very noble."

I paused sandwich making long enough to flip her off. "When I got him situated at home, he uncurled and dropped a large white pearl."

Her eyes narrowed. "The one you usually wear on the chain around your neck?"

I nodded. "I didn't think anything of it at the time, but it looked cool, so I put it on a chain. The next time I was practicing magic, I felt this strange sensation from the pearl. I eventually figured out I could push magic through it, and it would amplify the power."

"Really?" She leaned on the counter. "How much?"

I waggled a hand. "A magnitude of about four."

She whistled. "That's fucking awesome. Why don't you have it on now? It would've come in handy against Sigma."

I traced a hand down my blighted face. "Because it caused this."

"You didn't mention that when you told me about the girl," she said.

"Because I already looked stupid enough as it is." I blew out a breath. "Connecting the dots is pretty easy now, even for a moron like me."

Layla smirked. "Go on."

I kept talking. "Fred is a familiar. The pearl belongs to his master. Fitz said the pearl is a god relic."

"But the gods are dead," Layla said.

I nodded. "Yes, but Fred's master somehow got it."

"I think the dots are still pretty damned murky." Layla put a finger on the counter as if making a dot. "The master gave Fred the pearl and then planted him in a dark arts store that chops up animals for ingredients?" She shook her head. "That makes no sense. How was Fred supposed to give it to someone if he's dead?"

"Fred couldn't exactly steal the pearl and escape his master," I said. "Familiars aren't just free to do as they want."

"There's no way Fred was planted in that store just because of you." Layla tapped a finger on her chin. "Or is there?"

"First of all, why me?" I grabbed some ham from the fridge and began slicing it. "The pearl just seems to slowly corrupt the body until it dies. It hasn't turned me into a slave or anything. I wasn't even an assassin when I found Fred."

"Maybe it's supposed to control you, but a human body can't handle it," she said. "Maybe a fae was the target."

"I found Fred in this world, not Feary," I said.

Layla grunted. "Maybe the pearl was already in the store and Fred stole it."

"That makes the most sense," I said. "Fred steals shit from me all the time and then leaves dead animals as payment."

"But why would his master put him in a dark arts store?" Layla said.

"Because he can use Fred as a spy," I said.

"Let me remind you again that Fred was slated to be chopped up for parts," Layla said.

"Maybe his master didn't want him anymore." I shrugged. "Maybe we should just ask Fred if he ever comes up to the surface again." I yelled the last part at the pool.

Fred didn't appear.

I finished making ham and cheese sandwiches without further discussion and presented Layla with hers.

"All this time I thought you were such a badass, Cain." Layla took a bite of her sandwich and spoke with her mouth full. "But you're kind of sweet and pathetic."

I gave her a deadpan stare and bit into my sandwich. "You're anything but sweet, Layla." I reached across the counter toward her cheek.

Her hand whipped up and gripped my wrist. "What are you doing?"

I stared at her. "Will you just indulge me?"

Her eyes narrowed, but she released my wrist.

I tucked her hair behind a slightly pointed ear. "Are you half elf?"

Layla shifted uneasily on her feet and took another bite of her sandwich. She chewed it and continued to stare at me as if that might deter me from asking again if she didn't speak. After holding her gaze for a good minute, she relented. "My father is—was—fae. He was banished from Feary and made a life here."

"Wow." I hadn't been expecting that. "No fae would ever mate with a human."

"It's like bestiality to them," she said. "My father was basically booted from Feary because his fetish was fucking humans."

I laughed. "Damn, that's a good story."

"I know, right?" Layla held up her sandwich and regarded me over it. "So, you were like a pet dog to the fae?"

"I have no clue what I was to them," I said. "I still haven't figured out why they kept me instead of letting me die or dropping me off with humans."

She lowered her sandwich. "You fought for them in the war."

My phone vibrated. I put down my sandwich and slid the phone out of my pocket, mind racing with questions. Who else had this number and why were they texting me now? I looked at the phone and nearly dropped it when I saw who the text was from.

CHAPTER 19

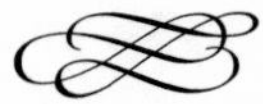

"Cain, you look like you just saw a ghost," Layla said.

I showed her the text. *Cain, are you okay? This is Aura.*

Layla scoffed. "Bastards stole her phone and are using it to track you down."

"Maybe." I stared at the screen for a moment then responded. *Where did we first meet?*

Voltaire's, she responded.

Easy enough, I figured. *What did you say to me then?*

I said you looked like a kid who lost his puppy.

It took all my restraint not to smile or shout in joy. "I think it's really her. She's not dead."

"How do you know?" Layla said.

I showed her the text.

"No one else would know that?" she said.

"We met years ago. It's not something anyone else would remember."

Layla pursed her lips. "What now?"

"I'm bringing her in," I said.

She snorted. "You really don't give a shit about privacy anymore, do you, Cain?"

I scoffed. "You're the one who forced me to bring you here at knife-point." I sent a message to Aura. *Where are you?*

She replied with a screenshot from her map app.

I replied. *I'll be there in twenty.* I checked the time on my phone and was shocked to see how late it was. "It's past midnight."

"Hot damn." Layla stared at my phone. "That little jaunt down memory lane must have lasted longer than we thought."

"Yeah." I nodded toward the guest room. "Keep an eye on Hannah for me?"

Layla nodded. "You're probably walking into a trap of some kind. If you're not back in two hours, I'm out of here."

"Just like that?" I said.

She nodded. "Just like that. Kid's on her own."

I scoffed. "No unicorn for you, then."

Layla frowned. "Good point. Maybe I'll give you three hours."

I grabbed my things and headed toward the door.

"Wait," Layla said. "How do I get past your wards?"

I went into my room and removed a small pouch from its hiding spot in the wall. I slid an ankh from inside and tucked the bag away. Then I went back to the main room and handed it to Layla. "Good for two passes through the wards. So you can go out and come back in."

"Wow, better than Hotel California," she muttered.

"Yeah, you can check out." I gave her a sarcastic salute and left. It took me ten minutes to drive to the area Aura had marked on the map. Dolores was already in disguise as a minivan. Anyone looking through the windows would see a harried mother desperate to get home and open a bottle of wine.

Aura sat on a bench at a bus stop. The location was a residential neighborhood with single-family homes. There were plenty of trees and bushes to conceal an ambush. I parked Dolores a block down from Aura so I could watch her and pulled up the floorboard in the back of the station wagon. I took out a remote-control car and powered on the magical battery.

I opened the door and put the car on the street, then used the remote to drive it across the street and into a front yard. Using the cameras on the car, I navigated it behind some bushes and activated the illusion spells on it. When I drove it from behind the bush, it looked just like me. The legs and arms only moved when the RC car moved. It wouldn't pass a close inspection, but it wasn't meant to.

I steered the RC car toward the road. To Aura, it looked like it was me walking toward her. She stood up and waved. The illusion couldn't wave, but the real me wouldn't have waved back anyway. She started walking toward me. I stopped the RC car and let it wait on her. Then I summoned my staff and peered at Aura through the scope.

It was her. No illusions. I switched to thermal and scanned the area for heat signatures. I found a dog, two cats, and a rabbit. There were humans inside the houses, but nothing else outside. There were plenty of supers who wouldn't show up in thermal, so I scanned a couple more frequencies to satisfy myself.

Aura reached the illusion and tried to touch it. When her hand went through my chest she backed away, eyes wide. I got out of the car. "Aura, I'm here."

She flinched and looked from the illusion to me. "What's with the trickery?"

I scoffed. "Do you really think I'd fully trust this situation?" I deactivated the illusion, revealing the remote-control vehicle. "Please bring back my car."

Aura leaned down and retrieved it, then walked over to Dolores. "Is this a minivan, or is it another illusion?"

"What do you think?" Part of me wanted to hug her. Another part wanted to punch her. I sat down in the driver's seat and her face lit up with confusion when I seemed to transform into a woman through the window.

She climbed in and shook her head. "It's no wonder you've lived this long."

"Yeah." I looked at the black mark on her shirt where the lightning hit her. "Now, tell me how you survived a full-on blast from Sigma."

Aura folded the shirt up to reveal silvery threads beneath. "I'm wearing mithril."

"Wow." I reached out and touched it. "You can afford a mithril shirt?"

"Agency issued." She slid closer to me across the bench seat. "How's the girl?"

"Alive." I narrowed my eyes. "How does Sigma have exemption from a fae safe zone?"

Aura shrugged. "No idea." She put a hand on my leg. "Can you take me to her?"

I pushed her hand away. "I've had enough of being manipulated today, thanks."

"I'm not manipulating you, Cain." She put her hand on my leg again. "I really do care about you."

I rolled my eyes. "Fuck you."

Aura gripped the sides of my face and pulled it close. Her soft lips pressed against mine. I breathed in her scent and grabbed a handful of her hair. Then I used it to pull her away.

She moaned. "I like that."

"Stop it!" I put my hands on her thigh and pushed her back across the seat. "I'll take you to her, but not because of this bullshit."

"It's not bullshit, Cain."

I huffed and shifted into gear. Aura watched me silently as we idled at a red light. I reached across her and opened the glove box. Pulled out a black hood and dropped it in her lap. "Put this on."

Aura's mouth dropped open. "Just so I can't stare at you?"

"No, so you can't see where we're going," I shot back.

Pouting, she slid it on. "You know I'm an elf, right?"

"Yeah, so?"

"And I work for an agency specializing in assassinations and bounty hunting," she said.

"You think your elven and agency skills will tell you where we're going?" I said.

"A hood won't matter," she replied.

I took a turn south. "Well, humor me, okay?"

"We were headed east at the red light," she said. "Right now, we're heading west for some reason."

I groaned. "Just shut up and keep the hood on, okay?"

She didn't shut up. When we turned east, she let me know we were headed southwest. When we went south, she said we were going west again. The disorientation spell on the hood was working great, provided she wasn't yanking my chain. When I got home and parked, I removed the hood.

Aura rolled her eyes. "We're about five miles northwest of the city center."

She was so far off it was almost funny. I threw up my hands. "You got me. Now don't give up my secret lair, okay?"

Aura reached for my hand again. "Look, Cain, this doesn't have to be just about business."

"Yeah." I took my hand back. "It does." I pushed her against the garage wall and held her gaze. "I liked you, Aura, but you played me for the fool I am." I huffed. "So just enjoy your victory and let's get the job done, okay?"

"The girl or the unicorn?" she said.

I shrugged. "Both." Then I took my hand off her shoulder and led her to and through the front doors. "Welcome to my humble abode."

The first thing I saw when I entered was Layla lounging on my couch in nothing but her bra and panties. A dragon tattoo coiled up one leg, across her rib and around to her back. I couldn't make out what was tattooed on her other leg but had to admit it was eye-catching.

Layla stretched languorously. "Is player three ready to enter the game?"

Aura's mouth dropped open. "What's she doing here? Did you fuck her, Cain?"

"Like a wild animal." Layla growled and snapped her teeth. "Want to join us, babe?"

I sighed and walked past Layla to the counter where I'd left my sandwich. Only crumbs remained. "You ate my sandwich!"

"You just left it there." Layla rose and stalked over to Aura, looking her up and down like a piece of meat.

I got out the bread and started slicing it.

Aura scowled at Layla. "I didn't realize you and Cain were a thing."

Layla circled Aura, a predator toying with its prey. She traced a finger up the elf's arm and put her mouth to Aura's ear. "I'm just fucking with you." Then Layla burst into laughter. "Gods, it was so worth it."

I shook my head. "Glad to know you'll strip half-naked for a laugh."

Aura pushed the other woman away. "You're such a bitch."

Layla shrugged. "Yeah, I know." She looked at me. "Guess I'm staying the night. You got any jammies for me? Maybe an octopus-themed onesie?"

I kept making my sandwich, this time with extra mustard. "All I have are oversized t-shirts."

"I guess I'm staying too," Aura said. She looked around. "Where's the girl?"

I pointed to the guest room. "By the way, the wards on the exit doors will paralyze you if you try to leave without me deactivating them."

"I wasn't planning on stealing her," Aura said.

I grunted. "Good."

Aura went into the guest room. I looked at Layla's half-nude form. She was small breasted with narrow shoulders and a petite but muscular torso. Her legs looked like they could crush a man's head. Given her fae blood, she probably could. I had to admit her dragon tattoo was hot, pun intended.

Her time as an assassin hadn't been all peaches and cream, though. A long scar crossed her chest, and one ran diagonally down her left cheek, narrowly missing the eye. Flogging scars crisscrossed her back.

She wasn't one of those gorgeous fantasy women from the movies, but a real-life killer who'd been through the thick of it. She was scarred inside and out, even more beautiful and seductive because of it. I hated myself for feeling so insecure in her presence.

Layla saw me looking. "Like what you see?"

I took a bite of my sandwich and nodded. "Of course."

She nodded. "Most men do. They think with their mini-mes." She tapped her crotch. "That's why they're so easy to kill."

"Yep." I kept eating. "Men are dumbasses. Thanks for the reminder."

"Anytime." She crossed her arms. "Where are the t-shirts?"

I went and grabbed a couple of extra-large shirts I used for disguises and tossed them on the couch. I pointed to the other guest room down the hall from Hannah's room. "You and Aura can share a bed."

Layla licked her lips. "Nice."

I felt a little jealous but quashed it. Pursuing anything sexual with Layla was idiotic. I finished the sandwich and locked myself away in my room. It was late and I was sore all over. I popped one of Fitz's pills and took a long, hot shower. When I slipped into bed and tried to fall asleep, Esteri's dead eyes and the leering gaze of the pedophile foster dad stared back at me. I must have fallen asleep at some point but jerked awake in a cold sweat as Torvin and I fought over Hannah's body in a dream.

"Fuck you, Fred." I wanted to strangle my conniving octopus. "I saved you and this is how you repay me?" I couldn't blame him. It wasn't his fault he was someone's minion, doomed to slavery until he died.

I dried the sweat with a towel and tried to go back to sleep. This time I didn't fight the nightmares—I welcomed them. I bore my own scars, but apparently, they weren't enough to protect me from Hannah's pain. It was almost refreshing to feel the deep cut of agony once more, to remind myself how pain molded me from a worthless human to something even the fae learned to fear.

And then, I slept.

I WAS the first one up the next morning, but not by much. The girl wandered out of her room, face still blue from the healer's potion, wounds crusted with dried green goop.

She looked at me and tears pooled in her eyes. "Cain?"

I was hungry, but it could wait. I walked over and put a hand on her shoulder. "How you feeling, kiddo?"

The tears flowed freely. "Awful." She looked up at me with hopeful eyes, then came closer and hugged me.

My heart skipped a beat. I knew I should push her away. Distance myself. But the time for that was long past. And a hug felt damned good. It felt awkward because I hadn't willingly hugged someone in so long. But I wrapped my arms around this human being and squeezed back. "It'll be okay, Hannah."

She shook with sobs and buried her face in my chest. "You said my name."

"Yeah." I sighed. "I'm fucked."

Face still against my chest, she shook her head. "Thank you."

I didn't answer.

"Well, this is touching." Layla smacked dry lips and wandered from the other guest room in the gray t-shirt I'd given her. "Got any orange juice?"

"I haven't squeezed any yet." I patted Hannah on the head and ended the hug. "Let me make breakfast."

"Can I help?" Hannah asked.

I nodded. "Grab the bag of oranges from the pantry.

"Did I hear something about breakfast?" Aura skipped into the kitchen, looking far too lively for anyone at such an early hour.

"How many women do you have here?" Hannah looked from Layla to Aura. "And what happened?"

I started the coffee machine and told Hannah everything while she sliced oranges in half for the citrus juicer. By the time everyone had a cup full of OJ, she was caught up. I gave Layla the dossiers and let her read them while the girl and I made pancakes, bacon, and eggs.

Layla tossed the pictures of the two mystery targets at Aura. "What's with the skimpy details, elf?"

"I didn't compile the folders," Aura said. "They came from the client like that. They said there was no further information."

"Lies," I said. "They're holding back for some reason."

"They don't want us to know the ulterior motive," Aura said. "But I don't think that will obstruct us too much."

"Us?" Layla raised an eyebrow. "Since when are you part of this?"

"I want Hannah to be safe," Aura said. "Cain needs to be healthy to protect her."

Hannah clapped her hands together. "Breakfast is served!" She set a plate piled with piping hot pancakes on the table in front of the women.

"Too many carbs." Layla got up and stalked over to the bacon and eggs. "This'll do."

"At least have one pancake," Hannah said. "I put almonds and cinnamon in them."

Layla munched on a slice of bacon. "Nah."

I yanked the bacon from her hand. "Eat a fucking pancake."

She growled and narrowed her eyes at me. "Fine, you sentimental idiot."

Layla went to the table, snatched a pancake, and tore into it savagely. "It's good, okay?"

Hannah beamed. "Thanks!"

I prepared myself a plate and sat down at the table. Then I took Mason Digby's folder and started reading where I'd left off.

It was time to plot an assassination.

CHAPTER 20

By lunchtime, we'd digested breakfast and the contents of Digby's folder. And no one liked what we read.

"His travel itinerary varies. He has no set patterns. His estate is nearly impenetrable, and the guild offices are just as hard to breach." Layla scoffed. "We need fresh intel."

"Agreed." I closed his folder. "Twenty-four-hour surveillance. I want to know everything he does." I slid the pictures of Greta Mead and Albert Ingram over to Layla. "Can you get these images into circulation and see if anyone else knows about these two?"

She took them hesitantly. "That kind of intel goes both ways, Cain. They'll hear someone is looking for them."

"Will they, though?" I tapped a finger on the table. "They're off the grid. That means their network of human intel will be limited to a very tight circle, if anything."

"Why don't you just hack some computers?" Hannah said. "Maybe the Digby guy has files on them."

"We'd have to hire someone to do that," I said. "Unless Layla or Aura have skills I don't know about."

"I know some people," Aura said, "but it would be expensive."

"Then ask them." I rapped my knuckles on the table. "Find out what they can do and get me a price."

She nodded. "I'll need an agency-capable computer."

"My laptop will work." I didn't use it for anything except agency work, so I wasn't concerned about her finding anything personal on it. I fetched it from my room and logged in. "The minute you connect to the agency, they'll see it's me."

"I'll use my login." Aura tapped on the keyboard. "I'm not burned as far as I know."

While she did that, I turned to Layla. "Can you get human intel for me?"

She nodded and held up the ankh I'd given her. "Got one of these with more than two uses on it?"

I shook my head. "We're not at that stage of the relationship where you get a key to my house."

Layla pouted. "You don't trust me?"

I snorted. "Hell no."

She grinned. "You're not as dumb as you look, Cain."

Hannah scowled. "You're such a bitch."

Layla smirked. "You know it, kid." She took pictures of the photos with her phone and got up. "I'll be back at some point." Then she left.

"I sent messages to my top two hackers," Aura said. "Guess we'll just have to wait now."

I turned to Hannah. "You need to continue training."

Her shoulders drooped. "But I want to help plan an assassination."

I held out my empty hands. "There's nothing left to do right now." I got up. "So, get moving."

The girl reluctantly did as she was told, and we marched downstairs to the training room with Aura trailing behind. I activated the training golem for ballet. "This is going to hurt. It's about building strength and balance."

"Ballet is for pussies!" Hannah said. "Why don't you just teach me to fight?"

I scowled down at her. "Do what I say, or you might as well cut your own throat right now."

She shrank back. "But it's ballet. It's stupid."

"Stand on your tiptoes," I said.

She tried but couldn't keep her balance. "When you tell me that's easy, then you can ditch the ballet." I pointed at the golem. "Begin training."

Hannah flipped me off, but when the golem started giving directions, she followed them. I walked to a stack of tumbling mats and sat down.

Aura sat next to me. "What's with the dance lessons?"

"It builds strength and dexterity." I sighed and looked heavenward. "Is this not a thing?"

"I've never heard of it," she said.

I turned to her. "Can you shadow dance?"

She waggled a hand. "A little. There are about five different elf variations on the fae original."

"Do you know the dance's origin?" I asked.

"Sure." She leaned back on her hands. "It was passed down by the elder fae when they left the gods and went to Feary."

I shook my head. "That's the textbook version. The shadow dance symbolizes the fae war with the gods and how they won their freedom. Zeus and the Olympians took the best parts of their world and used it to grow a new world for the fae."

"That's just legend." Aura scoffed. "Even my people don't believe in such fairy tales."

"I was taught by the Fae." I stood. "The story might be as ancient as legend, but it's true." I walked a distance from her and knelt, arms raised, palms up. "The fae beg for independence." I stood, put my fists on my hips, and frowned. "The gods disapprove of their servants." I held out my arms and spun away, spinning, twisting, and flipping. "The messengers escape the wrath of the gods." I played out the first act of the dance until my heart began to hurt. Then I ended it, fists upraised, standing on my toes. "The war begins."

Chest heaving, I sat back down on the practice mats.

Hannah clapped. "Holy shit! That was nuts!"

Aura stared at me, mouth slightly agape. "That's very different from the shadow dance I learned."

I finally caught my breath. "Yeah, well I can't do it like I used to." I lay back and wheezed for breath while staring at the ceiling. "Get back to work, Hannah."

She looked down at me. "Can I learn that dance, Cain?"

"The minute you prove to me you're capable." I wanted to stand up and give her a stern look, but I was too dizzy.

Aura touched my arm. "Cain, are you okay?"

I shook my head. "I'm dying, Aura. I'll be lucky to live long enough to complete the mission, much less eat a unicorn heart." I gathered my strength and got up, then labored my way up the stairs. When I reached the top, I went straight to Fred's pool and sat down next to it.

"Why'd you give me that pearl, Fred?" I splashed the water. "I saved your ass, and this is how you repay me?" I was dizzy, still reeling from the long climb up the stairs. "You're a fucking asshole, Fred!" My vision blurred and my head grew heavy as lead. I tumbled face-first into cold water.

I tried to move my arms. Tried to kick my legs. But I couldn't do anything except sink. As the pressure built in my ears, I realized this was how it was going to end. I was going to drown in my own house. I would have laughed but didn't want to suck in a lungful of water.

Something wrapped beneath my arms. Water rushed past me. Suddenly, my head burst above the surface. Strong arms dragged me from the water and left me gasping on the pebble tiles. I expected Aura to fill my vision, but instead, found myself staring into Fred's golden eyes. He slapped a tentacle across my forehead.

Sorrow. The voice was deep and somber.

The word echoed in my head along with a vision of the pearl.

For prophecy.

Fred stiffened and his eyes went black. Suddenly, I stood knee-deep in the underground ocean I'd seen at Fitz's. A giant silhouette stood before me, outlined by the brilliantly glowing fungi far above. A mass of tentacles writhed around its head.

"Where am I?" I shouted. My voice echoed back at me from the depths of the cavern.

A voice sounded inside my head. *You are mine. Submit and the agony ends.*

"Become your slave like Fred?" I shook my head. "Never!"

You will have power greater than the pearl.

"The price is too high."

Submit or die, mortal. There is no other choice.

I held up my fist. "Then strike me down, you fucking asshole!"

The monster raised giant arms and swung them down at me. I let them come. "End my pain and get it over with."

Its fists smashed down feet away from me. A torrent of water swept me off my feet, submerging me and dragging me into the bottomless depths of the sea.

I jerked upright with a shout. I was back in the church. Fred was next to me, his eyes once again golden. A tentacle reached out and gently stroked my hand.

No choice. Sorrow.

Then he slid back into his pool and vanished beneath the surface.

Fred wasn't responsible for my condition. That was all on his master and me. I'd used an artifact without knowing the origin. I might as well have been sticking myself with used needles found in an opium den.

At least the pain in my chest was gone for now. I peeled back my wet t-shirt, suddenly hopeful, but black veins still covered my skin. Whatever that monster was, it wanted me, body and soul. But it couldn't take me against my will. There was no way I'd agree to a bargain like that even if it gave me a few more years of life.

It took monumental effort to stand. Once on my feet, I made it to my room and downed two more of Fitz's pills. Then I lay down on the bathroom floor so I wouldn't soak the bedroom carpet. After a few minutes, I felt well enough to take off my clothes and dry.

When I emerged from my room in dry clothes, I found Aura sitting on the couch with my laptop.

She watched me for a moment. "Are you okay, Cain?"

I nodded. "Just dying a little more every minute." I sagged onto the other end of the couch. "Mind telling me the truth about your interest in the girl before I die?"

Aura tapped on the laptop keyboard. "One of my contacts got back to me. He says he can hack anything, but it'll cost extra."

"How much?" I asked.

"Ten grand."

"Is he up to the task?" I said.

She nodded. "Do you have that kind of money, Cain?"

"I can cover it," I said. "If you trust him, then hire him."

Aura gave me the laptop. "You'll need to wire him the deposit."

I read the message with the payment instructions and sent the money. "I hope he's as good as you claim."

"He is, I swear." Aura scooted closer to me. "You look awful."

I groaned. "Thanks, *Janice*." I put the laptop back on her lap and got up. "Keep me updated." Then I went downstairs to watch Hannah since there was nothing else productive for me to do at that point.

I felt like a sailboat adrift in an ocean on a windless day. Even if there were wind, I had no compass to guide me in the correct direction. I dropped onto the stack of practice mats and watched the girl go through a strength training routine. I sat there for five minutes before getting up and trudging back upstairs.

Even though there was a bounty on my head and my heart might give out any moment, I had to get out and do something productive. Wind and compass be damned. I'd pick a direction and row, row, row, until my arms fell off.

Aura looked up at me from the couch. "Where are you going?"

"Out." I tossed her an ankh. "This'll get you in and out once. Don't leave without telling the girl where you're going."

"Can I come with you?" she said.

I shook my head. "I need some alone time." I turned into my bedroom and threw on some enchanted clothes for protection, grabbed my dueling wands and blades, and left. When I slid into Dolores, I sat there for about five minutes, unsure where to go from there. Then I took a deep breath, backed out of the garage, and just drove.

I found myself heading toward Voltaire's, driven by a need to find Bill and threaten him, but also because it seemed a good place to ask questions. But no place frequented by the supernatural community was a good place for me to be asking questions. Besides, there was no reason to think these people lived in the Atlanta area.

The North American headquarters for the Mages Guild was a high rise in Manhattan in New York City. Digby lived in the penthouse, protected by layers upon layers of magical and mundane security measures. He also owned an estate in upstate New York about an hour from the headquarters. That didn't mean Mead and Ingram lived near there. They could be scattered anywhere across the globe. As the worldwide leader of the Mages Guild, Digby had abodes in other countries, too.

I pulled off the road and parked near a strip mall. I squeezed my eyes shut and tried to think of a starting point. Finding Hannah with the scant information I'd been given had taken weeks and a lot of footwork and travel. This would be no different, except this time, the agency would be hunting me.

I made a phone call.

"Cain." The man on the other end sounded surprised. "You already finished your last job?"

"Not exactly," I said. "I'm double-booked. Need another search in the federal database."

"You realize the FBI logs every search I make," he said.

"I do," I replied. "That's why I don't abuse your services and I pay well."

"Yeah." He paused. "What's the deal with this one?"

"You know I can't say."

Another pause. "Same price as last time plus ten percent."

"Five percent," I said.

"Done," he said. "Let me know when the money is transferred."

I logged onto my banking app and transferred the money to his offshore account. "It's pending."

"Hang on." He broke the silence a moment later. "Okay. What am I looking for?"

I sent him the photos and names via secure FTP link. It was kind of old school, but better than texting it straight to his phone. Even personal phones weren't safe from an FBI search.

"Hey," he said. "There are two people."

I grunted. "You got your money. Don't get greedy now."

My experiences with Agent Brines proved he wasn't great at bargaining, and he didn't break the trend this time.

"Okay, fine," he said. "I'll upload the report to the FTP if I find anything."

"Thanks." I paused. "Oh, and happy birthday."

He sucked in a breath. "You know it freaks me out when you get personal, Cain. I know it's just to keep me in line."

"Just a friendly reminder that I keep track of all my friends' birthdays and other personal info," I said. "Enjoy the money." Then I ended the call.

It was amazing how much a little personal touch could improve the behavior of my informants. Then I made a phone call to another agency. This one specialized in combing state and local databases for information. There was a lot of information, but it was scattered all over the damned place.

I placed an order with them and parted with another four thousand dollars. Between the two of them, they covered most law enforcement records in the United States. My next move was a longshot, but I decided it was worth risking the money. After all, I'd have no use for all the riches in the world if I didn't find these people in time.

After recruiting my list of contacts in child protective services and orphanages, I'd spent another sixteen grand. If Mead or Ingram had been through either system, they might show up. But it meant my contacts would have to sift through decades-old physical records. Digitizing paper files had not been a priority for most of those cash-starved organizations.

Now all I could do was pray this fishing expedition hooked something before I died.

CHAPTER 21

Praying for a miracle wasn't my style. Even if the gods were still around, it'd be stupid to rely on them to solve my problems. I wasn't a thoughts and prayers kind of guy. I preferred hunting the source of my problems and smiting them.

Because if smiting was good enough for the gods, it was good enough for me.

Without anything else to do at that moment, I indulged in something petty. I felt vindictive toward Bill for telling Sigma where to find me and Hannah and wanted a little payback. There wasn't much I could do to him inside the safe zone around Voltaire's, so I considered waiting for him to leave so I could follow him home and let him know just how much I appreciated him nearly getting me killed. While it might feel great, it'd be a huge waste of time, and I wasn't exactly in peak physical condition.

But there was another reason for me to stake out Voltaire's. Since I had no other firm leads, asking a few questions to the fine patrons there seemed logical. First, I needed some assistance. I called another number on my informant list.

"Oh, hey, Cain!" a cheerful voice answered.

"I need a makeover," I said. "You got time?"

"Always time for you." She made a smooching noise. "One hour, my place?"

"See you then." I ended the call and started driving that way. It took me thirty minutes to reach her side of town, so I pulled into a parking spot across the road from the rear of the apartment complex and waited. When it was time, I texted her.

Rachel met me at the back door of the parking deck with a hug and a firm squeeze of my ass. "Good to see you again, hot stuff."

"Yeah, same." I wore my illusion mask, but she knew what I looked like underneath. "Thanks for seeing me on short notice."

"Always." She took my hand and led me to the elevator. When the doors closed, she pressed herself against my chest. "It's been too long, Cain."

"Well, you know how I am." I stroked her long brown hair. "But it's good to see you."

When we reached her apartment, Rachel shut the door and shoved me against the wall. She put her arms around my neck and pulled me down for a long kiss.

"I don't really have time—" I started to say.

She put a finger over my lips. "Make the time or get the hell out."

I nodded. "Okay."

Rachel unbuttoned my pants and reached inside. She smiled. "See? You want this too."

"Of course I want to."

"Take off your mask," she said.

I dispelled the illusion.

Rachel tsked. "My poor baby."

"Want to put a bag over my head?" I said.

She giggled. "No. You're beautiful just the way you are."

We made our way to the bedroom and practically tore each other's clothes off. Rachel shoved me onto the bed and climbed on top. That was probably for the best since I didn't want to chance straining myself after my foolish display of the shadow dance earlier.

When we finished, I had to admit this had been an excellent idea. All the sexual tension with Layla and Aura had given me epic blue balls. I almost wished I'd come to see Rachel a little sooner.

Rachel lay next to me for a few minutes, sighing in pleasure. "You're still my favorite, Cain."

"Don't know why," I said.

She kissed my cheek and got out of bed. "No complications. We fuck, we do business, and you leave."

"I didn't realize that was an admirable quality," I said.

"If I could have you on demand, that'd be even better." Rachel slid a dress over her curvy body. "So, what's the deal today?"

"I need to go to a place where everyone knows my face," I said.

She smirked. "Cheers?"

I snorted. "I can't use illusion, so I need your skillset."

"Must be Voltaire's," she said.

I nodded.

Rachel took my hand and led me to her work room. She was a professional special effects artist, working regularly with studios that filmed locally. "How long do you have?"

"A few hours," I said.

"Good." She got to work.

Rachel took a couple of hours to make some minute changes to my face. She covered the blight, modified my nose with latex, and used a temporary dye to change my hair color a few shades lighter. Contacts shaded my eyes from blue to brown. When she finished, even I didn't recognize the man looking back at me from the mirror.

"Damn, you're good." I smacked her ass.

"You look good enough to fuck again, Cain." Rachel sighed. "But I'm not going to mess up all that hard work."

I paid her for the job. "How careful do I need to be about messing up the makeup and prosthetics?"

"Just behave normally," she said. "Everything will hold just fine unless you start rubbing your face against something or someone." She handed me a bag. "Use the masking agent in here to cover up your face as needed. I blended it for your skin tone, so you don't have to apply it perfectly."

I kissed her forehead. "Thanks."

When I left her place, I went straight to Voltaire's, and looked for a parking spot outside the safe zone. A Mercedes double-parked in a parallel space cock-blocked me just when I thought I'd found the perfect spot. I considered blasting it with my oblivion staff but didn't want to frighten nearby nubs. Instead, I dropped some slick potions around the car's tires and gave it a gentle shove to move it forward into one slot.

After parking, I made my way toward Voltaire's. The parking lot outside was cordoned off by police tape and covered in black marks and lumps of molten rubber from Sigma's rampage. I wondered how the cops would rationalize Sigma's lightshow. I also wondered if it was business as usual at Voltaire's given the violent disregard for safe-zone law the day before.

But when I knocked on the door and gave the password, Durrug didn't even give me a second look. I overheard some patrons at one of the tables talking about a fight the day before but couldn't make out the details.

Then I saw Bill's ugly face behind the bar. I fantasized about all the ways I could beat the shit out of him and decided to give my disguise a litmus test.

I took a seat at the bar. Bill glanced my way. "What'll you have?"

I responded with a little country drawl in my voice. "Vodka soda, partner."

"You got it, bud." He whipped it up and slid it down. "Don't think I've seen you in here before."

"I'm here on Mages Guild business." I chuckled. "Got us a couple of troublemakers."

His eyes brightened. "Does it have to do with Cain Sthyldor?"

I was shocked Bill knew my Fae last name. I rarely used it since coming to Gaia. "Nope. Just a couple of ghosts."

"That son of a bitch ought to be taken down like a dog." Bill grunted. "Just my opinion."

"Because he fought against us in the war?" I said.

"Yeah." Bill made a spitting noise. "Traitorous piece of shit."

I imagined smashing Bill's face down on the granite bar top. Imagined blood splashing as I slammed it repeatedly until he was dead. It was a satisfying daydream, but unproductive.

Plus, Bill might have value. "You get a lot of strangers through here?" I looked around at the small crowd. The people I'd hoped would be here hadn't arrived. Unless they broke their pattern, they'd be here sometime after six, roughly an hour from now.

"All the time." Bill waved a hand around. "It's the safest place in the metro area to meet, have some drinks, and conduct business. I'd be willing to bet most supers passing through the area stop by here at least once."

"How's your memory?" I asked.

Bill leaned on the counter and tapped his temple. "Excellent."

I showed him the pictures of Mead and Ingram on my phone. "I need to bring them in for questioning."

Bill's face twitched. "Nope. Never seen them."

"Ah, well." I put away the phone. "Worth a shot."

"Yeah." His demeanor suddenly became a lot less friendly. "Well, enjoy your trip." He moved down the bar, wiping it with a rag, but I could tell his mind wasn't on the task.

I hit a nerve. Bill knew something. It looked like I might have the pleasure of beating it out of him. That meant I'd be here for a while. I nursed my drink and waited. When dinnertime came, I ordered some food and waited some more. At long last, the people I'd been waiting on made an appearance.

Sirs Colin, Henry, and Francis took their usual table, pounded the table with their fists, and demanded immediate service from Rowena, the tavern wench. Rowena was not a small woman. She was of hearty Norse stock, part Viking and part giantess. She stomped over to the knights' table and spoke loud enough to wake the dead. "What'll you have?"

After they placed their orders, I ambled over to their table.

Colin glared up at me, proudly displaying his corncob teeth. "Who disturbs our repast?"

I refrained from a spurious response. "Sir knights, I'm looking for someone who knows the people of this community inside out. Someone who's well respected and might know how to find fugitives who disrespected guild knights in several states."

Colin grunted and looked at his companions. "You, sir, are looking at the most respected and knowledgeable knights of any guild."

"What do you want?" Henry asked in his usual delicate matter.

I noticed Bill watching me like a hawk, further confirming he knew something. I wished I could spirit him out of this place without violating the safe zone magic. Then again, there might be a way to make him leave of his own accord. I showed the knights the pictures. "Have you seen these fugitives before?"

Colin stared at them. "Nay. Nor have I heard of such scofflaws making trouble for other guild knights."

"Never seen them," Henry said.

Francis shook his head and turned back to his beer.

"Well, thanks for your help, sir knights." I bowed. "An honor to speak with you."

"Indeed." Colin flicked his fingers as if to shoo me away.

I went back to the bar and finished my drink.

Bill was there in a hot minute. "Any luck?"

I nodded. "I'm going to meet one of their comrades who apparently knows them." I flashed a grin. "My lucky day, I guess."

Bill stiffened. "Yeah, lucky."

I tapped the bar. "Can you tab me out?"

He brought me the check and I dropped some cash on the bar. "Have a good one, partner."

"Yeah, you too."

I headed for the door, pretending to talk on my phone, gesturing wildly for added effect. Bill said something to Rowena. She gave him a dirty look but nodded. I headed past Durrug, out the door, and upstairs. I walked slowly across the parking lot, giving Bill plenty of time to catch up.

He peeked above the top of the stairs and used a dumpster for cover. Then dashed across the parking lot and ducked behind a light pole when I reached the street. Bill was comically bad at stalking, but I gave him an A for effort.

A few minutes later, I crossed over the peace seal and kept going. When Bill crossed the line, I slipped through a dark alley and then doubled back on the other side, circling around behind him. Realizing he'd lost me, Bill jogged across the street and toward the alley. I stood right behind him and tapped him on the shoulder.

He shouted like an old man passing a kidney stone and stumbled against the alley wall. "What the hell?"

I pinned him to the wall by his shoulders. Keeping up my southern accent, I said, "Why are you following me, partner?"

"Y-you forgot your change," he stammered.

"Mhm." I let him sweat it out a minute then let him go. "You shouldn't be here. The people I'm meeting with are very dangerous."

He straightened and tried to regain a little dignity. "They know about your fugitives?"

"Yep." I played a bluff and hoped it paid off. "It seems they're connected to Mason Digby."

Bill scoffed but his eyes flared. "The Mage Supreme?"

"The one and only, partner." I folded my arms and watched him twitch. "Seems there's quite a scandal."

Bill reached behind his back and pulled a gun. I could've kicked him in the balls twice in the time it took him to draw. "Who are you meeting with and how do they know this?"

I held up my hands and feigned shock. "Hey, partner. What's the deal?"

He gestured with the gun. "Tell me who you're meeting with, now!"

"You know something, don't you?" I mocked disbelief. "Do you know those people?"

"You've got five seconds to tell me who you're meeting with." Bill aimed the gun at my leg. "Or I'll kneecap you."

"I have another suggestion," I said. "You tell me what you know, and I'll pay you five thousand dollars."

Bill didn't even hesitate. "Not interested."

"You have personal connection with them." I pursed my lips. "You're loyal to them."

"Shut it!" He pointed the gun at my leg again. "I'm counting down. Five, four—"

A streak of light flew between me and Bill and hovered in place. It took a moment for my eyes to adjust to the sudden brilliance. A pixie hovered before and slightly above me on gossamer wings. She was about six inches tall, clad in a sparkling cloud of pixie dust.

She looked down her nose at me. "An emissary of the high fae stands before you, human." Though one might expect a pixie voice to sound high-pitched like someone breathing helium, it sounded just as normal as a full-sized being.

I didn't kneel. "Greetings, emissary."

Bill's face turned bright red and the gun trembled in his hand. For a moment, I thought he might shoot the pixie.

The pixie glared at Bill. "On your knees, humans!"

Scowling, face purple with rage, Bill dropped to a knee, still pointing the gun at me. I stared at her and shook my head.

She scowled and dropped a tiny scroll on the ground before me. "You have been summoned to the court on high, one day hence. Present yourself or face consequences."

I'd had enough of her pompous attitude, so I leveled my gaze at her. "Do you know who you're addressing, pixie?"

Her stern look faltered. "Of course I do."

"Then you know what I'm capable of." I stepped closer and she fluttered back. "Why am I being summoned?"

"I don't know." She sounded a lot less sure of herself. "The scroll bears the peace seal. You have the guarantee of safe passage to and from the court."

I scoffed. "I don't have to worry about someone exempt from the seal showing up to kill me?"

She looked shocked. "There are no exemptions."

Either she didn't know, or she was being serious. I looked down at the scroll. "Pick it up and give it to me, emissary."

Her eyes flared. "How dare you!"

I nodded. "Yes, I dare. Now treat me with respect or I'll teach you a valuable lesson."

The pixie gulped. Then she flitted to the ground, picked up the scroll and held it out to me.

"Thank you." I took it. "How did you know who I was?"

"Your scent," she said.

"You've been waiting out here for hours, haven't you?" I asked so I could confirm the fae didn't have some other method of tracking me.

She nodded.

I nodded back. "You may go."

The pixie streaked away at top speed.

The weird shit was really piling up. I hadn't seen the high fae since leaving their service and now, out of the blue, they wanted to talk to me.

What in the hell was going on?

CHAPTER 22

Still pointing the gun at me, Bill stood. "Who the hell are you? No human speaks to pixies like that!"

I swatted the gun from Bill's hand with a quick backhand. Gripped his arm and twisted it behind his back. Before he could gasp, my arm wrapped around his throat. "I'm Cain," I whispered in his ear.

Bill shivered. "Oh, Jesus."

"I can be your own personal savior, Bill. But you have to tell me what you know about Greta Mead and Albert Ingram."

"I don't know nothing," he whimpered.

I sighed. "Well, shit. Guess I'll let you go then."

"Y-you will?" he said.

"No, Bill. I was kidding." I spun him around, gripped his neck, and slammed him to the brick wall. "You nearly got me killed yesterday, you cantankerous old shit."

"Serves you right, traitor." He squirmed in my grasp. "Let me go, you fae-loving bastard."

I shook my head. "No. You're coming with me. I'm going to enjoy torturing you."

"Oh, fuck." Bill gripped my arm and tried to free himself, wriggling like a worm on a fishhook.

I pinned him to the wall with a spell and let go with my hand. Then I unsheathed one of my silver blades and held it up to his right eye. "I like to get straight to the point," I said. "Pun intended."

"Help!" Bill shouted. "Help!"

"I cast a privacy spell, Bill. No one can hear you." I drew a scarlet line down his cheek with the blade. "Talk or lose an eye."

"Fuck you." He tried to spit in my face.

I pressed the tip of the knife against his closed eyelid. "Fine. Guess it'll be a pirate life for you, then."

"Jesus, fuck! No, wait!" He trembled. "I'll talk!"

I eased off. "Everything now or I'm going ham on your testicles next."

"They're our leaders," he said.

"Leaders of what?"

"The insurgency, you gods damned traitor." He spat but it missed me. "It didn't end with the war. We're going to free ourselves from your precious fae."

I barked a laugh. "You idiots really think you can defeat the fae?"

"We have a new leader. He's more powerful than you could possibly imagine."

I leaned in closer. "I trained with the Oblivion Guard, so I can imagine a lot, little man."

"Yeah." He laughed. "Try defeating a god, you puny ant."

"Enough with the bullshit, Bill." I put the knife near his eye again. "Where can I find them?"

"I don't know. They move around a lot." He bared his teeth. "I can't wait for the next war. We're going to slaughter your fucking masters."

"They're not my masters anymore." Bill seemed to be telling me the truth about not knowing where they were. But given everything he'd said, I had a pretty good idea how to go about tracking them down. "Sounds like Humans First didn't disband like they were ordered to. I wonder if the fae would be interested in that information."

"Traitor!" Bill shouted. "Fucking traitor!" He kept shouting until foaming saliva flecked his lips. "I'll kill you myself!"

I sensed another presence nearby and cast a flare down the mouth of the alley. A dark figure dodged from the light and dashed inside the perimeter of my privacy spell.

Layla regarded me with an arched eyebrow. "Well, it seems you went out for some human intel of your own."

"Couldn't just sit around," I said. "How did you find me?"

"Rowena told me Bill went to follow a suspicious character." She shrugged. "I spotted the pixie light when I was looking around, and that led me here."

"Turns out Bill knows our marks," I said. "They're leaders in Humans First."

Layla snarled. "Those filthy racists."

"Yeah." I shrugged. "He doesn't know where we can find them, unfortunately."

"He's going to warn them if you let him go," Layla said. "You know what you have to do."

"No, wait." Bill squirmed against the spell holding him captive. "I told you everything. I won't talk. I promise!"

"Bullshit." Layla turned to me. "Well, Cain?"

"Don't kill me!" Bill howled. "Please, no!"

I slapped a muffling spell over his mouth and approached him. A quick stab right beneath the left armpit would end him quickly. I pressed the blade against the spot and waited for the ghosts in my head to chime in. But this time, they remained silent. Did that mean they approved of killing Bill, or did they simply not care?

Or maybe I was insane.

Layla gripped my hand and shoved. The dagger slid home. Bill's eyes widened, his mouth formed a wide O, and he slumped against the magical bonds. I gave Layla a dirty look and pulled the dagger free. "Are you fucking serious, right now?"

Bill, the hateful old bastard, was dead. And I felt no satisfaction whatsoever. I wiped the blood off on his jeans and sheathed the blade.

Layla tried to look innocent. "You're kind of cute when you're pissed, Cain."

Surprisingly, the voices in my head remained silent. Maybe they thought Bill deserved it. Maybe they realized I hadn't dealt the blow myself.

I scoffed. "You realize his disappearance won't go unnoticed."

"Maybe. Maybe not." Layla sighed. "You've lost it, Cain. You're not a killer anymore."

"Not if I don't have to be," I said. "We could have found another way."

"Yeah, well it's a moot point." She nodded at the body pinned to the wall. "Want to let it down so we can dispose of it?"

"You talked to Bill almost every time you went to Voltaire's." I watched her face. "You seemed to enjoy the conversations. But now you don't even care that he's dead."

"First, I never liked him," she said, "and second, he was a racist asshole."

"Which you only just found out," I said.

"You think I had all those conversations with him and didn't already know how he feels about other races?" She rolled her eyes. "Can you let him down, please?"

I'd never carried on a conversation with Bill because he hated me so much the moment he saw my face.

I dispelled the binding and the body dropped to the alley floor. Layla opened a small pouch of gray dust and poured a sigil pattern. She flicked her fingers and cast a spark. The substance resembled gunpowder, but it burned slowly and put off an atrocious odor, like rotting meat in the hot sun.

I covered my nose. "I didn't know you had ghouls on the payroll."

"They're handy for cleaning up messes," she said. "They love corpses, bones and all."

"How appetizing." I was about to say something else, but Layla froze in place like a statue as another figure stepped into the light.

He wore black robes and a dark cowl covered his face, but the bony hands and gleaming scythe were total giveaways. A skeletal face regarded me from beneath the hood. It could have been smiling, but without flesh, it was hard to say. Seeing Death in his true form would loosen the bowels of most creatures, but after seeing him a few times, I'd gotten used to it.

"Another kill, but not yours." Thanatos pulled back the hood and his face once again had flesh. His eyes gazed at the air around me. He was probably looking at the ghosts. "You had a close call yesterday."

I nodded. "Do you know who controls Sigma? Can you help me find Greta Mead and Albert Ingram?"

Thanatos smiled. "Cain, a journey is no journey if you don't make the trip yourself." He reached toward Bill and clasped hands with something unseen.

"Other people don't see you, but I can," I said.

He nodded. "So you've noticed."

"I didn't know you could freeze people in place."

He looked at Layla. "Sometimes it's better that others don't think you're any crazier than you already are."

I scoffed. "True. Why can't I see the spirits or ghosts, but I can see you?"

"You're not looking hard enough, Cain." Death put a hand on my shoulder. "I like the path you're on. You've got a little longer before we meet in my official capacity."

"Not that much longer." I sighed. "You used to visit me when people weren't dying nearby. Did you lose interest?"

Thanatos shook his head. "A lot has changed recently. Business keeps me on the move with little time for idle interests."

Despite knowing one of the four riders of the apocalypse, it seemed I'd have to find the answers to my predicament all on my own. "Can you at least tell me if a unicorn still exists?" I wasn't sure I trusted Aura.

He nodded. "Yes, as a matter of fact, it does." Thanatos smiled and it sent chills down my spine. "Let's just say that this is the most interesting thing to happen in a very long time."

"To me, or in general?" I asked

His smile widened. "In decades."

A horse neighed, causing prickles of primal fear to draw goosebumps across my skin. I'd heard that neigh many times, but my body always reacted the same. A ghostly pale horse stepped into the light of my flare, its thin flesh revealing bones beneath. It snorted and nodded at me.

"Ghost says hello." Thanatos flickered from standing on the ground to suddenly being on the horse.

"Wait," I said.

Thanatos looked expectantly at me.

"If the gods are dead, where do you take the spirits?" I asked.

"To wherever they belong." He patted the neck of his horse. Ghost leapt forward and vanished in wisp of vapor.

The stench of the burning powder stung my nose once again.

Layla gave me a look. "How the hell did you move from here to there so fast?"

I blinked. "I didn't. Smoke must've gotten in your eyes." I dodged the smoke and walked toward the alley exit.

Layla caught up with me. "What exactly happened before I got to the alley? I saw a bright light."

"I've been summoned to the high court." I took out the tiny scroll. It grew to normal size when I unrolled it, displaying a paragraph written in Faeicht. The fae peace seal was stamped at the bottom. "Cain Sthyldor must present himself to the high court tomorrow at noon to speak about matters of great importance. His safety and that of an escort is guaranteed by seal, to and from court."

Layla gave me a sideways glance. "Not many humans read Faeicht."

"Not many humans were raised by them." I rolled up the scroll and it miniaturized once again.

Layla tapped a finger on her chin. "It said you can bring an escort."

I shook my head. "You're not coming."

She grabbed my arm and stopped me. "Why the hell not? We're in this together, aren't we?"

I glanced back at Bill's body and then to her. "How can I trust you when you pull a stunt like that?"

"You didn't object," she said.

"I did after the fact!" I sighed. "Besides, you just want to throw your existence in their face, don't you?"

"Maybe a little," she admitted. "I'll bet you they think even less of a half fae than they do of a whole human."

"They consider you an abomination." I had to admit it might be kind of funny to see their faces. "I'll think about it."

"Aw, come on, Cain." She pressed her body against mine and stroked her fingernails against my back. "You need a little arm candy to show off."

I scoffed. "You're a beautifully honed dagger, Layla. But you're poison, not candy." I separated myself from her. "Did you gather any information today?"

"I did, as a matter of fact." Layla took a step back. "It didn't seem useful until I connected it to what Bill told you."

I crossed my arms. "I'm waiting."

"It's not so much what was said, but what wasn't." Layla glanced at Bill's body. "I went to Ponce Underground since it's a good place to buy information. There must've been about ten people in the east wing who said they didn't know anything, but their body language told me otherwise."

"The east wing is full of Firsters," I said.

Layla grinned. "Exactly."

I frowned. "But Mason Digby ran on a political platform of tolerance between species. Why would he be in cahoots with Firsters?"

She shrugged. "I don't know."

I bit the inside of my lip and gave it some thought. "What was he doing during the war?"

"No idea." Layla shrugged. "I don't keep up with politics unless it pertains to my work. It seems unlikely he'd openly be a member of Humans First, though."

"The fae wouldn't stand for it," I said.

Humans First had been around long before the war, but it had been a niche group. Then a visiting high fae emissary killed a mage who accidentally touched him. The number of Firster members exploded, though it was primarily mages at the time. The fae cracked down and some vampires were caught in the crossfire. That was a catalyst for the vampires and the lycans to join the cause.

The wounds still hadn't healed even a decade after the war, but the fae had done a lot to appease humans, and Firster membership had dropped sharply. So why in the hell did Bill think they suddenly had a chance at a comeback?

"Bill hinted that the Firsters have someone with godlike powers as a leader now." I shook my head. "I don't think he was talking about Digby."

Layla snorted. "He was talking shit. Trying to scare you."

"I think it was more than that. Maybe they have someone like Sigma on their payroll." I blew out a breath. "Guess we'll need to figure it out without getting ourselves killed."

"The problem is, Firsters are a loyal bunch," Layla said. "I don't have any connections in that community."

"Do they know you're half fae?" I asked.

She shook her head. "I don't go around sharing that information with anyone."

"So, I should feel privileged?"

Layla nodded. "Damn right." She booped my latex nose. "Whoever did that makeup is really good."

"Yeah, she is." *And at more than just makeup.* I resisted the urge to scratch my fake proboscis. "You didn't know it was me in the alley?"

"Not at first," She said. "Once I got inside the privacy spell, your voice was a dead giveaway."

I grunted. "Maybe I can infiltrate Humans First with a disguise."

Layla scoffed. "Yeah, no. It takes months for new recruits to earn their trust. We need a shortcut."

"Then we sneak into a meeting," I said. "Surely they don't know everyone who's a card-carrying member."

"They'll be sure to have anti-illusion wards, mages, vampires, and more guarding the perimeter," she said. "You'd have to have fae-level glamor to make it past."

"Or just a damned good makeup artist." I pinched my nose and walked back over to Bill's body to gauge his height. He was about a head shorter than me, older, and somewhat gaunt. Even if my face looked like his, anyone who knew the man would do a double take at his newfound height and mass. "Well, I guess a disguise is out. We'll just have to go full ninja."

"We need to know when and where they're meeting first," Layla said. "And even then, we can't exactly question anyone about Mead, Ingram, and Digby."

"Then we capture someone and beat the info out of them," I said.

"Maybe." She nodded toward the alley mouth. "We should go. The ghouls will be here soon, and I don't want to watch them work."

I grinned. "Weak stomach?"

"Yeah, when it comes to them slurping down a human like a plate of spaghetti." She shuddered. "It's not for the strong or faint of heart."

We left the alley and started walking toward my car. I checked the time. "Maybe we could go to Ponce Underground since I'm still in disguise."

"No, I'll go back alone and see if I can nail down more info," Layla said. "Besides, your nose is crooked."

I touched it. "Did you do that?"

She winked. "Maybe." She booped my fake nose once more and left.

Since it seemed I'd done more than enough damage for one night, I went back to the car. A notification on my phone told me something was on my secure FTP. Agent Brines and four other assets had left messages informing me they'd come up empty. My hopes had been low, but it was still disappointing.

Agent Brines's message was more specific than the others. *I found nothing in any federal databases. But when I looked closer, I found a shell file that use to have information on Mead. I think someone deleted her records and accidentally left behind the almost empty file. Everything about these people was intentionally deleted. Sorry I couldn't find more.*

It wasn't good news, but at least I knew now that our other efforts probably wouldn't pay off. I contacted the hacker we'd hired via secure connection and sent him a query—*Find anything yet?* He responded almost immediately—probably normal for someone who spent most their waking hours behind a keyboard.

Two stub files in a database, and dozens of empty header records on the dark web. Someone scrubbed these people's data and tried to erase their existence. Still working on breaching the internal systems of the national Mages Guild, but I'll bet their records are scrubbed too. Two main dark web archives were also cleaned of references for them. Whoever did it is damned good. I can hunt for offline archives, but it'll take weeks.

I thought about it. *Do it and let me know if you find anything.*

Affirmative.

I disconnected from the secure messaging system and stared out into the darkness for a while. Since there was nothing else to do, I went home.

"Intruder alert!" Aura picked up my bread box and hurled it at me the moment I walked through the door.

I ducked and the wooden box struck the wall and splintered. "My bread box!" I shouted.

Aura did a double take. "Cain?"

I'd forgotten about my disguise. I peeled off the nose. "Yes, it's me, you idiot!" I knelt beside the crooked remains of the beautifully carved box and sighed. "I had this thing custom crafted."

"I'm so sorry." Aura knelt beside me and scooped up the splinters. She gasped and yanked back her hand. A splinter was wedged under a fingernail.

"Nice." I took her hand and inspected the finger. "Let me get some tweezers."

She watched me intently, as if looking for something in my eyes. Disappointment creased her brow. "I'll be okay."

I picked the bread out of the mess, but it was ruined. "Guess I'll have to bake another loaf."

Hannah dashed out of the door from downstairs, eyes alert "What happened?"

I took the ruined box and bread to the counter. "Aura tried to decapitate me with a breadbox."

"No, I thought..." Aura slumped. "You were in disguise."

"I'm almost always in disguise." I traced a hand down my cheek. "So I don't scare little kids and Keebler elves." I went to the bathroom and got the tweezers.

Aura snatched them from me and worked at the splinter.

"Did you find out anything?" Hannah asked.

I nodded. "Looks like Mead and Ingram are members of Humans First."

Aura flinched but said nothing.

"Oh, I read about them in the history books," Hannah said. "They wanted to throw off the yoke of fae oppression and free Gaia."

"Yeah." I picked up the broom and dustpan and swept away the splinters. "Layla's checking out some other angles."

"Layla was with you?" Aura looked hurt.

"Not at first." I dumped the splinters in the garbage. "I've got some bad news, Aura."

Her hurt turned to concern. "Oh, gods. What?"

"Layla killed Bill."

Aura looked confused. "Bill? But how? Voltaire's is in the safe zone."

I gave her the story.

Hannah clapped her hands. "Oh, snap! So glad you baited out that asshole and killed him after he ratted us out to Sigma."

"Layla killed him," I said. "I just happened to be holding the dagger."

Aura dropped into a chair. "I kind of liked that cantankerous old fart."

"Racist piece of shit, you mean." I landed my ass on the sofa. "I guess killing him was for the best, otherwise he would've warned the Firsters that we're onto them."

"What next?" Hannah said.

"A whole lot of planning." I looked up at her. "Have you felt any more energy spikes?"

She nodded. "I feel like my insides are warming up again. Just like they did that time in the library."

"Do you feel like it's something you can control?" I asked.

She shook her head. "No. It's like a rising fever. I can't do anything about it."

Sounded like the girl was headed toward another magical meltdown. If she didn't figure out how to control it soon, she might blow us all to kingdom come.

CHAPTER 23

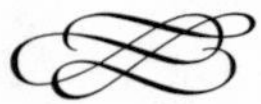

There were no two ways about it. The girl was an unstable nuclear reactor on the verge of going critical and she didn't have the knowledge to work the controls. Learning physical control was just one aspect of magic. The other was mind over matter. I was already working her hard, but she needed to go even harder.

"We need to move on to meditation exercises right now." I got up and headed for the basement stairs. "We'll keep at it until you figure it out."

"What if there is no figuring it out?" Hannah hurried along behind me. "What if I never get control?"

"Then you'll probably kill people," I said, "and those kids whose souls you swapped will never get their original bodies back."

"I don't think I'd swap them back if I could," Hannah said. "Let the bullies see what it's like to be picked on."

I raised an eyebrow. "What about the parents? Their kids aren't their kids anymore."

"Yeah, I guess that's true." Hannah shrugged. "But I'm pretty sure some kids are better off without the parents they have."

I couldn't argue that. Plus, what did I care about those nub kids? I took her through the training room and into a small chamber at the back with a stone pedestal in the middle. I suspected it had been used for sacrifices of some kind by the original builders of the temple. I'd cleaned and bleached the pedestal numerous times, but nothing could remove the black stains.

If I didn't think about the original use of the room, it was a pretty good place to learn meditation. I rarely used it for anything since I didn't need solitude and silence to meditate anymore.

Hannah shivered. "This place is creepy." She touched a dark stain on the wall. "What happened in here?"

"Used to be a wine cellar," I lied. "Probably broke some bottles and stained the floor and walls." I didn't mention all the stains splashed on the ceiling.

"Oh." She looked at the pedestal. "The people who owned this place were weird."

"Yeah." I sat cross-legged on the stone floor and patted a space next to me. "Let's get started."

Hannah sat down facing me. "Cain, do you think I'm dangerous? Is that why Sigma wants to kill me?"

I'd been too preoccupied with other matters to give it much thought, but in hindsight it was easier to make sense of the puzzle pieces. "I think you're like Sigma, except he can control his powers and you can't."

She brightened. "You mean I could shoot lightning from my hands too?"

I nodded. "Maybe. But you also hovered in the air. I think if Sigma could do that, he would've done it already."

"Wow, so maybe I'm even more powerful than him."

"Anything is possible." I put a hand on her shoulder. She flinched, so I took back my hand.

Hannah took my hand in both of hers. "I'm sorry, Cain. I'm not used to good touches."

I shuddered. "I've had a glimpse of the shit you've been through. It was awful."

"Is that why you decided to help me?" she said hopefully. "Is that why you started using my name?"

I looked down at her hands holding mine and sighed. "Maybe."

She held on tighter. "Why didn't you just let Sigma kill me to begin with?"

I bit my lower lip and tried not to think about it. But faces of the dead flashed in my mind before I could nix the thought. "I've got issues."

Hannah laughed. "God, Cain. Don't we all?"

I sighed. "During the war, the Firsters split into cells and used guerilla tactics since they couldn't defeat the fae forces head-on." My mouth became dry as the narrative marched toward the terrible conclusion. "My commander, Torvin Rayne, sent me to eliminate a cell."

"Alone?" she asked.

I nodded. "The enemy was hiding in rural Nevada, supposedly using an unknown Feary portal somewhere in the vicinity to carry out attacks." I tried to swallow. "Torvin told me that nearly fifty soldiers were in the house. He gave me a potion to put in the central air system that would kill the soldiers."

"That's dirty," Hannah said. "Why not just attack with the army?"

"Because they wanted to send a message," I said. "They wanted the humans to realize we could kill them anytime, anywhere without effort."

She grimaced. "A fear tactic."

I nodded. "I killed the guards around the perimeter of the target house, picked the lock to the crawlspace, and inserted the potion in the ventilation intake. The system wasn't on, so I used a spell to spin the fan and disperse the fumes." I shivered. "All I heard were bodies hitting the floors. No screams, no gasps, nothing. Just like that, they were dead."

"Holy shit." It was her turn to shiver. "How could you be sure you didn't accidentally breathe the fumes?"

"I shielded myself, of course."

Hannah nodded. "I see. So you killed a house full of soldiers. What's so bad about that, besides mass murder and all?"

I scoffed. "I used a neutralizing potion to clear the air upstairs so the fumes wouldn't kill anyone else who came to the house. They needed people to see the carnage, after all, or the Firsters wouldn't get the message."

"Make sense."

"Yeah." I cleared my throat. "I decided to take a body count even though Torvin expressly forbid me from entering the house afterward."

"To put more notches on your belt?" Hannah said.

I shook my head. "I didn't like being blindly used by authority. I had to know. So I went inside."

"How many soldiers did you kill?" she asked.

"Besides the guards outside?" I said. "None."

Hannah frowned. "But you heard bodies hit the floor."

I nodded. "There were maybe four men inside, but none of them looked like soldiers."

Her forehead pinched. "So you only killed four men?"

Killer, the voices whispered. *Murderer. Killer.* The chorus rose in my head as I spoke the final part of the story.

"The place was packed with women and children." My gorge rose in my throat and it was all I could do to keep it down. "I killed thirty kids and twenty-eight women." I lurched to my feet, taking deep breaths to fight back the nauseating sickness climbing up my throat.

"Oh my god, Cain." Hannah jumped to her feet. But she didn't run. She didn't curse me. Without even a moment's pause, she wrapped her arms around my waist and hugged me. "Fuck those fae!"

The sickness faded a little, but the accusing voices wouldn't shut up.

"You didn't kill me because you feel guilty?" Hannah said.

"It's more than that," I said. "I'm haunted."

"Killing that many people would haunt just about anyone," she said. "Except maybe Layla."

"No, I'm literally haunted." I put a hand over her back. It felt strange hugging someone for comfort, but it seemed to work. "I left a lot of ghosts in that house, but some of them came with me."

Hannah looked up at me. "Ghosts exist too?"

I nodded. "And they're almost always bad news."

"Dude, that sucks."

"Yeah," I said. "It does." I gave her one last squeeze and pulled away. "I've marked plenty of people for death since then, but I refused to pull the trigger myself."

"And it's different because I'm a kid?" she said.

I nodded. "Yeah, it's different."

"But I'm not innocent, Cain." Her lips trembled and tears pooled in her eyes. "I've killed."

"Not on purpose." I shook my head. "Besides, that fucker, Bob, deserved it."

Hannah's eyes flared. "What if Sigma has to kill me because I'm evil?"

"There's no such thing," I said. "People do shitty things and they do good things. No one is absolutely good or evil, I don't care what the fairy tales say."

"People do way more bad things than good, though." She sighed. "I'm sorry they tricked you, Cain. But I'm glad it means you didn't let me die. I guess that's selfish, but it's true."

I managed a half smile and mussed her hair. "It's self-preservation, kiddo."

Hannah beamed. "Underneath all that bad-assery, you're a good person."

I almost corrected her, but I didn't see the point. I'd disappoint her. Maybe not now, but later, I'd do something, and she'd see the real me. The monster who didn't try to hide in sheep's clothing. I knew for certain that my sense of self-preservation was trying to keep someone who'd done a lot of shitty things alive.

The ghostly voices faded to whispers and I was finally almost alone in my head again. I sat down and patted the place beside me. "Let's get started."

She nodded and dropped next to me. "Could we hurry things up with a montage?"

I snorted. "I wish. The spell I used will help, but it doesn't make miracles."

"I've learned dancing pretty fast," she said.

I nodded. "Yeah. Whatever kind of magic you have also enhances your physical abilities. That's why you healed so fast from those wounds. It's also how you can learn to dance faster than normal."

Hannah hugged her knees. "Your memory spell probably helped."

"Probably, but it doesn't account for how quickly you've learned," I said. "Let's hope it also holds true for training your mind." I sat cross-legged. "Sit like this."

She adjusted herself. "Okay, now what?"

"Usually, this kind of training takes weeks or months before a person achieves any kind of efficiency." I dispelled the sigil I'd put on her forehead earlier and traced a new one. "This one will help you focus your mind, but it tires most people quickly. Maybe your powers will allow you to use it longer."

She nodded. "I'm ready."

"Then let's begin." I lit a candle and set it in front of us. "Focus on the flame. Empty your mind of everything else."

"Uh, how do I do the second part?" she said.

"Narrow the world down to a single point of light, ignoring everything else." I put my hand on her chin and turned her head back toward the candle. "Don't look anywhere else until you've completed this."

"How will you know I have?" Hannah asked.

"Believe me, I'll know." I shut out everything except for the dancing tip of the flame. It became the only light in the world. It had been some time since I'd engaged in meditation in such a distraction-free environment. Shutting out the world around me was a well-practiced habit. Sigils required absolute concentration and focus. One mistake and a spell wouldn't work, or it could backfire on the user.

I changed my focus from sight to sound and listened to Hannah's breathing. As the seconds ticked past, it slowed, then quickened again as she grew agitated with the exercise. "Focus," I said. "Don't think, just stare at the flame."

"I am," she muttered.

Some thirty minutes later, I heard the change in her breathing. Her entire world was now the flame. The sigil I'd placed on her forehead served two purposes—it helped her concentrate, but it also exposed her subconscious to make her susceptible to hypnotic suggestions. I was certainly no specialist in the area, so I had to be very careful.

I turned to her. "Hannah, can you hear me?"

"Yes." Her eyes never left the flame.

"Do you remember the accident you had in the library?"

"Yes," she said.

This was the tricky part. "I want you to go back to that moment and tell me how it felt."

"My insides were hot. My skin burned." Hannah's eyes glowed gentle white.

"Go back to that moment, Hannah," I said. "Where is the heat coming from?"

"The white sun," she said.

I blinked. "Where is the white sun?"

Her gaze lifted. "In the sky."

An uneasy feeling formed in my stomach. "Where are you?"

"I am on the ground."

I was being too general with the questions. "Look around and tell me what you see."

"I am on a tall hill of red sand. There's a dead city next to a black ocean." Hannah's head turned as if she saw it in real life. "The other hills are red and streaked with gold and silver. There is a giant red lizard sitting on another hill." Her eyes flared and her breathing quickened. "Flames are coming from its mouth."

"You are safe, Hannah. Nothing here can harm you." I put a hand on her arm. "Do you understand?"

She calmed down. "Yes."

The world she spoke of was long dead, a place of ancient and terrible power. Only the most skilled of mages ever tapped into even a fraction of its power. Some sorcerers were able to do so with stolen blood magic, and of course, the few remaining ancient dragons.

"I want the sun." Hannah reached out with her hand and closed her hand around the candle flame.

I tried to grab her wrist. "No, Hannah, stop!"

But it was too late. Her body hummed with power, and her eyes burned so brightly it nearly blinded me. The room heated like an oven. I dove out of the door just as a wave of energy burst from her body. A shield saved me from becoming an overcooked steak.

"Hannah, let go of the power, right now," I shouted.

"Why?" she asked.

I cast another shield as my current one buckled. "Because you're hurting me!"

Hannah gasped. "Cain!"

The room went pitch black, all except for two pinpoints of white light. At first, I thought they were afterimages burned into my retinas, but then I realized they were Hannah's eyes looking out of the darkness at me.

I shivered in the focus of that gaze. This girl was more powerful than even Sigma, but far more dangerous because she couldn't control the power. The people who wanted her dead knew about her potential. Killing her, it seemed, was much easier than training her.

Hannah walked out of the room, eyes still unfocused from the hypnotic spell. "Cain." Tears sizzled from the heat in her eyes. "I did not want to hurt you."

"I know, I know." I walked over and pressed a thumb to the sigil on her forehead. "On the count of three, you'll wake up and remember everything, okay?"

"Okay, brother."

I paused. "Why did you call me that?"

"Because I always wanted a big brother to look after me." Her tears evaporated into steam before they could fall free of her eyes. "I wish more than anything that you were my big brother."

I choked up. "That's the nicest thing anyone's ever said to me." I took a breath. "One, two, three." I dispelled the sigil.

Hannah blinked and the light faded from her eyes. "Oh god, Cain. I'm so sorry."

"It's okay."

"I almost killed you again!" Without the light heating her eyes, the tears flowed freely. "I'm a fucking menace!"

I held out a hand. "No, Hannah. I'm here to help my…my little sister." It was hard to speak those words. I'd never had real siblings.

"Thank you." Sobbing, she hugged me tight around the waist. "I just want to be normal, Cain. Why does life have to be so awful?"

I stroked her hair. "I'll do everything I can to make it a life worth living, Hannah. I promise." I wondered if that was a promise I could even keep.

CHAPTER 24

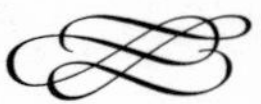

I decided that was more than enough practice for the day. "I think it's bedtime, okay?"

Hannah nodded. "Where was I, Cain? What was that planet?"

"It's another world like Feary." I headed toward the stairs. "But it's a dead world."

"I saw a dragon there," she said.

"There are some ancient beings who still inhabit it," I said. "Which makes it extremely dangerous to visit in person."

"So was I there or not?" she said.

"You weren't there." I wasn't sure how much I wanted to tell her. The concept of drawing magic from other planes was an advanced concept, at least for those who had to learn it instead of inheriting it. "There are multiple planes—Feary, Gaia, and so forth. Every plane has different levels of magic and magical energy. The Greeks called this energy aether—or the air the gods breathed."

Hannah drew in a breath. "Aether." When she exhaled, blue vapors drifted through the air.

I stopped walking. "Did you mean to do that?"

She shook her head. "I just wanted to see what aether looked like."

"Jesus." I watched the vapors dissipate. "Be really careful about what you want. It might just happen whether you want it to or not."

Hannah gulped. "Okay."

I started walking up the stairs. "Some people can learn to draw energy from other planes. Others inherit the ability, or they steal blood magic from someone who already can."

"I definitely didn't learn it," she said.

I nodded. "Yeah. You inherited it."

"But my mom didn't know anything about magic." Hannah ran a hand through her hair. "Does that mean I got it from my dad?"

"Possibly, unless the ability was dormant in your mom." I stopped walking. "But to access this particular plane through inheritance requires some seriously ancient blood."

"As in what?" she asked.

I wondered what her reaction would be to what I was about to say. "The most likely is that your father or one of your close ancestors is a dragon."

Hannah sucked in a breath. "Are you kidding me? My mom fucked a lizard?"

I laughed. "Ancient dragons can shapeshift into human form."

She looked even more confused. "But-but why?"

"Some are so old they get bored and try to live different lives." I shrugged. "Sometimes they just like to mess with humans."

"So I'm the result of a fling between my mom and a dragon?" Hannah looked at her hands as if they might grow scales. "It's weird, but kind of cool and disgusting."

"Yeah, it's something all right." I mussed her hair. "We'll explore it more after I get back from Feary tomorrow."

"Will I be able to shapeshift too?" she asked, suddenly a lot more excited. "Can I breathe fire?"

I snorted. "I'll use you to grill steaks from now on."

She giggled. "Sir, would you like that steak well done?"

"I'd like my burger flame broiled, if you please, Madame." I mocked eating a hamburger. "Tastes like dragon burps."

Hannah burst into more giggles. "That's gross!"

"Yep." I started walking again and wondered if I was right about her dragon heritage.

Hannah tugged my sleeve. "Cain, you never told me the name of that plane."

"It's one of the oldest places in the universe." I looked back over my shoulder. "It's the place the gods once called home." I summoned my staff and showed it to her. "This was named after the place where it was forged—Oblivion."

She reached out and touched it. "The gods came from Oblivion?"

I shook my head. "It was one of the first successful worlds they made." I sent my staff back into its pocket dimension. "According to legend, there were five or six other universes before ours. None of them worked out. Then Oblivion was created. Some say there was a single over-god who made it. Others say it was made by the gods we know so they'd have a home while they pondered how to create the perfect universe."

"Like Zeus and Odin?" Hannah said.

I nodded. "Yeah, something like that. Unfortunately, we only have mythological records for history. The fae claim there is no other historical account of the gods or what happened to them. I think they're lying."

"Why would they do that?" Hannah asked.

"Because the fae are our gods now," I said.

"*The History of Feary* claims the fae fought the gods and won their independence," she said. "Maybe the fae killed them all."

"Or that's what they want us to think." I shrugged. "No one but the high fae know."

"I don't know if I'm more excited about or frightened of my abilities." Hannah looked at her hands. "I don't want to hurt anyone by accident."

"Fear is healthy." I offered a reassuring smile. "Just be careful." I was certainly living a healthy lifestyle thanks to Sigma.

"I'll be very careful," Hannah promised."

"I'm sure you will." I headed for my room. "I'm exhausted. Gonna call it a night."

"Good night, bro."

I smiled. "Night, sis." It was weird, but it felt kind of good, too. But I had a feeling I'd pay like hell for all these positive emotions.

Layla was waiting in the kitchen the next morning when I went to make breakfast.

"I'm ready to go," she said.

I looked her up and down. "You're going to visit royalty in purple yoga pants and a tank top that says fuck the police?" She also wore her compact bow at her side and a quiver of arrows on her back.

She smiled. "Yep."

I laughed. "They're going to regret this so much."

Layla examined the wreckage of my bread box. "What happened to that?"

"Aura tried to kill me with it." I started heating up my cast iron pan. "When was the last time you went to Feary?"

"Few months ago," she said. "Costs a pretty penny to use the portals, so I don't go unless I have to." She frowned. "We get to use them for free with the summons, right?"

"Yeah." I hadn't decided if I was going to use a portal or not, but I didn't mention it to her. By the time I finished cooking, all my houseguests were awake, drawn to the kitchen by the pleasant odors. I set the table and stood back to watch as Aura, Hannah, and Layla dug into the food. It was the most surreal moment imaginable for me—even more so than seeing Sigma shoot lightning from his hands.

I have people living with me in my house. I never would have thought it possible. It was a far cry from having an actual family, but it was a good simulation of dysfunction.

"I want to come to Feary with you," Aura announced after she finished a stack of French toast. "I want to hear what they have to say firsthand."

"Too bad, so sad." Layla licked a sausage suggestively and then chomped down on it. "I'm going as his plus one."

"You're taking *her*?" Aura threw down her fork. "Gods be damned, Cain. She's got an active contract to kill you for ten million and you're taking her?"

"How the hell do you know about my contract?" Layla said.

"Because I poked my nose where I shouldn't," Aura shot back. "There's a running joke at the agency that you'll never kill Cain because you're too lazy."

"Too lazy?" Layla jolted to her feet, a butter knife clenched in one hand. "I'll fucking kill him right now."

"Whoa, hold on!" I cast a shield just in case the butter knife came hurtling my way. "Layla can kill me after we get back from Feary."

White light filled the room and all eyes turned to the source. Hannah floated about a foot off the floor, her body glowing. "If you try to kill Cain, I will burn you to ash."

The butter knife clattered to Layla's plate. She put her hands in the air. "Just a joke, love. Calm down."

"Hannah, look at me." I clapped my hands. "Look at me right now."

She rotated, glowing eyes watching me as if I were a friend and a stranger all at the same time. "I won't let Layla harm you." Hannah spoke as if in a waking dream.

I heard the power in her voice and realized it wasn't just her talking. Immense power had that effect on people, changing them without them even knowing it. And it was even more dangerous when the wielder had little control.

"Hannah, release the power." I smiled, trying to defuse the situation. "Layla's just joking."

The light in her eyes and surrounding her body flickered out and Hannah dropped to the ground. She stumbled, blinked, and shook her head. "Uh, why am I standing up?"

Layla and Aura exchanged concerned looks but remained silent.

"You touched your power again." I walked over and took her hand in mine. "Hannah, don't do that unless we're practicing. It's more likely to control you than you are to control it."

Her brow creased. "Oh, shit. I didn't mean to. I just got so pissed at Layla for threatening you."

I smiled and nodded. "It's okay. She's a bitch, but she's just kidding around, okay?"

Hannah cast a glare over her shoulder at Layla. "You'd better be kidding. Do you hear me?"

Layla held up her hands in surrender. "Loud and clear, love."

"I'd never hurt Cain," Aura said. "Just so you know that."

"Hah, hah." Hannah laughed mirthlessly. "I hope so." Then she sat down and started eating her scrambled eggs.

I'd had my fill of family drama for the morning, so I took my plate and ate in my locked room. After I finished eating, I logged into the agency. The key logging program had recorded Aura's username and password, so I used it instead of mine and accessed the bounty board.

There had been several private bounties placed on me over the years. All those who'd tried to collect had met with a quick end, driving the price from a few thousand up to the ten million sum Layla told me about. The public bounty board was a different beast, usually filled with names of escaped prisoners and wanted criminals.

Since I hadn't committed any crimes, I couldn't technically be placed on the public board. But it seemed someone had used the incident at Voltaire's as an excuse to list my name front and center. The reward for my capture, dead or alive, stood at a cool fifty grand. It wasn't a lot, but it was enough to draw crazies from the shadows.

I clicked on the link to find out who was brave enough to list a bounty. Only bonded individuals and companies had access to the board, so whatever account posted it would be named. I wasn't even surprised by the name I found there—*Gaia Enterprises*. It was a security and research company that employed mages, vampires, lycans, and other Gaia-centric supernaturals. The last I'd heard, nearly ninety percent of their employees were veterans of the war.

It was also a poorly kept secret that Gaia Enterprises were affiliated with or under direct control of Humans First. The organization had long since moved on from being a human-rights organization to something openly racist and xenophobic.

The fae didn't care. After a year of bloody guerilla warfare, they'd finally let Torvin have his way. His battle strategies used the dirtiest tactics imaginable, and I'd been one of his bloody instruments. I hadn't been the only one used to murder a house full of women and children. Others in the guard had done the same. The difference was that they'd been okay with it.

Humans First grew stronger in the face of such brutality and its membership had exploded. But once the war was lost, it had gone underground. The fae deemed it an illegal organization but hadn't done much to stomp it out. They probably saw no reason to antagonize humans any further now that the humans had learned their place.

If what Bill had said was the truth, it sounded like the fae underestimated the desire of humans to be free from their rule. Despite recent blood-soaked history, it looked like the Firsters wanted another shot at freedom.

"Those idiots are going to incite another war," I muttered. The Firsters might start it, but all the human supers would pay for it.

I connected to the dark web and went to the Gaia Enterprises site. I scrolled down the main page and clicked on the about section. The founder and CEO was a man named Herbert Banks. I'd never seen him before, but he looked vaguely familiar for some reason. I downloaded his picture along with that of the vice president, Marianne Harris, and other officers.

I ran a reverse image for Herbert's picture on the dark web and the public web. Nothing came up on the public side, but the dark web produced one news story. The headline caught my attention: *New Firm Takes Human Approach to Security*. I opened the story and read it.

The story was eleven years old, written just a month or two before the incident that sparked the Human-Fae War.

Albert Ingram and Greta Mead want you to know they're tired of seeing the supernatural security industry filled with trolls, goblins and orcs. That's why they decided to start a new company with a human approach to keeping clients protected.

"You can't take trolls out in public with you," Ingram says, "and it's impossible to disguise them as humans."

If you ask Mead, she'll tell you the same thing. "Lycans, vampires, mages, and feline shifters are every bit as powerful as their Feary-based counterparts," Mead says. "And in all cases, they're better to use in a world dominated by humans who know nothing of the supernatural. So why do major firms doing business in Gaia hire trolls when they could be employing hard-working humans instead?"

I read the rest of the article and clicked on the pictures. It only took a moment for me to realize why Herbert Banks looked so familiar. The hair, eyes, and ears were different, but the underlying facial structure looked too similar to be coincidence. Herbert Banks was Albert Ingram, and Marianne Harris was Greta Mead.

I ran a search on Gaia Enterprises and found dozens of articles, but all of them were from after the war. There were no mentions of Albert Ingram or Greta Mead in any of them. For some reason, the pair had assumed new identities and either had themselves surgically altered or were using illusion.

What did it mean?

I'd never heard of Gaia Enterprises until after I moved to Gaia and started looking for employment. I'd also never heard of Mead or Ingram in any briefings during the war. Which meant they hadn't been high enough in the Firster leadership to be primary targets. Torvin had exterminated the human resistance leaders along with their families. It seemed the snake had sprouted new heads since then.

It seemed improbable that there was only one story about the founding of Gaia Enterprises in the entirety of the dark web, which meant someone had to have purged all the information, just as Agent Brines suspected. If that was the case, how had this article survived?

A quick examination of the host website revealed that it wasn't affiliated with the news organization that originally published the story but belonged to a rabid Firster named Buster Jenkins. He had an archive of articles from the war, and a large collection of anti-fae memes. A short blog post buried in the archives told me how this one article had survived the purge.

Finally back up and running after being shut down for four years. Those bastards can't hide the truth anymore!

His website had gone offline a couple of months after the war started and reactivated four years and a few months later. Which meant the data purge had happened during that time, and whoever did it had never gone back to verify no other information had sprung up in the meantime.

I searched for a connection between Mason Digby and Gaia Enterprises, but found nothing. Digby's financial disclosures required by candidates for the Mage Supreme showed a complicated chain of corporations, most of which were certified common—the official term for normal humans and non-supernatural commercial entities.

But that didn't mean anything.

Common companies were used to hide illegal supernatural research all the time. The guild knights policed mages to some extent but relied too heavily on magic and not enough on technology and detective work to proactively detect illegal activities. The fae employed their own secret police to keep matters in line. Even I didn't know much about how they operated, but they consistently brought down criminal enterprises.

Was Digby hiding something illegal among his corporations, or was he somehow connected to Gaia Enterprises? It was yet another thread that might lead me to the life-saving unicorn heart.

CHAPTER 25

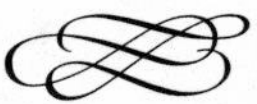

Further research would have to wait until after my visit to Feary. I locked the laptop and closed the lid. I slipped on my low-profile utility belt just in case the visit went to hell, though I doubted it would. The fae seal guaranteed me safe passage, and the fae couldn't lie. That didn't mean they couldn't deceive in other ways, but the invitation had been directly worded.

I went to collect Layla so we could be on our way and found her on the couch watching cat videos on her phone.

"Your octopus came out of the water and stared at me," she said without looking up. "Tell him I'm not into tentacle porn."

"You're not?" I sighed. "Well, that's a shame."

Aura still sat at the table reading one of my romance novels. "I don't like being stuck with babysitting duty."

"Then leave," I said. "Hannah will be fine on her own for a while."

"Leave and go where?" Aura threw up her hands. "I want to come to Feary and hear what the court has to say to you."

Something in her voice told me she wanted to be there a lot more than she let on. "I'm only allowed one escort," I said. "You've got an ankh, so you can leave anytime."

Hannah scoffed. "I'd prefer to be alone anyway." Staring at Layla, she savagely tore off a bite of sausage. "I don't trust either of these bitches."

Layla grinned. "Nor should you, girl."

I turned to Hannah. "I want you practicing with the dance golems again. Don't mess with meditation by yourself, okay? I don't want you to blow up the basement with an accidental burst of power."

She winced. Nodded. "Being buried alive sounds like the worst."

Layla growled. "Yeah, but rising back up and slaughtering the assholes who did it is satisfying."

"Jesus." Aura shuddered. "Someone buried you alive?"

"Save it for another time." I went to the pantry and put several jumbo-sized bags of gummy worms in my backpack, then headed for the garage. "We've got to go."

Layla winked at Aura. "Maybe I'll tell you what happened when we cuddle up in bed tonight, elf."

Aura scoffed. "You wish."

I climbed inside Dolores, closed the door, and moaned with contentment at the moment of silence before Layla slid into the passenger side and slammed the door.

"What's with all the gummy worms?" she asked.

I hissed between my teeth. "Don't slam the fucking doors!"

"Aw, I'm sorry." Layla patted the door handle. "Did I hurt Dolores?"

I resisted the urge to throttle her and shifted into reverse.

"Why'd you name your car Dolores, anyway?" Layla said. "Is she the only female you get inside of these days?"

"Yep." I wasn't going to play that game with her. I turned around on the driveway and headed toward the gate.

"Does your staff have a name too?" Layla glanced at my crotch. "Your oblivion staff, that is."

"No."

She quirked her lips. "But you named your car?"

"Yep."

My terse replies did nothing to discourage her questions.

"What are you into, Cain?" Layla leaned against the door and watched me. "You must be into guys. Aura practically threw herself at you and you turned her down. Or do you just not like good girls?"

I raised an eyebrow and spared her a glance as I turned onto the main road. "Why does it matter?"

"You're just…weird." She shrugged. "I remember the first time I saw you all those years ago at Voltaire's. Despite being on the most-hated list by supers, the women were all over you. But you didn't even seem to care."

I shrugged. "Sure, I cared. What straight man doesn't like all that attention?"

"You just hid it well?"

"I suppose. I don't even remember what you're talking about, to be honest." I was lying, of course. I was infamous in those days. The women who liked me were the same kind attracted to serial killers. They wanted me because I was considered extremely dangerous and because most supers hated my guts.

"Bullshit." Layla waved it off as unimportant. "In all these years, I've never seen you try to get into anyone's pants, male or female. Are you asexual?"

"Why all the personal questions, Layla?" I glanced at her. "Just trying to make conversation?"

"I want to know what drives you, Cain." She leaned closer. "Most men will do anything for sex or money. You don't seem to care about either."

I hated to admit it, but her question hit a tender spot. I'd left Feary with enough coin to live a lavish lifestyle for the rest of my life. I could have left everything behind and gone on to enjoy a common life. Instead, I'd stuck with the familiar and taken assignment after assignment from the agency.

It had been a comfortable life, but not very fulfilling. I entertained myself, I ate well, I worked on my car, and I tracked down some of the worst scum in the worlds. I felt satisfaction when I marked someone who'd been particularly hard to find, but that was about it.

"Truth is, I don't know what drives, me, Layla." I looked over at her. "I don't make friends. I like sex, but I don't want attachments. I just kind of move on from day to day, doing my job."

"Until now." Layla pursed her lips as if she'd nailed down something. "You care about that girl."

It had been bugging the hell out of me ever since the first time Hannah hugged me. I'd enjoyed it. Caring about the well-being of someone else felt good. And I hated myself for liking it. On the other hand, the odds were against me living much longer. I had to live every day like it was my last.

"Yeah, I do." I stared at the road ahead. "I didn't want to, but it snowballed on me."

"I can't stop myself from catching feelings either." Layla stroked my arm. "I tried distancing myself like you do, but it just doesn't work for me. I've got to express myself or I'll go crazy."

"I guess I'm just good at repressing emotion." I looked down at her hand. "I don't want you touching me, but I also do. So, I just push back emotion and keep going." I moved my arm, so her hand slid off.

Layla laughed. "Gods, we're fucked up, aren't we?"

"Makes life interesting." I turned down a dirt road leading deeper into the forest.

Layla frowned. "Where are we going?"

"To Feary, of course." I pulled off the road and into a clearing. "This is the best spot to travel from."

She grunted. "You're not trying to kill me in the middle of the woods, are you?"

I held up my hands. "Layla, do I look like I'm in any shape to actually win a fight against you?"

"Once you're better, I intend to put you to the test." She got out of the car and looked around. "Is there a Feary portal I don't know about?"

"Yeah." I reached over my shoulder and drew my oblivion staff from its pocket dimension. I reached out to her. "Take my hand."

"Oh, now you want to get frisky?" She looked at the staff. "Just so you know, I prefer real dicks inside me."

I let out a long sigh. "Gods, you're worse than a man. Take my hand, okay?"

Layla winked. "Kinky, but okay." She took my hand.

I concentrated on the thin veil separating the worlds, focused my will, and slashed down with the staff. The air in front of us warped and bubbled. Layla shouted in alarm and tried to reclaim her hand. I gripped it tighter. The bubble bulged toward us and popped.

There was a blink of darkness, a rush of cold air, and then we stood in a forest of giant trees.

Layla slid her hand free and turned in a circle, mouth hanging open, eyes wide. "What in the actual fuck, Cain?"

I spread my arms. "Welcome to Feary."

"B-but I thought you needed a portal," she said.

I spun my staff and banished it. "There are other ways."

Layla looked at the thin air where my staff had had been. "You never explained how you make your staff vanish. Is that how you brought us here?"

I nodded. "The staff allows me to travel to other planes."

"You can go to any world?"

"I have to know about the world first," I said. "There are other magical factors involved, so it's not as easy as waving my staff."

"Damn." She licked her lips. "I'd love to have a staff like that."

I couldn't resist. "That's what she said."

Layla groaned. "But really, where did you get it?"

"There aren't many in existence," I said. "They were forged by Hephaestus and given to the fae so they could be the guardians of man. Only a few staffs survived the war between the gods and the fae, and those few are in the hands of the Oblivion Guard."

"And they just let you keep one when you left?" Layla frowned. "Doesn't seem likely."

"Let's just say they didn't have a choice in the matter." I pointed to a tree scarred by claw marks. "Let's get a ride to town."

"You're really going to leave it at that?" Layla said. "How in the hell did the fae not have a choice?"

"A story for another time." I walked over to the tree and put my hand against one of the gouges. *Travel service requested*, I thought.

"What are you doing?" Layla looked at the tree. "Do we really want to be here when whatever made those marks shows up?"

I nodded. "If we want a ride, yes."

She stared at me blankly. "You love stringing me along, don't you?"

"Yep." I frowned. "Haven't you been here before?"

"I've been to the cities, but never ventured out in the middle of Murder Forest." Layla looked up and around. "To be honest, I've only been to Feary for very brief visits, so I don't know a lot about it."

I shrugged. "Oh, well there are a lot of creatures that'll eat you unless you know what you're doing."

Layla looked up and behind me at something. She went white as a sheet and drew her swords. "Incoming!"

I gripped her wrists. "Put them away. It's okay."

The ground shook as something huge landed behind me. I turned and offered a curt bow at the massive gryphon. "Greetings. We seek travel to the high court." I held out one of the bags of gummy worms. "Here is payment."

The gryphon turned its eagle eye on the worms. "Excellent, traveler." It spoke in Faeicht, but ambient magic in Feary acted as a universal translator, so beings from any of the worlds could be understood here. "It is rare I am offered such delicacies." It took the bag in its beak and deposited it in a satchel on its side. Then it turned its great lion body sideways to present a saddle. "Please get on."

Layla's eyes flicked wildly from me to the creature, then she took a deep breath and shook her head. "Well, this is definitely going in my diary." She hoisted herself up easily and I climbed on behind her and put my arms around her waist. Thankfully, her quiver was low profile and at an angle, so it wasn't right in my face.

The gryphon launched himself into the air with great thrusts from his wings, pressing Layla against me. She looked over her shoulder, a smoldering smirk on her face. "I can tell you like this, Cain."

I nodded. "What's not to like?"

"Please refrain from sex during the trip," the gryphon said. "Or I will drop you into the treetops."

Layla snickered. "Yes, sir." She laughed. "I've been on Gaia so long, I forgot what it's like to have talking animals."

Feary was full of intelligent animal species, but many of them weren't friendly. Some had once lived on Gaia but fled as mankind spread across the globe. At least that was what the history books said.

The forest spread out as far as the eye could see in nearly every direction. Mountains rose in the east, and the crystal city of Faevalorn sparkled to the north. A flock of geese veered away when they saw our approach. A gaggle of flying monkeys leapt from the trees, whooping and gibbering as they pursued us. The gryphon turned its head and screeched, but that didn't dissuade the chimps.

"Trouble?" I asked.

The gryphon turned an eye to me. "They'll rob you blind and smear shit on you, but otherwise, no."

Layla touched the compact bow at her side. "They're catching up. Is it okay if I shoot them?"

"Be my guest," he said. "But they'll probably do far worse than rob you when they catch up if you kill any of them."

"No need to kill them." I summoned my staff and whirled it. Here in Feary, it hummed with even more power than usual. I thrust it out behind me and sent gusts of hot and cold air toward the pursuers.

The monkeys howled as the turbulence tossed them about and caused them to lose speed while at the same time propelling the gryphon forward faster. He looked at me curiously. "That is an oblivion staff, but you're not one of the guard."

"Not anymore," I said.

His pupil widened. "You're Cain the Liberator! Why did you not tell me this?"

"I'm trying to keep a low profile," I said.

"Please, take your payment back," he said. "I will take you anywhere you wish."

"It's not necessary, really." I put a hand on his satchel. "Please, enjoy them."

"But, Liberator, I cannot—"

"Yes," I said. "You can and will accept them." I gave him a stern gaze. "I don't require special treatment."

He nodded. "Please let me or any of my kind know if you need our services."

"You're very generous," I said. "Thank you."

Layla gave me a perplexed look but said nothing.

The monkeys, meanwhile, had resumed their pursuit and were once again catching up. While they were capable of limited speech, they weren't on the intelligent end of the spectrum and were more likely to fling poop at us than listen to reason. We still had a good distance to go, so I resigned myself to casting the turbulence spell every so often to keep the chimps at bay.

"Seems like it would've been safer to just take a portal into the middle of the city," Layla said.

I shook my head. "Not really. The anti-illusion wards near the portals wouldn't let me travel anonymously. There's a public bounty on my head and the last thing I need is to be spotted at a public portal."

"Then why not drive us closer to the city and then take us through?" she asked.

I shrugged. "I didn't give it that much thought, okay? Besides, if I don't know exactly what's on the other side, we could end up inside a tree or worse."

Layla snorted. "Points for honesty, at least."

As the monkeys gained on us again, I once again drew my staff and prepared the spell. But this time, the gaggle had drifted apart into groups, making it impossible for me to hit them all at once. The spell took enough effort that I couldn't just cast it continuously in multiple directions. I also didn't want to tire myself before we reached the court.

Layla picked up on my indecision. "Now can I shoot them?"

I sighed. We hadn't even been here for twenty minutes, and things were already going to hell.

CHAPTER 26

The monkeys weren't smart enough to have realized drifting apart would save them from my turbulence spell—at least I didn't think they were. I had one more option before resorting to bloodshed.

I took out another bag of gummy worms and tore it open. Twirling my staff with one hand, I threw the bag into the air and hit it with the turbulence spell. Gummy worms shot through the air at the pursuing monkeys. Whooping and gibbering wildly, they dove after the treasure, snatching them out of the air and devouring them, or fighting their fellow chimps for a piece of the prize.

The gaggle scattered and it was every monkey for him or herself. Within minutes, they fell far enough behind that there was no chance they'd catch up again.

"Very wise tactics, Liberator." The gryphon screeched softly in approval. "It is refreshing to see one who avoids bloodshed when possible, even against the most obnoxious of the gods' creatures."

Layla blew out a breath. "Gummy worms are more valuable than gold, apparently."

The gryphon nodded. "Speaking of which, might you pass one to me, female?"

Suppressing a smile, Layla reached into the gryphon's satchel and procured a couple of worms from the bag. He snapped one from her grasp, raising his head and swallowing it with a sigh of pleasure. He devoured the second with equal gusto.

"So delicious," he said. "But I must eat them sparingly lest I become addicted to the sugar."

"I'll bring you some sugarless ones next time," I said. "If you like those, you can eat all you want."

"Uh, maybe," Layla said. "There are some that will give you terrible diarrhea."

The gryphon nodded sagely. "Then I will exercise utmost caution."

"What is your name?" I asked him.

The gryphon's head turned so one of his eagle eyes could look at me. "I am Pyroeis, at your service."

"It's an honor," I said.

Pyroeis blinked. "Nay, the honor is mine, Liberator."

Twenty minutes later, he swooped down for a landing in a wide plaza near the city center where other gryphons and flying beasts deposited their riders. Crystal buildings of all shapes and sizes dominated the cityscape. The turrets of the great crystal palace of the ruling fae rose higher than anything else except for the great sky towers all along the perimeter of the city.

One side of the palace basked in golden sunlight and the other frost and ice. Faevalorn was the combined capital, where the winter and summer courts shared power. It was where the Oblivion Guard spent most of its time protecting the governor and other high fae appointed by the summer and winter queens.

"Thank you for the ride," I told the gryphon. "I would ask one more favor of you."

He nodded. "Name it, Liberator."

I told him and he gave me a small token.

"Thank you," I said.

Pyroeis screeched and launched himself into the sky.

I hailed a horse-drawn carriage with a stubby dwarf at the reins. He took the local coin I offered as payment and then ferried us to the outer walls of the palace. I stood across the cobblestoned street for a while, watching the guards and other pedestrians to ensure I noticed nothing out of the ordinary.

Not much had changed since I'd been gone. Soldiers, mostly lower fae and elves, guarded the wall and patrolled the perimeter. A patrol of pixies buzzed above the grounds, serving as the primary aerial patrol. The Oblivion Guard would be inside with the ruling fae and their minions. Onwin and Frezia were the rulers of the capitol, but they usually left day-to-day affairs to a high fae governor. I wasn't sure who I was summoned to meet.

The populace of Faevalorn was a mix of mostly elves and Fae, but there was a smattering of dwarves, gnomes, and other little folk who called the city home. They made their living by metalworking and selling jewelry sourced from the mines in the far north and east.

Layla interrupted my thoughts. "When are you going to tell me about this Liberator business?"

"Well, it's nonya business, so never." I grasped the scroll the pixie had given me and headed across the street.

"Cain, seriously." She tugged my sleeve. "Don't be a dick about it."

"Later, okay?" I was trying to remain alert. The fae peace seal supposedly guaranteed safe passage, but I remained comfortably suspicious and ready to flee at a moment's notice. Sigma's complete disregard for the rules made me think that perhaps the fae didn't have as much control over everything as they wanted us to believe.

The pixie patrol dove toward us the moment we stepped onto the edge of the plaza near the walls. The female leader held up a hand and halted us. She wore her green hair exactly like most others of her kind, pixie style of course, though I did notice a rebel with long pink hair hovering behind the others.

She summoned glowing orbs of energy in her hands. "Halt, and announce your business."

I opened the scroll and turned it toward her.

Her eyes flared. "I will conduct you at once to the palace." She dismissed the other pixies with a wave of her hand, then flitted ahead of us toward the gates. The elven guards in their shiny mithril armor saw the scroll and parted to open the massive alabaster gates.

Braided strands of platinum and gold formed a road to the palace doors. Smooth marble paths led through lush gardens and tall hedges on one side, and a maze of ice and dead trees on the opposite.

If an intruder tried to pass through anywhere except the braided road, they'd find a series of deadly challenges waiting for them, the least of which were centaur warriors and cecrops—reptilian humanoids who could kill with a quick sting from their tails and fangs, or simply spit poison in the face of the intruder.

The pixie looked back and down at me. "I am astonished to see you here, Cain. After all you did, I can think of no reason for those on high to ever allow you back on these hallowed grounds."

I didn't recognize the pixie and not because nearly every female sported the same hairdo, but because she hadn't been around when I'd been here. At the time, I'd known every single entity that walked these grounds. Not because I was a friendly guy, but because it was my duty to be ever vigilant for threats of any kind.

I grunted. "I'm as surprised as you, pixie."

Her gaze sharpened. "Had you not that scroll, I would teach you respect for your superiors, human."

I let my eyes grow cold as frost. "I take it you never heard what happened to the pixies of Evanor when they saw me as easy prey."

She scowled. "I have only heard of your crimes, human scum. You cannot frighten me with tales."

I smiled. "I would welcome a duel, inconvenient though it might be for me."

Her eyes blazed with anger. "Human filth!"

Layla raised a hand. "Hey, I'm half fae, half human. What do you think of that?"

The pixie gagged. "Such foul creatures! How could they allow you to despoil our land?"

Layla burst into laughter. "Man, if the fucking pixies think they're such hot shit, I can't wait to meet the high fae."

The pixie balled her fists. "I would destroy you here and now were I as dishonorable as Cain. Only that seal saves you from destruction."

I bared my teeth. "Believe me when I say this, little one. It is you this scrap of paper saves, not me."

Her face turned scarlet, but she turned away and flew faster toward the palace. The guards at the entrance asked no questions when they saw the seal and admitted us at once. The interior was every bit as magnificent as I last remembered. Sunshine refracted off the crystal dome hundreds of feet above, casting rainbows on a sparkling waterfall.

A small stream wound its way through lush gardens to our left. Bees bummed to and fro among flowers as tall as trees. Butterflies of every kind fluttered about the massive atrium. Multiple species of birds and other lower animals wandered about the miniature paradise.

Ice and snow dominated the atrium to the right and the stream was frozen solid. Ice bees settled on frost flowers. Crystal birds sprinkled snow beneath their beating wings. Penguins waddled across frozen water, dipping through a hole in the ice.

The braided path continued into another chamber, this one filled with craggy trees and sand that glittered like flecks of gold.

"What in the hell is all this?" Layla said. "I thought we were entering a palace, not a wildlife preserve."

"The fae were originally created as caretakers of nature, but the gods changed their minds about that," I said. "They've adapted and changed over the years, but the fae still cling to their old ways."

Layla scoffed. "Might as well live in trees."

I nodded. "Many of the low fae do."

We passed through several more chambers, each with its own natural theme, each one divided into summer and winter, and arrived in the throne room. On one side, the walls and floors consisted of woven strands of living wood that grew up the sides of the crystal dome. Ice and snow covered the opposite side. The sunlight from one side of the dome was yellow, and cold white on the other.

I knew from experience that if one departed the braided road, they would feel warm on the side with wood and cold on the side with ice. The path was the only neutral place in this treacherous environment.

There was no one in the room, which came as little surprise to me, since fae royalty would never deign to wait on or meet with such low company. I expected that, after a sufficiently long wait, lower dignitaries from the governors would eventually enter the room from their respective sides and tell me what they wanted.

The pixie cried out, "Visitors of the court have arrived."

Strands of fire twisted and whirled in the yellow sunlight while glittering ice and snow performed a dance of its own in white frost light. A glowing throne of gold coalesced on the left and a throne of icy platinum solidified on the right.

The air rippled and bubbled to the sides of each throne.

A woman in a billowing green dress, hair as golden as the sun, face more beautiful than humanly possible appeared on the left. Another woman in white, with long, platinum locks appeared at the same time on the right. Her face was beautiful, but cold. The woman on the left was dark and tanned, while her counterpart was pale as ice.

The women regarded each other for a moment, then sat on their respective thrones, looking down at me as one might regard an ant.

"Holy shit," I whispered. "What in the hell is going on?"

These were no lower dignitaries at all, but queens Solara of the summer court and Mayce of the winter court. I'd witnessed a dual court only once before. To draw both queens to the throne room was unheard of.

And where was the Oblivion Guard? The fae queens would never visit Faevalorn without escorts, which meant this meeting was completely off the books. There was something going on here they didn't want anyone else to know.

A door opened behind the thrones and a pair of pixies flitted out. One wore green and gold, a nimbus of golden fire around her. The other wore gray and white, a halo of frosty light around her. They came down the stairs leading up to the thrones and spread their arms.

"Come closer and stand in the presence of the queens," they said in unison.

Our escort pixie bowed to them. "I shall take my leave, your highnesses."

They didn't reply, but the ice and fire pixies nodded, dismissing the escort to leave us alone with royalty.

"Um, are those the actual queens?" Layla whispered to me.

I nodded. "I'm just as surprised as you are."

"Should I bow or curtsey or something?" she asked.

I shook my head. "Whatever you do, don't accept any deals they offer."

Layla made a zipping motion across her lips. "This is your show."

"Yeah." I gathered my wits and walked to the stairs leading up to the thrones, pointedly ignoring the pixies.

The pixies spoke in perfect unison again. "The queens have, in their grace, decided to offer Cain Sthyldor a complete pardon for his crimes against the kingdom."

It suddenly became crystal clear why I'd been brought here. I stared at the queens, refusing to acknowledge their little minions. "Then let the queens speak," I said. "I would hear it straight from their mouths and not the utterances of their familiars."

The pixies gasped, but Solara waved a hand and the pair flitted away to hover behind the shoulder of their respective rulers.

"You were once the most noble and obedient of the guardians," Solara said warmly. "Before you became the disobedient child who ran away."

"We have been long in deciding what to do with you," Mayce said coldly.

I remained quiet, determined to let them make the offer I knew was coming instead of preemptively throwing it in their faces.

Solara's golden eyes glittered as she observed me.

She knows that I know, I thought. The fae weren't all-knowing, but thousands of years of experience gave them an edge when it came to reading the intentions of others. In the ancient times they'd been much closer to humans, always looking to strike one-sided deals and gain power over their wards. Like everything else, they'd evolved into something much different than their past selves.

The silence lingered, but I continued to wait.

Mayce finally spoke. "You do not look pleased to hear of our decision, Cain."

"Because I know it comes with a price." I held out my hands. "Tell me, what do you require?"

"You already know," Solara said. "You will receive a full pardon and we will provide you with a cure for your ailment, provided you hand the girl, Hannah, over to our associates."

Layla sucked in a breath but didn't speak.

"You have a spare unicorn heart?" I said.

"I fear there are no more unicorns in Feary," Solara said. "But fae magic can cure most ills."

"This is perhaps the fairest deal I have ever received," I said. "I can enjoy a healthy life as a law-abiding citizen once again, provided I hand over a lamb for the slaughter."

Mayce raised an eyebrow. "What makes you think she would be harmed?"

"Who are your associates?" I said. Fae couldn't outright lie, but they were experts at tangling the truth into unrecognizable knots.

"She would be in the care of our pixies," Mayce said. "I promise she would come to no harm by their hands."

"And who would they hand her over to?" I asked.

"You bargain for more information?" Solara said. "What would you offer in return?"

"I would know everything about this deal before agreeing to anything," I said. "Full disclosure."

"And if we provide you with this information you agree to be bound to the deal?" Mayce said.

"No." Despite growing up in this environment, it was still a challenge dealing with the masters of manipulation. "I want full disclosure as a precursor to my decision. I would know who is involved in hunting the girl and why she is so valuable dead."

The pixies looked mortified and outraged that I would question the queens so. But judging from the amused expressions on the queens' faces, they couldn't help but enjoy bending yet another mortal into one of their convoluted bargains. Even the most noble of cats would still pause to play with a bit of string dangled in its face.

And I was the string.

"Dead?" Mayce scoffed. "As I said, the girl would be perfectly safe in our custody."

I held up a hand. "Then guarantee that she would never leave your custody and you would never allow her to come to harm from any source as part of the bargain."

"Life is so fragile," Solara said. "Not even we can guarantee such a thing."

Even if they agreed, it might also mean they could simply throw Hannah into a cell somewhere and keep her in isolation until she went mad from loneliness. Through trial and tragic error, I'd found that the best way to make a good bargain with a fae was to never do it in the first place.

I shook my head. "I have made a bargain with Hannah that guarantees my protection. Accepting your deal would subvert that agreement."

"Then come with her and be her guard here," Mayce said. "She would certainly be safe with you."

I shook my head again. "I must decline your offer."

The amused smirks vanished from their faces.

"It would be wise to reconsider." Frost crackled on Mayce's words. "There are many in the worlds who have grievances against you, Cain."

"Many who would see you suffer and die," Solara added. "Why does the girl matter to you?"

"It's nothing you'd understand," I said. "Since you've refused to answer my questions and allay my concerns, I will be going."

"If you leave without striking a bargain, you will be hunted and killed by your enemies in Feary," Mayce said. "And the girl will be alone and vulnerable."

I took note of how she specifically mentioned my enemies in Feary and not Gaia. There was something subtle at play that I'd missed. And I suddenly realized what it was. I looked at the scroll and read the second line: *His safety to and from the court is guaranteed by seal.*

Solara 's eyes flashed with pleasure. "I think you understand the situation."

I did, and it was even worse than I thought.

CHAPTER 27

I'd never received a summons like this, but I should have been more attentive before agreeing to it. The moment I'd taken it from the pixie and acknowledged it, I'd sealed the bargain. I'd agreed to come here. They'd agreed to keep me safe to and from the court. Which meant the moment I stepped off the palace grounds, they'd fulfilled their bargain.

And I'd be fair game to all my enemies in Feary.

"Fucking fairies," I growled.

Mayce rose to her feet, glaring frostily at me. "Remember your place, human."

The time for playing nice was over. "Oh, I remember my place. I remember what I did the last time you forced my hand too."

"You are no longer that man, Cain." Solara stood as well. "You are sick and weak. Accept our bargain and you will be healthy and whole in body and spirit."

I considered it for a second. At least until Layla elbowed me in the ribs.

"Cain, what the hell is going on?"

"The moment we step off the palace grounds, I'm fucked." I sighed and accepted the truth. I wasn't giving up Hannah, and I wasn't the same person physically or mentally who'd forced the fae to accept his resignation from the Oblivion Guard. But I also wasn't the same man I was two days ago.

I'd made a decision. I'd fought my fate. I'd finally accepted responsibility for a life that was not my own. And I felt good about it. So maybe in the grand scheme of things, I was coming out ahead for the first time in years.

"Cain, you've got that look," Layla said.

I blinked. "What look?"

"That you're okay with dying." She gripped my arm and whispered. "You don't have to die yet."

I shook my head and whispered back, "Hannah is your responsibility now. No one will harm you. Just go to the nearest portal and take it back to Gaia, okay?"

Layla slapped my face so hard the crack echoed. "Shut up, you idiot. You're not setting me up to be a single parent. I'd rather kick the girl into the streets than deal with that."

"You don't mean that," I said.

She nodded vigorously. "Oh, I do. If you don't make it back, I guarantee I'll hand her over to Sigma myself. Good riddance to the little shit."

I bared my teeth. "You fucking bitch. I'll kill you here and now if you don't agree."

Layla grinned. "There's my badass little Cain." She patted my cheek. "Now, gird your loins, and let's get out of here."

I threw up my hands. "Why is everyone out to screw me over?"

"Agree!" Solara's voice boomed through the chamber.

"Agree!" Mayce echoed. "Agree or lose your life."

The high fae couldn't directly harm a human, but they had plenty of minions who could do the job for them. I had a feeling there would be a small army of them waiting outside the palace walls. Which meant I had to squeeze every bit of mileage out of the peace seal that I could.

I shook my head. "It's obvious someone put you up to this. Someone who's even more powerful than the almighty fae." I held up my middle finger. "So, use those royal lips for something useful and kiss my hairy ass." Then I took Layla's hand, turned us around, and walked out.

"You will regret this," Solara shouted. "For a very short time after you leave the palace grounds."

I ignored her and kept on walking.

Layla giggled like a girl. "Holy shit, Cain. Did you really tell the high fae to kiss your ass?"

"Might as well enjoy my last moments of life." I marched us through the desert chamber.

"Damn, that was hot." She reclaimed her hand and slapped my back. "Too bad you're a man."

I frowned. "What's that supposed to mean?"

She rolled her eyes. "It means you're an idiot, but sometimes you impress even me."

I looked back and saw the summer and winter pixies following us. "Well, I'll certainly have an impressive death after we leave the palace."

"Then let's camp out here for a while." Layla grinned. "They guaranteed you safety on the grounds, so doesn't that mean they have to feed us too?"

I scoffed. "Safety doesn't mean comfort. They'd make us miserable."

Layla sighed. "Just when I think we can have some fun with a situation, you have to go and ruin it."

"That's me," I said. "Party pooper." We left the palace and stepped onto the outside grounds. This was where things got tricky. I checked the scroll to make sure the seal was still there. I was pretty sure the grounds extended all the way to the plaza outside the walls. But the moment I stepped onto the street, I was fair game.

Which was why I needed to change the rules.

I took a right, heading into the summer gardens.

Layla rubbed her hands together. "Oh, we're going on an adventure."

"Yep." We entered a hedge maze.

Layla drew one of her short swords. "Allow me." She chopped at the hedge. Metal dinged and the blade bounced off the bushes. Layla grimaced and massaged her hand. "What the hell?"

I snorted. "It's enchanted. Almost nothing can cut through these." I summoned my oblivion staff and activated the brightblade. "Almost nothing." Then I sliced open a neat hole.

The light from the blade reflected in Layla's eyes. "That is one impressive weapon. It can be a magic staff and a laser sword?"

"It's multifunctional," I said. "You can use it for sniper magic and more."

She sheathed her sword. "Okay, you lead the way."

I plowed straight ahead, slashing a neat tunnel through the thick hedges. Our luck ran out about fifty yards in when we reached a small clearing with a massive beast in the center. The centaur rose up on hind legs and drew a battle axe large enough to cleave a car in half.

"Halt, intruders!"

I showed it the seal on the scroll. "You cannot harm us."

He glared at it and scowled. "You think this grants free license to destroy the queen's garden?"

I held up my glowing brightblade. "Yeah, pretty much." I shoved the scroll in his face again. "So, go eat some grass and relax."

He stomped his hoofs and clenched his fists but backed off. "May your doom find you."

I winked. "Thanks, buddy." Then I slashed open another hole and kept on going.

Layla grabbed my arm. "Hey, why don't you just open a portal back to Gaia with your staff instead of all this running around?"

"It would blow up in my face." I waved a hand around. "The wards here prevent opening a portal within a wide radius of the palace grounds. Only authorized fae can do it."

"Shit." She sighed. "I should've known it couldn't be that easy."

"Never is." I started slashing my way forward again. "And like I said, I can't just open a portal anywhere. We might end up three hundred feet off the ground or inside a car."

A pair of green-scaled females waited in the next clearing. The cecrops hissed and bared poisonous fangs. I held up the seal and their aggression turned to almost comical confusion.

"Why are you destroying the hedges?" one asked.

I shrugged. "I needed a shortcut."

"He bears an oblivion staff!" The other one's eyes flared. "Liberator! You have returned!"

The first bowed. "You are always free to pass through here, Liberator. It is an honor to see you again."

"The honor is all mine," I said. "I apologize for my haste, but this is a matter of life and death."

"We are at your service," the first one said. "How can we help?"

I waved them off. "I appreciate the offer, but—"

The second slashed a hand through the air. "Do not deny us this honor, Liberator."

I sighed. "Call me Cain, please." A quick glance back found the pixies from court tailing us. I had a feeling my enemies would be circling the wall to meet us wherever we emerged.

"As you wish, Cain." The second one bowed. "I am Morgina."

"And I am Dusana," the first said.

Layla clucked her tongue. "What's this Liberator stuff about?"

"Not now." I sliced another hole in the hedge. "We need to get to the street before the pixies alert whoever is waiting for me."

"There is a faster way," Dusana said. "Follow me." She turned down a corridor between hedges, took a left at a fork, and then stopped at a dead end. She tugged on a branch in the hedge and the section opened to reveal the crystal wall on the other side. At twenty feet tall, it was a formidable hurdle.

Layla sighed. "Great. We have to climb over that thing?" She turned to our newfound allies. "Can you get us up there?"

"Of course," Morgina said. "But the top is coated in razor-sharp crystal. You do not want to try that route."

"Uh, then what was the grand plan here?" Layla turned to me. "Well?"

I turned down the narrow space between the wall and the hedge where I found a small outline in the wall. "There's a secret exit here."

"It's not very secret," Dusana said. "Not if you work here."

I ran a hand along the crack and found the latch. A slab of wall slid in and to the side, leaving a narrow corridor through the wall. The cecrops slipped past us and went out first.

"It is clear," Dusana said. "Come."

I went through and poked my head out. A couple of curious elves watched us from across the street, but there was no murderous crowd waiting to behead me. I took out the small token Pyroeis had given me and rubbed the claw mark on it. Now all we had to do was wait for the gryphon. He couldn't land here, so we'd have to meet him in the street.

I grunted. "Maybe this'll be easier than I thought."

The pixies flew over the wall and threw orbs of dust into the air. They exploded like flares, brilliant even in the daylight.

They smirked at me. "Enjoy your final moments, traitor." Then they ascended higher and hovered, presumably to enjoy the show.

"Enjoy waiting," I shot back. "Because I'm not stepping off the palace grounds until I'm ready."

Dusana spun, eyes alert. "We are no longer on the grounds, Cain."

My mouth went dry. "Um, what?" I checked the scroll and witnessed the seal slowly fading away. "Oh, shit."

Six goblins dashed from the shadow of an alley across the road, rusty blades clenched in knotted, hairy fists. Like most goblins, they were short by human standards. Their skin was scaly, mottled green and brown. Had it just been them, I wouldn't have been too worried, but a group of dark elves clad in black cloaks and hoods approached from the north, and a pair of orcs from the south.

It seemed the fae had killers stationed at all corners of the perimeter.

Dusana and Morgina hissed and leapt in the way of the goblins.

"Halt, or feel my sting." Dusana whipped her reptilian tail forward, displaying the glistening barb at the end.

"Get out of our way," one of the goblins said, "or feel the sting of our blades."

I brandished my brightblade. "You mean the stink of your blades?"

"Stink?" the goblins looked at each other, not quite getting the insult.

"Yes, because goblins stink and—" I waved it off. "Forget it. It was a bad joke."

They resumed their rush.

"Am I allowed to kill them?" Layla asked.

"If you really want to commit," I said. "Because once you do, you'll make enemies and won't have a free pass out of here."

She bit her lower lip. "Hey, goblins, will you let me pass?"

"You are with him," the lead goblin said. "You will die with him."

Layla smiled. "Thanks for clearing that up." She unpacked her compact bow. Hands a blur, she shot three of them in the eyes before they'd made it halfway across the street. I spun my staff and beheaded one with a vicious strike. The last two fell convulsing with barbed stingers in their chests.

Layla grunted. "That was easy."

I looked up and around for our ride. "The dark elves won't be." They were only fifty yards away. The orcs were further out, but their long strides would get them here about the same time as the elves.

And then a loud screech echoed. Pyroeis swooped low over the buildings and came to a running landing nearby. "Hurry, Cain!"

"Thank you for your help," I told Dusana and Morgina. "Now, go back to safety."

"It was an honor, Cain." Dusana bowed and ran back through the crack in the wall. Morgina bowed and followed her.

Layla leapt on Pyroeis's back. I banished my staff and climbed up after her. My chest ached, warning me that I'd already strained myself too much. The gryphon launched skyward. Elven arrows flashed after us but fell short. The orcs roared and raised their fists after us.

"It was as you predicted," Pyroeis said. "The fae have no honor."

"They have honor," I said, "but they know how to leave enough wiggle room for a good double-cross."

"Shall I deliver you to where I picked you up?" he asked.

I scanned the horizon and saw a dark cloud rising behind us. I gritted my teeth. "Can you outrun harpies?"

Pyroeis glanced back. "With only one rider, yes. But not two."

Layla bumped me with her ass. "Get off, Cain."

I held onto her waist a bit tighter. "Ladies first."

She smirked. "What a gentleman."

I wasn't sure how far out the anti-portal wards extended. They didn't affect established Feary portals, but we couldn't go to a station and use one without risking a violent death, especially since I'd have to purchase a ticket and get through security.

Layla looked behind us and shuddered. "Gods, those things are disgusting!"

I snorted. "Never seen a harpy before?"

"No." She grimaced. "Are they dangerous?"

"Not alone," I said. "But they usually travel in flocks. This kind carries some pretty nasty diseases as well. A scratch or bite will do you in if you don't treat it immediately."

"And they let those things in the city?" she said.

I shook my head. "Not normally. Solara and Mayce must have sent invitations to all the groups that hate me."

"You're not the Liberator to them?" she said.

Pyroeis screeched. "The harpies do not value freedom. If not for Cain, many gryphons would suffer under their yoke."

Layla gave me another look, but I shook my head. "Save it for later."

There were different tribes of harpies. Some were more humanoid than others. Our pursuers were the worst, with the heads and torsos of men and women, and wide wings with gnarled claws at the ends. Their legs were proportionate to human legs but covered in scaly skin. They had three-toed feet with yellowed claws, used for grasping prey when they swooped in for the kill.

The harpies were close enough for me to hear their squabbling as they argued over who would slurp meat off which bones and who would peck the eyes from our skulls. The turbulence trick I'd used on the flying monkeys wouldn't help against them. So, I decided we had to take a chance that the portal-blocking wards didn't extend throughout the city.

I pointed to a plaza below. "Land there, Pyroeis."

"As you wish, Cain." He angled down so sharply that Layla gasped and gripped the saddle horn with both hands. He made another running landing smoothly, raising his wings to avoid striking pedestrians, and stopped.

The harpies dove after us, claws outstretched, shrieking their victory.

I hopped down and slashed my staff downward. The air rippled and bubbled. "Layla, get down here!"

She leapt off. Pyroeis galloped away and leapt into the air, but the harpies didn't care about him. They wanted us. The bubble swallowed us. Layla cried out. We snapped through the cold void and rolled onto a city street. A terrible scream cut off and a harpy leg flopped onto the asphalt behind us.

Rubber screeched and a horn blared. I looked behind us and saw a cement truck barreling toward us, tires smoking. I staggered to my feet and yanked Layla up and out of the path of the truck. It screeched to a halt five feet past us. The wide-eyed driver shouted in Spanish through the open window, then drove away.

I picked up the huge harpy claw in the street. It looked like garbage and stank even worse. I heaved it into an alley dumpster. Layla moaned and sagged against me.

"Are you okay?" I said.

She gagged, pushed me away, and heaved her half-digested breakfast on the sidewalk. There was a nasty cut tinged with green on her right shoulder. The harpy claw had slashed her just before we made it through.

If the wound wasn't treated soon, Layla would die.

CHAPTER 28

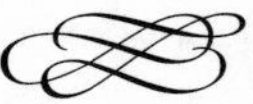

"Son of a bitch." I tried to help her up, but she heaved and retched.

Pedestrians gave her disgusted and concerned looks.

"She's drunk," I explained, and tried to hail a taxi. But one look at the barfing woman and the drivers refused to stop.

I waited until Layla finally got her heaving under control, then helped her up. "We need to get you to my place ASAP."

She groaned. "Antibiotics?"

"Probably won't do anything to the diseases in your blood right now." I moved her along while trying to find another taxi. We were on the outskirts of downtown Atlanta which should've made it easy, but it seemed no drivers wanted to deal with a sick passenger. I was on the verge of carjacking someone when I decided it'd be easier to just steal a parked car.

The problem was finding one not locked up in a parking deck. Layla's knees went weak and her feet dragged until I was practically carrying her. Her face blanched and her lips turned blue.

I'd just settled on a car parked roadside when a siren whooped behind me. I turned to face the police car. The cop turned on his lights and got out. "What's wrong with her?"

"Drug overdose, I think." I gripped her waist to keep her upright. "I can't get a taxi to stop for us."

He unbuttoned his gun holster and approached slowly, hand ready to draw. "Let me see her arm."

I gripped a wrist and showed him the insides of her arms. "She doesn't have track marks. I think she took them orally."

"And you didn't call nine-one-one?" He frowned but seemed to come to a decision. "Put her in the rear of the patrol car. Then I'm going to have to secure you until I have a chance to verify your story."

"I understand." I dragged her to the car and lay her on the backseat. Then I got on my knees and put my hands on my head.

The cop approached from behind, cuffs clinking. I waited until he was right behind me, then energized my power sigils. I shot up from my knees, spun behind him, and punched an electrical spell into the nerve bundle at the base of his neck. He slumped and I caught him.

A nearby vagrant shouted in alarm. "What the hell happened to him?"

There were at least four other witnesses nearby, so I hurriedly jammed the cop into the passenger seat of the patrol car, then slid across the hood and got behind the wheel. I drove off before too many people realized what had happened. Traffic wasn't heavy, but I turned on the lights and barreled forward.

Layla's face had gone from stark white to green. I'd been scratched by harpies before, but I'd never seen an infection catch on this fast. I had a feeling they'd dipped their claws in poison or a fast-acting infection potion. Harpies could eat just about anything. Even bloated, poisoned carcasses would taste just dandy to them.

Cars swerved out of the way when they saw me coming, so I went faster than was advisable on the narrow four-lane road. "Hang on, Layla. We're almost home."

I had a supply of anti-poison potions at home. I just hoped one of them worked, because we were too far from Layla's emergency healer to get there at this rate. I made it home in record time but waiting for the outer gate to open felt like an eternity. I skidded to a halt outside the house, then rushed inside.

Aura leapt up from the couch when I burst inside. "What's wrong?"

"Emergency." I raced past her and into my room. I grabbed three potions and ran back outside. I poured the first one on Layla's wound. It bubbled and fizzed. Green fumes rose from the flesh, filling the patrol car with a rank odor.

Aura stood behind me. "Oh gods, what happened?"

I took a blue potion and dribbled it into Layla's mouth. She coughed weakly but swallowed it. I chased it down with another anti-poison potion and hoped something worked. Her breathing steadied after a moment and she began to moan softly. The sickly tint to her face began to fade.

I checked the cut on her back. It looked inflamed, but the greenish hue was gone. "I think you're going to be okay."

She moaned again. I slid Layla out of the car and carried her inside, Aura close at my heels. I put her on the couch and put a hand on her forehead. She was warm, but not burning up like earlier.

"Aura, get her some water. I've got an errand to run."

"Taking that police officer somewhere else?" she asked.

I nodded. "I can't leave him close by."

"Let me help. You can get your car on the way back."

I considered it for a moment then nodded. I went to the basement stairs and yelled, "Hannah, I need you up here."

Apparently, my shouting voice was good, because she appeared a moment later.

"You're back?" She looked from me to Aura. "What happened?"

"Layla was injured," I said. "I need you to watch her while Aura and I remove some evidence from the property."

"Sure, okay." Hannah blew out a sigh. "I'm glad you got back okay. I was really worried something might happen."

I grunted. "Everything went smooth as silk."

Aura raised an eyebrow but said nothing.

Aura and I went outside and climbed into the police car, me in the front, her in the back. Then I drove us out to where Dolores was parked.

Aura leaned against the grate separating the front from the back. "Do you need to handcuff me, officer?"

I rolled my eyes. "Are you serious right now?"

She sighed. "I thought it was funny."

I got out and opened the back door to let her out. "Hilarious."

Aura slid behind the steering wheel of the patrol car and I climbed into Dolores.

We drove to a shopping mall five miles away and left the cop slumbering with the car on, air conditioner running, and the doors locked. He'd probably wake up in another twenty minutes, give or take. Then we went back to the house.

Layla was sitting up and drinking water when we came in, while Hannah sat in the easy chair across from her.

"Remind me to kill every fucking harpy I ever see," Layla said. "I can't believe I almost died from a scratch."

"A harpy?" Aura sat on the sectional couch closer to Hannah. "Cain, what happened?"

I put a hand on Layla's forehead, then checked her pupils. I wasn't a healer, but she seemed to be on the road to recovery. "We had a little adventure." I went around to the kitchen counter to make a sandwich and remembered I hadn't baked another loaf to replace the one Aura destroyed with my breadbox. I let out a long sigh and stared at Aura for the duration just to let her know how I felt. Then I retrieved ingredients so I could make another loaf.

"The fae played me like a fiddle," I said. I told them everything.

Hannah teared up halfway through and ran over to hug me. "Thank you, Cain."

"I'm trying to make bread." I held my flour-coated hands in the air so I wouldn't soil her clothes. "A little space, please." I tried to sound exasperated but was disgusted with myself for sounding happy instead. I knew I shouldn't be upset with myself for enjoying her hug. I should just experience all the moments from here until the point where I either expired from my disease, or we both died screaming at the hands of Sigma.

Because that was exactly what was going to happen, sooner or later.

She stood on tiptoe and kissed my cheek. "I can't believe you turned down a pardon and a cure for me."

"Cain's a big softie." Layla groaned and tried to stand, but her knees wouldn't hold her up. "It's going to get him killed."

"Well, he saved you and your bitch self," Hannah said.

Layla scoffed. "That's just because he owes me."

I finished the story while Hannah stood nearby and watched me with big eyes. I wondered if she'd be okay after I was dead. I didn't think I could count on Layla or Aura to make sure she stayed safe. But maybe she'd be okay if I just left her my place. I certainly wouldn't need it if I didn't find the cure.

Maybe I was a fool for not taking the faes' offer. Maybe there was a good reason for killing people as powerful as Hannah. But the queens hadn't seen fit to give an explanation. As usual, they'd kept their cards close to the chest and tried to play me for a fool. They might pretend to be all-knowing and powerful, but they were still mischief makers at heart. They might have evolved, but they hadn't fundamentally changed.

"You never explained that Liberator nickname," Layla said.

I didn't much feel like talking or sharing my past, but I also didn't relish Layla bugging the shit out of me until I finally told her. It seemed telling her was the best way to get her to shut up about it.

"When I left the Oblivion Guard, I was badly injured and went into hiding." I tossed the dough on a board and began kneading it. "At the time, it was legal to own certain sentient creatures the fae deemed lesser beings. Gryphons, cecrops, hippogriffs, pegasi, and so forth. A pair of gryphons owned by dark elves kept me hidden while the fae and Oblivion Guard searched for me." I flipped the dough and started on the other side. "I saw how the dark elves mistreated their slaves and it infuriated me, so I killed the elves. When I healed, I went from place to place freeing slaves and threatening the owners that didn't release them voluntarily with a slow death."

"Jesus," Hannah said. "That's awesome!"

I nodded. "Ogres owned the lion's share of slaves. They made their gold by actively hunting and breeding gryphons until there were almost none left free in the wild. I couldn't directly confront the ogre clans, but the males are idiots, so I was able to infiltrate their villages and open the cages."

Hannah grimaced. "Wow, ogres for real?"

I nodded. "But the Oblivion Guard was always hot on my trail, and I grew tired of running." I shrugged. "So, I confronted them. I killed half of the guard along with their high fae commander. I left a message for the queens that while they might eventually catch me, I would wage war on them until my dying day unless they made a bargain."

"And the fae love bargains," Aura said.

I nodded. "I used their own nature against them. They agreed to my terms, including that no sentient creatures could be owned. The fae signed the Freedom Accords and that was that."

"How in the hell did you kill half the Oblivion Guard?" Layla said. "That's impossible!"

"I wasn't alone," I said. "I'd amassed a small army of freed slaves. The queens realized that fighting back would only lead to a brutal war they couldn't afford to fight, especially since they were still waging the war against humans. So, they agreed to the bargain. I was allowed to leave Feary, and sentient creatures were liberated."

"That's amazing, Cain." Hannah sighed. "See, you're a good person."

I shook my head. "I didn't do it for altruistic reasons, Hannah. I knew my only chance for survival was finding allies. I saw the opportunity and took it. I used them for my own personal gain."

"Bullshit." Hannah shook her head. "You did something good and noble."

"No, Cain's telling the truth," Aura said. "Something good came from his actions, but he was entirely pragmatic about it."

"Don't think for a moment he's a good person," Layla said. "He's a killer, kid. If his brain wasn't infected with magic cancer, he'd have seen how stupid it is to keep you around."

Hannah scowled. "Keep opening that stupid mouth and I'll burn it shut."

Layla raised a trembling hand. "I ought to smack your smart mouth."

I ignored them and continued kneading and rolling the bread dough. I really wanted a sandwich after the day I'd had.

After they traded a few more insults, I got back to business. "I did some searching this morning and think I tracked down our ghosts."

They stopped bickering and flicked their gazes to me.

"How so?" Layla asked.

"Ever heard of Gaia Enterprises?" I said.

Aura nodded. "Yeah, they're a security company that only hires supers."

"Yeah, humans only." Layla scoffed. "I was approached about a job until they found out I wasn't pure."

"Not human enough?" Aura said.

Layla scowled. "Not by half."

Hannah frowned. "I've heard that name before. My mom mentioned it when we were on the run."

I stopped rolling the dough. "You sure about that?"

She nodded. "Mom kept a metal box filled with pictures and documents. I don't remember much about them, but one of the documents had a picture of Earth and it said Gaia Enterprises on it."

Layla tried to spring to her feet, but her legs still weren't ready for prime time. "Where is this box, girl?"

"Last I saw, it was in the abandoned house in Detroit." Her eyes glistened. "Where Mom killed herself."

I hissed between my teeth. If my hands weren't covered in flour, I probably would've put a hand on her shoulder or something to let her know it was okay. But it wasn't okay, not in the slightest. And I hated what I had to ask her next. "Do you remember where that house is?"

Hannah shook her head. "No, but the cops probably have a record of it since it burned down and Mom's body was inside." She wiped her eyes.

"You okay?" I asked.

She shook her head. "No, but it is what it is."

I figured I'd kneaded the dough enough, so I tossed it in a pan and put it in the oven. "Looks like it's time for a field trip to Detroit."

"I'm going," Hannah said.

"No way," Layla said.

But I saw the anger and pain in Hannah's eyes. The kid had open wounds that might never heal if she didn't get to confront the past. She'd been through some terrible shit, but I knew without a doubt that when her mom tried to murder her and committed suicide it left a deep, jagged scar across her soul.

I nodded. "Yeah, you can come."

"Are you crazy, Cain?" Layla tried to stand again and failed.

"Yeah, maybe I am." I washed my hands and looked at Aura. "If you ruin this loaf of bread, I'll feed you to Fred."

Aura smiled sheepishly. "I'm sorry, Cain."

I turned to Hannah. "How's practice going?"

She shrugged. "I can dance my ass off now."

"Good." I nodded toward the stairs. "Go downstairs and warm up. I'll be down in a minute to test you."

I had to do whatever it took to keep her focus off what was to come because I had feeling Detroit would be hell for her.

CHAPTER 29

I went to my laptop and bought tickets. One for me, one for the girl. I didn't want Aura and Layla tagging along. They might be good backup, but Layla was bad for Hannah's mental health. She was probably bad for mine too. If she weren't such a formidable fighter, I would've already tried and failed to kick her out.

Afterward, I went downstairs and found Hannah stretching. Aura watched from her seat on the practice mats.

"It's amazing how fast she learns," Aura said. "I'm a little jealous."

I set the golem to ballet mode and put on a short piece of music, *Dance of the Sugar Plum Fairy*. The golem began the routine. I nodded at Hannah. "You're on."

The piece wasn't complex but required a great deal of strength and precision. Hannah mimicked the golem, doing it so well that I realized the few times she'd practiced with this piece had been enough to burn it into her muscle memory. Though the golem taught the moves, I hadn't programmed it to teach the names of techniques. That was primarily because I'd never learned them myself.

To me, it was the physical aspect that mattered, not labeling every move. But whatever the moves were called, Hannah performed them impeccably, taking short, quick steps on her toes, then leaping and spinning as effortlessly as she might tie her shoes. I'd seen a lot of crazy things in my lifetime, but this girl's physical and magical abilities took the cake. Only the high fae could match it.

When the piece was over, Aura and I clapped, and Hannah bowed.

"That was amazing," I said. "It took you days to accomplish something that takes most humans a lifetime."

"Your memory sigils make it easy," Hannah said. "I don't think it's really because of me."

"Let's move on to something a little spicier." I switched to salsa music.

Hannah partnered with the golem and went through the dance moves. Though she followed the golem's lead without issue, the look on her face was one of pure boredom. About halfway through, she pushed the golem away. It staggered back and stood in place, its spell unable to cope with the break from the routine.

Hannah turned to me and motioned me over. "Come show me what you've got, Cain."

"He nearly killed himself with the shadow dance," Aura said. "Is that wise?"

But I got up and took Hannah's hands. We started the basic footwork, then I spun her one way, then another, and flipped her over my arm.

She shouted with joy. "Now *this* is dancing!"

By the time the song ended, we were both sweating and grinning like idiots.

Aura shook her head. "You need to be careful, Cain."

I rolled my eyes and held out a hand to her. "Come here."

"I don't know this dance," Aura said.

Hannah laughed. "Don't be a wuss, Aura. Just follow his lead." She started another song.

I motioned Aura. "Come on, I won't hurt you."

"I'm worried about you dropping dead." Aura sighed and took my hand. I took her left hand and put it on my shoulder, then held her right hand. "Be firm but flexible. Don't try to lead."

She nodded. "I'll do my best."

"Do you know the basic steps?" I asked.

"Yes, I practiced them with Hannah."

"Good. Then this'll be easy." We started moving, forward and back, forward and back. I experimented with a spin. She yelped in surprise but didn't fight my lead. The uncertain frown on Aura's lips turned into a wide grin as the song went on and the tempo increased. I spun her backward so we danced side by side, our arms tangled, and then reversed the spin and flipped her. Aura giggled like a girl.

When it was over, I was done for. Salsa wasn't nearly as draining as shadow dancing, but it was hard enough.

Aura stood on tiptoes and kissed me on the lips. "That was amazing, Cain. Thanks."

I blinked in surprise. "Um, sure."

"Have you two slept together yet?" Hannah asked, amusement shining in her eyes.

I snorted. "Nope." I grabbed a water from the mini-fridge and took a drink. "Not a good idea."

"I think it's a good idea," Aura said. "But Cain's afraid of falling in love."

"Let's remember that up until a few days ago, I didn't even know you were my agency handler, *Janice*." I tossed her a water. "So, don't bullshit me with your sweet and innocent act. I don't even know the real you."

Aura caught the water and sighed. "Cain, I'm not evil or anything. Just because I was secretly your agency handler doesn't mean this is all an act. I'm the same bartender you've known all these years."

"Janice was completely different," I said. "She was cold, impersonal, and straight to the point—just like a handler should be." I waved my hand at Aura. "Your Aura persona, however, is a chatty bartender who loves to flirt. Is Aura even your real name?"

"Yes, it is." Aura huffed and stuck out her chin. "And I'm actually chatty and love to flirt. Janice was my fake persona, not this."

Hannah laughed. "Just screw already. It would make this hot mess even more dramatic."

I scoffed. "Yeah, it would." I shook my head. "I'm going to take a shower and hit the hay."

"Are we going to Detroit tomorrow?" Aura asked.

I shook my head. "Hannah and I are. You and Layla are staying behind."

Aura's jaw dropped. "What? You can't be serious."

"Serious as a heart attack," I said. "We'll be safe unless the agency can somehow track my moves."

"Why are you always leaving me behind?" Aura said. "I need to make sure you're safe."

"Because you're non-essential," I said. "Layla's a pain, but she can fight. What do you really have to offer?"

"Wow, that's mean." Aura shook her head. "Give me a chance and I'll prove myself."

I was too damned tire to spar with her, otherwise I would've made her prove herself then and there. "You'll have a chance, but it won't be tomorrow." I headed upstairs. The delicious odor of baking bread reminded me that I couldn't go to bed until it was ready. I decided to take a shower and get ready in the meantime.

Layla was passed out on the couch, so I let her keep on sleeping.

I went into my room and turned to close my bedroom door only to find Hannah close on my heels. "What's up?"

"I just want you to know that I'm excited about going on a trip with you tomorrow," she said.

"Yeah?" I offered a tired smile. "Our last trip together wasn't exactly to your liking."

She laughed. "When you kidnapped me?"

"Is it really funny to you?" I asked. "Because it was only a few days ago."

"Best thing that ever happened to me," she said. "I just didn't know it at the time. I didn't know the world was full of monsters and that I was one of them."

"You're an entirely different breed of monster," I said. "You're a teenager, and I've heard they're the worst."

Hannah giggled. "Yep. But I am really happy you kidnapped me, Cain."

"Well…I'm glad it's working out for you."

She rolled her eyes. "Don't get all gushy on me."

I grunted. "Don't worry, I won't."

Hannah cleared her throat. "I've been reading the history books in your library. The weird thing is, I haven't found a single mention of people as powerful as me or Sigma."

I pursed my lips. "We should have you genetically tested. Maybe you inherited some strange blood magic I've never heard of."

"Maybe." She shrugged. "Whatever you think is best."

"Yeah, we'll see." I nodded toward the oven. "Keep an eye on my bread, okay? I'll be out in a few minutes."

She nodded. "I won't let Aura get near it."

I closed the door and went into the bathroom to turn on the shower. I sensed a change in air pressure, like a door opening and shutting. I'd forgotten to lock the bedroom door. When I turned to go see who'd entered, I nearly ran into Aura as she came around the corner.

"What the hell?" I said.

Aura wrapped her arms around my neck and stood on her toes. Her lips pressed hard against mine. I knew I'd regret it later, but I didn't fight her off. She was my handler. She'd lied to me. She might not even really be a cute and somewhat sweet elf, but someone far more sinister. I'd checked her out through the scope on my staff, so I knew she wasn't hiding behind illusion. But even the scope couldn't tell me someone's true intentions.

Aura sighed. "You're overthinking this aren't you, Cain?"

"How do you know?"

Her hand rubbed against my crotch. "Because you're soft."

"Maybe I've got erectile dysfunction," I said.

She scoffed. "I know you don't." Her fingers worked at my belt buckle. "I want you, and I know you want me."

I raised an eyebrow. "You're a mind-reader?"

Aura shoved me. "Fuck you, Cain. Can't you at least be nice to me for a minute?"

I snarled and wrapped my hand around her throat. Pushed her against the wall. Steam swirled around us because I hadn't turned down the hot water yet. I reached down with my other hand and yanked down her jeans, revealing pink panties.

I leaned forward and whispered in her ear. "Is this what you want, Aura?"

She whimpered. Nodded. "Gods, yes. Take me."

My hand tightened on her throat. She gasped and trembled. Her hands fumbled with my belt. Undid it and reached inside. This time she found no softness. I spun her around, ripped down her panties, and wrapped my arm around her neck. I squeezed tighter. Ran my hand up her soft backside.

Gods, I wanted her so much right then. I'd fantasized about her more times than I'd ever admit to anyone. I was too weak to resist even though I had a feeling this would be one of those stupid decisions I regretted later.

I thrust deep inside her. Her back arched and she moaned.

"Oh, Cain." She reached her arms up behind her and gripped my hair. "Fuck me."

I proved to her I was good at following simple instructions and obliged.

By the time we were done, the bathroom was hot as a sauna and full of steam. I spun Aura around to face me and pinned her to the wall by the neck. "Don't think this means anything." My words rang hollow, at least to me. Because it meant something to me. She was one of the only people in the world I'd ever considered close to being a friend, at least before I found out she was Janice. And now that I'd had her, I wanted her again and again. But I couldn't afford these emotions. Not now. Maybe not ever.

Aura's eyes clouded, but she nodded. "I understand, Cain."

I released her and turned the water all the way to cold. Then I got in and shivered in the frigid water. The cold washed away the sweat and the heat, but I felt as if I'd crossed a line I shouldn't have.

Aura got in and hugged me from behind. "You've always liked me, Cain."

"Was it that obvious?" I said.

She pressed her cheek to my back. "I was the only person you talked to. The only person you smiled at."

"You broke my trust, Aura. Just because we had sex doesn't mean I trust you."

"But it does mean you still like me even if you hate yourself for it." She kissed my back. "Can I sleep with you tonight?"

I shook my head. "No."

"But—"

"I said no." I pulled her arms off me and turned around. "Maybe someday, but not today."

Aura smiled. "So, you're saying there's a chance?"

I refused to smile back. *Gods damn it, what am I doing?* "Maybe." I made a shooing motion. "Now leave me alone."

She leaned up and kissed me, then got out and began drying off. "I'm not opposed to a round two later." Aura winked. "Let me know."

After she left, I gently banged my forehead against the tiled wall. "Cain, you're a moron." But then I remembered something—I was going to die in a month. Why not go out with as many bangs as I could? Deep down, I didn't believe we could pull off a three-way assassination within the short amount of time we had, especially with my physical condition. Since my death was all but guaranteed, I needed to enjoy the time I had left and let the others deal with shit after I died.

It was a sound plan in theory, but it rang hollow in my chest.

I finished showering and went out to the kitchen to find Hannah had already removed my bread from the oven. She smirked when she saw me come out. Layla was still asleep on the couch and Aura wasn't there.

Hannah walked over and raised her hand for a high-five. "Score one for the Cain-meister."

I shook my head. "You're not right, you know that?" After all the sexual trauma she'd been through, I wondered if it helped her to make light of it. I wondered if deep inside there was a bubbling cauldron of hurt and despair she did her best to ignore. I smiled and didn't leave her hanging.

I didn't know what else I could do to heal the hurt she'd suffered except to just be kind to her. To just let her know that at least one person in this miserable world cared about her, even if he hadn't wanted to in the first place.

"How was it?" Hannah asked.

I shook my head. "It was none of your business." I grinned. "Thanks for taking the bread out. I'm too tired to let it cool so I can finally make my sandwich, though."

"That's sad," Hannah said. "Want me to make you something else?"

I shook my head. "No, I'm good." I should have been starving, but the magic cancer seemed to be sapping my appetite. "I'm going to bed."

She hugged me. "Goodnight."

I patted her back. "Goodnight."

I went into my room and locked the door this time. My body couldn't handle a round two, and I didn't want Aura thinking she could just come in here whenever she wanted. I opened my laptop and ran some searches to prepare for the trip tomorrow. It didn't take long to find a news story about a body found in a burned down house fourteen years prior. I located the local police and fire precincts just in case.

If Hannah's mother had kept a file and it survived the fire, then it might be a treasure trove of information. It might also explain where Hannah got her powers from. Maybe Gaia Enterprises was meddling with supernatural DNA and they'd had something to do with creating her. Maybe they were the demons Esteri had been so afraid of.

It seemed unlikely Hannah's case would somehow link to the targets of my assassination job, but stranger things had happened.

CHAPTER 30

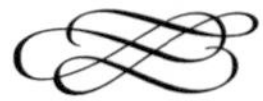

The next morning, Hannah and I took the first flight out to Detroit.

Hannah waited until the plane took off to ask the difficult questions. "Cain, are you catching feels for Aura?"

I shook my head. "Nah."

"Are you sure?" She stared at me until I answered.

"I don't want to," I said.

"Mhm." She grinned. "So you are."

I sighed. "Maybe I've always had feelings for her. But I know I shouldn't."

"Why not?" Hannah nudged me with an elbow. "I think you need to live a little."

"I'm living more than I planned to recently." I grunted. "I don't know how I should feel. I think I need to wait it out."

"Bad idea." She tapped on the in-flight entertainment screen and scrolled through movies. "You were a real grump when we first met. Now you're practically giddy."

I scoffed and shook my head. "Watch a Disney movie or something and let me think."

Hannah found a horror movie on her screen and picked the same one on mine. "Watch it together?"

I sighed long and loud. "Fine." I put in the headphones she gave me, and we started the movie at the same time.

Hannah moved the armrest between us up and leaned against me. "This is nice. I could get used to having a big bro."

I didn't know what to say, so I just nodded. It felt nice having someone to protect. Someone who looked up to me even though I was a terrible role model. I would kill for her, even if it meant murdering another kid. Judging from how quiet the ghosts in my head remained, they approved.

After landing in Detroit, I rented a car at the airport and drove us to the address of the burned-out house. Over the last decade and a half, parts of the neighborhood had seen a revival. New houses replaced condemned structures. Neatly mowed lawns and white houses brightened up the otherwise dismal landscape.

Thankfully, the house where Esteri had squatted hadn't been touched. It was little more than a heap of charred wood and brick. The ashes had long since been washed away by the rains and snow. I doubted we'd find anything, but it was the best place to start.

Hannah grew still and quiet when I parked on the road in front of the house. Her body stiffened and her breathing quickened. This place was a trigger point in her life. A place where her mother, her only protector, had tried to kill her and ended her own life.

I'd experienced the horror through Hannah's eyes. Even then it hadn't imprinted on my cold, dead heart. To experience that as a child would leave deep scars that might never heal.

I took Hannah's hand and squeezed. "Are you okay?"

Tears trickled down her cheeks. "No. But I expected this." Her shoulders shook with the effort of holding in sobs. She was trying hard to keep a stiff upper lip, but it wasn't working.

"Don't keep it in," I said. "Just let it out. It's okay."

She buried her face in my shoulder and wailed. "It's not fair!" Her hands tightened on my arm. "It's not fair!" Hannah sucked in a ragged breath. "Why couldn't I be normal? Why did Mom kill herself and leave me all alone?"

I didn't remind her that Esteri tried to end both their lives. "Life sucks. People suck." I'd seen someone comfort another human by rubbing their back, so I did it. "Let's kill the assholes who drove your mother to this and even the score, okay?"

Hannah's sobs turned to rough laughs. "Cain, you have a strange way of looking at things." She sat up and rubbed her red eyes. "But I approve."

My shirt was soaked from tears, but I didn't really care. "Good. Because once we get a handle on your powers, we're going to clean house, okay?"

She nodded. "I just wish I wasn't so emotionally weak."

"Hey." I squeezed her hand. "You're the strongest kid I know."

Her forehead pinched. "You don't know any other kids."

"Doesn't matter," I said. "You bend, but you don't break. That's how you survived all these years. Your mom did her best, but she eventually broke. You won't."

Hannah wiped her damp cheeks. "I hope you're right, Cain. I feel like I'm going to break all the time."

"You're braver than me," I said. "I ran away from my past and tried to never go back."

"But you did go back to Feary." She watched me carefully. "Wasn't that your past?"

"Kind of." I shrugged. "I don't even know who my real parents were. I don't know where I came from or where my adoptive parents found me."

"Have you ever been back to the house?" she said. "The one with all the people you killed?"

I shook my head and looked away. "I've got enough ghosts in my head already, thanks." I opened the car door and got out. "Let's go take a look."

I summoned my staff and peered through the scope at the ruins. Everything looked normal. No magical signatures or wards to indicate anyone else from our community had been here recently. That didn't mean they never had. Small amounts of magic usage had a short half-life. If someone had leveled the house with magic, that signature would've lasted for years.

The neighboring houses were boarded up, but discarded trash and broken boards indicated they'd hosted squatters at some time or another. I doubted anyone living in them now would know anything about what happened all those years ago, but it wouldn't hurt to ask.

I banished the staff and walked across the patchy lawn. "What do you remember about the files?"

"She kept them in a metal lockbox." Hannah held her hands apart to approximate the size. "Like one of those old-timey folder carriers with the flimsy metal handle."

"Did she have a car?" I asked.

Hannah nodded. "I don't remember much about it except it was full of clothes and canned food." She squinted as if trying to see the past. "It was old, faded red, and it rattled a lot."

"Compact?" I said.

She nodded. "Yeah. Like one of those eighties Japanese cars."

"Do you remember where she parked it?" I asked.

Hannah bit her lower lip. "Probably behind the house to hide it from the street."

"Smart." I walked up the concrete stairs to the skeletal remains of the foundation. There had been a crawlspace, not a cement slab. Few of the joists had survived so I was able to walk around. I found the tattered remains of blankets, rotted and half-buried in the hard-packed dirt, a few blackened cans without labels, rotted remains of clothing, and some half-melted candles.

I traced a sigil in the dirt and powered it. A pulse rumbled through the ground. Wherever it found something harder than dirt, it projected an illusion above the ground. The images weren't detailed, but judging from the sizes of the objects, most were rocks and bricks. Nothing matched the size of a metal case.

Hannah stared at the burned blankets, unmoving and unblinking.

A figure stepped up beside me. "This neighborhood is filled with ghosts." Death wore jeans and a t-shirt.

"This your day off?" I said.

"Death doesn't take days off." He watched Hannah closely.

"Is her mom's ghost still here?" I asked.

He shook his head. "Most of the ghosts here died of suicide or overdoses. Esteri was ready to go."

I looked at him. "Where did she end up?"

"Where she belongs." Thanatos shrugged. "I'm just an intermediary. I don't judge them."

"What the hell am I supposed to do?" I sighed. "Am I doing the right thing by helping her?"

He pursed his lips. "You want my opinion?"

"Yes, dammit. Enough with the riddles."

"I think you are, Cain." He put a hand on my shoulder. The touch didn't chill me to the core, meaning he wasn't Death incarnate at the moment. "Maybe for the first time in a while."

"Who's trying to kill her?" I said.

"Who pulls Sigma's strings?" Thanatos shook his head. "Believe it or not, I haven't kept up with divine affairs in a while, so I don't know."

"Do the fae queens control him directly?" I said.

"I don't have many connections with the courts." He glanced toward a pale motorcycle parked at the curb. "But if I hear something, I'll be sure to tell you."

I nodded. "I haven't heard from you in almost a year, so whatever is happening must be pretty significant."

Thanatos smiled. "Yes, I think it is." He walked through tall weeds back to his motorcycle and drove off.

Hannah unfroze, but she'd been so overwhelmed with her thoughts, she didn't seem to notice her brief pause. I let her be and strolled next door to a house with broken boards on the back door. The inside stank of rotting food and mold. I found a few filthy sleeping bags, some rusted needles, and discarded food containers, but no people.

I left the house and went in the opposite direction to the one on the right of the burned down house. Hannah blinked and looked up from the blankets as I walked past. She squared her shoulders, wiped her eyes, and left the spot where her mother had died all those years ago. I held up a hand in the stop gesture and pointed to the ground. She nodded and waited while I went through the back door of the other house.

Three people slumbered on the floor inside what had once been the family room. Judging from the blackened tar on a spoon and the needles nearby, they were sleeping off their last hit of heroin. Even if I woke them, they'd be useless. I doubted they remembered what happened twenty-four hours ago, and it was unlikely such transients had been here all those years ago.

The next step was visiting a local police precinct and seeing what I could find out. I left the house and motioned Hannah toward the car. She watched me for a moment, then got in the rental. I climbed in a moment later.

"Who was that man you were talking to?" she asked.

I blinked in surprise. "You saw him?"

She nodded. "I saw him walking to his motorcycle. I didn't see his face, but something about him sent chills up my spine."

As amazed as I was that she saw Thanatos, I didn't think bringing him into the conversation was the best thing for her right now. "He was looking for someone too."

Hannah pressed her lips together. "Oh. Well, did you find anything?"

I shook my head. "Nope. Let's hope the cops still have a report on file." I reached into the back seat and fumbled with my duffel bag. I finally dug out a leather wallet and dropped it in the cup holder.

Hannah opened it and examined it. "It's empty."

"Yep."

She quirked an eyebrow. "What's it for?"

"Identification." I winked. "You'll see."

The nearest precinct office wasn't too far away. I parked in the front and altered my appearance with an illusion spell.

"A business suit?" Hannah frowned. "What are you doing?"

"Come with me and find out."

"Uh, how are you going to explain a random kid with you?" she asked.

I shrugged. "Maybe it's take-your-daughter-to-work day."

Hannah laughed. "That's weak."

The precinct office was housed in a two-story brick building that looked as if it had been around a while. The officer behind the front desk was young and clean-cut. He smiled and nodded at us when we entered, a far cry from what I'd seen in most city precinct offices. The name on the badge was Officer Hill.

"How can I help you, sir?" he said.

I took out the black leather wallet and flipped it open. "I'm Special Agent Burns. Looking into some cold cases of human trafficking and hoped you might have some records I could look through."

Officer Hill looked closely at the wallet then nodded. "Sure. What year?"

"They'd be from fourteen years ago." I took a pen and pad of paper from the desk and wrote down the address of the burned down house. "The body of a woman was found here. She had a red car."

Officer Hill looked at the address and jotted some notes of his own. Then he turned to his computer and began typing. His eyes flicked to Hannah a couple of times as he worked. "Who is the young lady with you?"

I smiled. "I'm teaching my daughter about old-fashioned police work. She thinks computers are the only way to find things."

Hill grinned. "Well, they make it a lot easier. But it seems there wasn't much done on the case." He motioned me around the desk and pointed to the screen. "They figured it was just a dead squatter."

There were pictures of a body so badly burned, there was no way to identify it. I forced myself not to look at Hannah, because I didn't want her to come around the desk and see her mother's body. Hill scrolled down to pictures of an old compact car. The hatchback was stuffed with clothes and boxes of canned foods.

"Can I get this printed out?" I asked.

"Sure." He hit some buttons and a printer in the back hummed to life.

I read the printout and found what I was looking for. The car had been towed to a city impound lot. The odds were it'd been long-since destroyed and sent to a junk yard, or auctioned off.

Officer Hill gave me a folder with the documents. "How does this relate to human trafficking?"

"It's just a hunch," I said, "but there were reports some abandoned houses were being used as temporary places to hold people. It's a long shot, but I figured I'd check it out."

He nodded. "I hope to be a detective someday. I'd love trying to solve a challenge like this."

I chuckled. "Some days it makes you feel like you're chasing your own tail." I tipped an imaginary hat. "Thanks for the help."

"You're welcome, Agent Burns."

We left and got back in the rental car.

Hannah snorted. "That was super easy, barely an inconvenience."

I scoffed. "Would you prefer it went down with shots fired and a city-wide police chase?"

"I mean, of course not." She shrugged. "I'm glad it went so smoothly."

"Nubs believe what they see," I said. "Even bad illusions work well with them. But some of them are by the book and would have called a number to verify my ID. Thankfully, this guy didn't go by the book."

"What would you have done if he tried to verify?" she asked.

"How many cops did you see in the front office?" I asked.

"None, but there was one in the break room down the hall, and I heard voices from the room down the hall on the left."

I gave her a thumbs-up. "Good job. What alternate plan would you recommend if he'd verified the ID?"

Hannah tapped a finger on her chin. "Knock out the cop behind the desk, search the computer and get out."

"That's it?" I entered the impound lot address into my phone and started driving.

Hannah bit her lower lip and thought for a moment. "Were there cameras?"

"You didn't see any?" I asked.

"I didn't look."

"There were two on the ceiling in the corners behind the desk." I turned onto a highway. "Two more at the ends of the hallways to the left and right." I glanced at her. "And the room with the monitors was through the door behind the desk."

"Knocking out the cop would've been recorded," she said.

"Yeah." I flicked my fingers in a pattern. "But you can't use an EMP spell because you don't want to fry the computer you need to use."

"Wow, okay." Hannah pursed her lips, deep in thought. "I guess knock out the cop, go to the security room and erase the footage, then go search the computer and leave."

"Complicated," I said. "Your window of time would be extremely short."

She threw up her hands. "Blow up the station then?"

"Exactly." I gave her another thumbs-up.

Hannah scowled. "Okay, Mr. Smartass. How would you handle it?"

I waved a hand over my face and changed my illusion mask to that of an old man. "Let them record away. Remember, they believe what they see, and they don't see me."

She slapped her forehead. "Duh. The cameras record the illusion. They wouldn't know what you really look like."

"Yep." I switched back to the square-jawed persona of Agent Burns. "Don't over-complicate things."

Hannah smiled eagerly. "Teach me how to disguise myself and I won't."

I checked the map and took another turn. Something nagged at me. At first, I couldn't quite place my finger on it, but when it hit me, I wanted to punch myself in the face. Traffic was heavy, but I should have noticed it a long time ago.

We had a professional on our tail.

CHAPTER 31

I thought back to leaving the airport. There had been dozens of rental cars like the one behind us. I suspected the driver had been tailing us from the beginning. I'd been so focused on Hannah and the traumatic event she was about to relive that I hadn't been vigilant.

But how would anyone even know we were here? Only Layla and Aura knew where we were, and I doubted they'd burn us. It didn't make sense. As I tried to wrap my head around the possibilities, I realized I was overlooking the same someone I'd overlooked for years.

Fred.

Maybe his master had eavesdropped through his familiar while I talked about coming to Detroit. Maybe his master had other minions who'd waited here. That was the only likely explanation. The burned house would've been an ideal ambush spot, but we hadn't remained there for long. Even so, there had been plenty of time for a posse of minions to attack while we were in an isolated area.

I saw only one person in the car following us. So maybe it wasn't that kind of mission. Perhaps they were simply following and observing—for now. I decided to give them a false sense of security. Let them think

I didn't know about them for now. But if they tried anything, I'd be ready.

The impound lot looked like most other government-owned properties. It was in a rundown part of town and consisted of little more than a few acres of asphalt surrounded by chain-link fence topped by razor wire. I didn't see any point to avoiding our destination. Whoever was following us might have trouble getting in unless they used the same tricks I did.

I parked outside the security office and went inside. The chubby guard behind the front desk was stuffing his face with a handful of Cheetos when I walked in. He wore a blue shirt with a badge that read *Security*. The holster at his side held pepper spray. As usual, the city had farmed out the duty to a low-paying private firm. I gave him the same spiel as Officer Hill.

"Oh, wow, the FBI?" The guard got up and saluted. "I'd love to help, sir."

"I just need to know if this car is still at the lot." I showed him the paperwork.

He wiped Cheetos dust on his pants and started typing on the computer. The keys on the keyboard glistened orange. There were corpses I'd rather touch before putting my fingers on that thing.

After a moment, he nodded. "Yep. It was supposed to be auctioned off a few years ago, but the city had a huge budget crisis and cut back on personnel. Most of the cars in this lot have been here way longer than they were supposed to be, but they don't seem to care anymore."

"Great." I walked around to look at the monitor. "How do I get to section forty-six F?"

He gave me directions. "I'll buzz you through the gate."

I went back to the car and drove to the gate. It rolled aside and let us in. Our tail had pulled into a rundown shopping center across the road. I wondered if there was a back gate leading out of the impound lot. It'd be the perfect way to give them the slip.

The lot was so packed that most cars were boxed in and unable to be moved without shifting other cars out of the way. Esteri's car was hemmed in by two other compact cars. The color had faded from red to light orange. Peeling paint had given way to rust, and the tires were flat and dry-rotted. The doors were locked, but it was an easy matter to carve out the lock of the hatch with a spell. I opened it and the odor of musty clothes tickled my nose.

Hannah stared at the car pensively, but she didn't seem to be suffering another emotional episode. "It's so strange seeing the car again after all this time." She shook her head. "It still has my child seat in the back."

The fabric was rotted, the plastic faded, but it was still there. So were all the clothes and canned goods. But I didn't see the metal box. I tugged on a striped sweater and it tore apart like paper. I grabbed an armful of clothes and pulled them out, filling the air with dust and mold spores.

I started sneezing uncontrollably, much to Hannah's amusement. Once I regained control, I cast an air purification spell around my nose and mouth and resumed unloading the car. It was the spell that prevented me from smelling the smoke just before I saw it. A pinpoint of light was focused on the clothing in the back of the car, causing the dry material to catch on fire.

It only took a moment to see the source. A figure in black clothing stood on a building adjacent to the lot. They held a tubular device with a glass lens on their shoulder. But they seemed to be intentionally aiming it at the car and not us. The device was a spell focuser, used to magnify energy spells over longer distances when the mage wasn't close enough to do it with a staff or wand.

That was when I realized the light had burned a hole through the metal in the side of the car to reach the clothes. If the user aimed it at me or Hannah, it'd burn through our skin in seconds. The figure on the roof realized he'd been seen. But he didn't swing the focuser on us. He tapped on the side of the device with a gloved hand.

Whoever it was wasn't a mage. He was using a device enchanted with preset spells. An orange ball of flames emerged from the lens at the end of the focuser. It was small, but super-concentrated and would blow the car to bits when it hit. I tore out another clump of clothes and threw them aside. A metal handle protruded from beneath a torn blanket.

I grabbed the file box and yanked it out, then spun, grabbed Hannah, and threw myself on top of her. She went down with a yelp.

The fireball smashed through the rear driver-side window. Gouts of flame burst through the windows. The metal blackened and sagged. Within seconds, the car was nothing but a pile of molten metal and ash.

Hannah wheezed beneath me. "Ouch."

I rolled off her and dragged her behind a neighboring car, then peered through the filthy windows at the attacker. The figure in black was gone from the rooftop. But I knew he hadn't gone far. At least I didn't have to worry about him taking aim at us. It didn't take much imagination to piece together what he was after. He'd wanted to destroy the evidence in the car without killing us.

"That was close!" Hannah put her back against the car. "What happened?"

"Someone didn't want us to get this." I tapped the lock on the file box and pried it open with a spell. I prayed it held answers. The papers and pictures inside were yellowed and brittle. But they remained intact when I pulled them out and spread them on the asphalt in front of us.

There was a cover letter inside written by Elizabeth M. Ward, paranormal investigator.

Ms. Esteri Kabiri,

Please find enclosed all materials related to the requested investigation. It would seem the incident at school caused gossip to spread. The people who approached you have ears everywhere and investigated rumors of the incident. That caused Hannah to become a person of interest to them. They didn't know at first that she was special, so that was why their first attempts were gentle probes.

They escalated their efforts once Hannah suffered another incident. This investigation has taken me through a complex web of individuals, corporations, and other connections. The people I discovered are powerful. I know of no legal antidote to this problem. I have provided the facts for you, so the decision is yours.

My advice is simple: Run.

I have contacts who can provide you with new identification. But the cost is prohibitive. Unfortunately, I have no way to discount it for you. I wish I could be of more help.

Yours,

Elizabeth M. Ward

"Oh my god, I remember that woman," Hannah said. "I was maybe three or four. After Mom saw her, she freaked out and put the house on the market. But I don't think we ever sold it."

"Probably didn't have time to," I said. "Your mother must have taken you on the run with whatever money she could scrape together."

"I was still so little when she killed herself." Hannah looked at the stack of papers. "She didn't last long on the run."

"It's a hard, hard life." I put a hand on her shoulder. "Believe me, that kind of life would break most people."

"I don't blame her." A tear pooled in her eye. "She did her best."

"That she did." I kept an eye on the rooftops and nearby area in case the mystery man made another move. Unfortunately, it looked like there was no rear exit to the impound lot, so for now, staying here was better than leaving. "Let's get in the car."

I put the file box in the car and drove us further back into the impound lot until I found an old moving truck to hide the car behind. It didn't guarantee safety, but it felt better than remaining in the open. I pulled out the files and shuffled through the papers.

I had to hand it to Elizabeth M. Ward. She did a damned thorough job. I hadn't heard of her before, but I could tell by reading her work that she had divining skills—an innate prophetic ability that couldn't be learned. They were rare, but her ability to winnow facts from speculation was far too precise to be true intuition.

The summation page told me we were in even further over our heads than I'd thought. The fae weren't the only ones with their sights set on Hannah. Ward outlined four distinct factions that were hunting not only for Hannah, but for others like her.

Hannah leaned over the center console to read with me. "This can't be right."

"This is bad. Really bad." I read out loud. "The factions have names for people like Hannah. They call them divines or demis. Demi is short for demigod. The four distinct factions I've uncovered refer to each other by the following nicknames: Killers, Underlords, Firsters, and Enders."

Hannah scoffed. "They think I'm a demigod?"

I shrugged. "I mean, you and Sigma are ten times more powerful than any mage I've ever seen. The shoe fits."

"But a demigod is offspring from a god. I thought they were all dead."

I waved a hand. "Let's keep reading, okay?"

She nodded.

I continued reading out loud. "The Killers want all demis dead. They believe humans like Hannah will end the world as they know it. The Underlords seem to be worshippers of demons. They want demis to become minions to their masters." I grunted. "That sounds familiar somehow."

"Keep going," Hannah said.

I read further. "The Firsters want demis to help them overthrow the fae. The Enders want demis to end the world and reset the natural order."

"That must be why Gaia Enterprises is in the folder." Hannah dug through the papers and found the section titled *Firsters*. The first picture had four people in it. I knew three of the faces all too well: Greta Mead, Albert Ingram, and Mason Digby. They sat around a table. The fourth person, a middle-aged woman, stood in front of a large screen with a map on it. The map wasn't of Gaia, but of Feary.

"Damn, kid, you're popular." I shuffled through more pictures. There was a lot on the Firsters, but almost no info on the Killers. The reason became apparent when I read the dossier. "The Killers are linked to Eclipse, an agency specializing in assassination, espionage, and bounty hunting. I've only discovered two names tied to the faction: Torvin Rayne and Sigma. I don't know who they are, but I'm certain they're extremely dangerous. I have been unable to penetrate their organization for more information. They are, without a doubt, the most dangerous and well-funded faction."

"Aura works for Eclipse." Hannah looked worried. "You don't think Aura is with them, do you?"

I frowned. "If she is, then Sigma would have already been at my front door."

I went to the Overlord dossier next. "This group is the most insidious, using a small army of minions to locate and identify demis. Though they don't seem to be overtly aggressive, they have eyes and ears throughout the magic community. Their minions range from ravens to rats and everything in between."

"Like Fred," Hannah said.

"Yeah." I sighed. "Gods damn it, Fred."

"He's the scariest octopus in the world," Hannah said. "You need to dump him in the ocean."

"I think you're right." Fred wasn't in control of himself. And if he was linked to the man following us, I couldn't afford to have a spy in my household.

Hannah read the Enders dossier. "This faction seems the least dangerous, but they will kill anyone who threatens the demis. Their goal is to rescue threatened demis and put them in hiding so they can learn to control their powers. The Enders believe in the same prophecy the Killers do, that a demi will bring about the end times. But they think a grand reset is the best way to create a fair world."

I scoffed. "Fucking nuts."

Hannah shrugged. "I mean, maybe it'd force the fae to start off on even terms with everyone else."

"I doubt it. If anything, humans would be even more vulnerable." There was too much to go over in the parking lot, but we had a pretty good overall picture at least. And it looked as if my mission to kill Mead, Ingram, and Digby tied in with Hannah's predicament. I had a feeling that was no coincidence. Whoever hired me was trying to kill two birds with one stone.

I tucked the files back in the box and put it behind my seat. "We got what we came for. Let's get back to the airport."

But first, I had something or someone to take care of. When I pulled back onto the road it only took a few seconds to spot the mysterious man following us in his rental car. I pulled into a busy gas station.

"Go inside," I told Hannah. "Act normal."

She frowned but did as requested.

Our stalker pulled into the parking lot and drove to the other side, parking where he could keep an eye on us. I started filling the tank and went into the building through the front. I ducked out the side door to my left and ran around the back of the building. The stalker was still in his car when I peeked around the corner.

He wore a hoodie with the hood pulled up, so I couldn't get a good look at his face, but he seemed to be weighing his options. Probably deciding if he should run over and inspect my rental car. He'd probably seen me pull the metal box from the car before it melted.

Using the other parked cars for cover, I crouched and made my way behind his car. A quick peek told me the man was still watching the rental car and not paying attention to his rearview mirrors. I traced a sigil on the sidewall on the right rear tire as I passed, then crouch-walked around the back and repeated the procedure on the other rear tire. This earned confused looks from passersby.

The man flinched and threw his car into reverse. He'd seen me, but it was too late. I powered the sigils I'd traced on the car tires and they burst. People screamed and scattered, apparently thinking someone had fired a gun. The stalker tried to drive on the flat tires, but a passing pickup truck blocked him in.

I jerked open the car door and yanked back the hood. The man was middle-aged, with a wide nose and a shaved head. He held up his hands but said nothing. It only took me a second to realize why. The face didn't show fear, concern, or any other emotion. It was a canned illusion spell, the cheap kind.

I wiped away the illusion. And the face beneath it made me want to unleash hell.

CHAPTER 32

The face hiding beneath the illusion was no man at all, but a cute red-headed elf I knew all too well. "Gods damn it, Aura!"

Her face twisted through several emotions—fear, sadness, and embarrassment. "Hey, Cain."

"What in the actual fuck?" I kept my voice low so the nubs watching wouldn't freak out. I didn't know how to handle the situation without it turning ugly real fast. Yanking her out of the car would only land me in a video on someone's social feed. I couldn't cast a wide enough hex to hit all the phones in the vicinity.

"I hope you're not mad." She managed an uneasy smile. "I really wanted to come, so I took the same flight as you."

I'd been too preoccupied to notice someone with a bad illusion spell boarding the plane. I knew for sure Aura had access to better spells at the agency, but she apparently hadn't brought any with her since taking refuge at my place. "Well, I hope you're taking the same flight out, because we have a lot to talk about."

Aura tried to play innocent. "Like what?"

"Like you slagging the car." It was all I could do not to slap that sheepish smile off her face. "Like why you didn't want us to get those files."

"That wasn't me, I swear!" She held up her hands in surrender. "Can I catch a ride to the airport anyway since you popped my tires?"

That was a definite yes. But I didn't want her anywhere near the files. I was a hundred percent sure it had been her on that roof. Which meant there was something in the files she didn't want us to find. I decided to play along.

I let my shoulders relax. Nodded. "Following us was really stupid. I don't suppose you saw who blew up the car did you?"

She shook her head. "I was in a parking lot across the road. But I thought I saw another car ahead of me that was also following you."

Damn, she sounded convincing. My heart wanted to believe her, but my brain told me she had an agenda. An agenda that required her getting close to me. What better way to get close to someone than sex?

"Is this car a rental?" I asked.

Aura shook her head. "I stole it."

I nodded. "Smart. We'll just leave it here then." I glanced at my rental car. "Meet me over there in a minute but look happy about it so the nubs don't think I'm coercing you."

She reached out and squeezed my hand. "Thanks, Cain."

"Yeah." I walked back to the car, my stomach twisting and turning with anger. I'd know in a minute if Aura bought my act. If she didn't, she'd probably flee on foot. Then again, she might want to destroy the files so badly that she'd come with me no matter what.

I got in the car and glanced over at her. Some nubs had approached her and were apparently making sure she was okay and that I wasn't a menace. I used the moment to grab the files from the folder box. I flipped through the papers, scanning a page at a time and turning each one over on the seat. There wasn't enough time to read them thoroughly, but I hoped something would catch my eye.

About halfway through, something did. I made sure Aura was still talking to the nubs and read what I'd found. When I was done, I knew without a shadow of a doubt what Aura's role was in all this. And it broke my cold, dead heart.

"Fuck!" I repressed the urge to fling the papers to the floorboard. A part of me wanted to forget what I'd found. To burn everything and damned be the consequences. Those urges told me a lot about how I felt about Aura. I cared for her more than I'd cared for almost anyone. Because of one simple thing—she'd been my friend.

But it had all been an act. A way to get me in her pocket.

I put everything but the papers pertaining to Aura in the folder box. Those documents I photographed with my phone and put in the glove box.

Hannah came out of the store and did a double take when she saw Aura walking toward the rental. She hurried to catch up to her. I got out of the car and waved Hannah over. "Hey, did you get me a big guzzler?"

"What?" Hannah blinked a couple times.

Aura tensed, perhaps sensing that I didn't want Hannah near her. But she continued walking to the car. She didn't think I knew and hoped she could destroy anything pertaining to her before I got to it. I had a feeling she wasn't sure if there was anything about her in the files but wanted to play it safe.

I motioned Aura to the front seat. I didn't want her messing with the metal box. I also didn't want her sitting next to Hannah when I dropped the bomb.

Hannah climbed in the back. "What's going on? Why are you here, Aura? Did you follow us?"

I kept silent and pulled onto the road, headed back to the airport. When

I reached the highway, that was when I let it all out. "Aura is with the Enders, Hannah. She's been using me to get close to you."

Aura sucked in a breath.

Hannah gasped. She leaned back as if trying to put distance between her and Aura. "No." Tears pooled in her eyes and streamed down her cheeks. "Aura, no!"

Aura looked away and out the window. "When did you find out?"

"Just a minute ago." I reached over. Aura flinched as if I meant to hit her, but I opened the glove box and grabbed the photo of Aura and the document with it. In the photo, Aura was talking to someone at the bar in Voltaire's. The accompanying document identified the man and Aura as members of the Ender faction.

Surprisingly, Aura was her real name.

I handed it to Hannah. "I'm sorry she turned out to be a traitor."

"I'm not a traitor." Aura wiped her damp eyes. "I'm just doing what I think is best. I want Hannah to survive just like you do. I want her to have a life."

"Now I understand why you wanted to spare kids like her." I gave her a side glare. "It wasn't because you cared, but because your faction wanted you to."

"I do care!" Aura turned to face Hannah. "You have to believe me. I don't want more kids to die. That was why I tried to get the demi jobs assigned to Cain."

I blew out a breath. "You used me to stay close to Hannah."

Aura bit her lower lip. "I like you, Cain."

"Don't bullshit me, Aura." I dodged around a slow car in the fast lane and repressed the desire to take my anger out on the driver. "You did anything and everything to stay close to me."

She huffed. "Yes, Cain. I'm sorry, but I had to. We want to save every demi possible."

"Because you care about us?" Hannah said. "Or because you want to use us to end the world?"

"Because nature needs to take its course." Aura turned in her seat to face Hannah. "I like you, I truly do. And it's my job to make sure you remain safe so you can fulfill whatever destiny awaits."

"Well, your job is officially over." I pulled to the side of the road, leaned over, and opened the passenger door. "Get out."

"No, Cain, please." Aura shut the door. "I can help you. I'm still in Eclipse and there are people in my faction who can help too."

"I can't trust you." I jabbed a finger to the door. "Get out. You're done."

Hannah wiped her eyes and nodded. "You betrayed us, Aura. Just go."

"But I'm on your side!" Aura clasped her hands in prayer. "Please, Cain." She looked at the folder box. "I don't know what information you have, but I know things that will open your eyes to what's really going on."

I considered it. Aura had her own agenda, but at least it was mostly benevolent. Still, I couldn't trust that she wouldn't try to spirit Hannah away somehow. Since she knew where I lived, that put another wrinkle in things. It meant I'd have to keep her close to ensure she didn't return with an army of Enders behind her.

Or, I could kill her.

I looked into her sad eyes and knew there was no way I could ever do that. *Fuck my life*. Emotional connections sucked ass.

"Tell me everything, or you'll never see us again," I said.

Aura looked back and forth between me and Hannah and nodded. "But I'd like to—"

"No!" I slammed the flat of my hand on the dashboard. "No deals, Aura.

Tell us everything or get the fuck out. Promise me you won't conduct any Ender business without my express consent or get out."

"All that." Hannah's eyes glowed. "Or I'll burn you, Aura. I swear it!"

Aura's eyes lit with fear.

I touched Hannah's hand. "Don't do that. Don't even think about killing with your powers, okay?"

The glow faded. Hannah shook her head. "Why not? You use your powers to kill."

"Could you really kill Aura after all this?" I said.

Hannah looked down and sighed. "No. I hate her, but I still kind of like her too."

"Then don't ever threaten to kill her, okay?" I rubbed her hand. "This is about keeping you alive, not burning others to the ground."

"I know." Fresh tears glistened. "But I trusted her, and she betrayed us."

"I'm so sorry," Aura said.

Hannah's sadness morphed to anger in an instant. "Shut your lying mouth, bitch."

Aura gulped.

I sighed. "Hannah, put on your seatbelt." I steered onto the road and started driving again. "Do you promise not to do anything Ender-related without my express permission, Aura?"

Aura nodded. "Yes."

"Then tell me everything," I said.

Her shoulders relaxed, but her eyes settled on the road ahead, as if not looking at the people she lied to would make it easier. "Years ago, I became aware of a disturbing pattern of children being marked for termination by the agency."

"How would a handler know about contracts that aren't assigned to them?" I asked.

"Most contracts come through central handling," Aura said. "They're posted to our internal board and handlers recommend specialists for each job."

Hannah scoffed. "Cold-blooded."

"Efficient," Aura replied. "Most targets are criminals."

I glanced back at Hannah. "Back to the story."

"I began to see a pattern of about two to three children a year ending up on the board. They weren't criminals as far as I could tell. In fact, their dossiers were quite small." Aura shook her head. "Only a select few contractors will even consider killing kids. Torvin usually rotates these jobs among them. I tried inserting Cain into the pool, but Torvin never chose him. It wasn't until Hannah's case that Cain was finally chosen, primarily because no one else could find her."

I grunted. "And Torvin didn't know who I really was, right?"

"No, he only knew your agency code name and behavior profile." Aura shrugged. "No one could track Hannah, so they finally gave in and assigned you the job."

"Mom kept us on the move," Hannah said. "I don't think she even knew where we were most of the time."

"It saved you," Aura said. "Most of the other children were killed within days of being posted because the Council found them first."

I blinked. "Council?"

"The Divine Council, also known as the Killers." She folded her hands across her lap. "I assume you know about the other factions?"

I nodded. "The Underlords and Firsters."

"The Killers are driven by the Oblivion Codex, a prophecy that claims a demigod will bring about the end times." Aura glanced back at Hannah. "But some among them are also driven by jealousy and hatred of illegitimate divine offspring."

"They sound like wonderful people," Hannah said. "But I'm not a demigod. I can't be since the gods are dead."

Aura winced. "That's actually a lie. The gods are very much alive, and most are thriving."

I scoffed. "Bullshit. They died in the Fae-God War."

She shook her head. "Propaganda spread by the fae to solidify their rule."

"And you know this how?" I said.

"Because I've found gods living among the mortals," Aura said. "They didn't abdicate their thrones because of the fae—they became bored and went on to try new things."

I scoffed. "Like selling door-to-door insurance?"

"Some run companies. Others live in solitude." She shrugged. "I don't know exactly what they're all doing, but I can tell you one thing, some are still making babies with mortals."

Hannah made a raspberry. "That's ridiculous."

I shook my head. "No, it's normal. Imagine how bored gods must be after hundreds of thousands of years."

Hannah frowned. "They don't care about the prophecy?"

Aura shrugged. "I don't know all the details, but our people have discovered that some gods do it out of spite, and others simply don't care." She looked at me and then back to the road. "The Divine Council, is ruled by Hera."

I nearly veered off the road. "Say what? The queen of the gods is the one having kids killed? But she's the freaking goddess of childbirth!"

"Hera runs everything now," Aura said. "She sees the demis as a direct threat to her rule."

"Who else is on the Council?" I asked.

Aura shrugged. "The fae queens and possibly some other gods, but there is no definitive list. The Council hires the agency to track down the demis and sends Sigma to kill them."

I grunted. "They're using a demi to kill other demis."

She nodded. "Zeus is among the gods who doesn't believe in or doesn't care about the prophecy. Hera stalks him relentlessly and scoops up his children the moment they're born. Then she's able to brainwash and use them for a time before disposing of them."

Hannah gasped. "That's awful!"

Aura sighed grimly. "Sigma's name comes from the Greek alphabet. It's his designation."

"Because he's the eighteenth of his kind?" I said.

"We aren't sure, but we think he's Sigma Three," Aura said. "Which means this is the third time through the alphabet since the Divine Council began its ungodly project."

I glanced at Hannah through the rearview mirror and saw the hope draining out of her eyes. I knew exactly how she felt. How in the hell were we supposed to win the fight for her life against a coalition of gods?

And it also begged another question. Who was Hannah's father?

CHAPTER 33

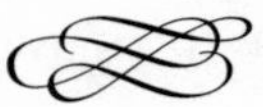

"Where did Hannah come from?" I asked Aura.

"We don't know," she said. "Maybe those documents you found will tell you."

"Mom never mentioned my father," Hannah said.

"Maybe not to you." I reached behind my seat and tapped the metal box. "Maybe she did to the investigator."

Aura held up the dossier about her. "I'd like to know how an investigator was able to photograph me and write an entire file on me."

"She's a scryer," I said. "A very skilled one, judging from how many files are in that package."

"I'd like to see the other files," Aura said.

I scowled at her. "Hands off. The only reason you're not walking home is because you've got info we need."

"And I also want to help you get your unicorn heart." She reached over as if to touch me, but apparently thought better of it. "I want you to live, Cain."

"Because I'm useful." My hands clenched the steering wheel. "And because I'm apparently going to be taking out three high-level Firsters which will directly help your faction."

Aura nodded. "I honestly didn't know Mead, Digby, and Ingram were Firsters when I got the dossier. I had nothing to do with selecting the targets."

"How am I supposed to believe you?" I said. "Is there even a job with a unicorn heart as payment, or did you make it up so I'd weaken a faction for you?"

"I swear it exists, Cain!" Aura gave me a pleading look. "It's fae verified. I can access the certification from your laptop when we get back to your place."

I slapped the steering wheel. "You expect me to let you back in my house after using me all this time? Fuck that!"

"Yeah, fuck you, Aura." Hannah practically spat the name. "Cain really liked you, and you broke his heart."

"I wouldn't go that far," I said.

Hannah didn't relent. "You broke his heart and stomped all over it, Aura!"

I groaned.

Aura bowed her head. "I'm sorry, I really am. I had to do whatever was necessary to keep you safe, Hannah. Cain was the only way. I always felt bad for him because so many people in Feary and Gaia hate him for what he was and what he'd become. I thought he needed a friend. And then I saw that he could help at least one of these demi kids, so I used his abilities for good."

"Wow." The lead weight in my chest tripled in size. "You felt sorry for me? That's even worse than just using me."

Hannah's grimace reflected in the rearview mirror. "Maybe I should be grateful, Aura, but I actually like Cain. I think you're a first-class bitch."

Aura's chin rose. "As long as you're alive, I don't care what you call me."

"What other ulterior motives do the Enders have?" I said. "Do they want to control the demis?"

Aura shook her head. "Demis should be allowed to live their lives and seek their own destinies."

I kept a straight face even though I felt sick to my stomach. I couldn't believe Aura had just used me like a tool. But when I thought about it, as my handler, she'd been doing it for years. I just hadn't realized it was her. I was furious at myself for feeling the way I did about her. For letting her compromise me.

Aura took a deep breath and turned to me. "Cain, I want you to join us. You can help save a lot of kids the Council wants to murder."

"No." I didn't even look at her. "I'm not getting any more involved than I already am."

"But—"

I put a finger over her lips. "Shut it."

Hannah's eyes met mine in the mirror. She seemed to be considering Aura's proposal. Maybe I was about to lose her to the Enders too. Maybe it was for the best. I'd allowed myself to care for two people and, so far, it sucked ass.

I changed subjects. "If the Firsters want to use demis to fight the fae, what do the Underlords want?"

"The Underlords are very subtle in their manipulations." Aura cleared her throat. "Their use of minions and familiars means they don't need to trust anyone because they literally mind control them."

Hannah shuddered. "Poor Fred."

Aura nodded. "I suspected he was one of them, but I couldn't be sure."

"He's not one of them," I said. "He's their fricking slave." I shook my head. "Can they mind control humans?"

Aura shrugged. "I don't think so, but the Underlords can compel them to do things."

"Same thing," Hannah said.

"Not quite." I turned onto the airport road. "You can resist, but it's not pleasant."

"The Underlords do have human collaborators," Aura said. "There's even a fifth faction called the Pandora Combine."

"Like Pandora's box?" Hannah said.

Aura nodded.

"That sounds very reassuring." I glance at Aura. "None of the other factions are good enough for them?"

"They have more extreme goals," Aura said. "The Combine wants to find the lost armory of Hephaestus and use the weapons there to enslave the gods."

"Not gonna happen," I said. "No way the gods would sit back and let them do that."

"Rumor has it some gods are helping them." Aura clasped her hands across her lap. "Ares, for one."

I wasn't surprised. "The god of war thrives on chaos and strife. It makes sense that he'd be happy unleashing the weapons from the armory."

"Yes." Aura leaned against the window and watched planes taking off from the nearby airport. "The more demis we keep from the others, the better."

I frowned. "Sounds like the Pandora Combine wants the end days too, just like your people."

Aura shook her head. "They want to enslave everyone. We can't let that happen, no matter what."

That was the moment I knew she'd take Hannah away if she had the chance. The Enders couldn't afford to let the demis go unused—not until they ensured the other factions were no longer a threat. What better way to do that than by forming their own army of godlike kids?

I kept that opinion to myself, mainly because I wasn't sure if that would be a bad thing. Maybe Hannah would be safer with the Enders than with me.

THE PLANE RIDE home was a quiet and somber affair. I took my window seat and went to sleep. I didn't want to watch a movie. I didn't want to talk. I just wanted to be left with my own thoughts so I could purge all the negative emotions roiling inside of me. The fae were a very emotional people, but excellent at hiding it. Everything they'd taught me revolved around trickery and deceit.

The Oblivion Guard, on the other hand, had taught me how to repress all emotion and only release it when no one was watching. I had chosen another method: avoiding emotional entanglements altogether. It had worked until now. It seemed the magic cancer was eroding my wits and my will.

When we got home, I took the box with the files into my room. Layla lounged on the couch, looking much better than before, but still a bit pale.

"Fun trip?" she asked as I stalked past.

"Yep." I went into my room and locked the door. It was time to plan the hit on the Firsters and get my damned unicorn heart.

Gaia Enterprises was far more than just a security company. According to the scryer's dossier, they owned dozens of other corporations—technical services, a garbage collection company, and even a massage parlor. Out of everything on the list, there was one company that caught my eye: Iron Age Steakhouse.

One might wonder why a restaurant would catch my eye. First, it was the only restaurant on the list. Second, it had the word *iron* in it. The fae hated iron. Touching it caused them immense pain. If not for that glaring weakness, they would have won the Human-Fae War even faster. While iron wasn't exactly their kryptonite, it prevented them from using their magic to escape or fight.

Gaia Enterprises wouldn't house anti-fae projects at their corporate headquarters, and certainly not at their security firms. A restaurant, on the other hand, seemed like an excellent place to hide their secrets. The name practically spit in the faces of the fae.

I checked the hours on the website. It opened daily at five and stayed open until eleven. Either they did amazing dinner business, or they just didn't care about the lunch crowd. It was almost nine and I was tired. But I needed to get out there and beat the bushes if I was going to beat the clock on my magic cancer.

Because I certainly couldn't count on anyone else to do it.

I changed into jeans and a button-up shirt. I slid my dueling wands into the hidden pockets in my jeans and applied the masking agent Rachel had given me over the black veins on my face. I planned to use illusion for a disguise, but if they had anti-illusion wards, I wanted a backup plan.

I powered the sigils on the table in the center of my walk-in closet and pulled up on the edge. The floor swung open, table and all, revealing a staircase descending into darkness. I'd discovered several such secret tunnels beneath the church and modified them. One of them led to an underground crypt. Another wound its way for miles and emerged inside a hollow tree in the forest. I'd connected most of the tunnels to give me escape routes in all directions.

Since taking Dolores would only alert my house pests, I took one of the escape tunnels leading to a small underground cellar about a hundred yards from the house. I pulled the cover off the motorcycle hidden inside and started it. The engine rumbled to life. I cast a muffling spell to keep the noise from travelling and activated the sigils on the door. It swung open, and I drove up the ramp and into the night.

Iron Age Steakhouse stood alone on a service road about a quarter of a mile from the next closest restaurant. I parked across the street and summoned my oblivion staff to study the area. The scope didn't reveal anything magical. The people entering and leaving appeared to be nubs, and I didn't see any obvious wards. Judging from the packed parking lot, the place seemed to be hopping.

Maybe I'm wrong, I thought. This might just be a plain old restaurant. Unless I was missing something subtle. I walked across the street. Staying at the edge of the parking lot, I began to circle the building, inspecting it through my scope. I finally had a hit when I reached the service entrances. One of them was guarded by a sigil pad, and the other was not.

Three security cameras watched the back—one on each corner and the third directly over the door with the pad. The cameras on the sides were angled so they could see the entire service area. Cameras on the sides and front of the building made approaching it unseen difficult. My scope didn't detect any magical signatures on the cameras, meaning they were ordinary nub technology.

By circling the outer perimeter, I'd stayed out of camera vision, but there didn't seem a good way to approach any closer without being seen. At least not without magic. A camouflage blind like the one I'd used to remain undetected at Hannah's school would suffice since the perimeter wasn't warded. I'd have to wrap the blind around me so the corner cameras wouldn't glimpse me from the sides.

I cast the illusion. To anyone watching the camera feeds, it would look like a smudge on the screen. But the closer I approached, the larger and more obvious it would become. Anyone with a sharp eye wouldn't be fooled long. I was probably counting too much on the incompetence of their security but didn't have much of a choice.

I reached the door without incident—no alarms blaring and no squad of armed men bursting from inside and riddling me with bullets. The sigil pad to the side of the door resembled a keycard pad but was a smooth-polished stone commonly used by magical security companies. This model was, of course, manufactured and sold by Gaia Enterprises.

The only way to unlock it was by tracing the proper sigils in the correct order. I'd seen plenty of these pads over the years. They worked well and were nearly impossible to crack since the combination and number of sigils required varied by model and could be customized by the owner.

As with computers, the weak point of security wasn't the device itself, but the users. The required sigils could be anything, but the vast majority of users chose simple patterns so it didn't take twenty minutes opening a door. Even so, the list of commonly used simple sigils numbered in the hundreds—too many to guess.

It was a good thing I didn't have to.

I slid a small bottle out of my utility belt, shook the contents, and sprayed a fine mist of glowing liquid onto the pad. The mist adhered to oily residue left behind when fingers pressed against the pad. Dozens of crisscrossing lines appeared, nonsensical scribbles to anyone without experience deciphering them. Using clues from the edges of the patterns I was able to discern five distinct sigils.

That meant a permutation of five without repetition—still too many to guess. I didn't want to lock out the pad or set off an alarm by entering an incorrect code too many times. I had no choice but to try a different approach. I sprayed another liquid on the pad. It dissolved the glowing mist and cleaned the oil residue from the surface.

I could get the code in one of two ways: by capturing someone and torturing it out of them, or by concealing myself and watching for someone entering the door. The latter course of action held the lowest risk, but I needed to set myself up for success first. I removed a pinhole camera from my utility pack and affixed it to the dumpster next to the other service door. Then I backed up across the delivery zone, keeping the camouflage blind between me and the cameras until I reached safety.

A small strip of bushes and trees at the edge of the asphalt gave me a place to remain concealed without use of the blind. I made myself as comfortable as possible and waited. Thirty minutes passed, then an hour. During that time, three people emerged from the normal service door for smoke breaks. No one approached the secured door.

Closing time came and went. The parking lot emptied, and still nothing. I considered blasting open the door, but then the Firsters would know their cover was compromised. There was another way, but it was extremely risky. I could go to the door, portal through to Feary, walk forward a few feet, and portal back in.

But planeswalking held serious risks. The portal bubble didn't allow me to see what lay on the other side. Once it swallowed me and took me through, there was no way to turn around and jump back. Portal bubbles weren't like doorways or open windows. You were essentially shifting blindly from one plane to the next.

For all I knew, there was a thousand-foot cliff, or a scalding lake of fire in this very spot on Feary. Even if a placid field of daisies greeted me on the other side, there might be something solid or dangerous on the other side of the door in this plane. I'd seen a man partially embed himself in a wall after he tried to planeswalk without knowing what waited on the other side.

Whenever I needed to planeswalk from somewhere new, I scouted the location extensively from both sides by first travelling from a known spot. That precaution had saved my life a dozen times over.

All things considered, waiting all night sounded preferable to risking my life with a shortcut.

The distant thrum of an engine dragged me from my bored stupor around three in the morning. A windowless black van parked in front of the special door. I watched through my scope as the driver and passenger hopped out, walked around to the back of the van and opened the doors. They pulled a laundry cart from the back and rolled it down a ramp that extended from beneath the bumper of the van.

"Son of a bitch," I muttered. It was the damned laundry crew. But the workers didn't go to the normal service door. The van blocked my view, so I switched on my phone and watched the video feed from the hidden camera.

The driver slowly but precisely traced his finger through the patterns on the sigil pad. Though the side view wasn't the best, it was enough for me to guess the order of the patterns since I'd already deciphered which ones they used.

The door opened and the men pushed the cart inside ahead of them. I was on the move the moment the door closed, using the blind to hide me from the cameras. I didn't go to the door right away. Instead, I opened the van door. The interior was sparse—rubber floors, vinyl seats, and an empty space in the back. There was nothing else to indicate they used the van for laundry, not even another cart.

I dug through the glove compartment and examined the documents inside. The registration card claimed the van belonged to Allman's Cleaners, one of the companies owned by Gaia Enterprises. The address was only a few miles away from Iron Age. I scanned the rest of the interior with the scope on my staff. A few specks of dried blood lit up. A splash of unknown residue stained the rubber-coated floor, but I couldn't determine what it had been.

I banished the staff and slid out of the van. Hoping the laundry men didn't make a fast return, I went to the secured door and traced the patterns in the order I'd seen. The latch clicked. I cracked open the door and peeked inside. I'd expected stairs, but instead, I found a ramp leading down.

I had to find out what lay below.

CHAPTER 34

Distant voices echoed from somewhere ahead, but they were far enough away that I risked creeping down the ramp after them. When I reached bottom, I found a dim hallway leading into a room with a metal tank and utility equipment. There were no doors to be seen, but the men from the van stood before a sigil pad nearly hidden by the tank.

One of the men from the van paused to trace the same patterns from the outer door onto the pad. The tank slid aside almost soundlessly despite its size. The other man pushed the cart through the opening and into another room. The tank didn't slide back into place after them, so I assumed they meant to leave it open because they were coming back this way soon.

I slipped into the room after them and found a space behind a neighboring tank on the left wall. The pipes led up into the ceiling, but I doubted they connected with anything. The tanks were props, nothing more.

The men returned with the laundry cart fifteen minutes later. The driver tapped once on the sigil pad and the tank slid back into place. I wished they were more talkative so I could glean information about this place, but they went up the ramp without saying a word. I listened for the van to leave, but the room was apparently soundproofed. I waited five minutes, then left concealment and used the patterns on the sigil to move the tank aside.

The room beyond was nothing but bare concrete with a single door and another sigil pad next to it. The same code opened it too. I didn't understand the point of multiple locked entries if they all opened with the same code. It was likely that, at one time, they had used multiple codes but had become lazy over time when no threats materialized.

As usual, the users were the weak point in any security system.

I crept through the door. A hallway on the other side led past rows of windowless metal doors. Bright light shone from a room ahead and voices drifted down the corridor toward me. I continued down the hallway, putting an ear to some of the metal doors as I went. I heard faint moaning from one of them, confirming that these were holding cells.

I reached the end of the hall and peered around the corner. Three coffin-sized stainless-steel tanks lined one wall. Two metal tables occupied the middle of the room, along with an assortment of hospital equipment. Metal shelving held potions, medicines, and small devices.

A terribly thin and naked man was strapped down to a table, eyes filled with misery and defeat. He had the look of someone wishing for death. A short, bald man in a black lab coat stood opposite the table from a taller man with brown hair and a petite brunette.

The bald guy inspected the man on the table, grunting as he shined a flashlight into the prisoner's eyes. "I think he's awake enough to begin."

"How many tonight, Vincent?" the woman asked the bald man.

"Two. Young and fertile. We've got thirty minutes to get this done." Vincent slapped the prisoner's cheeks. "How are you feeling, Rupert?"

The prisoner moaned and blinked. "Awful. Why don't you let me sober up, and I'll let you experience it yourself?"

Vincent smiled. "Rupert, you're doing work that will save our species. Imagine how enjoyable it would be if you did it voluntarily."

"Fuck you," Rupert slurred.

Vincent nodded at the woman. "Alicia, let's get started."

The brunette traced her fingers along Rupert's chest. "Hey, Rupert," she said in a seductive voice. "Miss me?"

He groaned. "Fuck you."

She laughed. "You could fuck all the women you wanted if you played along." A sigh. "Sorry it has to be this way." Alicia began to stroke his crotch. I couldn't quite see it from here and I really didn't want to, but I was flummoxed.

What in the hell was going on here?

Alicia lowered her head and from the sounds, I could tell she was giving the guy head. Rupert's groans turned to moans of pleasure. He began to convulse. Alicia pulled back her head and Vincent moved his hand to Rupert's crotch.

When he pulled it away, he held two large vials filled with sperm.

Rupert apparently took his vitamins, because that was a hell of a load.

The other man disappeared and returned with a gurney loaded with an unconscious young woman in her twenties. He left her next to Vincent and returned with another gurney bearing another slumbering woman who looked about the same age as the first.

Alicia went to a sink and rinsed her mouth, then began assisting the other men in disrobing the women from the waist down. Vincent took a vial and loaded it into a plastic tubular device. He coated it with lubrication and inserted it into the vagina of the first girl. A squeeze of the trigger and the sperm shot through it. He repeated the process with the other woman.

The other man tilted the gurneys so the women's legs were elevated. Then he tapped a digital timer and set it.

"Gods, I hope this is worth it," Alicia said. "This is the most humiliating job ever."

"I think the odds are much better than with the previous subjects," Vincent said. He looked at the other man. "Harvey, how many confirmed pregnancies do we have?"

Harvey consulted a tablet computer. "We're at eighteen out of one hundred and fifty-three. That's much better than the original subject."

"Does this guy even have decent powers?" Alicia said. "I don't want to be sucking off a low-quality demi."

"He's got lightning powers is all I know," Vincent said. "You know they don't tell me much."

"Another one of Zeus's kids?" the woman asked.

Harvey shook his head. "They said it's probably Thor." He lowered his face toward Rupert's. "Is your daddy Thor?"

Electricity crackled along Rupert's fingers. Vincent's eyes flared with alarm. He grabbed a syringe filled with golden liquid and jabbed it into the prisoner's neck. Rupert went limp.

"Jesus, his body burns through that stuff fast." He picked up a jar and refilled the syringe. "They're not bringing us any more tonight, so let's lock him up."

Harvey nodded and pushed Rupert's gurney toward the hallway. I backed up to the far corner and hoped the darkness and my camouflage blind kept me concealed. Harvey stopped at the first metal door, opened it, and pushed the gurney inside. He returned a moment later with an empty gurney and traced a sigil on the pad next to the door to lock it.

The timer went off and the trio tilted the women's gurneys back to level. When they started clothing the women, I figured it was time to leave. Vincent tapped on his phone and spoke to it. "They're good to go."

"Coming down," a voice replied.

That was when I realized the men from the van hadn't left. They'd just gone somewhere to wait.

Shit! I tested the nearest door. It was locked. I didn't have time to mess around, so I traced the sigils on the pad, and the door clicked open. I slipped into the dark room on the other side and closed it. Since Harvey had manually locked the other one, I assumed this one wouldn't lock behind me.

I'd only been in there for a second when I noticed the smell. I wasn't alone. I cast a ball of light and illuminated the room. The room was more crowded than I'd realized. Dozens of unblinking and unseeing eyes stared back at me. They belonged to dead pixies suspended in preservation fluid in large glass jars on a shelf.

Puncture wounds along their small arms told me that the Firsters had been draining their blood so they could extract pixie dust and convert it to concentrated liquid mana. The amount extracted that way wouldn't amount to more than a few grams, but it was enough to work some serious magic if the users knew what they were doing.

Movement in the back of the room caught my eye.

Holding my staff before me, I stepped past the shelf and found metal cages. Only one had an occupant, a red-headed pixie covered in bruises and cuts. The bruises were from puncture wounds, probably IV needles where they'd drawn as much blood as possible without killing her. They apparently had no patience when it came to the procedure, or else they just enjoyed killing pixies. Probably a little of both.

The pixie's eyelids cracked open. She mumbled something, but it wasn't coherent.

I heard talking in the hallway and pressed an ear to the door.

"We need more than two a night," Vincent said. "Rupert can produce enough sperm for up to six women. He's extremely virile."

"Do you know how hard it is to abduct the exact type of female you want?" It was probably the driver speaking. "We've got vampires luring them out of clubs, but we have to spread it out, or people start asking questions."

"Greta Mead is not the type who forgives missed quotas," Vincent said. "If you want to keep getting paid what you do, I suggest you pick up the pace."

"We're doing the best we can," the driver said. "And it's not for the money—it's for the cause, so you can shut your dick sucker, you bald little fuck."

"Yeah," another man said. "Fuck off and let us do our job."

"Get out!" Vincent shouted. "Get out before I call Greta myself!"

Booted feet stomped away. Vincent grumbled and moaned to his colleagues before stomping away. Alicia spoke a moment later, but her voice was faint enough I figured she was somewhere down the hall in the lab. I tested the door to my room and was relieved when it opened.

The hallway outside was clear, so I crept back down to the corner and began eavesdropping again. It took a moment for me to figure out the researchers were talking about blood. As they talked about mixing reagents and test subjects, I realized they were formulating a potion from Rupert's blood. While they didn't specifically say why, it seemed reasonable to assume they were trying to figure out other ways to give humans godlike powers.

There were computers further back in the lab, along with other equipment I didn't recognize. I couldn't risk going for the computers. There simply weren't any places to hide in the room. I'd have to come back another time. It stood to reason that the researchers worked late hours because that was the prime time for their people to abduct women, bring them in, and get them back out before anyone knew they were missing.

"Did you get the summons yesterday?" Alicia said. "I can't wait."

"I wasn't invited," Harvey said. "Guess I'm not as important."

"It has nothing to do with that," Vincent said. "We're going to observe and collect data."

"They're bringing a professional camera crew too," Alicia said. "It's going to be a major event."

"I'm part of the team," Harvey whined. "Why would they leave me out?"

"They told me that space is very limited," Alicia told him. "But they wouldn't be more specific than that."

"Be happy, Harvey," Vincent said in a condescending tone. "Daphne's reveal is going to be huge. She's our first major success and I can't wait to see her operating in the real world."

"All the bigwigs will be at the convention," Alicia said. "Even Mason."

"Of course he will be there," Vincent said. "This is the moment we've all been waiting for."

"Two more days." Alicia giggled. "I can't wait!"

"Yeah, have fun," Harvey grumbled. "Such bullshit."

"Oh, shut up, Harvey." Alicia huffed. "You're technically just an assistant."

Harvey grunted. "Give me a break. You're not a scientist. You just give blowjobs to demis."

She sighed. "Because it's the easiest way to collect his sperm, jackass."

I peeked around the corner and watched them as they continued talking about the convention where Daphne was scheduled to make her first appearance. It sounded like the perfect place to catch the targets together, but not once did they mention where it was held.

After bitching for another five minutes, Harvey looked at his wrist. "I'll take the latest batch to the pharmacy so they can start testing. See you tomorrow." He gathered vials of blood and loaded them into a carrying case.

I wasn't ready to leave just yet, so I slipped back into the prison cell with the pixies and waited for Harvey to leave. When his footsteps passed by, I waited another few minutes and then went back to eavesdrop some more. When I tuned into the conversation, Alicia was talking about having kids.

"I told Alan I want at least five kids. We've got to keep our numbers up as much as possible especially with all the half breeds on the rise." Alicia made a gagging sound.

"It's frightening," Vincent said.

"Yeah, but get this," Alicia said. "Alan told me that he doesn't want kids, especially if we're about to start another conflict."

"Children were our weak points last time," Vincent said. "You remember the safe house slaughters. The Oblivion Guard murdered so many women and children, it forced us to our knees."

Their talk woke the ghosts in my head. *Killer. Murderer.* I tried to block their voices, but their whispers grew louder.

"Fucking evil bastards," Alicia said. "Gods, I hope Daphne lives up to the hype. I want to do to the fae what they did to us."

"Oh, she will," Vincent said. "Greta told me that our efforts have paid off."

I wondered how many atrocities the other guardians and I had committed, all in the name of the fae. After all the killing I'd done for them, I still didn't understand why the slaughter of those women and children was the one thing that made me call it quits.

Alicia and Vincent continued talking as they worked, but never returned to the subject of Daphne's reveal. About six in the morning, they started packing up to leave.

"I won't be in until four tomorrow," Alicia said. "I've got to make a special trip to the pharmacy first. They tweaked the fertility pills again."

"Let's hope they actually work this time," Vincent said. "I'm just happy we're closing up shop early so we can be rested for Thursday."

I hid in the cell again and waited until they left. When silence persisted for long enough, I went into the lab and began taking pictures. The computers were password protected. I wasn't a hacker, so I didn't bother trying to crack them. From what I could tell, they kept their test subjects here, drew fluids, ran tests, and then sent batches over to the pharmacy for processing. I hadn't seen a pharmacy listed in the companies owned by Gaia Enterprises, so it was probably hidden inside another businesses.

A notepad next to a computer listed quantities of ingredients going to the pharmacy. Two quarts of pixie blood, one liter of Rupert's blood, an orc horn, a goblin testicle, and various organs from an elf. It listed captives that had come from the laundry—nearly eleven women in the past seven days. A street address without a city or zip code was scrawled in the margin. I took a picture and flipped back to the first page. The pages before then had been torn off, so I took pictures of what I could, then put the notepad back exactly as I'd found it.

After a thorough investigation of the lab, I took a moment to investigate the other cells. One held a heavily drugged orc. The next one had a dead but preserved elf on a shelf. The other cells were empty, but the stain-covered floors led me to the conclusion that nothing good had happened in them.

I left Rupert's cell well enough alone. I entertained the thought of letting him go but had no idea what the man was capable of or how his moral compass swung. He might go on a killing spree. Plus, releasing the

Firsters' prize possession would alert them that someone had infiltrated their lab.

I had to admit the Firsters had a first-class operation going. They'd kidnapped dozens of pixies, gods only knew how many elves, orcs, and other creatures, and they had their very own demigod breeding program.

With that much power, I had a feeling the next war would break all the worlds.

CHAPTER 35

I'd uncovered a plot that would shift the balance of power heavily in favor of some very bad people. But I wasn't here to save the world—just my life. Maybe killing the trio of Mead, Ingram, and Digby would delay their plans for another war, but I doubted it. I'd collect my unicorn heart and let them kill each other all they wanted.

On the way out, I paused in the hallway. "Don't do it, you idiot." It was a horrible idea. But after dithering outside the door, I realized I couldn't help myself. I went inside the room with the pixies and examined the contents of all the jars, using the small stepstool to see the top shelf. I found the perfect subject two jars back on the top. It took some major effort to wrestle the lid off without upsetting the other jars. Formaldehyde fumes stung my nose when I extracted the damp body. I used a drying spell to get rid of the moisture. The body was in good condition —at least good enough for what I planned.

I closed the jar. Unless someone climbed on the stepstool and pushed the first two jars aside, they'd never know it was empty. Another spell opened the simple padlock on the cage with the living pixie. I reached in and gingerly cupped her in my hand, then put the dead one in her place. Hopefully, they'd assume she died of blood loss and injuries. I didn't much like pixies and they didn't like me, but being used as a lab rat was a fate I wouldn't wish on my worst enemies.

After making sure I'd locked the cell doors and left nothing else undisturbed, I made my way out, the pixie cradled in one arm. I took out my phone and checked the dumpster cam feed to make sure no one waited outside, then unlocked the exit.

Without the van blocking the corner cameras, I was concerned they might see the door opening all by itself since I was hiding behind the camouflage blind. I opened the door a crack and cast a different kind of illusion spell. A bird fluttered in front of the cameras, blocking them for the few seconds it took for me to open and close the door. By the time the fake birds fluttered away and vanished, I was already backing across the delivery zone and out of range of the cameras.

The pixie's breathing was shallow, and her skin felt cold and clammy. I imagined she could have endured only about one more blood-draining session before she expired. It was nearly five in the morning, but I figured it was best if I got her some help right away. The pixie nestled perfectly into one of my motorcycle's saddle bags so I could drive her to Layla's emergency healer.

After several minutes of knocking, the healer finally came to the door, eyelids heavy. "This isn't a twenty-four-hour ER," she grumbled. She saw the pixie in my arms and her eyes blinked fully open, suddenly alert. "What in the hell?"

"Can't explain, but she's lost a lot of blood," I said.

"Gods almighty, bring her in." She opened the door and led me to the room where she'd treated Hannah. I laid the small female on the table and backed up.

"I never got your name," I told the healer. "Seems like I might as well ask since I'm a regular client now."

"Danni. Now be quiet and let me work." She scanned the pixie with a wand and dribbled potion over her. Green vapors rose from the pixie's skin. "She's lost so much blood. I don't know if there's anything I can do about it."

"She's still breathing," I said. "Can't she recover on her own?"

"I need blood to be on the safe side." She took a drop of blood from the pixie and examined it with another spell. "At the very least, I need plasma." She looked at me. "Human plasma will suffice."

"Wonderful." I bared my arm. "Take what you need." I'd really gone off the rails, first saving a pixie and now donating blood plasma. What was next, starting a foundation for the prevention of pixie haircuts?

Danni pointed to a chair in the corner. "Have a seat. I need to make sure your blood isn't tainted by your condition."

"Oh, yeah." I hadn't thought about that. I took the seat and let her draw a sample. She ran some tests and frowned. "I thought you were human."

"I am human." I wiggled my fingers. "I've had genetic tests done before. I'm not mixed."

"But your blood type is exceptionally rare." Phyllis ran her test again. "You're a universal donor."

"Um, isn't that type O?"

"Pixies, elves, and fae have certain magical qualities to their blood that humans lack." She frowned. "You carry minute traces of aphora in your blood, a trace element found in Feary. Its non-medical term is pixie dust."

"I grew up in Feary," I said. "Maybe eating their food did it."

"Doubtful," she said. "I've met other humans who lived there most their lives and they certainly didn't have it." She frowned. "Did you use scientific genetic tests to determine your heritage?"

"No." I strained to remember the company name. "It was one of the major magic tests—the same one sorcerers use to prove they inherited their magic."

"Twenty-three and Magic," she said.

I nodded. "That one."

"While that will tell you if you have genes from other races," she said, "it doesn't require a blood sample. That means their genetic tests wouldn't detect this anomaly."

"I don't know what to tell you." I shrugged. "I was raised in Feary, so maybe that's why I've got aphora in my blood."

"Well, whatever the reason, it doesn't matter." Danni pushed me back into the chair and drew two vials of blood. She hooked up an IV to the pixie and let it drain into her veins.

"Does that mean my blood isn't contaminated?" I said.

"Your blood is fine," she said.

"How much do I owe you?" I asked.

"I'd prefer an explanation as to what happened to this pixie," she said.

I thought about tossing her a bone, but it was too risky letting anyone, even her, know what I'd been up to. "She was caught and tortured by some fae haters is all I know."

"Bastards." Danni checked the pixie's vitals, then turned to me. "I don't charge for good deeds, Cain."

"Oh." I was at a loss for words. "Well, thanks." I tapped my arm. "Need more blood?"

She shook her head. "Her small body doesn't need much."

I got up. "I need to get going. Thanks again."

"Don't you want to be here when she wakes?" Danni said.

I shook my head. "Probably best if she doesn't know where the blood came from. I'm not well-liked by pixies."

"That could change," Danni said.

"Doubtful." I tipped an imaginary hat and left. When I got home via my secret tunnel, I collapsed into bed and fell asleep soon thereafter.

BANGING AND SHOUTING on my bedroom door woke me up around noon.

"Cain!" Hannah shouted. "Cain, are you okay?"

I pushed up groggily out of bed, nightmares about dead pixies still shrieking in my head. "What's the fucking problem?"

"Oh, thank god! He's okay," she said to someone else. "Layla said you probably died in your sleep, so I got worried."

"Tell Layla I'll murder her in her sleep for getting you to wake me up," I said.

Muffled laughter came from the other side of the door, then Hannah spoke again. "Layla says that's a good way to get your dick cut off."

"Whatever." I sank back onto the bed and tried to sleep, but my stomach rumbled, and hunger pains prodded me awake. I got up and threw on some clothes, then went into the kitchen.

"Cain!" Hannah grabbed a plate off the counter. "I made you a sandwich with your new bread." She displayed a ham sandwich with lettuce, tomato, and mustard. "Do you want me to cut the crust off?"

Layla guffawed from the comfort of the couch. "Gods, what a perfect little family you are."

Hannah ignored her. "I hope you like it."

I bit into it and let the tangy mustard wash over my taste buds. "It's perfect, Hannah. Thanks."

Her face flushed and she beamed with pleasure. "You're welcome!"

A pair of golden eyes I hadn't seen in a while watched me from across the room. Fred sat just outside his pool as if uncertain if he should go any further. It was high time to flush the spies out of our midst. I pointed at him. "You and me are gonna have a talk."

Fred slipped back into his pool and vanished.

"I hear you got your heart broken, Cain." Layla pushed up from the couch, wincing when she moved her shoulder. "Elves are the worst, but you just had to go and fuck Aura, didn't you?"

"It seemed like a good idea at the time," I said.

Layla groaned. "Men are so easy to manipulate." She looked at my quickly vanishing sandwich. "Hey, girl, can you make me one too?"

"Make your own," Hannah said with a bright grin. She pointed to the bread. "Maybe make me a sammich while you're at it?"

"I'll make myself one, you snarky little bitch." Layla gripped the bread knife like she wanted to slash a throat with it, then deftly cut two slices and started piling ingredients on them.

"Why'd you sleep so late?" Hannah asked me.

Layla's eyes narrowed. "Cain's been outside. There's grit in his hair and a dead bug on his forehead." She sliced the tomato. "Go on a motorcycle ride last night?"

I rubbed my forehead. "Do I really have a dead bug on me?"

"It's just a black smudge," Hannah said. Her smile faded. "Did you really go out last night?"

"Recon mission." I picked up the bread knife and cut more slices because I was starving. "Got some useful intel for our operation."

"I'm listening." Layla took a bite of her sandwich. "You're a terrible assassin, Cain, but you make excellent bread. I think you're in the wrong business."

"I'll open a bakery if I survive," I said.

Aura emerged from the guest bedroom and stood in the doorway. "What did you find out, Cain?"

"You can go sit in the corner with Fred," I said. "I'm not saying another damned word in your presence."

Aura's eyes turned pleading. "But I can help. I promise! I'll do anything you want."

"Ooh, anything?" Layla rubbed her hands together and grinned maliciously. "Cain needs another booty call."

Hannah snorted.

I did my best to ignore them. "This is the second time I found out you've been lying to me, Aura." I angrily slapped a piece of ham on my sandwich. "Never again."

"We don't need you, elf." Layla took another bite of her sandwich. "You and Fred can go make some tentacle porn while we do the heavy lifting."

I groaned. "What is it with you and the tentacle porn?"

Hannah chortled. "You're sick in the head."

"Yep." Layla licked mustard off her lips. "And proud of it."

I examined the bandage taped over Layla's shoulder. "How are you feeling?"

"Like I had too much to drink and got into a bar fight," Layla said. "Remind me to never get near a harpy again. I'd rather eat maggot-infested garbage than smell those old birds."

Hannah gagged. "Are they really that bad?"

"Worse." I made another sandwich and motioned the pair toward my room. "Let's go in there. I want to talk without spies in the room."

"Cain, please!" Aura stepped closer to us. "I'll do anything you want. I'll keep everything secret and not tell my people a thing unless you say it's okay."

"A rim job might change his mind," Layla said.

I stifled a laugh. "No, it won't." I put my hands on Aura's shoulder. "Do you know what will change my mind?"

Her eyes became huge and innocent. "Just tell me, Cain. I'll do anything."

I stroked her hair. "Good." Then I turned her around and gave her a nudge. "Go to your room and think about how bad it is to betray people."

Hannah and Layla burst into laughter.

Aura spun back, face twisted with anger. "Gods damn it, Cain, I can help! I've got valuable information."

"Not the kind we need," I said. "Unless you can tell me when and where the targets will all be together, you've got nothing to offer." Thanks to Alicia and Vincent I had a when, but I didn't yet have a where.

"My people might know something," Aura said. "Just let me help."

I shook my head. "Not now." I headed to my room and the others followed. I closed and locked the door, then cast a muffling spell so Aura couldn't overhear anything.

Layla eased onto the leather couch against the wall and looked around at the mostly empty space. "You could fit two bedrooms in here."

I dropped into the chair at my desk and Hannah sat on the edge of the bed.

"So, what did you do last night?" Layla asked.

I told them about my little adventure and showed them the pictures on my phone.

Layla shook her head. "You've gone soft. Why would you go out of your way to save a pixie?"

"Because he's a good guy," Hannah said.

I shook my head. "Don't mistake me for one of those."

"Too much blood on his hands." Layla sighed. "Just the way I like them."

"Daphne is a weird name." Hannah bit her lower lip. "Is she a member of the Scooby gang or something?"

Layla snorted. "I think she's named after Apollo's Daphne."

"Yeah, it makes sense." I recalled my Greek history. "Daphne was a naiad, an indirect daughter of Gaia. The Firsters probably think her name is symbolic for children of Gaia."

"What kind of powers does she have?" Hannah said. "Does she grow plants or something?"

Layla mimicked grabbing someone. "I'll bet she controls plants and makes them kill people."

Hannah shuddered. "Wow, that's awful."

I looked up the street address I'd found on the notepad last night. I didn't have a city or zip code to go with it, so I ended up with two possibilities. One was a bar in White House Springs, Alabama, the other a mansion on a remote strip of beach near Los Angeles.

Hannah watched over my shoulder. "You think one of those places belongs to the Firsters?"

I nodded and turned to Layla. "Tell me if this sounds right."

"I'm listening," she said.

"These researchers deal with the same people all the time, right?" I tapped a finger on my chin. "They wouldn't write down the address to the pharmacy or the laundry or one of their other regular suppliers. But if they got an invite to the unveiling of a secret weapon, it would probably be somewhere they hadn't been before."

"Which means they'd write it down," Layla said. "Where would a bunch of fae-hating Firsters meet in secret?"

"Probably a mansion," Hannah said. "I'll bet Mason Digby wants to throw a fancy dinner and everything."

"Maybe." I ran a search on the mansion and found out it was owned by an actor. The bar in Alabama wasn't listed with the other companies owned by Gaia Enterprises, but the name caught my attention. "I think it's the bar."

Layla raised an eyebrow. "Why?"

"Because it's called New Hope Bar and Grill," I said.

Hannah exchanged a look with Layla. "That definitely doesn't sound like the name of a place for the Firsters."

"It does if you know your history," I said. "Led by a young man with great powers, rebels destroyed a mighty empire's most powerful weapon."

Hannah groaned. "Are you for real?" She turned to Layla. "He's talking about Star Wars!"

"Specifically, the movie, *A New Hope*." I folded my arms, a smug smile on my face. "Prove me wrong."

"I think you've watched too many movies," Layla said.

"Why Alabama?" Hannah said. "That seems awfully remote."

"Gaia Enterprises was founded in Atlanta, primarily because it's the largest hub of travel to and from Feary in North America." I displayed a map on my laptop with all the Feary portals highlighted. Red dots covered the Atlanta area and became fewer and farther between as they spread out. There were none in Alabama. In fact, the closest one to the bar was five hundred miles away.

"The reason Atlanta is such a hotspot is because Faevalorn is in the same geographic area," Layla said.

"Yep," I said. "Portals are located near towns, villages, and cities in Feary. They could put them anywhere, but they're for fae convenience, not humans." I traced my finger around the big blank space in Alabama. "And if you want to make sure you rarely get unexpected fae visitors, then you keep your secret weapon in the most remote place possible without keeping it too far from your headquarters."

If I was right, then this bar would soon host all three targets. It was the perfect spot for a triple assassination.

CHAPTER 36

Layla pursed her lips. "I'm sold. Let's check it out."

Hannah opened her mouth.

I spoke before she could. "You're coming with us."

Her mouth hung open for a moment. "Oh, I was about to demand you let me go with you." Her eyes narrowed. "Why am I coming along?"

"Because I'm not leaving you alone with Aura or Fred." My jaw clenched. "I can't believe I have two traitors in my house." I flicked my gaze to Layla. "Anything you want to tell me?"

She grinned. "Yeah, you're soft and stupid and you got played. How's that for starters?"

I flinched. "Are you hiding a secret affiliation with one of the groups after Hannah?"

"No." Layla tilted her head and stared at Hannah. "Wonder who the baby daddy is."

"Mom never said, and I didn't find anything in the files," Hannah said.

"Which god can switch souls between bodies and shoot rays out of his eyes?"

"Hell if I know," Layla said. "All of them?"

A yawn cracked my jaw. "Well, let's get going. It's a long drive."

"Yeah, five hours," Layla said. "How about we fly into Birmingham and drive from there instead?"

I ran some searches and was surprised to find an international airport in Huntsville, only an hour away from our destination. I booked our tickets for an afternoon flight. "Go get packed."

"I've got nothing here to pack." Layla tugged on her dirty yoga pants and torn shirt. "Guess I'll buy something when we get there."

"Just go home and change," I said. "We've got time."

She sagged into the couch. "I'm still way too out of it to go traipsing across town right now."

"Maybe I have something that will fit you," Hannah said. "You're a little tall, but I picked up some cute dresses when Cain took me shopping."

Layla groaned. "Do not drag me into this little fantasy family of yours, okay?"

"Jesus." Hannah scoffed. "Cain saved your life, in case you've forgotten already, and you didn't even thank him. You don't have to be our best friend, Layla, but at least be somewhat nice until you leave us."

Layla snored loudly. "Oh, what was that? Sounds like a child whining."

Hannah bared her teeth and shook her head. She gave me a *what can you do?* look and walked out of the room.

Layla struggled to her feet, wincing and flexing her shoulder. "You know, I was injured because of you, Cain, so don't expect gratitude. I was there because you needed someone like me around to watch your ass, and Hannah isn't that someone."

"I'm also relying on someone who's party to a ten-million-dollar contract to kill me." I snorted. "If my other slipups haven't proven I'm an idiot, I guess that would."

"Yeah, it's a proven fact already." Layla put a hand on my chest. "So, was fucking Aura fun at least?"

"I enjoyed it," I admitted. "But sex is usually enjoyable."

"Sure." Layla started to walk away.

I touched her arm. "Why? You interested in some fun?"

Layla chuckled. "Cain, I don't want to break your heart again, but you're not my type."

I blinked. "Well, okay then."

She pressed herself against my chest and ran a hand slowly up my leg, stopping at my crotch. "Oh, the little guy is perking up."

I bared my teeth. "You play dirty."

"I know." Layla gently patted my crotch, then spun on her heel and left me alone with my unfortunate boner.

"Fuck my life," I muttered. I wished I could make another visit to Rachel, but there wasn't enough time, and I sure as hell wasn't going to Aura for a round two. I took my mind off sex by packing my carryon bag and preparing for the trip. Then I went into the den to have a heart-to-heart with my octopus.

Fred floated to the surface when I got to the edge. I sat down and held out a hand. His tentacle touched it.

Sorrow, he said.

I nodded. "I know you're sorry, Fred, but you can't stay. I can't have your master watching me."

Understood, he said. Inky black clouded his golden eyes and the world flickered to darkness.

I stood once again before the underground ocean. The massive figure hovered ominously about thirty feet offshore. It towered three stories tall, a mass of tentacles writhing around its face. It stepped forward and the glow from the cave roof brightened, allowing me to see Fred's master clearly for the first time.

The monster was thick and muscular with the mass of a dozen elephants. His head was that of an octopus with glowing red eyes. Great bat wings spread from his back, and his hands were webbed with wicked claws at the end.

The beast raised its hand and the rocks beneath my feet rumbled and shot up, forming a pedestal that brought me almost eye level with it. I'd heard legends of the beast, but I could hardly believe he was real.

"You're Cthulhu," I said.

He stepped closer, sending giant waves crashing onto the stony shore, and stopped just feet away. He spoke in a guttural language I didn't understand, but English words flowed into my head. *I am the king of the deep ones, master of the dark reaches where even Poseidon holds no domain.*

"Why do you want me to become your slave?" I said.

I seek useful minions. I will make you a trade. The girl for your life. If you will not submit to my rule, I will accept her in exchange.

I scoffed. "Don't play games with me. You're already after her, and you'd use me to get her if I agreed."

Submit and become more powerful. I will grant you access to my powers and my plane of power. None will stand against your might.

It was a very tempting offer. But I shook my head. "For better or worse, I'm my own master." I turned my blighted cheek toward him. "So kill me and be done with it, or shut up and leave me alone."

Brave little man. He leaned closer, wafting his hot stank-ass breath over me. *You will keep my minion, or I will kill him and you.*

Damn, he was playing hardball. "You'll leave me alone if I keep Fred?" I said.

For now.

In a blink I was back in my house and Fred's eyes were once again golden. He shaded white. *Sorrow.*

I sighed. "Yeah, me too, buddy. But at least you get to stay for now."

His skin turned light blue as he slipped back into the water.

I got up and nearly ran into Aura when I turned around.

"Cain, please let me come," she said.

"Come where?" I asked.

She huffed. "I know you're going somewhere because Hannah is packing. Take me. I can be an asset."

"Nope."

"Fine," she growled. "I didn't want to have to do this, but you leave me no choice. If you don't let me come, you'll never get that unicorn heart. I'm the only connection you have to the agency. I'm the only one who knows the client."

"I'll find them eventually," I said.

She shook her head. "No, you won't. Even if you kill the targets, you'll never get the reward without my help."

It seemed everyone had an ace up their sleeve except for me, and I was the joker. I had no choice but to keep Fred around, and there was no point in assassinating the targets if Aura didn't tell me where to find the client. So, I came up with a palatable alternative. "You can come, under one condition."

She nodded. "Name it."

"Be right back." I went into my room and retrieved a dagger.

Aura's eyes flared with alarm. "What are you doing?"

I snorted. "Relax and give me your hand."

Arm trembling, she held out her hand. I poked her finger to draw blood and then used it to trace a sigil on the floor. I powered the sigil and held my thumb to the center. "Swear that you will do nothing to betray us and you will not communicate with anyone about anything without letting me know beforehand."

Her eyes flared. "That's a very broad oath, Cain."

I glared up at her. "Swear it or stay behind."

She pressed her lips together. Nodded. "I swear it."

"Twice more," I said.

"I swear it, I swear it."

"Thrice spoken, the bond is secured." I stood and pressed my thumb to her forehead. "If the bond is broken before I have released you from it, you forfeit your life."

Aura sagged. "Now, can I go?"

I took her hands. "Yes. Would you like to come to my room first?"

Forehead pinched, she looked at me. "For sex?"

I nodded.

"No, Cain, I wouldn't like to. You just made me swear a blood oath because you don't trust me."

"You're right, I don't trust you."

"And you want to sleep with me again?"

I nodded. "I like you, Aura."

"Well, I'm sorry, but it wasn't personal, Cain." She took back her hands. "It was duty."

"That's what I thought, and that's why I asked." I watched her carefully. "I needed to know the truth."

She huffed. "You were testing me?"

"Yeah." I nodded toward her room. "Now go get ready."

"Fine!" She threw up her hands and walked away.

I walked toward the kitchen. Thankfully, Hannah and Layla were in another room, so no one saw the disappointment on my face. It had been a test, but the truth fucking hurt. "All because you let someone in," I muttered. "Play stupid games, win stupid prizes, die a little more inside."

I went to my laptop and purchased another ticket for Aura. I chose the seat across from the lavatory at the back of the plane because I was feeling petty.

Layla and Hannah emerged into the den, each with a single bag. Layla wore a form-fitting blue dress that didn't quite reach her knees. The same dress would have gone several inches below Hannah's knees.

"Isn't this adorable on Layla?" Hannah said to me.

"She's cute as a button," I said.

Layla scowled. "I'll shove a cute little dagger between your ribs."

Aura came out in the same clothing she'd been wearing for the past two days. "Can I borrow a dress, Hannah?"

Hannah bared her teeth. "Fuck off."

I rubbed my hands together and faked a smile. "Alright, kids, let's hit the road."

When Aura started to follow us to the car, Hannah stopped and gave her a look. "Where do you think you're going?"

Layla laughed. "She took a blood oath. I heard the whole stupid thing."

"You can trust me because I have no choice," Aura said.

"Wow, how reassuring." Hannah looked at me. "You are really dumb sometimes, Cain."

"Understatement," Layla said in a sing-song voice.

"Road trip!" I said with feigned excitement and hurried to the garage.

The tension in the car on the way to the airport was thick as shit gravy. Thankfully, everyone remained mostly silent, aside from a few snide remarks from Layla. The only brief joy I got was watching Aura do the walk of shame to the back of the plane when we boarded. When a heavy-set man rushed into the lavatory a moment later, I felt even better.

Layla wasn't too happy to be consigned to coach while Hannah and I took first-class seats.

"You cheap asshole," she muttered to me on the way back.

"You don't have to come," I said.

Eyes narrowed, she took the middle seat a few rows back from first class. I was a little disappointed that her row mates weren't overweight men.

The flight wasn't that long, but I managed to sleep the entire way, trying desperately to catch up on the missed sleep from last night. After landing, I rented a car and drove my lovely companions to a motel not far from the bar.

The man at the desk whistled. "Man, you came on the right day."

"How so?" I asked.

"We're booked solid for the next three days." He shrugged. "Some kind of convention, I guess."

My interest piqued. Layla gave me a knowing look.

It seemed we'd found the right place. "Do you have many conventions here?" I said.

"Yep. This time every year there's a big convention. Bunch of folks dressed up like fantasy characters." He chuckled. "They told us it was going to be even bigger this year. Some kind of special event."

I went from being eighty percent sure about this being the right place to ninety-nine percent. This had to be the spot where Digby, Ingram, and Mead would unveil Daphne. All three targets would be here in the next couple of days, making this the prime location to kill them and claim my prize unicorn heart.

I took the keycard for my room and handed another one to Layla. "Thanks for your help, sir. I guess we'll have to find other accommodations if we decide to stay."

"Afraid so," the clerk said. "There ain't many hotels in town, so you might have to go a town over."

I thanked him again and went outside in search of my room. The motel wasn't very large, but it looked well-kept for such a place.

"Do I really have to stay in the same room as the others?" Hannah asked as we walked.

"Sorry, but I like my space." I shrugged. "Why don't you all do what girls do and have pillow fights or something?"

Layla scoffed. "Oh, Cain, you know us girls all too well."

Hannah followed me into my room anyway and closed the door. "Cain, what made you decide to bring Aura along?"

"Because she threatened to withhold the client payment from me even if I complete the contract," I said. "Which means I'd never get the unicorn heart."

"That bitch." Hannah huffed. "But the blood oath won't let her screw us over, right?"

"That's the hope," I said. I decided it best to tell her about my encounter with Cthulhu since it involved her. "I had another encounter with Fred's master. He threatened to kill me and Fred if I didn't let him stay."

Her eyes grew big. "Whoa, really?"

"I met his master face-to-face and he scared the hell out of me." I blew out a breath and sank onto the creaky bed. "He offered to release me from the curse if I handed you over to him."

Hannah's eyes flared. "Because he's with the Underlords. He wants demis like me."

I nodded. "I wouldn't be surprised if he's the actual Underlord himself."

She bit her lower lip. "What's his name?"

"Oh, he's no one big," I said. "Just Cthulhu."

Hannah frowned. "Like baby Cthulhu?"

I shook my head. "Not the internet meme. This is the real deal. He's a giant and there's not a benevolent bone in his fishy body."

"Damn, that's freaky." She shivered. "What did you tell him?"

"I told him he can have you."

Hannah stared at me wordlessly.

I winked. "Just kidding."

She rolled her eyes. "Duh. We wouldn't be here if you gave me up." Her lips pressed into a flat line. "If this doesn't work out, maybe you should give me up. I don't want you to die."

"Not gonna happen." I offered a reassuring smile. "We've got this."

Hannah looked toward the window. "What's our next move?"

"We recon the bar."

"Can I even get in?" she asked.

"It's also a restaurant, so yes." I got up and went to the bathroom mirror so I could apply some concealer to my blighted cheek.

Hannah frowned. "Why are you doing that? Why not just use illusion?"

"They might have wards around the perimeter," I said. "This is my fallback."

"Oh, that's smart." She continued to watch. "You're not very good at putting on makeup."

"I'll get better." I glanced at her. "Go tell the others to be ready to head out in ten minutes."

We didn't have much time to plot and execute an assassination.

CHAPTER 37

New Hope Bar and Grill sat off Main Street on an acre of land, right across from a farm equipment store and an automotive repair shop. The lot next to the repair shop was crammed with vehicles that hadn't made it out alive. The bar was a far cry from the kind of redneck dive I'd expected. The parking lot was big enough to host at least a hundred cars or more, and the building itself was two stories tall and several thousand square feet. I was a bit disappointed that, given the name, it didn't have a Star Wars motif, but that was probably expecting too much.

I parked in the vacant lot where a Western Grill restaurant used to be and took a moment to examine the exterior of the bar through my scope. I didn't see any wards, but the sigil pad just outside the front door confirmed they used magic locks like the ones hiding the underground lab. It meant my hunch had been right and that we'd found the place where Mead, Ingram, and Digby would gather to show off their new secret weapon.

Judging from the busy construction workers in front of the building, the Firsters weren't taking any chances. The workers were erecting a long metal carport with covered sides in front of the entrance. Once finished, it would shield cars and their occupants from being seen from the road, allowing them to enter with almost zero exposure. There was a car dealership on the right and a gas station on the left, but neither offered a good vantage point for sniping.

It was going to be a tough nut to crack.

We strolled through the gas station parking lot for a look at the back of the bar. There we found workers covering the back deck. Even without the covered deck, sniping three targets without concealment or elevation would be nearly impossible.

"They're prepping this place like it's about to hold the G Eight Summit," Layla grumbled. "No chance of getting them outside. We'll have to infiltrate."

I took pictures of the back entrance and put my phone in my pocket. "Let's take a look at the inside."

I gave everyone illusion masks, except for Layla, since she could do her own. Unless they had anti-illusion wards somewhere on the inside, we'd be fine. The workers cast a few appreciative glances at Layla as we walked past, but no one seemed to care about the group of strangers headed for the bar.

"What's all this for?" I asked one of the men.

"A swanky convention," the guy said in a southern accent. "They invade our town every year this time."

It seemed the Firsters hired the same local workers for their annual shindig. "This place looks real fancy," I said. "Hope the food is good."

"Oh, it's damned good," the worker said. "Their pork barbeque is right tasty."

"We'll give it a try." I headed inside.

The floor inside was polished concrete. Wooden booths lined the walls, and high tables dotted the floor in between. The bar formed a circle in the center. Glass shelves loaded with enough alcohol to inebriate an army of goblins towered behind the bartenders. Stairs to the left and right of the entrance led up to the second floor. The kitchen door was on the right side of the bar, and the restrooms were on the left.

A smiling teenaged girl showed us to a booth on the left side of the restaurant. Another girl showed up a moment later to take our orders. I got the barbeque. When she left, I slid out of my seat. "I'm going to take a look upstairs. Be right back."

"Yup." Layla took a sip of her soda. "We'll be here playing family time."

No one glanced twice at me as I sidled my way toward the stairs. At the top I found a locked door with a sigil pad next to it. I sprayed revealing mist on the pad and found nothing. It was clean. I twisted the doorknob and was surprised when it clicked open.

I cracked open the door and peeked inside. A large pedestal stood at the back of the room. The rest of the space was wide open, aside from a few support columns that ran up to the fifteen-foot ceiling. A long buffet table ran along the opposite wall from me. This seemed the most likely place for the gathering and unveiling to take place since the room downstairs was packed with tables.

I counted four windows in each wall, but each one had a set of curtains hanging to the sides. Once they closed them, there'd be no way for me to see inside and perform a long-range hit. I walked around the room, looking for anything to give me an advantage.

I found a closet in the back corner. The shelves held party supplies, but there was nowhere to hide in the cramped space. After doing two circuits around the room, I couldn't find anything that might give me a way in. If the construction work was any indication, this place would be locked down tight.

I could possibly capture an attendee and assume their identity. But they'd certainly have other security measures in place. Illusion disguises and other magical means of entry would likely be blocked.

The assassination would be nearly impossible to pull off from either outside or inside this location. That meant I had to hit them before they got here.

I slipped back downstairs without the wait staff noticing and sat next to Hannah in the booth. "This place is going to be a fortress."

"It's odd they'd have so much security if this place is secret," Layla said. "We're far from any Feary portals and almost no one except the Firsters know about this place."

"Maybe we could blow it up," Hannah said. "Just burn everything to the ground."

Aura's eyebrows rose. "That's overkill, don't you think?"

Layla grinned. "I like the way you think, kid."

"We don't have access to those kinds of explosives," I told her.

"You have me." Hannah tapped her temple. "I can unload on them and kill them all."

I couldn't help but smile. "You'd do that for me?"

"I'd do just about anything for you, Cain." She glared at Aura. "Except be nice to her."

"You've got spirit, I'll give you that." Layla sipped her water. "But you don't have that kind of control over your abilities, and we also need to identify the bodies when it's all said and done."

"True." I shrugged. "Keeping their heads intact helps."

"Any private meeting rooms up there?" Layla asked. "There are usually VIP rooms at conventions so the bigwigs can have some privacy before they go on stage."

I shook my head. "Not that I saw. Just a broom closet."

Layla pursed her lips. "The kitchen, maybe?"

"Doubtful," I said. "There's a buffet table upstairs. I imagine they'll have the kitchen staffed, and I doubt Digby and the others will want to talk in front of them."

The server returned to the table and took our orders. I studied the girl. She and the rest of the staff seemed to be nubs, not supers. I doubted they even knew their town was about to be invaded by vampires, werewolves, and mages. Something about this operation bugged me, but I couldn't put my finger on it.

Layla grunted. "Firsters don't seem the type to hire a bunch of nub rednecks to run one of their places."

"Maybe there's an underground lab here," Hannah said. "They could be meeting right under our feet."

"I did see a few extra doors on the outside," Layla said. "I'll go check them out while we wait."

I nodded. "We'll be here." I went back to mulling over the situation.

Layla returned a few minutes later. "There are two other doors, but both are emergency exits. They were locked, but I could see through the windows."

"Maybe there's something hidden with illusion," Hannah said.

I shook my head. "My scope would've detected any active wards or illusions."

"Only magical items I saw were the sigil pads," Layla said.

Aura shrugged. "If this place will be so hard to penetrate, maybe we should try to hit the targets when they arrive or find out where they're sleeping."

"Hate to admit it, Cain, but the elf has a point." Layla crunched on a piece of ice. "There's only one main highway into and out of this town—three if they go out of their way by forty miles."

I examined the map on my phone and nodded. "We'll station someone on either end of town, and then what?"

"No, we'll position someone at these intersections." Layla tapped two locations on the map. "Put the girl at one end and the elf at the other to let us know when a car is coming, then we ID the occupants."

"What if there were two elves or two girls in this group?" Hannah said. "Would you call us by our names then, *Layla*?"

"I'd call you girl one and girl two." Layla crunched another piece of ice. "If I knew your last name, I'd just use that."

"What if I called you halfling?" Hannah said.

"Then I might slice off your tongue," Layla said sweetly, and crunched yet another piece of ice.

"Bitch," Hannah muttered.

Layla bared her teeth in a smile.

"What are we looking for?" Aura said.

I shrugged. "Fancy cars, I guess. I'll know for sure in a few minutes." The food still wasn't there, so I went outside to the workers. I saw a guy leaning against a pickup truck with a company logo on it. Since he wasn't doing anything productive, I figured he was the boss. I strolled over to him. "Some kind of big deal going on here?"

He grunted and nodded. "Out of towners with all their money like to grace our little town with their presence." He hawked up a gob of brown spit. "Last four years they closed off everything for a mile like they own the place."

"That's insane." I shook my head. "It's like the president is visiting or something."

"Yeah, you'd think." He spat again. "One of the Bucknell boys tried to sneak in a couple years back. Said he saw some guy with a magic wand throwing fireballs." The man chuckled. "Kids and their imaginations."

"I'll bet they pack this place with fancy cars," I said.

"You'd think they would," the boss man said, "but most of 'em come in normal rental cars."

"No limousines?" I said in a disappointed voice.

"Nah. Guess it's harder to rent those nearby." He spat another brown wad. "The whole mess of 'em probably fly into Huntsville and get their cars from there."

"That's where we flew in," I said. "It was the closest place with commercial flights."

"Yep." He looked past me at a man wrestling with a steel pole. "Bobby Lee, I don't care how strong you think you are, I told you to get help with them things." He motioned at another man. "Clyde, get over there before that kid gives himself a hernia." He shook his head.

"Do any locals attend this shindig?" I asked.

"Not from these parts." He spat another glob. "Mind you, we all have to clear out at the close of business today. They have their own security team that comes in first thing in the morning to lock the entire town down even tighter."

I whistled. "Well, looks like it brings in some money at least."

He nodded. "Yeah, I don't mind that part. They pay double the going rate."

"So, they block off the entire town?" I looked at the main road. "What about all the traffic on the highway?"

"They'll detour people back out to Old Register Road," he said. "Course, if you really want to get into town anyway, there's a dirt road about a quarter mile south." He pointed in the general direction. "It'll take you across Hipps Creek and get you to White House Lane. But I wouldn't bother. All the businesses will be closed."

I grunted. "Yeah, doesn't sound worth the trouble." I started back inside. "Have a good one."

I rejoined the others and told them what I'd learned. "I'll bet most of the attendees are coming in from the south like we did."

"You want to put all our eggs in one basket?" Layla said.

"In a sense, yes." I patted my shoulder as if indicating something strapped to my back. "The scope on my staff can penetrate illusion. If they're entering town in a regular car, then I need our lookout to see through the disguises."

"Makes sense," Layla said. "If the event is tomorrow, we need to keep watch this evening."

Finding the targets as they came into town and finding out where they were staying marginally improved our chances of making this work. After eating, we returned to the motel. There wasn't much else to do but wait. I took the opportunity to do a little more fact-finding and went to the motel office. The office manager wasn't behind his desk. I heard a television in the adjoining room and peeked around the corner to find him snoozing on a beat-up old couch. At least I wouldn't have to invent an excuse to get him away from the office.

The computer on the desk looked about a decade old. It wasn't password protected and the scheduling software was open. I opened the reservation list for today. Aside from my party, there were only two other people staying here. The list was considerably longer for the next day. I scanned the names, but none were familiar. Mead and Ingram weren't listed, and neither were the aliases they used on the Gaia Enterprises website. Then again, this motel was probably too low rent for them.

Something else was hard to miss, though. There were three different Jones parties, four Smith parties, and two Robinsons. The number of Janes, Johns, Toms, and Dicks was uncanny, especially considering most mages legally changed their names to something stylish to bolster their reputations.

In other words, the list was mostly comprised of aliases.

Considering the extreme security at the bar, it made sense that the attendees would hide their true identities. The Firsters weren't just careful, they were downright paranoid. I didn't blame them. The fae secret police had a knack for tracking down criminals. It was almost impossible to believe they hadn't uncovered the Firster annual convention.

I took a couple of pictures and left, then made my way to the three other hotels in town. Using trickery and illusion, I took pictures of all the bookings and found more half-assed aliases mixed in with what might be real names.

I shared my findings with the others when I returned.

Layla huffed. "You went off and had fun while I sat here and watched game shows all afternoon?"

Aura examined the pictures. "They're not very inventive when it comes to fake names."

"They don't need to be," Layla said. "An assassin can't figure out where the targets are by looking at the computer records."

"I guess so." Hannah shook her head. "Otherwise, you could just kill them in their hotel room."

But there was no other way to do it. Somehow, we had to find out where the targets were staying. It was our only chance to take them out.

CHAPTER 38

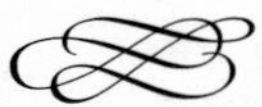

"Got to admit I like this plan," Layla said after I explained the latest revision to the plan.

Aura huffed. "Except I'm solo."

"Yeah, well deal with it," I said. "Let's get going."

I drove us down the road to the farm equipment place and rented a pickup truck for Aura. I sent her north while Hannah and I set off for the south side to keep a lookout for incoming cars. Using my scope, I'd identify the occupants and relay information to Layla.

Layla would remain in town to tail the marks to their respective hotels and get their room numbers. Aliases or not, we'd know where the marks were staying and could eliminate them in their sleep.

The biggest problem was the terrain. The land was heavily forested and mostly flat, with very few rises from which to watch the road without being seen. I puttered down the highway, slowing whenever I found a field or other spot that might afford me a good view. We were a couple of miles out of town when Hannah pointed to a water tower at the edge of a field.

The metal was rusted, and the structure wasn't as tall as the modern UFO-shaped towers, but it rose higher than the nearby trees and offered a good view of traffic coming from the south. That was all I needed.

"I haven't seen a single car going into town yet," Hannah said as I found a place to park. "This place is like a ghost town."

"Good for our purposes." I grabbed my utility sack and the insulated lunch bag with our food. "Let's go."

I let Hannah climb the ladder ahead of me as we scaled the tower. The catwalk at the top wasn't terribly wide, but by angling myself just right, I was able to lie down and watch the road through my scope.

Traffic was light, and most of it looked local. It wasn't until after lunch that I spotted a car with a rental plate on the front. I zoomed in on the driver. He had a bluish aura around him indicating he was a mage, but not a particularly powerful one. I checked for other heat signatures but detected no other passengers.

Another car came into view a few minutes later, this one carrying a female mage and a nub passenger. A short time later, cars began passing by in droves, most of them carrying multiple passengers. I scanned each car and Hannah took pictures. Of the few occupants using illusion, none were our targets. One car carried werewolves, and a large black SUV with heavily tinted windows ferried a flock of vampires.

It seemed the Firster crowd was coming out in force.

On and on they came. We counted over a hundred and fifty people, but none were on my kill list. As the sun began to set, I wondered if Mead, Ingram, and Digby were arriving today. It was possible they wouldn't arrive until just before the big event tomorrow.

I phoned Aura. "Anything?"

"No," she said. "Just a couple of beat-up old pickup trucks."

Layla reported nothing of interest when I phoned her, so Hannah and I kept watching, idly chatting about nothing in particular between waves of cars.

"I should've checked the airport schedule," I grumbled. "Then we would've known who was arriving from where."

As the last rays of sunlight reddened on the horizon, Aura called me. "There's a convoy of ten black SUVs coming from the north. It's too dark for me to see who's inside."

"Shit!" I pounded a fist on the catwalk. "That's got to be them." I hung up and phoned Layla. "Convoy incoming from the north. Can you get to the edge of town and ID them when they roll past?"

"Sure." She disconnected.

I dithered for a moment and made up my mind. "Let's get back to town."

"What if that's not them?" Hannah said. "Maybe we should wait just a little longer."

I blew out a breath. If it was them, Layla would track them to their hotels. I didn't need to worry about her screwing anything up. But if the targets were disguised with illusion, she wouldn't be able to see through it.

"Why would they all arrive together?" I said. "With so much security, it seems stupid to throw all their eggs in one basket."

"Governments use convoys to hide important people all the time," Hannah said. "Some cars might have no one but drivers, or the people might be spread out among the cars."

She was right. I'd seen enough spy movies to know that, though I'd never actually tried to take out someone in such a convoy. It was always easier to find them in places of leisure.

So, we waited. Layla contacted me some twenty minutes later. "Cain, something isn't right."

I raised an eyebrow. "Explain."

"I couldn't see through the tinted windows on the SUVs," Layla said, "so I followed them. They didn't go to a hotel. They went to a large house at the edge of town." She paused. "The place is heavily guarded, but I saw the people getting out of the cars."

"Our targets?" I said.

"No. I don't even think they're human." Layla paused again. "I'm almost positive they were elves and fae."

"You're shitting me," I said. "What would they be doing here?"

"They were surrounded by guards in gray suits," she said. "Judging by the way they moved and looked, I'm certain they're Oblivion Guard."

"My god," Hannah said. "They're going to attack the Firsters!"

"Yeah." I hissed a breath between my teeth. "A shit storm is on the horizon."

My phone vibrated because Aura was calling. I conferenced her into the current call with Layla and told her what we'd found out.

"Oblivion Guard?" Aura's voice rose in pitch. "My gods, there's going to be a battle!"

"Good for us," I said. "All we have to do is swoop in and nail the targets during the confusion."

"Yeah, but we still haven't seen Digby or the others," Hannah said.

I gave the scenario some thought, piecing the jigsaw together. "The fae came from the north because they know most people are arriving from the south. Sounds like they brought in an entire army with ten SUVs."

"Yeah," Layla said. "The SUVs were loaded with personnel. Fifteen looked highly trained and dangerous. Most of the others didn't look like soldiers at all, so they might just be magic casters."

"Any dark elves?" I asked. "Orcs?"

"None," Layla said. "Not surprising, though. The fae don't usually deploy them in Gaia since they're so conspicuous."

"Layla, find a place to get things set up near the bar. Aura, you keep an eye out for anything else. Hannah and I will watch the south a while longer." I checked the Huntsville airport schedule and noted that the last flight would arrive within the next hour. "Digby and gang have to show up soon."

"Or they might not arrive until tomorrow," Layla said, "since their little choir retreat doesn't start until then."

"Since we don't know for sure, I have to keep watch." I spotted incoming headlights from the south. "Let me know if anything changes." I ended the call.

"This is kind of exciting." Hannah giggled. "All hell is gonna break loose."

"Looks like it." I found it hard to believe the fae would order such a bold attack. "The fae must have found out about Daphne and sent a force to kill her and the Firsters."

"I guess you can't hide anything from the fae." Hannah shook her head. "It's amazing you've kept me alive this long."

"Positively miraculous." I scanned the next car and the next, but no sign of our targets. Around nine-thirty, another group of cars came, probably the people from the last flight into Huntsville. None of them held our targets.

I groaned. "Looks like we're going to be out here all night." I wasn't going to chance that our targets slipped past us.

"I don't think they're coming tonight," Hannah said.

She was probably right. "All the motels are full. We've got nowhere else to go."

"Actually, we do." Hannah took my phone and opened map app. "I looked around and found this bed and breakfast about a mile outside of town. I checked and they've got rooms available."

"Maybe I'll drop you off—" I started to say, but she interrupted.

"Cain, they're not coming tonight. I guarantee they won't get here until tomorrow, okay?" She stared at me as if daring me to contradict her.

I stood up and stretched. "Fine. But I think waiting for the fae to attack tomorrow is a mistake." I phoned Layla and Aura and told them about the change in plans.

"Makes more sense than spending the night outside," Layla said. "Doesn't look like they're coming tonight anyway."

"Guess not." I headed toward the ladder. "Aura, pick up Layla and meet us at the bed and breakfast."

Layla made a smooching noise. "See you soon, darling."

I ended the call.

Hannah and I arrived at the bed and breakfast a short time later. I reserved two rooms and gave Hannah a key to one. Then I went straight upstairs to mine. I didn't want to see Aura or Layla. I just wanted to shower and sleep.

The stakeout had been a massive failure, despite uncovering the fae plot to kill Daphne and the Firsters. The fae might very well kill Digby, Mead, and Ingram before I had a chance. The client might not award me my prize if they knew I hadn't been responsible for the kills. There were just too many threads in motion and not enough information to work with. It seemed likely I'd come out of this with nothing.

Despite my worries, I slept soundly and woke to delicious odors drifting upstairs. I got dressed and was the first to get a seat at the dining room table for breakfast. A middle-aged woman served pancakes and bacon and poured me a steaming mug of coffee. Layla arrived a moment later, followed by Aura and a tired-looking Hannah.

Hannah downed a cup of coffee as if her life depended on it. "Cain, please don't make me stay in the same room with them again."

My mind immediately went to the gutter. I grimaced and glared at Aura and Layla. "Gods, what in the hell were you two doing to keep her up?"

"Layla snores like a pig!" Hannah said.

Layla rolled her eyes. "It's a gentle snore, you little bitch."

Hannah ignored her. "And Aura's farts smell like cabbage."

Aura blushed. "Ladies don't fart, so hush your mouth."

"You're no lady," Hannah shot back. "So, lay off the broccoli and cabbage, okay?"

I hid a grin behind my coffee cup, then cleared my throat and forced myself to look serious. "Just eat so we can get an early start, okay?

Hannah huffed, but dug in.

Aura shook her head again. "I do not have stinky farts."

Layla snorted. "The girl's right. You've got digestive issues, elf."

"Did someone say digestive issues?" The B&B owner returned from the kitchen. "You should try probiotics. My husband's farts don't even smell anymore now that he takes them."

Aura's face turned bright red, but she didn't hang her head in shame. "What's the brand name?"

Layla and Hannah burst into laughter.

I wished I could enjoy the moment, but shit was about to get real. I was far too stressed out about what lay in store for us. There might be an all-out battle between fae and Firsters in the middle of the small town. More than likely, it would be a massacre, and then the fae would clean up the mess, leaving no proof that Mead, Ingram, and Digby were dead.

Everything we'd done to get here might have been for nothing.

CHAPTER 39

Our trip back to town was cut short by a roadblock. Sheriff's deputy patrol cars flagged us down when we approached.

Deputy Higgins stepped up to the window. "You with the conference?"

I shook my head. "Just passing through."

He nodded and pointed back down the highway. "Go about a quarter mile back and take Old Register Road. It'll loop you around town by about five miles and take you to the north side."

"Must be some kind of big deal to close down the town," I said.

He shrugged. "Just the way it is, sir."

"Weird." I glanced back. "Guess we'll take the detour."

Higgins touched the brim of his trooper hat. "Appreciate it, folks." He went back to his patrol car and watched as I executed a five-point turn to get us going the opposite direction.

I slowed down about fifty yards away and summoned my staff. I flicked up the scope and took a glance at the roadblock. There were no troopers or patrol cars—just two mages and a pair of rental cars.

"It's an illusion," I said.

"Lemme see." Layla took my staff and peered through. "How the hell do they get away with this? You'd think the townsfolk would be in an uproar."

"See that light blue glow in front of the cars?" I said.

She frowned. "Yeah."

"Aversion wards." I took back my staff and banished it. "Probably have them scattered around town."

"Why not choose a place in the middle of nowhere instead of a town?" Hannah said.

I shrugged. "I'm sure they have their reasons."

"They're using the nubs as human shields," Layla said. "The fae won't openly attack if they think normal humans might witness it."

Aura blew out a breath. "Judging from the size of the fae convoy, I don't think they care. There's no way they can approach without being seen."

"Something doesn't mesh." I started driving again. "And it's really bugging me."

"I think it meshes nicely," Layla said. "The fae found out about Daphne, and all hell's about to break loose."

The dirt road the contractor had mentioned the day before was blocked by a cattle gate. I got out and inspected it. It wasn't locked, so I swung it open, drove through, and closed it behind us. A surprisingly sturdy wooden bridge took us over a small creek. After a short distance, we stopped at a point due east of the bar and got out of the car.

We walked through the woods and reached the creek again. It was wide and deep enough to prevent us from jumping across. I summoned my staff and powered the brightblade. A couple of quick slashes turned two small pine trees into a makeshift bridge. We crossed and continued until we reached the junk car lot across the road from the bar.

Keeping low, we made our way south to the woods and took up a position with a good view of the target building. I checked the area with my scope and spotted numerous aversion and anti-illusion wards. Mages guarded the entrance to the parking lot. They stopped cars, scanning the occupants and the vehicles before allowing them entry.

I scanned all newcomers with my scope, but none of the vehicles held the targets. Despite the extra security measures, the parking lot filled rapidly. All we could do was sit and wait. Even if the targets showed, I had no idea how to take them out without dozens of mages descending on our position.

Almost an hour later Hannah squeaked. "Oh my god, it's about to happen!" She pointed to the north. A line of black SUVs thundered down the road toward the bar.

"Oh, shit." Layla tensed.

"Those are the cars with the Oblivion Guard!" Aura said. "They're about to attack!"

"Son of a bitch." I turned my scope on the SUVs. The first one held five people, all of them Oblivion Guard. I couldn't see past the lead SUV from this position, so I got up and backed further into the woods for another angle.

"What the hell is their plan?" Layla said. "Drive up and unleash a full-frontal assault? That's stupid, even for the guard."

I caught a glimpse of more familiar faces in the middle SUV and they shocked me to my core. "Onwin and Frezia are in that convoy!"

"What in the hell are they doing with an assault team?" Layla said.

Before I could come up with a rational answer, the SUVs turned into the parking lot and drove under the shelter. The first SUV emerged from the other side and drove a distance before stopping so the vehicle bearing royalty could remain under cover. The lead vehicle disgorged a group of grim-faced people in gray suits. Even with the sunglasses, I recognized two of them.

Alwyn had been a low-level grunt like me all those years ago, but a pin on his suit indicated he was now a section leader. The elf female next to him was Jadeen, the leader of the guard. They casually scanned the perimeter like they belonged there, not like they were about to attack the occupants.

"What in the hell is going on?" Layla said. "They're not attacking—they're going in!"

Aura frowned. "I don't understand."

Hannah pointed at a group of people getting out of a rental van. "Maybe this has nothing to do with it, but I've seen several people wearing the same t-shirt."

Even from this distance, it was easy to spot the logo—two globes next to each other. I zoomed in on the shirt and examined it. I'd been so busy looking for familiar faces that I hadn't noticed the shirts. The globes were of Gaia and Feary. A curving blue arrow went from Gaia to Feary, and a curving green arrow went in the opposite direction.

"Why should we care about the shirts?" Layla said.

I shrugged. "I've never seen them before."

Aura's eyes flared. "Actually, I believe I've seen that logo before."

Layla's eyes flicked to her. "Yeah? Well, what is it?"

"Did you feel that?" Hannah looked up and around. "The air is vibrating."

I sensed a faint thrum in the distance. "They must be fighting inside."

"No, it's not coming from in there." Aura pointed up and to the northeast. "It's a helicopter!"

I followed her finger and saw the large aircraft flying low over the trees. Aside from a faint vibration in the air, it was almost silent. The guards standing outside the bar didn't seem to see it. I turned my scope on it and found out why. A camouflage illusion concealed the chopper from the front and a muffling spell silenced the sound of the blades.

All the Oblivion Guard had gone inside with the others, so there was no one with a scope to see it. The mages in the parking lot seemed oblivious to the incoming aircraft.

"It's using illusion and a silencing spell," I told the others. "No one in the bar can see it coming."

"Why hide itself from the bar?" Hannah said.

The chopper was a Blackhawk, large enough to ferry a dozen or more people. I zoomed in to the window and spotted a familiar face looking out. "Because Mason Digby is on board."

"Flying first class," Layla said.

"But why is the chopper only hiding from the bar and not from other angles?" Aura said.

Camouflage spells of that magnitude took an awful lot of power to maintain, especially on a moving object. Wrapping the blind around the chopper would be nearly impossible for one person to manage. But given the extreme security protocols in place, why not go the extra mile and hide the chopper? And why in the hell were Firsters meeting with the fae?

There were too many conflicting facts for me to form any kind of theory about what was happening in that bar.

The chopper set down just north of us in the junk car lot and disgorged a large group of people, including my old pals, Alicia and Vincent from the secret lab beneath Iron Age Steakhouse. Four men brandishing ivory staffs came last, followed by the three people I'd come all this way to kill: Digby, Mead, and Ingram.

"Holy shit." Layla shivered with delight. "We just hit the jackpot!"

I aimed my staff and envisioned the shot that would kill them quickly and efficiently before their comrades knew what happened. The scope told me they were a hundred and thirteen yards away, give or take. That was an easy shot for one target. Multiple targets in quick succession were another matter entirely. I'd have to focus my will and unleash the power with less than half a second between shots.

Depending on their reflexes, I had anywhere from a half second to a full second before the other targets reacted and the guards shielded them. I needed the shots to hit in quick succession to avoid that. I also didn't have a clean shot on Digby from this angle. I'd have to wait for him or the guards to move, or I'd have to shift position until I could line up on all of them.

"I hope you can hit them from this distance," Layla said, "because I don't think we can close the distance before they head across the street."

Digby spoke to Alicia. She nodded and walked to the chopper. She appeared a moment later, towing a young girl behind her. The girl had dark brown hair, olive skin, and stood maybe five feet tall. I guessed she was anywhere from nine to eleven years old.

"Is that Daphne?" Aura whispered behind me.

"It's got to be," Layla said. "Why else would you bring a little girl to this shindig?"

"I'm going to hit them when they cross the road," I said. "Be ready to rush them if I miss."

Layla grunted. "If the airline let me bring my bow and arrow, this would be a hell of a lot easier."

Hannah rolled her eyes. "You could've put it in checked luggage."

Layla scowled. "I wouldn't trust my precious to those buffoons."

"Just be ready to rush them," I said.

Digby patted the girl on the shoulder, and she started walking toward the bar, leaving the others behind.

"Say what?" Hannah rubbed her eyes. "Why are they sending her alone?"

Daphne answered the question when she reached the road. She spread her arms and golden light coalesced around her, lifting her in the air like an angel.

"Wow," Layla breathed.

Aura oohed and Hannah gasped.

"My gods, that's insane," I whispered. "She can fly!"

The people in Digby's crowd watched with proud smiles and congratulatory pats on backs. Digby exchanged pleased looks with Mead and Ingram.

The guards in front of the bar shouted in alarm when they saw the little girl floating in the air above the street. In that moment, I realized I'd completely misjudged the situation. Judging from the look on Layla's face, she realized it too.

Daphne thrust her arms forward and unleashed hell. Massive golden beams of sunlight obliterated wide swaths of the building, burning each swath to ash in an instant. The guards out front raised wands and fired spells back at the girl. She shifted her focus and engulfed them in murderous heat.

Digby's crowd cheered.

"They're not here for the convention, they're here to destroy it!" Aura said.

Layla scoffed. "No shit!"

"I remember what the logo on those shirts means." Aura turned to us. "It's the symbol for the Human-Fae Alliance. They're a fringe group that's been trying to promote peace and cooperation with the fae."

Everything suddenly made sense. This convention had nothing to do with the Firsters. They were here to reveal their new secret weapon so Daphne could obliterate everyone involved. I was nothing if not an opportunist, so I powered my staff and lined up Digby in the scope. I took a breath. Focused my will. Unleashed the power. Shifted to Ingram and repeated. Flicked to Mead and focused once more.

Digby's head exploded. The back half of Ingram's head sheared off. But Mead stepped forward at the last instant and the shot sliced through the neck of the man standing behind her. Guards shouted. Firsters dropped to the ground screaming and covering their heads.

Oblivion Guards rushed from the burning bar, staffs firing beams of searing energy at Daphne. She dodged back and forth on wings of sunlight, blasting golden rays back at them, but the guardians hadn't earned their positions for being slow. They dodged back and forth too quickly for her to hit them.

The Firster mages began rounding up their panicked wards, herding them toward the still-running chopper. I fired a blast at one of the guards shielding Mead. His arms flew out when it struck him in the back. He face-planted on the ground. Another guard replaced him before I could get off another shot. My chest began to hurt. I tried to power the staff again, but my lungs constricted.

I fell to my knees, gasping.

"Cain!" Hannah knelt next to me. "Are you okay?"

"Fucking magic cancer," I wheezed. "Someone get Mead! She's getting away!"

"I'll kill her myself!" Hannah roared and dashed away.

My vision blurred. I sucked in another breath and looked for Aura and Layla, but they weren't there. More screams echoed. I looked up as Daphne fired more blasts into the bar and at the guardians coming for her. She flicked her head back and saw the ruckus at the chopper.

Daphne dove lower, and I lost sight of her. I used a sapling to pull myself to my feet. Layla and Aura fought the Firster guards. Mead scrambled onto the chopper. Hannah raced toward Layla and Aura. None of them saw Daphne diving at them.

I tried to shout a warning, but a wheezing cough stole my breath. My chest felt as if it were locked in a vice and my vision swam from lack of oxygen.

Layla shouted. Hannah looked up at Daphne. Her eyes glowed white. That only made the other demi focus on her as a target. Daphne raised her palm toward Hannah. Something silver flashed through the air, narrowly missed a startled bird, and struck Daphne in the chest. The girl screamed and plummeted twenty feet to the ground.

Mead screamed at the helicopter pilot, but the remaining guards ran for Daphne. Gasping, I raised my staff. With trembling hands, I aimed. With a weak heart, I focused all I had left and fired. Mead's body convulsed and her clothes caught fire. Screaming frantically, Alicia kicked Mead's burning body off the chopper.

I managed a weak smile and collapsed on the ground.

CHAPTER 40

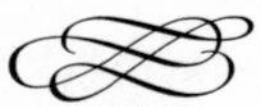

A moment later, Layla stood over me, a frantic look on her face. She yanked me up and threw me over her shoulder. My labored breathing became even more difficult as my stomach bounced off her shoulder with every running step she took.

"The pine tree bridge is back there," Hannah said. "Are you going to jump the creek?"

"Hell no," Layla said. "I'm running through it!"

Water splashed into my face a moment later. I sputtered and tried to breathe. My vision went blurry and darkness took hold for an instant, then I woke to shouts for another instant before passing out again.

When I opened my eyes again, I was on my back, my head in Hannah's lap. She smiled down at me. "Who's a little sleepy head?"

I groaned and managed to speak. "Where?"

"We're in the rental car," Layla said. "You passed out about fifteen minutes ago."

"They're all dead!" Hannah said with glee. "Well, Mead, Ingram, and Digby are. Daphne and some of the others got away on the chopper."

"I almost killed that little bitch," Layla said. "But I hit her shoulder, not her heart."

"It was a great throw," Aura said. "You hit her with a dagger from thirty yards!"

Layla grunted. "Should have been child's play."

"You saved my life," Hannah said. "I was trying to blast the girl, but my powers didn't work."

Aura peered over the back of the passenger seat at me. "How are you, Cain?"

"Peachy," I groaned.

"I took pictures for proof," she said. "All we have to do is submit them to the client."

"Digby's head exploded," I said.

"His face was mostly intact," she said. "It was lying on the ground next to his body."

"Gross!" Hannah shuddered. "That's so nasty."

"Good shots, Cain." Layla whistled. "I've never seen anyone hit three long-distance targets in such quick order."

I groaned again. "I missed Mead."

"Because she moved." Layla blew out a breath. "Too bad you're half-dead from the attempt."

"I feel completely dead." I closed my eyes. "No guardians after us?"

"No, we made it out clean." Layla clapped her hands. "Hot damn, I get to see a unicorn!"

"I can't believe it. Those people at the bar were in peace talks?" Hannah said.

Aura nodded. "The HFA—Human-Fae Alliance—is a fringe group, or so I thought. I heard about them a couple of years ago, which is why I didn't recognize the logo right away."

"Not so fringe if they're talking to the upper crust of the fae," Layla said. "Guess those peace talks are trashed."

Aura blew out a breath. "Yeah. The Firsters practically declared open war on the fae."

By the time we reached the airport, I felt marginally better, but nowhere near the seventy percent I'd felt lately. I was so out of it I didn't even bother to make Aura sit next to the airplane bathroom again. I barely remembered the flight home. Even half dead, I refused to let anyone else drive Dolores home once we landed.

"I need to use your laptop to confirm the kills," Aura told me when we got there.

"Fine, but I'm watching you like a hawk." I got the laptop and stood over her shoulder the entire time. She uploaded the pictures and digitally signed the certification.

She turned to me. "It'll probably be a while before—" The laptop chimed, and a response appeared on the screen.

Confirmation accepted. Instructions to follow.

Aura frowned. "That was fast."

A moment later an address, time, and date appeared. The meeting was scheduled at eleven the next morning.

Hannah laughed and clapped her hands. "Cain, you're going to be healed!"

"There's no guarantee it'll work," I said.

"Actually, there is," Aura said. "Unicorns were among the first magical creatures made. They have the magic of creation in them. That's why a living unicorn heart can heal almost anything."

Despite my weariness, I was almost too excited to sleep that night. I popped a couple of Fritz's pills to tide me over, and somehow managed to sleep anyway.

THE NEXT MORNING, the four of us piled into Dolores and I drove us to the meeting spot, a small farm north of the city.

"What kind of being accompanied the unicorn last time?" I asked Aura.

"A human," Aura said. "It's possible she was just a front."

I nodded. "Wouldn't be surprised."

"What does that mean?" Hannah asked.

"It means she was a temp hired to be the face for the initial transaction." I pulled onto the gravel road that led to the farm. "Some clients don't want anything linking them to the contracts. Most avoid any kind of personal meeting, but in cases like this, it can't be helped."

Hannah shivered. "I'm so excited. I always thought unicorns were just make believe."

Layla clicked her tongue. "Hard to believe one survived extinction."

Hannah turned to face the back seat. "How'd they all die?"

"Lots of reasons." Layla shrugged. "Mostly because practitioners of black magic poached them for their parts and sold them."

Hannah scowled. "Humans, as usual."

"Afraid so," Layla said. "The fae cracked down hard, and that was one of the reasons the humans started the war."

I blew out a breath. "Yeah. Wasn't all that long ago, either. Maybe fifteen years, I think. I remember hearing something about the fae trying to stop unicorn poaching."

Hannah raised a fist. "Mother fucking humans. Even the supernatural ones are like roaches."

"Thanks," I said.

Hannah put her hand on my arm. "You're not. You're one of the good ones, Cain."

Layla snorted.

Aura shook her head. "Hannah, dear, there are no good ones, just shades of gray."

Layla scoffed. "That's about the only sensible thing you've ever said, elf."

Aura narrowed her eyes. "Go to Hades, Layla."

"Been there already." Layla inspected her fingernails. "Wasn't impressed."

I pulled onto the long drive leading to the farm and parked in front of a quaint craftsman cottage. Constructed of gray stone, it resembled something out of a fairy tale. When a dwarf stepped onto the front stoop to light his pipe, I wasn't even surprised.

He nodded at me when I climbed out of the car. "Ghostwalker."

"Just call me Cain, please."

He looked over our group. "I'm afraid only you and one guest are allowed inside."

I frowned. "The details didn't mention a limit."

"Yes, but—"

I waved off his reply. "Are you really going to give me a hard time about this?"

The dwarf shrugged. "Well, if you insist, I suppose it doesn't matter at this point." He sighed. "Claim your prize, assassin."

I approached the door. "The unicorn is inside?"

He nodded. "Yes."

"You don't seem happy about this," I said.

The dwarf looked up and blew a puff of aromatic smoke in my face. "Unicorns are about to become truly extinct. Why would I be?"

"You offered him as a prize," I said. "It's your fault."

The dwarf looked down. "No, it wasn't my choice." He turned to the door and opened it. "Go inside and get this over with, you murderous bastard. I wish I could have talked her out of this arrangement, but it was her decision. Her sacrifice."

"Who are you referring to?" Aura asked.

"You'll find out soon enough." The dwarf motioned us in. We entered and he closed the door without following us in.

A girl in a white dress sat at a large oak table. Her hair was black as night and her skin fair as snow.

Hannah beat me to the question. "Are you Snow White?"

The girl wiped tears from her eyes and shook her head. "Follow me," she mumbled. The girl stood and shuffled toward a door.

"Are you okay?" Hannah asked.

The girl whimpered and spun on us. "No, I'm not okay!" She began sobbing. "Just follow me, please. My mistress commanded me to make this quick."

Hannah teared up and looked at me. "Cain, I don't understand."

I cleared my throat. "I do."

Layla rolled her eyes and shook her head. Aura frowned but said nothing.

I barely noticed the details in the next room except that it was spacious and had a vaulted ceiling. Besides the girl, there was only one other being in there, and it was magnificent. The unicorn was as large as a Clydesdale, with pure white hair and a golden mane. A horn as black as onyx rose from the center of its forehead, shining like polished obsidian.

Even Layla gasped.

The girl leaned against the beast, sobbing and rubbing its mane. She held out her hand. "Assassin, come to me." She flinched as if struck and spoke again. "I'm sorry. Cain, please take my hand."

I looked at the others.

Lips trembling, Hannah nodded at me. "Go, Cain."

Layla clenched her jaw and rolled her eyes again. Aura stared at the unicorn, eyes glistening with tears.

I approached and took the girl's hand. A faint shock passed through me.

Thank you for your service, a gentle female voice said inside my head.

I looked into the big brown eyes of the unicorn. "Is that you talking?"

The unicorn nickered. *Yes. I am Shraya, the last of the first unicorns.*

"Last of the first?" I tried to make sense of it. "You were one of the originals?"

Yes.

"Are you the one who wanted me to kill Digby and the others?"

Yes. They were responsible for mass murders of my herd. They discovered our last refuge and planned to use us to create super humans for another war. Shraya nickered. *I worked so hard to revive our species, but they slaughtered them with no mercy.*

"Wait, so you're not the last unicorn?" I said.

She shook her head. *There are just enough of us left to continue our species. I am one of four females, and only five males remain.*

"And the last of the first." I said. I nodded at the girl. "Who is she?"

A virgin. I can speak to you through her.

I grunted. "Didn't realize the virgin thing was true. Does that mean I can't touch you myself?"

You can, but I can only communicate through a virgin.

I grunted. "Talk about a rare creature."

Shraya nickered. *You have done a great service. Without leaders, Humans First and Gaia Enterprises will be rudderless. It will give us time to hide and replenish the herd.*

"Why not hide in Feary?" I said.

There are many in Feary who would poach us as well. With no place left to hide, I realized that my life for the continuance of our species is a price worth paying.

I swallowed a lump rising in my throat. "You sure about that?"

Absolutely. She regarded me with her dark eyes. *My heart will cure your curse, Cain. It will remove the dark stain from you and free your soul from Cthulhu.*

"It's my fault I have it." I touched my cheek. "My thirst for power did this."

You are no worse than any other, Cain. Man seeks power. It is the way of things. Shraya stomped a hoof. *Patricia, bring forth Carnwennan.*

Sobbing even harder, the virgin girl released my hand and drew a silver blade with a white hilt from an ornate sheathe on a table nearby. She knelt before me and held it aloft. "This blade will cut through any flesh as easily as if it were paper." She picked up a chunk of charcoal and drew a circle on the left side of the unicorn just above and behind the foreleg.

Sobbing, she continued. "Cut carefully so you might pull out the heart while it still beats. You must then bite off as much as you can and swallow the living flesh quickly."

I took the dagger. It felt unnaturally heavy, and the hilt tingled with power. It truly seemed to be Carnwennan, the mythical dagger of King Arthur himself.

Patricia choked back her sobs. "Please make it quick so my queen does not suffer."

I looked back. Tears poured down Hannah's face. Aura's shoulders shook as she strained to keep sorrow at bay. Layla looked constipated.

I took Patricia's hand. "Let me speak with her again."

I turned to my companions. "I want to be alone. Leave."

"But, Cain—" Aura held out a hand.

"Leave!" I roared.

"Go." The girl shoed them out.

"Cain?" Hannah backed out of the room, confusion pinching her forehead.

Patricia shut the door and turned back to me, face red with tears.

I touched Shraya. An unpleasant jolt met my fingers, like the mother of all static electricity, but it passed. Her hair was soft as down and smooth as silk. I let my hand linger for a moment, mind racing with what I had to do. I motioned Patricia over. "I want to talk to her again."

She wiped her eyes and took my hand.

I thought my words to Shraya instead of speaking them aloud. *You are the most magnificent being I have ever met, even more beautiful than the fae queens. I am but a human, unworthy of such a gift.*

And yet, you have proven your worth, Shraya said. *You have won my life fairly.*

I held up the dagger. *Is this the dagger of King Arthur?*

It is, Shraya replied. *It is powerful enough to kill even a god.*

I cannot take your life. I held the dagger in my palm. *I request Carnwennan instead.*

Patricia gasped and stared at me.

Shraya blinked. *You will die, Cain.*

I nodded. *The world could use one less human, Queen Shraya. I wish you success in your endeavors.*

A sparkling tear rolled from the unicorn's eye. *I cannot say that you are good, Cain, but I can say that you are worthy of a longer life. The dagger is yours. I will also give you some of my blood. It may prolong your life, but the dark power polluting you has already progressed so far, I doubt it will delay the inevitable.*

I nodded. *Long life to you and yours, Queen Shraya. I don't welcome death, but I deserve it far more than you.* I took the sheath from the table and slid the dagger inside. "Thank you."

The girl launched herself at me, hugging me so tightly I almost lost my breath. "Thank you, Cain. My world is once again whole."

"I didn't do it for you." I separated myself from her.

"Then why?" Patricia asked. "You're a mercenary—an assassin."

I grunted. "Yep. And no one else should have to pay for my mistakes." I went to the door and opened it.

Ears pressed to the door, Aura, Layla, and Hannah nearly fell inside.

Layla saw the living unicorn and scowled. "Why is it still alive?"

Hannah's mouth dropped open. "You didn't take the heart?"

I shook my head, unable to speak. I felt incredibly stupid and relieved at the same time. Living at the cost of Shraya's life would have filled me with sadness for the rest of my days. But how could I explain that to the others?

Hannah seemed uncertain how to feel. She looked from the unicorn and back to me. "But you'll die, Cain. You have to do it!"

"I can't," I said. "I'm not worth the price."

"Cain, you have to!" Hannah burst into tears. "I don't want to lose you!"

I held up my hands in surrender. "Hannah, I'm sorry."

Patricia took Hannah's wrist and dragged her over to Shraya. She pressed Hannah's hand to the unicorn's neck. Hannah's eyes widened and her sobs subsided. Her eyes dropped to the floor as if ashamed.

"I'm sorry, but I want Cain to live." She wiped a stray tear. "Isn't there another way? I don't want Cain to die."

"Are you kidding me?" Layla threw up her hands. "After everything we went through, you're not taking the prize?"

I spun on her. "You got to see a unicorn. Isn't that enough?"

Layla's jaw worked back and forth, and a single tear pooled in her eye. "Fuck you and your humanity, Cain. Since you just gave yourself a death sentence, maybe I should end you here and now and collect my money."

Hannah's eyes glowed. "Try it and I'll kill you!"

Aura put herself between the pair and held out her hands. "Can you save the hostilities until we leave, please?"

Shraya nickered. Patricia connected us. *Humans are so strange.*

I snorted. "Yeah, we are."

"Wait here a moment." Patricia bowed, and she and Shraya left. When the girl and unicorn returned moments later, the virgin held several vials of blood. "You can drink it, but injecting it is more effective."

"Thank you." I took the vials and led my companions from the room. Patricia and Shraya followed us.

A teary-eyed dwarf waited in the foyer. His jaw dropped open when he saw the queen. "Y-you didn't claim her heart?"

I shook my head. "There's a shortage of perfect creatures in this world. Be a shame if I killed one."

CHAPTER 41

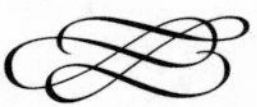

The car ride home was deathly quiet. Hannah curled up next to me on the bench seat. Layla stared out the window, refusing to look at anyone else in the car. Aura watched me through the rearview mirror but said nothing.

When I got home, I went into my room and wrote a brief will.

I leave everything except twenty million dollars to Hannah. To Layla, I leave twenty million dollars, provided she makes sure Hannah remains safe.

I signed and dated the document, made a copy, and went into the den. Layla sat on the couch, staring blankly at a wall. I sat next to her and gave her a copy of the will. "Is this enough for you to keep Hannah safe?"

Layla looked at it and tossed it aside. "Sure."

"Can you seal it with blood?" I asked.

She pricked a thumb with a dagger and pressed it to the document. "I promise to keep Hannah safe, Cain. Now, can you go ahead and die so I can collect my inheritance?"

"You could kill me and end up with a cool thirty million," I said.

"Fuck off." She crossed her arms.

"Layla, will you for once tell me what's on your mind and cut out the tough girl act?"

She worked her jaw back and forth. "I just think life would be a little more interesting with you around, Cain." She stood and looked down at me. "And I think you're an idiot." Then she produced the ankh I'd given her. "I'm going out for a drink."

"Voltaire's?" I said.

She nodded. "Where else?"

There was one more thing I had to take care of before I died, and this seemed like a good time to do it. "I'll come with you."

Layla raised an eyebrow. "It doesn't matter how much I drink. I'm not sleeping with you, Cain. Not even as your dying wish."

I chuckled. "A pity fuck is the last thing on my mind right now. Besides, what's the point if you're not even into me?"

She pursed her lips. "As long as you understand that."

Hannah emerged from her room, eyes red, face blotchy. "Are you going out?"

I nodded. "Yeah. Be back soon."

"I want to go," she said.

I shook my head. "Not today. We'll do something tomorrow. Something normal, like ice cream."

She whimpered and wiped her eyes. "Okay."

I threw up my hands. "Gods damn it, I'm not dead yet, okay?" I held up one of the vials of unicorn blood. "This is really helping. Hell, I might last another six months on this stuff."

Hannah's lips trembled. "Ice cream and a movie tomorrow?"

I nodded. "Whatever you want, sis."

She laughed and fresh tears spilled down her cheeks. "Thanks, bro."

I hugged her tight, fearing it might be the last time I saw her. Then I pulled away, keeping a stiff upper lip. "Where's Aura?" I asked.

Hannah's shoulders sagged. "She left. Said she was going back to her life."

Layla scoffed. "Well, at least we'll have a decent bartender at Voltaire's tonight."

I went into the bathroom and loaded a syringe with a dose of Shraya's blood. Seconds after the injection, I felt strength pouring into me. For the first time in months, I felt a hundred percent. I hoped it would last long enough so I could finish off the night with a bang.

Layla and I headed out in Dolores. I parked the car just outside the fae safe zone near Voltaire's and climbed out.

Layla frowned. "You're not in disguise, Cain."

"What's the point?" I shrugged. "Once we enter the zone, my illusion will vanish."

"Yeah, but shouldn't you at least use the makeup your girl gave you?"

"Nah." I shook my head. "Not today."

"Well, whatever." She started walking without me.

I hurried to catch up.

Durrug's little red eyes narrowed through the speakeasy door when he saw me. "Cain?" he said in his deep voice.

"The one and only," I said.

Layla groaned. "Open the damned door, Durrug. We're thirsty!"

The troll swung open the door and bared his teeth at me. "We almost died because of you."

"Little old me?" I feigned surprise. "I wasn't the one blasting this place to hell. That was Sigma."

He sat back down on his stool. "He came for you. Evil kid."

"Wasn't my fault." I looked past him and saw the usual crowd, including Sir Colin and his knights. Aura stood behind the bar, regarding me with confusion.

Layla nudged me. "Gods, this place is a sausage-fest tonight."

I nodded toward a table of young women in black dresses and pointy, but stylish hats. "What about the witches over there?"

She pursed her lips. "I call dibs on the redhead."

"Do you even like men?"

She nodded. "Sure. But tonight, I'm in the mood for a woman."

"You swing both ways."

"Provided I like the person." Layla pursed her lips. "Look, I'll be your wingman. Maybe hook you up with a witch too."

I snorted and touched my blighted cheek. "Yeah, right. I don't stand much of a chance looking like this."

"Because you never try, Cain." She rolled her eyes and in a mocking voice said, "Boo-hoo-hoo. Everyone hates me because I'm an ugly fae-lover."

"Didn't know I sounded so girly," I said.

Layla punched my shoulder hard enough to hurt it. "Just buck up and try to get laid, okay? Might as well have some fun with the little time you have left."

"Yeah, sure." I pointed to the bar. "Drinks first, then we get laid."

Layla slapped my back. "That's the kind of talk I like to hear."

I went to the bar and sat down. "Give me an extra-large mangorita, barkeep."

Aura frowned. "What are you doing here, Cain? There's still a bounty on your head."

"Yep." I raised my eyebrows. "Can I get my drink with an extra pirate sword?"

"Yeah, elf." Layla slapped the bar. "Get me a unicorn sunrise and hurry it up."

Aura put her hands on her hips. "You can't just order me around."

Layla's mouth dropped open in mock confusion. "Last I checked, you work here. So, get me a drink, you pointy-eared little liar."

"Fine." Aura stalked off to the liquor.

"And don't spit it in," Layla shouted after her.

I sat with my back to the bar, and casually flicked my left ear with an amplification spell. The safe zone wards didn't care if someone used magic so long as it wasn't for offensive purposes. I eavesdropped on some conversations the best I could with all the ambient noise. The glares from some people told me I wasn't welcome here as usual, but that was to be expected. I was searching for something else.

With the price on my head, I doubted I'd have to wait long.

Layla eyed the witches. "I'll be over there. Let me know when the elf finishes my drink."

"Sure."

She strolled over and casually took a seat next to the redhead. Layla said something and the women laughed.

"Why are you here, Cain?" Aura hissed from behind me. "Someone is going to report seeing you. There's no way you'll get out of here without someone trying to capture you for the bounty."

I figured I'd waited long enough. I stood and faced her. "It's been fun,

Janice. I'll be back for my drink in a minute." Then I went outside.

I paced in the parking lot behind the bar. It was still blackened and scorched, but most of the debris had been cleaned up.

"I didn't think you'd come back," said a familiar voice behind me.

I turned and faced Sigma. "Consider this my last act."

He frowned. "What's that supposed to mean?"

"It means the girl is under my protection. Tell Hera to leave her alone or things will get ugly."

Sigma scoffed. "You dare to threaten the queen of the gods?"

"Yes, I very much dare it." I readied myself in case he launched an attack.

"Where is the girl?" Sigma said.

"Her name is Hannah, and she's safe. I'm teaching her to use her powers safely and responsibly." I held out my hands. "I could give you a safe place too, Sigma. I know Hera and her people treat you like a slave. Come stay with me. I'll protect you too."

Uncertainty flickered across his face. "They don't treat me like a slave. I'm a soldier doing my duty." His shoulders stiffened. "I do what has to be done."

"Yeah?" I shook my head. "There were other kid soldiers before you. Do you know what happened to them?"

He shook his head. "There were only two others before me, and they died in the line of duty."

I shook my head back at him. "No, you are the sixty-sixth demi they've used. Once your predecessors hit a certain age, Hera had them killed."

Sigma slashed a hand across his chest. "Lies. I've seen the pictures and the trophies."

"I have pictures and documents to support me," I said. "Hera despises you and all the demis. For her, it's not about preventing the prophecy, but about jealousy and power." I wasn't sure if that was true or not, but I figured it was okay to lie if it made the kid change his mind.

"Don't talk that way about my queen!" Sigma thrust his hands at me and unleashed bolts of lightning.

The instant I saw the look on his face, I'd dodged out of the way. Asphalt bubbled and boiled from the assault of superheated electricity. I kept moving, fueled by the unicorn blood in my veins.

I shielded myself from another lightning strike and ran for the safe zone border. Sigma might have an exemption, but I didn't. If I struck back, Feary soldiers would portal in and help him kill me.

I made it to the park where I'd fought the knights the last time. Homeless people and panhandlers looked dazed and confused as I sprinted past. The moment bolts of lightning ripped through trees behind me, they panicked and scattered with almost supernatural speed.

Dark clouds gathered in the sky, casting random bolts in my path. It seemed Sigma had upped his game.

I drew my oblivion staff and ignited the brightblade. For the first time in months, I felt the strength to do what I needed to do. Sigma was powerful, but Layla's dagger in Daphne's chest and my previous interactions with Sigma had taught me something about these wunderkinds. They weren't well trained. Their masters thrust them into the world relying almost entirely on godlike powers and brute force.

For ninety-nine percent of their targets, that probably worked. But it was time to teach this kid a lesson. I spun my staff and cast a shield. Sigma caught up to me, face red with anger, chest heaving, and violent balls of electricity crackling around his fists.

I held up a hand. "Sigma, remember when you asked me why I'm called Ghostwalker?"

"The others told me it's because you murdered women and children during the war." He bared his teeth. "You have blood on your hands."

I shrugged. "Sure. I'm haunted by the innocents I killed." Thankfully, they remained silent as I contemplated what needed to happen with Sigma. "But that's not why I'm called Ghostwalker."

Sigma frowned and held up lightning-laced fists. "I will make you a ghost unless you give me the girl, Cain. Then you can ghost walk for eternity."

I groaned. "Gods damn it, kid, you're wrecking my dramatic reveal."

"I don't care!" He thrust out his fists and blasted my shield. It cracked and shattered, but I was already on the move again.

I took cover behind a thick tree. "You've ruined the moment, you little bastard!"

"You've ruined everything!" Sigma screamed back.

It seemed I'd just have to show him how I earned my nickname. When I'd learned to shadow dance, I'd discovered a strange talent that not even my mentor could explain. She'd told me to keep it a secret, but I'd used it on occasion during my duties. The other guardians began to call me Ghostwalker. The name spread in whispers and rumors. Despite being a human, I gained notoriety as the most feared guardian because of my strange ability.

I hopped out from behind the tree and flipped off Sigma. He snarled and aimed another blast at me. I focused power into that special part of my mind and ghostwalked. A puff of black smoke drifted where I'd been an instant before. Now I stood behind Sigma. I raised a hand and chopped his neck.

But my hand never reached his neck. Instead, it met an invisible barrier of electricity around his skin. Brilliant light flashed. A burst of energy flung me backward at incredible speed. I rolled across the ground and my back struck a tree. My hand felt as if it were on fire and my mind reeled. I gathered myself and pushed up to my knees.

It seemed I'd ruined the big reveal even more than Sigma had.

Sigma stared at me with wide eyes. "How did you—" he looked behind him and back at me. "That's why you're called Ghostwalker!"

I had a witty reply on the tip of my tongue, but my mouth refused to work. I was fucked. I'd underestimated the kid. Instead of going for the killing blow, I'd tried to knock him out. It seemed I was an even bigger fool than Sigma.

He smirked. "Too bad it doesn't help you against me." He thrust his fists forward and fired another strike.

I rolled behind the tree. The thick trunk splintered and smoked, but it held. I remained still as a frightened squirrel, trying to recover my senses. It seemed like there was only one way for this to go down, provided I could focus enough to make it happen. But a peek around the tree revealed Sigma racing my way, eager to finish me off.

I staggered to my feet and tried to run, but my knees felt like rubber. I stumbled. Looked back. Lightning crackled around Sigma's fists. He raised them for the killing blow.

"Hey, kid. Catch!" Layla dashed through the trees. Hand blurring with speed, she fired a volley of arrows at Sigma.

He yelped and threw out a panicked ball of lightning. The arrows shattered and burned. Layla loosed another volley, then dropped the bow and threw daggers so fast, I could barely follow her hands. Sigma gathered his wits and summoned a lightning shield.

Arrows splintered on impact. The daggers sparked and bounced off.

It occurred to me that the electrical barrier around his skin wasn't a shield, but probably a normal occurrence when he used his powers. It meant I had a chance as long as I didn't touch him. I summoned my wits and ghostwalked behind him. In one smooth movement, I drew Carnwennan and threw it. It plunged into the left side of Sigma's back, right through the heart.

CHAPTER 42

"I'm sorry," I said. And I meant it. Sigma was a brainwashed kid. It wasn't his fault he was a murderer. That onus was on Hera. But I couldn't let him live. Couldn't let him hunt Hannah. Because I wouldn't be around much longer to protect her.

Sigma screamed. An electrical shockwave slammed into me and hurtled me through the air. I hit the same tree again and fell to the ground. My face and arms felt sunburned. The odor of burning hair stung my nose. A vice clamped around my lungs and heart, and it was all I could do just to breathe.

"So stupid." Layla's blurry form knelt in front of me. "I don't know what you did, but that black shit is crawling across your face now."

Ghostwalking used a lot of power. Between that and the massive electrical discharge from Sigma, I'd probably accelerated the magic cancer. It didn't really matter. "Sigma dead?" I wheezed.

"As a doornail." Layla looked back at someone and growled. "Can't you leave us alone, you little twit?"

"What happened?" Aura rushed up behind Layla. "He killed Sigma!"

"I did most of the work," Layla said.

A tall figure shrouded in darkness stepped from the shadows, a giant scythe gleaming in his skeletal hand. Aura and Layla started arguing, unaware of Death looming behind them. He knelt next to me and they froze in place.

"It's time," I said. There was no question about it.

Thanatos nodded. "It's been a long wait, old friend, but the time has finally arrived."

I sighed. "Thank the gods. I'm ready."

He slid back his cowl to reveal his normal face. "In the end, you made me proud. Made us all proud."

"All?" I said.

"Your passengers." He flashed a grin. "Selfless acts from a selfish person."

"It's not enough, though." I sighed. "My soul is too black."

He nodded. "Blacker than most, but not the blackest."

I looked up at Layla's and Aura's faces, both frozen in an argument. "Is it dumb that I'm going to miss listening to those two?"

"Miss them?" Thanatos chuckled. "Cain, I think you misunderstood." He held out a hand. Dozens of hands reached out for him. He stood and began pulling them one by one. Women, children, and even a pair of ghostly men lifted from my body. They stood behind Thanatos, looking down at me. The emotions on their faces was strange—not quite happy or sad.

Their mouths moved, but no sounds emerged.

"It's time for them to find peace, Cain." Thanatos waved a hand and the spirits faded away. "But it's not yet your time." He grinned and slid his hood back into place. The leering skull stared out at me. "Until next time."

I was still mostly dead and somewhat frozen with shock, so I had no reply. He hopped on Ghost and rode away.

Aura and Layla unfroze.

Layla shook her head. "Let's get you home, hero."

Thanatos must have done something to allay the pain from my injuries because agony rushed back in. Suddenly, it was all I could do to keep my eyes open.

Layla and Aura hefted me, and I passed out. I didn't remember most of the car ride home, but every time I woke, I cursed at Layla for driving Dolores.

Breathing became harder and harder, like sucking air through a clogged straw. I wondered if Thanatos had been right about me surviving, because it didn't feel like I was going to make it. With Cthulhu's curse gnawing me to the bone, it didn't seem likely that I'd have more than a few hours left. My ghosts had only a short head start on me.

Layla dumped me on the couch. "Hannah!" Layla shouted and pounded on the bedroom door. "Get your ass out here."

"Why?" Hannah shouted back.

"Because it's time to say goodbye." Layla's voice lowered. "I think Cain is almost done for."

A door slammed open and footsteps pounded. Hannah leaned over me, tears pouring from her eyes. "What happened? Why is the cancer moving across his face?"

"The dumbass used himself as bait to draw out Sigma," Layla said. "He killed the kid, but I think it took everything he had left."

"No!" Hannah touched my face and smoothed back my hair. "Why, Cain, why? All you had to do was eat the goddamned unicorn heart!"

I managed a smile. "I'm not worth it, kiddo." My lungs started to seize up. "Stay in school, okay?"

Hannah screamed. Tears poured down her cheeks. "Cain, don't leave me!" Her eyes glowed and power leaked from her hands. "I'm a demigod. I can save him!"

My skin burned as she ran her fingers across my face. "Ow," I groaned. "Not working."

"I'll pull out his soul and put it in Aura's body!" Hannah said. "She deserves to die more than he does."

I took as deep a breath as I could and managed a stern shout. "No!" I gripped Hannah's wrist. "No."

Her hot tears dripped on my face. "Fuck you, Cain. You're not leaving me." Hannah vanished.

"Kid, what are you doing?" Layla said.

I started to lose consciousness. "Don't be stupid," I rasped. My eyes closed and my body grew incredibly heavy. This was it—my final moment.

Something wet slapped across my face. I couldn't pry open my eyes to see what it was.

"I accept," Hannah said. "I'll do it, on a few conditions, but only if you save him now."

I didn't know who she was talking to. Just before I lost consciousness, I heard a single word in my head.

Sorrow.

I JERKED awake and sucked down a healthy lungful of air. I felt good—no, I felt amazing. I felt right as rain. A look around told me I was in bed, naked. The sheets were soaked with sweat and stank like someone had soaked them with moldy seawater. My arms and legs looked atrophied, as if I hadn't used them for weeks.

I swung my feet out of bed and pushed myself up, then made my way to the bathroom. The mirror reflected a young man, all skin and bones. Gone were the blighted veins and the wrinkled skin. I looked like someone in their early thirties, not a man only two years removed from forty.

It was me, the way I'd looked years ago, but how?

I showered off the film of stale sweat from my skin, dressed, and went into the family room. "Hello? Is anyone here?"

I looked through the guest rooms, but they were empty. Dolores was parked in the garage. I walked downstairs down to the library. Grunting and clanging metal echoed from the training room.

I found Layla clashing blades with a practice golem. She disarmed it and booted it to the floor, then turned to me.

She grimaced. "You need a sandwich, Cain."

"W-what happened? Where's Hannah?"

Layla bit her bottom lip. "Cain, you've been asleep for four days. Maybe you should eat something and then—"

"Where's Hannah?" I wanted to roar, but I was so weak, I barely managed a whisper.

She swallowed hard. "She's gone."

That last word I'd heard before oblivion claimed me echoed in my mind. *Sorrow*. "No. Please tell me she didn't."

"She did, Cain." Layla grimaced. "Stupid kid."

I slumped against the practice mats. "Why, Hannah? Why would you do that?"

"She loves you." Layla scoffed. "The girl accepted Cthulhu's bargain to save you."

I stumbled over and gripped Layla's t-shirt. "She has a fucking name."

"I know."

"Say her name!"

A single tear trickled down Layla's scarred cheek. "Hannah."

I couldn't hold myself up any longer. I leaned against Layla and fought back the agonizing pain ripping apart my heart. "Should have let me die."

Layla sighed. "I didn't have a choice in the matter." She threw my arm over her shoulder and dragged me upstairs where she dumped me on the couch. A moment later, she brought a bowl of warm soup. "Eat it, and don't talk 'til you're done."

I drained the bowl in seconds. I felt marginally better in body, but my soul felt like it'd been trampled by a herd of buffalo. "Where did Hannah go?"

Layla took my bowl and replaced it with a sandwich. "Talk to Fred."

I ate the sandwich and went to Fred's pool. He appeared the moment I stepped close to the edge, almost as if he expected me. I knelt and he put a tentacle in my hand.

Sorrow.

"Yeah, I know." I wiped my face with a free hand. "Where's Hannah?"

His eyes went black. I stood on the shore of the underground ocean. The looming presence of Cthulhu was absent. Instead, I found Hannah.

"Cain!" She wrapped her arms around me. "You look terrible, but I'm so happy to see you."

I kissed her cheek and backed away. "Am I really here? Are you?"

"No. I'm on Gaia somewhere."

"Where?" My fists clenched. "I'm coming to get you."

Hannah wiped tears from her eyes. "You can't, Cain. I accepted Cthulhu's price to save you."

A lump built in my throat. "Why, Hannah? I saved you from Hera, and you just jumped into the arms of another god?"

Shoulders shaking, she looked down. "I'd pay the price a thousand times to save you."

I put a finger under her chin and lifted her gaze. "You're the little sister. I'm supposed to protect you, not the other way around."

Hannah smiled through the tears. "It works both ways, bro." She glanced to the side and nodded as if someone unseen spoke to her.

"What is it?" I asked.

"Time to go."

I growled and made a fist. "Tell Cthulhu I'm not done with this. I won't let him have you."

She laughed and cried at the same time. "You're not supposed to get emotionally attached, remember?"

I shook my head. "Too late."

Hannah kissed my cheek and hugged me tight. "I love you, Cain."

Tears stung my eyes. "Love you too, Hannah."

And then she was gone.

I was back in the church staring at Fred. His golden eyes regarded me for a moment, then he slipped back into the water.

Layla sat next to me. "You're so stupid I actually feel sorry for you."

I took her hand and squeezed it. "Thanks, Layla."

She rubbed her eyes. "Gods, why am I even still here?"

"Because you're stupid too."

Layla laughed. "Must be contagious." She stood and helped me up. "I'll make you another sandwich, but then I'm gone, okay? Maybe I'll come back and collect that bounty when you're up to a fair fight."

"Okay." I felt numb. Death sounded like a real bargain just then.

I should've been happy to be alive. The old me would have forgotten about Hannah and moved on with his life. But my life had changed the moment I'd spared her. I'd grown into someone different. I was still Cain, but with purpose. I had a reason to live. A reason to care.

And I would save Hannah from her fate, no matter the cost.

BOOKS BY JOHN CORWIN

CHRONICLES OF CAIN

To Kill a Unicorn

Enter Oblivion

Throne of Lies

THE OVERWORLD CHRONICLES

Sweet Blood of Mine

Dark Light of Mine

Fallen Angel of Mine

Dread Nemesis of Mine

Twisted Sister of Mine

Dearest Mother of Mine

Infernal Father of Mine

Sinister Seraphim of Mine

Wicked War of Mine

Dire Destiny of Ours

Aetherial Annihilation

Baleful Betrayal

Ominous Odyssey

Insidious Insurrection

Utopia Undone

Overworld Apocalypse

Apocryphan Rising

Soul Storm

Assignment Zero (An Elyssa Short Story)

OVERWORLD UNDERGROUND

Soul Seer

Demonicus

Infernal Blade

OVERWORLD ARCANUM

Conrad Edison and the Living Curse

Conrad Edison and the Anchored World

Conrad Edison and the Broken Relic

Conrad Edison and the Infernal Design

Conrad Edison and the First Power

STAND ALONE NOVELS

Mars Rising

No Darker Fate

The Next Thing I Knew

Outsourced

For the latest on new releases, free ebooks, and more, join John Corwin's Newsletter at www.johncorwin.net!

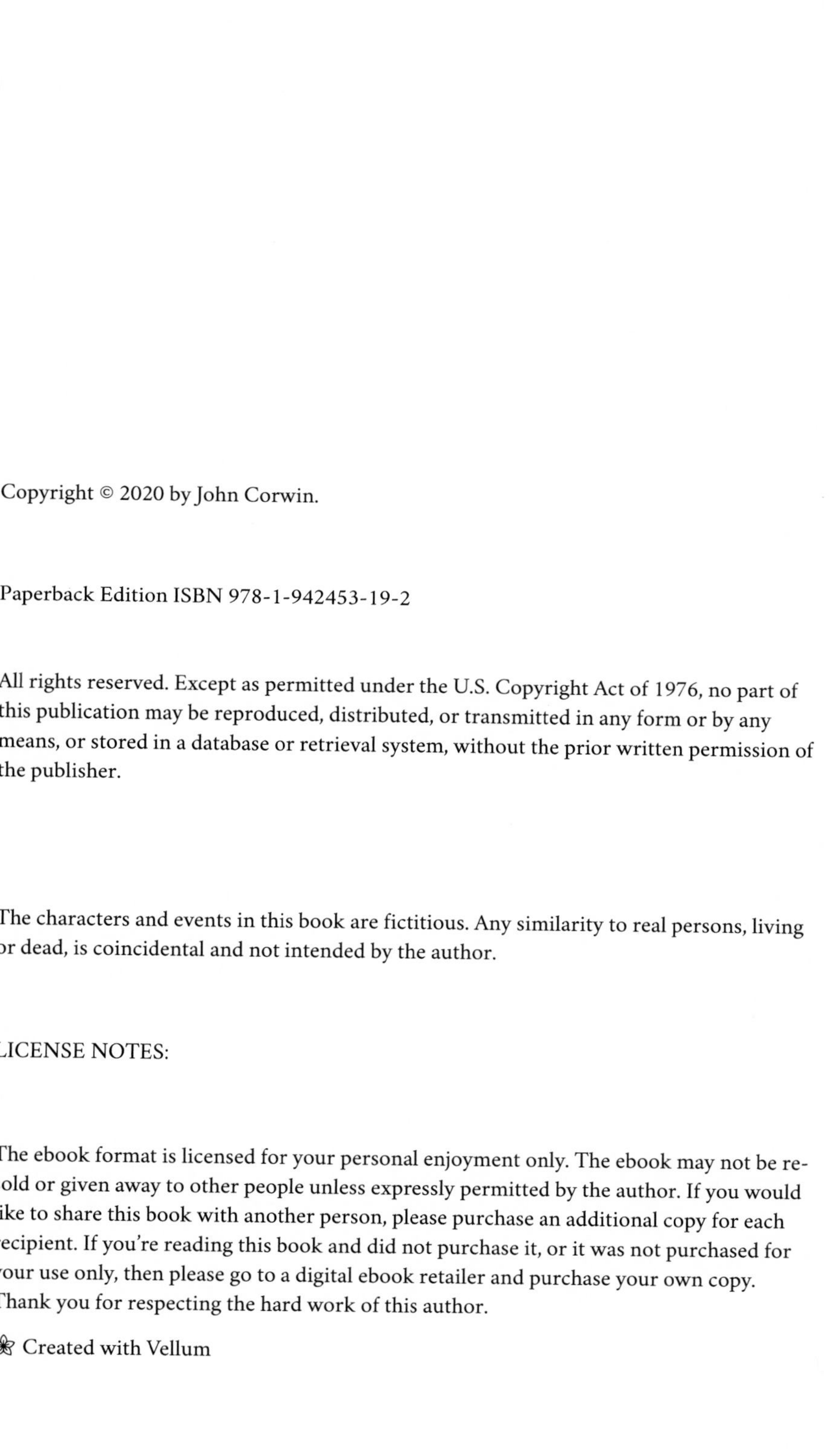

Paperback Edition ISBN 978-1-942453-19-2

The characters and events in this book are fictitious. Any similarity to real persons, living or dead, is coincidental and not intended by the author.

❀ Created with Vellum

ABOUT THE AUTHOR

John Corwin is the bestselling author of the Overworld Chronicles. He enjoys long walks on the beach and is a firm believer in puppies and kittens.

After years of getting into trouble thanks to his overactive imagination, John abandoned his male modeling career to write books.

He resides in Atlanta.

Connect with John Corwin online:
Facebook: http://www.facebook.com/johnhcorwinauthor
Website: http://www.johncorwin.net
Twitter: http://twitter.com/#!/John_Corwin

Made in United States
North Haven, CT
27 October 2023